I0972762

Previously published Worldwide Mystery title by
JULIE HYZY

DEADLY BLESSINGS

DEADLY INTEREST

Julie Hyzy

W🌐RLDWIDE®

TORONTO • NEW YORK • LONDON
AMSTERDAM • PARIS • SYDNEY • HAMBURG
STOCKHOLM • ATHENS • TOKYO • MILAN
MADRID • WARSAW • BUDAPEST • AUCKLAND

For Paul,
who survived Susie, Sni-a-bar and much, much more.
Love you, Bruds.

Recycling programs
for this product may
not exist in your area.

DEADLY INTEREST

A Worldwide Mystery/August 2014

First published by Five Star Publishing in conjunction with
Tekno Books and Ed Gorman.

ISBN-13: 978-0-373-26906-8

Acknowledgments

A very special thanks to my patient family, who still insist they enjoy having me around, even though I sequester myself at my keyboard for hours and then fall asleep in front of the TV.

ONE

"THANK GOD," I said under my breath when the garage door lurched upward, responding to a quick press of the remote. The opener had been misbehaving recently, often taking half-a-dozen tries before activating. It needed new batteries—but I didn't have time to deal with that tonight.

Shutting off the engine, I gathered my purse and reached up to my visor, hitting the control button again.

Nothing.

I made a face, and pressed again, this time holding for an extra second—hoping for a strong enough signal to catch. Still nothing.

"Fine," I said aloud, getting out and slamming the car door shut. I started around the front of the Escort, when I heard someone calling my name over the steady drizzle.

"Alex?" The high-pitched voice held a touch of urgency.

I peered out into the rainy night. One of my neighbors, Mrs. Vicks, held a folded newspaper over her wiry carrot-red hair, shuffling along the alley in what, for her, had to be warp speed.

A quick glance at my watch told me it was ten minutes before six. I needed to rush inside, make myself look gorgeous—as much as that was possible—and be out the door by six-thirty for the first newsmagazine awards dinner where I was a contender for the prestigious Davis Prize.

Mrs. Vicks' expression was at once eager and apologetic, the wrinkles in her face so dense they formed crisscross patterns on her cheeks, pink with exertion. She had on a dark plaid raincoat, its silver snaps clipped shut from hemline to neck. Beneath it, she wore shiny sweatpants gathered over her extra-wide gym shoes that splashed up shots of water as she made her way toward me.

"Made it," she said, with obvious relief, ducking into my garage to get out of the rain. "I'm locked out." She shook out the newspaper, sending sprays of water across my car's hood, and I got a mouthful of her cologne.

I was about to explain my rush, but she interrupted. "Diana must've locked the front door. She was sitting at the kitchen table when I got home from work, and I thought she was staying in. I was sure of it. I told her I was going to be right back. I don't know what goes on in that girl's head, sometimes."

Mrs. Vicks' roommate, Diana, had been a troubled teen, and was now a troubled young woman. I knew Diana well enough to say hello and exchange quick pleasantries. She didn't strike me as vindictive, or the type to purposely lock Evelyn Vicks out of her home for laughs, but I could believe she was sufficiently scatterbrained to forget about her landlady when leaving the house.

Digging out my cell phone, I offered to call my Aunt Lena who lived just a few houses down. "She has a key, right?" I asked, my voice a mite too hopeful.

Mrs. Vicks inspected her gym shoes. They were dappled with dark spots and she tried cleaning them by rubbing the tops against the fabric of her pant legs. She had difficulty maintaining balance and latched onto my forearm for support, holding me frozen in her iron grip. "Nah," she said, not looking up. "Lena and Moose aren't home. I tried them first. Nobody else is around." She finished her futile effort and finally glanced up at me with a hopeful smile. "Well, nobody who's agile enough to get through my back window."

She let go as I put my phone back in my purse. I glanced at my watch. Five minutes had ticked by already.

"Mrs. Vicks, I'd love to help you out, but I'm really in a hurry tonight. How about you stay at my house till my aunt and uncle or Diana get back?"

She was shaking her head even before I finished talking. "I put a pork roast in the oven," she said. "Told you I wasn't going to be gone long. I just walked down to the strip mall to pick up my prescription. Half hour, tops." Her eyes widened as she proffered a stapled-shut white bag that had been tucked under her arm. She held it out with a look of determination, as though I doubted her. "I'm afraid it's going to dry out—you know pork does that real quick—or, heaven forbid, it could start a fire if it's in there long enough."

The last time I helped her get back into her house, it'd been a Saturday morning in the fall, and I'd been out trimming my yews and raking maple leaves. Suitably dressed in jeans and a T-shirt, I'd been perfectly willing to prop a ladder up to her back porch windows and shimmy inside.

Tonight was one of those almost-warm March evenings, the protracted rain pulling fresh growth smells from the new-green ground. Having shucked my lined coat because it was too heavy, I had on a brand-new navy blue skirt suit with matching pumps. There was no way I could see myself climbing up a wet ladder in this miserable weather. Not to mention that the clock was ticking. Even if I ran into my house this minute I'd never get my hair done in time.

"Really, Mrs. Vicks, I have to be somewhere by seven and I still have to get ready."

She scrutinized me. "You look fine, honey. You always do." Her eyes raked me up and down and she sighed, as though for her lost youth. "Your aunt told me about this dinner thing you're going to. Isn't this the one where you're up against the jerk who cheated your station out of a big story?"

I winced. "Something like that."

Mrs. Vicks pursed her lips and wrinkled her nose. "Well, I hope you beat him good," she said. Her glance slid down the alley toward her house, four garages away. "I mean," she said, "your aunt told us all about how that TV big-shot fellow got all the credit for the work you did. You're not dating him anymore, are you?"

I scratched my eyebrow. Mrs. Vicks could talk all night.

"Wait here," I said, dumping my purse onto my car's passenger seat. I pulled on my coat in an effort to protect my suit, and hoisted my extension ladder from its hangers on the garage wall. This house and all its finery had belonged to my parents. Now safely ensconced in a retirement village in Arkansas, they'd seen fit to leave the whole kit and kaboodle to me. Mostly it came in handy. Tonight I wished I lived in a north shore condominium with a doorman named Joe.

The rain had let up, but Mrs. Vicks, determined to accompany me in my rescue quest, tottered alongside, holding the folded newspaper over me. Since she was at least four inches shorter than my own five-foot-six, the newspaper kept whapping against my head as we walked through the narrow passage that separated her garage from my aunt and uncle's.

"How are your parents enjoying the leisurely life?" she asked. Not waiting for my answer, she continued. "And your sister, Lucy. What about her? I can't help but feel— don't tell your folks this—that the poor girl is going to be lost in that retarded institution."

Her mouth made a clucking sound, and she watched her feet, rather than the hand carrying the newspaper. I suffered another whack, and cringed at the word "retarded." If Lucy had been here, she'd have been hurt.

"Sorry," she said, meaning the hit in the head, and not the terminology. "It's just that poor Lucy doesn't seem like she should belong there. Not that she isn't 'special.'" Evelyn Vicks glanced up at me then. "Of course, she isn't exactly normal, either."

"She's doing great. Loves it." My tone was abrupt.

Mrs. Vicks shuffled as fast as she could to keep up with me, but all I wanted was to get in, get out and get moving. I heard her heave a long sigh. "Lucy is such a sweet girl. I miss her."

A moment's pang. I missed her too.

Once in the small yard, I headed toward the back porch. Not watching what I was doing, I inadvertently skimmed the top rungs of the ladder against her massive fir tree. The bouncy branches slingshot back at me, showering my head with rainwater and my last chance for decent hair washed away.

"It's okay," I said, pushing away her hand, trying hard not to let my impatience show. I raised the ladder till it bonked against the back of the house, next to the right-hand window. Things would have been easier if Mrs. Vicks hadn't outfitted all her basement windows with glass-block panes.

I tried not to think about balancing on wet metal rungs as I stripped off my shoes. "You're sure this back window's unlocked?" I asked.

"I know it is," she said, holding the paper over herself again. "I had it open this afternoon for a bit, when I got home from work."

I sighed, handed my heels to Mrs. Vicks, and started up.

I was only three rungs up when a bright crack of lightning, just north of us, shot me with renewed urgency.

Standing on a metal ladder, the ridged rungs digging into the soles of my pantyhose-covered feet in the middle of a storm was not how I'd planned tonight's festivities.

As if to berate me for my foolhardiness, the sky rumbled, then boomed, shaking the already unsteady ladder. Above me, a trio of windows awaited, set into the vinyl-sided back porch add-on. All large and double-hung, I knew from experience that even from the inside, these heavy panes were often hard to lift.

"I've got you," Mrs. Vicks said.

I glanced down long enough to see her eager, upturned face, squinting against the steadily growing drizzle. One hand was wrapped around her prescription bag and newspaper, her fingers tucked into the backs of my shoes, the other hand gripped the ladder.

Three more upward steps and I was in position. My left hand grabbed the white-painted wood frame of the window and I peered over the center to verify that the lock was unlatched.

She was right about that, thank goodness.

The wind whipped my skirt around, shooting blasts of damp air up my butt and making me feel for a moment like Marilyn Monroe must have over that subway vent, except cold. I tucked the excess fabric between my thighs in front, and tried to hoist the window upward.

No luck.

I heard the oncoming torrent before I felt it. Like the sound of a thousand spirits shushing at once, it moved from the north like a wave. Seconds later, we were drenched.

Grimacing, I dug my fingers between the upper and lower panes, and pushed the bottom half of the window upward with all my might.

It gave, about a half-inch.

Encouraged, I pushed again, till there was enough

room underneath the frame to sneak my fingers in to get the leverage I needed to open the window full wide. The wrenching noise led me to believe that it'd gone off its track, and I felt like I'd broken something. A half-second later I realized I had—one of my brand-new acrylic fingernails. Getting them done on the way home from work was what made me run late in the first place. They'd been gorgeous—long and French-tipped. Now the middle fingernail on my right hand was short and ragged. I clenched my eyes shut, less in pain than in aggravation, but at that point, all I could think of was how fast I could straddle the windowsill and heave myself inside.

As I made it through, I heard Mrs. Vicks shout in glee that she'd meet me around the front door.

She was gone before I could argue that the back door was closer.

I ran a hand through my wet hair and took stock as I made my way to the front of Evelyn Vicks' house. I glanced at the clock in the kitchen, where the table was covered with paperwork, and I could smell delicious heat coming off the pork roast. The room was bright and warm, plastic yellow tiles framed with a black border about three-quarters of the way up the wall.

My stomach growled.

Six-fifteen.

I made my way to the front door, and let a very grateful Mrs. Vicks inside.

"Oh, Alex, honey, thank you so much. You're a dear."

She handed me my shoes as she kicked off her own by the front door, stooping to place them neatly on a ribbed rubber mat right inside.

I smoothed back my hair again, pushing at its slick wetness till the water dripped down the back of my neck. "Not a problem," I said, lying through my teeth. I headed toward the back door, but she stopped me mid-stride in the kitchen.

"Hang on, let me give you something."

Her purse, a massive bone-colored vinyl bag with a long, wide strap that I'd often seen her wear strapped across her chest, was slung along the back of one of the chairs. She started to dig into it and I wondered why she hadn't taken it with her to the drugstore. Or why she always seemed to be losing her keys.

Before I could say a word, she held out a five-dollar bill, shaking it to show she meant business.

"That's okay," I said, striving for polite, but wanting nothing more than to race home and get moving. I inched toward the porch pulling my pumps back on. I'd be sorry tomorrow that I put them on with these dirty wet feet. "Really, it was nothing."

As I turned, I knocked over some of the papers on her table and cursed my bad luck. More time wasted, picking them up.

I mumbled to myself, as I snagged all the papers that had fallen, and I placed them on the table trying to arrange them neatly.

Bank statements, all of them. From Banner Bank with the distinctive double-B logo. I knew Mrs. Vicks worked there. She'd been taking the bus downtown everyday since I was a kid.

"Don't worry, I'll take care of it," she said, taking the bunch from my hand. She stopped for a moment, as though considering something, the five-dollar bill forgotten on the table, much to my relief. "Alex..." she said, "while you're here..."

I turned. Almost out the door, I thought. Almost.
"Yes?"

"You're still a news reporter, right?"

I still needed to get the ladder back to my garage before I could even hope to get dressed for tonight.

"I'm a researcher. It's not really the same thing."

"Would you be the person to talk to if I knew something?"

I winced at her question. Another clap of thunder shook the house and the sound of the pounding rain let me know the storm's intensity had increased. People always ask me what to do if they know something. The "something" they're talking about can run the gamut from a neighbor who leaves his dog out all night to howl at the moon, to a con man who's plotting to talk an elderly parent out of retirement savings. My stories are assigned to me by my boss, Philip J. Bassett, not-so-affectionately known as Bass. I rarely find anything on my own that warrants the local Chicagoland coverage that our television newsmagazine provides.

"Ahh," I said. "That would depend."

I inched toward the stairs that led down to her back door. She stayed with me, hovering close, her brow furrowed and her lips tight, staring at the sheaf of bank statements in her hand.

She glanced up then, and her eyes were clouded. "It's just that there've been some," she looked askance and tsked, "I don't know. Just some things going on that I thought my boss ought to know about."

My left hand was on the metal doorknob. I reached my right up to casually flick the flybolt open. "Well, you should say something then," I said, my words bland. A quick glance at my watch. Six-twenty-five. Damn.

She cocked one hip and set her hand full of paper on it, as though settling in for a talk. "But I did. And, well, it's like this—"

Desperate, I pulled open the door. "I'll tell you what,

Mrs. Vicks," I said, knowing I'd be sorry later for making hasty promises now, "How about I stop by tomorrow and you can tell me all about what's going on?"

Her face brightened, the deep crisscross grooves in her cheeks settling into cheerful smile lines. "You're a sweetheart, Alex. You always have been, even when you were a little girl. Okay, it's a date then."

I grabbed the ladder and flinched at yet another flash of lightning overhead.

She called after me, "I'll make dinner, would you like that?"

I opened my mouth to decline, thought better of it, and said, "That would be great."

She beamed. "I'll make it something very special."

TWO

BASS WAS PACING the foyer of the Convention Center when I got there. As I passed through the second set of glass doors, held open for me by the studly young valet, I watched my diminutive boss taking short-man strides across the dense maroon carpet. A wide set of double staircases leading to an empty loft above, curved like huge parentheses around his pacing area, keeping him contained. Centered high above, a crystal chandelier the size of my kitchen sent glimmers of brightness throughout the spacious entry-way, but did nothing to brighten his obviously sour mood.

Bass was alone, head down, hands gesturing as though in conversation. People passing by might think he was talk-ing on one of those cordless headset phones, but I knew better. Bass talked to himself often. Indeed, from the look on his face and the movement of his lips I could tell he was muttering. About me, no doubt. Behind him, along a gold-brocade wall, three sets of open double doors framed the busy ballroom beyond, like three giant animated pictures. The guests were seated, chatting in low tones as the wait staff mingled, trays balanced atop gloved fingers. Soup was being cleared away, salads were looming; I was later than I thought.

Bass looked up. He scowled.

"Where the hell have you been?"

Ignoring him, I headed toward the coat check to the foyer's far left. I handed two young girls my shawl, tak-ing a plastic token in return. Turning toward the ballroom, my eyes scanned the sea of round tables, all covered in white linen, with light-refracting crystal held by manicured hands. I felt the tip of my own ripped nail close in on my fist and I grimaced.

Bass scurried to walk with me as I ran my hands down the sides of my indigo blue gown, smoothing it. My dress was the only thing that hadn't gotten screwed up tonight. It was silky and cut on the bias with a demure slit that slithered up from its calf-length hem. I'd pulled back my damp hair into a chignon, and the last glance I'd taken in the mirror before I tore out of the house made me believe that I'd at least managed a little bit of elegance.

Bass had a nervous jumpiness about him that made him look, in his black tuxedo, like a sixty-year-old ringbearer with ants in his pants. "Do you have any idea what it would've looked like if you hadn't shown up?" he asked for the second time.

"I'm here, aren't I?" I took a deep breath, centering myself before moving toward the open doors.

Every woman knows that her attraction is in her mind—people will react to her based on how she feels about herself. Tonight I was determined to dazzle.

"Everybody's been asking where you are. Where were you, anyway?"

I was a few inches taller than Bass most days. Tonight, in my three-inch heels, I felt like an Amazon woman. Standing close, forcing him to tilt his head far up to look at me, I pasted on a smile and ignored his question.

"Just show me to our table."

WILLIAM ARMSTRONG, MY partner at work, stood as we approached. "Alex," he said.

Holding out the chair next to his for me, his expression was one of concern, eyebrows close together over sparkling blue eyes. When I shot him a crooked grin, his face relaxed and I watched his eyes move up and down my body, as though seeing me for the first time.

Something about that man's smile turned my knees weak. I'd never seen him in a tux before, but his just over six-foot frame wore it so splendidly, that I had to bite the insides of my cheeks to stop myself from saying "Wow!"

"You look great," he said in a low voice as he pushed my chair in.

I let out the breath I'd been holding. "Thank you."

As William sat to my left, Bass took a seat next to his long-time girlfriend, Mona. I murmured apologies for my tardiness to them. Two chairs to my immediate right were currently unoccupied but had been claimed, as evidenced by a wineglass with red-lipstick marks, and two crumpled napkins lying on the vacant seats. A man's Armani jacket, draped so that the tag faced outward, shouldered the chair next to mine.

"Can I get you something?" William asked, leaning forward, his fingers poised on the tabletop as though to boost himself upward at my command.

William's solicitousness took on a peculiar quality when I realized we were seated together, like dates. I managed to say, "No thank you," and turned to my boss, who smirked.

Bass had made comments in the past about William and me having a secret fling going, and when I realized my protestations to the contrary only served to encourage him further, I shut up about it and let him believe what he chose.

Mona reached past William toward me. "It's so good to see you again, honey," she said. Her fifty-something care-worn face was mottled from years in the sun, her black hair a shade too dark to be natural, but the creases bunching up near her pale brown eyes and the deep grooves around her mouth made it clear this was a cheerful lady.

I clasped her little-girl hand, half-concealed under rock-studded gold rings. "You too," I said with feeling. "How's the big guy been treating you?"

"He better treat me real nice," she said, her eyes twinkling, "I booked us a reservation in one of them Sybaris swimming pool suites tonight." She leaned back and slapped Bass playfully on the arm. "Didn't I, honey?" She laughed then—deep-throated and merry—a surprising sound from such a small person. Next to her, Bass looked away, reddening. How a fellow as cranky as Bass could have snagged a gem like Mona had always been a mystery to me.

I spied our station's anchor, Gabriela Van Doren, and her date seated at the next table, chatting it up with the general manager from our competing station. I turned to William. "Why is Gabriela over there?" as it occurred to me that she had apparently been invited to bring a guest.

William shook his head and shrugged.

Perplexed, I placed my hand on the back of the empty seat next to me and addressed Bass. "Then who's sitting here?"

A cool hand covered mine. "Hello, Alex."

My stomach clenched, but I forced a smile as I looked up. "Dan," I said, trying to keep the surprised disappointment out of my voice. I pulled my hand out from under his, but I wasn't quick enough. He snagged it, long enough for his eyes to flick over my ragged nail, and lift an eyebrow in disapproval. I maintained eye contact, smiled, and returned my hand to my lap, pretending that it was the height of fashion to have a splintered middle fingernail.

"How have you been?" I asked, my voice flat.

Behind him, his new girlfriend Pamela hovered with blond perfection. She and I had met, just once, under strained circumstances.

"Great," he said, flashing a bright oh-so-sincere smile. "And you?" Without waiting for my answer he half-turned toward his date. "I'd like to introduce you to—"

"Pam," I finished. "We've met."

"That's right," Dan said, smoothly.

She blinked a couple of times in feigned confusion, smiled faintly, and wrapped her hands around Dan Starck's shirt-sleeved biceps. "I prefer Pamela," she said. She gave his arm what was obviously meant to be a proprietary squeeze.

He glanced back toward her with a sly smile, running a finger along his own jawline the way men do sometimes, as though to verify that they really did remember to shave that morning.

Like a model from the cover of GQ, he wore local fame like an inner glow, radiating brilliance from his perfect white teeth to his golden-tanned and trim body. As beautiful as his latched-on accompaniment was, however, she paled in comparison to his confident radiance. The way she held on to him, two-handed, protecting him from my evil clutches, delivered a welcome boost to my self-confidence.

It had been a while since he and I were an item, and despite the fact that the breakup had been a mutual decision, in retrospect I couldn't help but believe that the relationship that had preceded it had been all his doing. He'd sought me out, wooed me, and when I responded to this handsome hunk's undivided attention by moving in with him, I discovered that in addition to clothes and toiletries, he expected me to bring all my station's stories, informants, and secrets into the relationship, too.

That didn't happen.

I drew my line and he drew his. It was when I stepped back to get a better look that I realized there was no overlap.

A gloved hand placed a chilled salad in front of me

and I picked up my outermost fork. Dan leaned close, his shoulder skimming mine. "Good luck tonight," he said. His eyes caught the light from the crystal chandeliers above us.

Sincere or mocking—I still couldn't tell.

I stabbed a cherry tomato and brought it to my lips. "The same to you."

THE MOMENT WE'D all been waiting for came just as the last remaining parfait glasses disappeared—stolen away by quick-fingered busboys. The table before us emptied so quickly and unobtrusively that it went from cluttered to clear as though by magic. As final crumbs were scraped off white linen, the master of ceremonies took the podium in front of tall, crimson curtains. A local author, he'd been tapped for duty after his latest book hit the New York Times Bestseller list. He scratched his trim beard and began his introductory remarks.

William inched his chair closer to mine; we'd angled them a bit when the speeches began. He wasn't much bigger than Dan, just over six feet tall, but he was broad-shouldered and trim. Sitting between these two, I couldn't help but compare. Dan's Abercrombie and Fitch good looks were stunning, but almost feminine-pretty. William with his smile lines and solid build, was handsome in a real-man way. His light brown hair had a tendency to curl in humid weather, and I found I couldn't get enough of looking at him. When he and I worked together, I felt a level of comfort I'd never achieved with Dan.

I almost wished he could read my mind right now. I envisioned him grabbing my hand, whisking me out of this stuffy party, and taking a long drive out to where the harsh lights of the city didn't interfere with the bright skyshow of stars.

I sighed, but it was lost in the audience's polite applause.

"The nominees for this year's Davis Award for excellence in reporting are…"

The master of ceremonies spoke slowly. One at a time, he named three feature stories and those in the media responsible for bringing them to light. I waited. I knew we were fourth on the nomination list.

"*Midwest Focus NewsMagazine* for 'Crowning Glory.' Gabriela Van Doren, anchor, and Alexandrine St. James, reporting."

William reached over and squeezed my hand.

His simple gesture made my breath catch.

"And our final nominee tonight is…*Up Close Issues* for 'Scandal in the Catholic Church,' Dan Starck, anchor."

No reporter named on Dan's story. I found that interesting.

The crowd settled into an anticipatory silence. I watched everyone at our table lean forward in unison, as though straining to hear the announcement one half-second sooner than anyone else.

The man at the podium grinned out at the crowd, peering over his half-moon glasses. "And this year's Davis Award for Excellence goes to…"

There was no drum roll, but I felt the hard beat in my heart.

"*Up Close Issues*, for 'Scandal in the Catholic Church.'"

The gentleman at the podium smiled and gestured toward our table as I sat back in my chair. My perfunctory clapping was lost in the roar of the room's applause.

Dan stood as the bright spotlight found him. He didn't blink, but I did, as the searing whiteness accidentally hit me first, before moving to capture his look of surprise. It was as practiced as my smile, I'd bet. He turned toward Pamela, kissed her, and then made his way, grinning, through the round tables full of beautifully dressed people, clasping outstretched hands, eager to touch their perception of greatness.

William leaned over. "You okay?"

The taut strings of my smile were still working, and I spoke between closed teeth. "No surprise," I said, not looking at him. "I'm fine."

The spotlight clicked off, leaving us with that immediate-loss-of-light blindness. I worked my mouth to loosen it, and strove for serene.

Dan stood there, gazing out, looking like the Reverend Jim Jones might have, right before urging his followers to drink the Kool-Aid. As if born for this moment.

I felt a sudden, vicious stab of fury.

This was his moment. But it should have been mine.

"Thank you," he said, waiting to begin until the crowd quieted. His manicured hands were wrapped around a crystal, flame-shaped trophy he hefted twice, as though weighty. He spoke briefly about how wonderful it was to be surrounded by so many pillars of the community.

He was right about that. There had to be over a thousand people present, only a quarter of whom were media folks. The rest were lawyers, bankers, business-owners, and philanthropists who attended Chicago gala affairs as part of their job descriptions.

I had to give Dan credit; his speech was engaging. He came across as sincere, speaking in a modest manner of how much this award meant to him and how he chose every single day of his life to do the best job he could and how he'd never dreamed of being awarded for such humble efforts.

"Of course," Dan was saying now, "I owe a great deal of gratitude to so many people."

Here it comes, I thought.

Dan began summing up. He hadn't yet mentioned our

station, *Midwest Focus*, and he hadn't mentioned me. I told myself I didn't care. But I knew Bass did. The little fellow's head stretched out, straining, and even from here, I could see the glitter of anger in his eyes. Mona kept one hand on his back, making small circles as though quieting a nervous animal.

"And I would be remiss if I didn't mention Alex St. James, over at our competing station, *Midwest Focus*."

Bass leaned further forward.

For the first time all night, I lost awareness of William next to me. He faded as the room dissolved and I could see nothing more than Dan standing there, bathed in the only light on the planet. Would he really admit that this story had been mine? That through luck and conniving he'd stolen it from me? That I'd killed a man in the process and had nearly been killed myself?

"Her tenacity is remarkable," he said. "Like the little engine who says, 'I think I can,' she works very hard at her job."

I felt my mouth open.

He flashed a smile in my direction that I wanted to slap off of his smug face.

"She was determined to cover this story, and even though she couldn't, her efforts should be an inspiration to all of us to not let stalling and wheel-spinning get us down." He nodded in pontification. "She's quite the determined little thing, and she 'thinks she can.' That's an attitude I hope she's able to maintain forever."

He smiled, said a few more insipid things, then bowed to the crowd amid more applause, to head back to the table.

Behind the stage curtains, a band had set up. Now with Dan's speech complete, the heavy red draperies parted and the sounds of tuning began.

"Dan, dinner, and dancing," I said. "What more could anyone want?"

No one missed my sarcasm, and even as I heard the tone of my own voice I felt petty and small.

"Excuse me," I said, standing.

William stood up, following me through the obstacle course of tables blocking my path. I knew I couldn't stay in the ballroom for one more minute. As I scooted to the open doors at the far right of the room, I smiled with the grace of an automaton at the people reaching to tap me and laugh as I passed.

A man I recognized as a defense lawyer in our building—one whose practice came under our station's scrutiny a year or so back—stood up, effectively blocking my path. His well-fed face broke into the ugliest smile I'd ever seen. Raising his wine glass as if in toast, he wiggled his bald head in a drunken way, slurring his words when he spoke.

"The little engine that could," he said, attempting a leer. "I like that."

I didn't break stride. "Excuse me."

He moved, but I caught the drift of his deep chuckle as I passed and I wondered if my face flamed as hot as it felt.

All I wanted was to grab my shawl, pull off my heels, and run, not walk, to my car. I wouldn't, of course. I'd never give Dan that satisfaction. What I needed was a moment to pull myself together—the ladies' room was just about a hundred feet ahead. Duck in, pretend to do my business, and walk back out. Maybe then I'd be able to fake it.

I almost laughed out loud when I remembered my plans to dazzle.

William caught my elbow just as I crossed the ballroom's threshold.

I half-turned, but kept walking.

"Hold on a minute," he said.

Like I hadn't understood the tug on my arm. Couldn't he take a hint?

"What?" I snapped.

Bass came through one of the other sets of double doors. He and William corralled me far off to the side, tucked into the shadowed area created by the left-hand curved staircase. "What?" I asked again, but my voice was weaker.

Bass's hazel eyes glittered in the scant light. He pointed the way we'd come; his hand shook. "Get back in there."

Slow-motion, it dawned on me that William hadn't let go. He'd adjusted himself, however, and instead of gripping my elbow, he held a hand steady on my shoulder and his fingers moved slightly on my back, almost in a caress. I watched him shoot a look of fury in Bass's direction.

"Give her a minute," William said. Then to me, "Are you okay?"

With one man ordering me around and the other trying to be Mr. Supportive, I nearly lost it with both of them. I didn't need either of them to tell me how to behave. What I needed was to be alone and the two of them in the tiny space were crowding me. I felt the rise of anger like bile in my throat, and it took all my self-control to keep from slapping William's hand away and telling my boss to go to hell.

"I'm fine," I said with a calm I didn't feel.

Twin looks of disbelief on their faces made me doubly determined to seek refuge in the bathroom and pull myself together.

"I need to use the washroom," I said. I turned to William and gave a quick arm-wiggle, effectively dislodging his hand. "Do you mind?"

They both stepped aside. I squared my shoulders and strode away.

THREE

I SHOULDN'T HAVE been surprised, I suppose, when Bass and William's panicked eyes met me upon my return.

"Can I get you anything?" William asked, for the second time that night.

Dazzle, I told myself.

I braved a smile. "White wine. A Riesling, if they have it. If you don't mind."

He moved to his feet with a swiftness that surprised me. Relieved, it seemed, at being assigned a task.

Mona reached to grab my hand the moment he left. "You hang in there, honey."

I'd been about to thank her, when two men stopped by the table. Both were older, businessmen types and evidently good friends of Bass'. One clapped our station manager on the back while keeping up polite conversation with the other. The other fellow kept a more reserved stance but smiled and shook hands all the way around as Bass introduced them.

Their names were familiar. More bigwigs. The chattier fellow, slim but rather short, pointed his finger at me, gunlike. "So you're the little engine, huh?"

Bass shot me a warning look. I clenched my teeth and said, "Apparently."

The man chucked his friend on the shoulder again and said something under his breath that I couldn't completely catch. It sounded like he said he wanted to see exactly what my engine was capable of.

William returned, and placed a sparkling glass of white wine in front of me. Its bowl was twice as large as the other wineglasses at the table. I shot him a questioning look.

He shrugged. "I asked them for their biggest glass. You looked like you could use it."

There was a hint of amusement in his face. I reached for the glass with a grin and was warmed both by the first sip and by his smile in return.

The second sip went down like warm honey, and I let out a long sigh of resignation. I'd be stuck here for at least another half-hour or so. To leave any sooner would be tacky, and obvious.

The houselights had dimmed, the music began, and waiters were now lighting large candle centerpieces at each table.

Mona whispered to us that she hoped to get her boy up on the dance floor soon and that getting him out of his chair was half the battle. "Warm him up for tonight, you know," she said with a wink. I grinned at her and hoped Bass had remembered to pack the Viagra.

Eyeing my wineglass, I thought about getting myself warmed up. I pushed it farther toward the middle of the table by its base, and wrinkled my nose. Nah. I didn't need to risk losing inhibitions tonight. I'd be liable to say something I'd regret later.

"Alex. William."

We both glanced up toward Bass at the sound of our names. Mona had drifted off and Bass gestured us forward, with an eager smile of encouragement. Rising, we obliged him by coming around and joining the group.

"These are two of my staff," Bass said to a gentleman who he'd called over. Close to fifty, and tall, with a big-man's build, he had a gray mustache, a receding hairline, and wore circular frameless spectacles that were a shade

too small for his round face. Still, there was an attractive-
ness about him that I couldn't dismiss. I watched his glance
touch lightly on William, as Bass made introductions. They
shook hands and spoke briefly before he focused on me.

"You're Alex St. James," he said, without the customary question mark at the end of the statement. His right
hand gestured vaguely in the direction of the stage. "The
reporter Dan Starck mentioned in his speech."

I was biting the insides of my cheeks, wondering how
long I'd be forced to deal with the aftermath of tonight's
remarks, when he offered his thick hand.

"The same, I'm afraid," I said, shooting him a lips-only
smile. My dad taught me young to have a solid handshake,
telling me that it didn't matter that I was a girl, that people
respected a good grip. He'd made me practice with him
until I got it right and then started goofing with me with
all sorts of silly handshakes until I started giggling. This
man shook back with a firmness that matched my own.

"David Dewars," he said. He was more adept at covertly
assessing women than most men, but I caught his all-over
glance just the same.

Mona returned, and Bass invited her to the dance floor.
I took a half-step back from David Dewars, and fingered
the low neckline of my gown with a glance William's direction.

He'd turned away, his attention claimed by a group by
the bar. His profile offered an expression I couldn't read
and I thought about asking him to dance.

"Alex?"

I turned. David opened his hand toward the couples
gliding across the shiny wood floor. "Would you do me
the honor?"

I opened my mouth to thank him, to politely decline,
when I saw William walk off, headed toward a crowd of

Sun-Times writers I recognized as his former colleagues. That told me where I ranked.

"I'd love to," I said.

It'd been a long time since I'd danced with a man, and at first I found myself concentrating solely on staying light on my feet. Soon, however, I loosened up, letting myself move with my partner's rhythms. He must have sensed the change because his hand, flat against the small of my back, pulled me in closer and he took control of our movements as though we were but one body. David Dewars, beneath his exquisitely cut tux, felt precisely how he looked. Solid, strong, and warm.

"Your dress is lovely," he said.

"Thank you."

I hadn't expected conversation, so it surprised me when he continued. "I think Dan Starck is an ass, if you'll pardon the expression."

I had one hand on his right shoulder, the other tucked into his left hand. I leaned back far enough to make eye contact. There was laughter there; we were sharing a joke. Wary, I said, "He's something, that's for sure."

"Ah…being careful are we?" he said, grinning, turning me. "Don't worry. I can keep secrets." He pulled me in, his hand firm on my back, his cheek close to mine. When he spoke, his breath grazed my ear, sending surprising shivers down my spine. "Bass just gave me a quick rundown about what really happened."

"Did he?" My voice came out several decibels too high.

"Mm-hmm," he said. "I'd love to hear the whole story sometime."

"Well," I hedged, as the final notes of the song ended and we parted, "it would be my side of it. And it's vastly different than Dan's version. You'd have to decide for yourself which story to believe."

Still holding my hand, he stared at me for a moment. "Did you really kill a man?"

I closed my eyes. "Bass told you a lot."

"Not nearly enough." He guided me ahead of him as we headed back toward the table. His voice was husky as he leaned in to be heard over the next song. "I'd welcome the opportunity to know more about you. Perhaps we could have dinner sometime?"

Taken aback, I stopped, glancing at him over my shoulder to decide if he was joking. And, to my great chagrin, I stammered. "I'm not…sure," I said.

He finally let go of my hand, turning me as he did, to face him. "You're a careful girl," he said. "That's good. I certainly wouldn't want to scare you off." Taking hold of both my shoulders, he brought his face just close enough to mine to invade my personal space. Resisting the urge to push away, I caught a twinkle in his dark brown eyes.

"It's the ones who get too close, too fast, you have to be afraid of," he said, winking. "We'll do lunch instead. It'll make you feel safer." He held me a half-second longer. "I'll call you, is that all right?"

I opened my mouth, with no idea what I was about to say. Not that it mattered.

With a grin and another wink, he was gone.

THE DAVIS AWARD celebration was still blazing in rowdy elegance when I decided to duck out at ten-thirty. Enough was enough, and if one more person were to make a "little engine" comment, I knew I would embarrass myself. I reasoned that it was better to go home, kick off the dress that hadn't had any effect whatsoever on its intended target, and catch some much-needed sleep.

To my great surprise, William followed me out.

He walked with me through the quiet parking lot, giving

me a "we'll get 'em next time" pep talk. Behind us, the pillared entryway stood bathed in hazy light, with glittery people milling about outside, catching their smokes. The sounds of them chatting and laughing faded as we made the long trek to my car.

Having arrived so late, the only spot I'd been able to find was in the lot's farthest reaches, where pavement met farmland. Our slow pace and the buzz of high-beam lights in the foggy March night gave me the first feeling of freedom I'd had all evening. I took a deep breath of the cool dampness, finally feeling myself relax.

"What did you think of David Dewars?" I asked as we reached my Escort.

William shrugged, his gaze on the clouded moon. "Not much." Moving closer, as I fitted my key into the door, he added, "But then again, I didn't dance with him."

"Oh," I said. My voice would have gone perfectly with eyelash-batting, but I exercised restraint. "You noticed."

"Of course I noticed."

I thought I detected a note of jealousy in his reply—but it was probably just my wistful imagination.

Stillness settled in around us like a conspiratorial cupid and the very air felt different to me. I moved closer to him, just a bit. Even with my spiky heels on he was taller, and I couldn't help but think our heights were perfect. "Interesting evening," I said, just to fight the silence.

"It was," he said, just as blandly.

We hadn't broken eye contact since we'd gotten to my car's door. I waited, hearing the swish of the wind over the nearby wheat tips, and the beat of my heart, fast and deep.

I thought about how easy it would be to lean up and kiss him right now, but I couldn't. It was his move.

His move… If he ever was going to make one.

He opened his mouth and took a sharp breath, as though

to say something. But one moment later, he closed his lips, flashed a quick smile, and looked away, obviously changing his mind. And when his eyes came back to meet mine, there was friendliness in them. Nothing more.

He leaned in, kissed me on the cheek.

"Good-night, Alex. Sweet dreams."

Great, I thought, as he walked away. The perfect end to a perfect night.

I wondered if he heard the frustrated slam of my car door.

I'D BEEN ABOUT to turn into my alley when I changed my mind, deciding instead to park out front. With the way my luck was going, I'd be hitting my remote for a half-hour and it still wouldn't open. One night without the shelter of the garage wasn't going to kill my little car.

As if to make me sorry for my words, rain began, dropping in heavy patters on my car's roof. I allowed myself a long sigh. Every move today had been a mistake of some sort. No reason to expect things to be different now.

I began to accelerate into the left turn that took me onto my street, when I stopped short. Four squad cars formed a rough semi-circle mid-block, their warning blue Mars lights flashing across the fronts of all my neighbors' brick bungalows, flashing against their picture windows.

A female police officer approached my car, her black-gloved hand raised to halt my progress.

I rolled my window down and she leaned in.

"You a resident?" she asked. Her hat was sheathed in a clear covering and she had on a dark raincoat, open over her uniform. Her blond hair was tucked behind her ears and she wore an inquisitive expression.

"What happened?" I asked, pointing, "I live right there."

I noticed belatedly, an ambulance parked behind the

last squad, and a crowd of neighbors all staring the same direction, heads together, arms folded in worried fashion. I couldn't decide whose house it was, and all thoughts of my miserable evening vanished as I searched the faces for family. My aunt Lena and uncle Moose were getting up there in age. But even if they'd taken ill, that didn't account for all the squads.

The officer straightened and assessed the street, shaking her head. "I can't let you in."

I spotted Aunt Lena breaking from the group of onlookers, and I sighed my relief. She hurried toward my car, waving. "This is my niece," she shouted in a breathless voice, pointing as she ran up to meet me. Her tan raincoat flapped in the wind and she held a dark umbrella aloft. I noticed that she had on her pajamas and house slippers.

The officer turned to her. "I'm sorry ma'am. There's nowhere for her to park."

"I'll go to my garage," I said, then addressing Aunt Lena, "What happened?"

"It's just terrible," she said. Then, with motherly scrutiny, she asked, "You still having problems with your door opener?"

I nodded.

"Park in our garage. I'll tell Moose to open the door for you. I'll meet you there." She'd turned to run back to the gathered crowd. "Just terrible," I heard her say again, but the rest of her words were swallowed up in the night.

FOUR

UNCLE MOOSE MET me at the garage. He'd positioned his massive frame half-in, half-out of the structure, straddling the threshold of the small service door, his hair a dark wet helmet.

"Come on," he said with a peculiar look on his face, as I came around the front of the Escort. Then, "Where were you?"

"At a big dinner." No sense in getting into detail. "What happened? Why are the police out front?"

He dropped his gaze to my high heels. "You going to be okay standing out there in those? Maybe I should get Lee to find you something more comfortable."

"Uncle Moose," I said, with urgency in my voice, "tell me what happened." I caught another wary glance at my legs. Exasperated, I added, "I'm fine."

How many times had I said those words tonight. And not once had they been true.

He popped open an umbrella over my head as we trekked through the gangway that separated houses from one another. Uncle Moose had been a professional wrestler—fairly well-known in Chicago. Though he'd slowed down over the years, he maintained the sort of lifestyle that kept him moving. He was taller than my dad—heavier too. And while my dad's hair was beginning to fade from light brown to gray, Uncle Moose's stayed dark. Of course that might have had something to do with the used coffee grounds he massaged into his head each night.

"There was an incident today," he said. I could feel him choosing his words, like I was a little girl again, like he needed to protect me.

"Just tell me. About a million possibilities are racing through my brain right now, and I'll bet they're all worse than what really happened. So just tell me. I'll handle it."

In the dark, I felt his skeptical glance more than saw it. "It's Evelyn Vicks," he said.

"Mrs. Vicks?" We were walking pretty fast through the gangway that separated my aunt and uncle's bungalow from the two-story next to it. It took me double-steps to keep up with him and I rethought the wisdom of wearing these strappy heels. "Oh my God, what happened?"

He shifted the umbrella to his left hand and pulled me in with his right as we navigated the narrow passageway. I noticed he kept his eyes focused at some middle-distance in front of him. He licked his lips, then bit them. "Somebody broke into her house today."

I blinked, not understanding. "That was me."

"What?" His face scrunched into a frown of confusion, but he didn't stop walking.

"She was locked out this afternoon. I went in through her back window to unlock the front door. She didn't tell you that?"

He was about to answer when we emerged from the shadowed gangway, and a quick gust of wet wind made me shiver. My aunt Lena looked up from a conversation she was having with another neighbor. She leaned in to the woman, said something, then headed in our direction.

A voice yelled, "Moose," and my uncle turned.

"Talk to your aunt," he said, and started to walk off. A second later he came back, handed me the umbrella and disappeared into the anxious crowd.

"What is going on?" I asked Aunt Lena with an emphasis on each word.

Women will tell women things; they don't try to hedge and protect the way men tend to. I watched resolve come over her features. Her dark eyes tightened, making them seem smaller within deep wrinkles. She'd been crying. Her words came out trembling, pained: "Evelyn Vicks was murdered."

My mouth dropped. I'd just seen her a few hours ago. How could this be true? It seemed surreal…some sort of joke.

I tried to wrap my mind around her statement feeling like I didn't completely comprehend. I started to say, "You're kidding," but stopped myself when I realized how stupid that would sound. All I could do was repeat the word that hit me hardest. "Murdered?"

Aunt Lena nodded; she bit her lip. "Someone broke in."

Evelyn Vicks had been a good friend to all of us for as long as I could remember. I couldn't imagine who would murder such a sweet, helpless woman. I shivered again, this time from more than just the cold night air.

"Broke in," Aunt Lena repeated, then stopped herself short with a strangled laugh. "What a joke, huh? You know she always kept her doors unlocked."

Well, most of the time, I thought. "Yeah."

She shook her head again. "Someone just waltzed in, killed her, and took off." The squads' blue lights flashed on my aunt's face like an uneven strobe, illuminating the tight pain in her expression. "The bastards." Though her body faced me, her attention stayed directed toward the movement in and out of Mrs. Vicks' house.

"A robbery?" I asked. The rain had slowed enough for me to lower the umbrella. Thank goodness; I was fighting a sense of claustrophobia. I wanted to know what had happened. I wanted to know it all. Now.

"Nobody's telling us anything. But, you remember how Russ Bednarski used to be a Chicago cop?" She gestured with her chin toward a cluster of people. Mr. Bednarski had his hands out in front, gesturing as he spoke. "Well, Russ was able to talk to some of the officers over there, and they said it didn't look like a robbery to them."

"But I just saw her," I said, as though my words could somehow change the events of the evening. With a stab, I remembered the smell of the steaming pork roast, and the way she'd promised me a special dinner tomorrow night. I felt my eyes sting, my throat tighten. I pulled my shawl snug around my body, suddenly craving the warmth and comfort I'd felt at her house earlier. And then I remembered something else. "Diana? What about Diana?"

Aunt Lena shifted her weight from one foot to the other. She wasn't a heavy woman, but standing out on the wet cement wearing only house slippers had to be uncomfortable for someone in her late sixties. "That's who found her. They're talking to her now, inside one of the squad cars. She called 911, and then she called us."

"When did it happen?"

My aunt shook her head and shrugged, glancing at me briefly. "Moose picked up the phone around nine. I could hear the poor girl screaming, and I was all the way in the bedroom getting changed for bed. I came out to see what was wrong, but Moose couldn't get her to settle down. We came over here right away. I thought she might've made some mistake and maybe Evelyn had just fallen, or something."

I nodded. "I talked to her," I said, almost to myself. "Around six-thirty."

My aunt made a sympathetic noise. "You never know,

do you? You just never know." A half-second later, I heard her sharp intake of breath. One of the squads had moved forward, to allow passage of a black van with the telltale FH on its license plates. Funeral Home. A suited man threw open the van's back doors, and pulled out a wheeled silver cart that expanded to body-transporting-size in seconds. "Oh my God," my aunt said, her voice cracking. "Oh my God."

"I'll be right back," I said, starting toward the police perimeter.

"Where are you going?" she asked, reaching her hand out as if to hold me back.

I turned, shrugged. "I might have been the last person to see her alive," I said, thinking: except for the murderer, that is. "I think I ought to let somebody know that."

Another young officer, this one male, stopped me as I scooted between the bumpers of two squads. His name-tag read: Randall.

"Hey, there," he said. "Hold on a minute."

"Who's running this investigation?" I asked.

His dark eyes took in my formal dress, spiked shoes and far-too flimsy shawl. "And you are…?"

Switching into professional mode gave me more comfort than I had any right to expect. "Alex St. James," I said, leaving off the added information that I worked for *Midwest Focus Newsmagazine*. That'd get me bounced in a hurry. "I was here…with Mrs. Vicks earlier this evening. I thought I could be of some help?"

I ended the statement with a question. Officer Randall nodded once, told me to wait there, and disappeared into a crowd of uniformed officers standing near the funeral home's van. Neighbors I'd known since I was a kid all stared at me with what seemed a combination of respect for approaching the authorities, and confusion as to why. I offered them a somber smile and turned to wait for Officer Randall's return.

A moment later, he did, stopping at Mrs. Vicks' tiny front yard and gesturing me closer. Her home had been roped off with bright yellow crime scene tape that caught the light in snatches as the wind tilted it back and forth. As I walked past her house, I looked down at the foot-high white plastic chain she always kept strung around her lawn to prevent kids from trampling, I felt yet another pang. Mrs. Vicks was part of my life, and I'd blown her off this evening when she needed to talk to me.

"This way," he said, leading me toward a squad. "Detective Lulinski wants to see you."

I'D NEVER BEEN in the back seat of a police car before, and while the warmth from its idling engine was a welcome change from the wet chill of the night, I couldn't help but feel uncomfortable. I'd landed in a cloud of aroma, not at all good. It was such a combination of odors, ones I could imagine and others I'd prefer not to, that I blinked, hoping I could get used to it fast.

The entire seat was one piece of gray molded plastic. My backside slid as I got in, and I wound up accidentally pinning the long edge of my shawl under my butt. Officer Randall waited patiently for me to get myself settled, but I must have looked like the most uncoordinated passenger he'd ever had. Digging my heels into the floor, I lifted myself enough to loosen the shawl.

"You okay?"

"Yeah," I answered, realizing I would have been happier waiting for the detective in the drizzle.

Randall looked as though he was about to close the door, but my left foot still hadn't cleared. All this took mere seconds, but in that time, I watched Mrs. Vicks's roommate, Diana, being helped from the back seat of the squad across from us.

Both her hands gripped the car's doorframe in an effort to pull herself out. A man I assumed was Detective Lulinski alighted moments before. He held out his hand, offering assistance, but with her face positioned downward, Diana didn't see it. Her stringy dark hair fell forward, and I could imagine the look of concentration she wore as she struggled to make her way outside. I couldn't see her face, but her large build and lumbering manner made her identity clear.

I put Detective Lulinski in his late forties or early fifties. He was tall, with a thin build; his gray suit pants hung so loosely that I was glad he wore a belt cinching them at the waist. He had on a white long-sleeve dress shirt, the collar opened, tie loosened. His hair was crew-cut short, and he scratched at gray eyebrows while he waited for Diana to step out.

"Thank you, Ms. Grady," he said, finally able to grip her hand and help her as she stumbled.

She righted herself and stood, blinking in the blue flashes. Her lips moved, working as if to say something. She opened her mouth, closed it, then opened it again, her eyes wide with childlike terror. "I...don't have nowhere to go."

Diana had pulled her thick arms around her waist, in an effort to close a too-small sweater around her large frame. She lifted one hand to smooth damp hair behind her ear, and her drooping lips trembled.

The detective held her elbow, scanning the crowd. "Who were those people who came to help earlier? Maybe you can stay at their house tonight."

Like a little child who realized she has the right answer

for a trick question, she straightened, her eyes suddenly alert. "Lena Szatjemski," she said.

I wiggled back out of the car's smooth seat. "That's my aunt," I offered, moving toward them. "She's over there, Diana." I made an exaggerated "come here" gesture with my arm and Aunt Lena swooped in to take Diana safely away.

"We'll need to talk to you again, later," the detective said to her departing figure. I doubted she or my aunt heard him.

He turned to me and gestured toward the car that Diana had just vacated. "I'll be just a minute. Have a seat."

I did. The backseat of this squad was identical to the other, and the smell pretty close, too, though a bit less intense.

The detective conferred briefly with Officer Randall and then returned to me.

In the short amount of time he was outside the car, he pulled a cigarette from a pack in his shirt pocket, lit it and smoked it down to the filter, faster than I'd ever seen anyone do that before. The entire time, he maintained conversation with the uniformed officer, mouthfuls of expelled smoke accompanying his crisp directives.

He lowered himself into the back seat next to me. Up close, I could smell the freshness of the cigarette he'd just finished.

I slid over, making room, taking in this entire backseat experience. A clear Plexiglas panel separated us from the front seat, and a small handle at its center could be used to push it closed. Open now, I heard flat voices repeating information on the radio, but I couldn't make out all the words.

"You were in the house today?" Detective Lulinski asked me, jerking his head and eyes toward Mrs. Vick's home.

I nodded.

"What time?"

"I left about six twenty-five."

He'd flipped open a notebook—the kind with the silver wire spiral at the top. From the looks of its bent shape, and the leftover shreds of paper where he'd pulled sheets out, he'd had this one for a while. "And the victim was alive to the best of your knowledge?"

My words caught in my throat. I wanted him to call her Mrs. Vicks. Not "the victim."

Outside I watched raincoated young men lead a black-zippered bag on the silver cart toward the open back doors of the dark van. Next they'd be calling her "the body." At what point does death change a vibrant living person into "remains?" I shuddered, and blinked. "I'm sorry," I said. "This has been too much of a shock. Can you repeat your question?"

He did. He asked me several questions about my relationship to Mrs. Vicks and then he asked me about Diana's. I focused my attention on him. Despite being a thin man, he had paunch in his face. His jowls drooped ever so slightly, bringing his mouth into a downward scowl. Close up I could tell this was more a force of nature than of personality. His eyes were alert and he asked me again about Mrs. Vicks being alive when I was there.

"Yes, very much so," I said, willing my voice to steady itself. "She was grateful to me because she'd locked herself out and I helped her back in."

His hand stopped moving and he glanced up at me. "Neighbors have been telling me all night that she never locked her doors."

I nodded, a presage to my answer. "That's true. She never did. But Diana…" it was my turn to gesture into the dark outside, "she always would lock the doors, even when Mrs. Vicks asked her not to. And sometimes she did it when Mrs. Vicks would forget her key..." I let the sentence hang.

"And that's what happened today?"

I nodded again.

"How did you get in?"

I told him. He'd stopped writing and was watching me as I spoke, his eyes expressionless. Somehow that encouraged me to tell him more. I did. I told him about how grateful she'd been, and how I'd smelled the food and how she'd promised to make me dinner tomorrow night.

Out of habit I glanced at my watch. "It's tomorrow, now," I added.

"Where did you go afterward?"

I opened my mouth, reluctant to let on that I was part of the media. "A big dinner," I said finally. "From work."

His eyes took on a skeptical look as though he knew I'd held back. Again I felt a gaze taking in my outfit, heels and shawl.

"How was she killed?" I asked. "What were the circumstances?"

Back to scribbling, Detective Lulinski didn't look up. He held up a finger, indicating I should wait. A few seconds later he asked me for my address, date of birth, and home, work and cell phone numbers, jotting them all down as fast as I spoke. Then, remembering my question, he finally answered, "We're not releasing any details yet."

"Did someone actually break in, or did she let them in?"

His expression impassive, his eyes blank, he repeated, "No details."

Exasperated, I sat back, and let out a long sigh.

He had another question for me. "You said you picked up some papers in her house. Papers that fell?"

"Bank statements," I said. "Yeah."

"We're going to need to fingerprint you. For elimination purposes." He gazed at me with that flat expression, pulled out a business card and handed it over. "Come down to the station tomorrow."

I nodded. I was being dismissed.

He got out of the car and looked at his watch. "Or, like you said—today."

FIVE

I TOOK THE stairs, as usual, up to the second floor of our building. Constructed during the prohibition-era, the thirty-five-story edifice was home to our *Midwest Focus* staff. I loved the place. I loved walking up the marble stairs with their center carpet of deep red print, the kind I'd expect to find in a British nobleman's castle. The effect wasn't dispelled by the rest of the lobby. Gold-leaf paint trimmed the crown moulding above, and the gold elevator doors gleamed.

I cleared the top step, gazing ahead through the doors of our office. I could see everyone moving around, silent through the heavy glass. Like a bunch of office-mimes. Busy already.

A long night of rehashing poor Mrs. Vicks' demise left me sleepless, and now I'd have to run the gauntlet of well-meaning colleagues.

"Alex!"

It started immediately as I pushed through the doors. The center of our spacious office was taken up by the "hub" where the entire support staff answered phones, prepared reports, and pretty much kept our craziness on an even keel.

I pasted on a smile, trying to answer all their exclamations with appropriate responses.

"I'm so sorry, Alex. You should have won that award."

"It's a shame, isn't it? You okay? How did Bass handle it?"

"Oh, Alex, I heard about what that lowlife Dan said in his speech. What an idiot. Just wait till it's your turn."

I tried nodding, agreeing, thanking, but all I wanted to do was bolt into my office. My assistant, Jordan, would help me sort through my morning jumble. A beautiful black girl just a few years younger than I, Jordan was one of my best friends. She waved to get my attention and I could tell from the look in her eyes that it had to be important.

"What's up?"

She wheeled back a foot or two and swiveled in her chair to hand me one of those pink "while you were out" notes, her feminine handwriting spelling out a detailed message. "Your sister's home called. A Lester Raymond," she said, summarizing. "He tried to get ahold of your folks, but couldn't reach them."

Lucy's institution, The Riverside School, was more of a halfway house than an actual educational establishment. The place had an incredible reputation. Despite our initial misgivings about leaving her in the care of others—with the benefit of hindsight, we knew placing her there had been exactly the right decision. She'd flowered and matured in the past year—more than we could have expected.

Downstate, the residence sat about halfway between Chicago and my parents' home in Arkansas. They made it a point to visit her monthly, as did I, but the school only called when Lucy needed something unexpectedly. "He say what he wanted?"

"No. And I asked," she said with a little frown. "This new patient confidentiality thing."

I glanced down at the name. "I'll call him."

"How come he couldn't get ahold of your parents? Are they okay?"

Out of the corner of my eye I saw William making his

way toward his office. "Yeah. Very okay. They left this week for a month-long trip to Europe with their pinochle club friends. Can you believe it? I hope I'm as energetic as they are when I get to be that age."

With a twist in my stomach, I thought about Mrs. Vicks—my parents' age, now dead—killed in her home in cold blood.

"Um," Jordan said, interrupting my musings, "you read today's paper yet?"

I had a copy I'd shoved into my briefcase before I left the house. I'd brought it with me to read the coverage of Mrs. Vicks murder—although I had my doubts that it would've made the morning edition. "About to," I said.

"Um," she said again.

Immediately, my guard was up. "What is it?"

Her left hand reached over to a stack of files, and she turned to pull a cut-from-the-paper article out from beneath them. Swiveling back to face me, her expression was apologetic. "Probably better you hear it here, first." As I grabbed the paper from her, she whispered, "Nobody's going to take this seriously, okay?"

Sandra Stanek, gossip columnist extraordinaire, stared up at me from her photograph at the top of her daily column. In today's writings, devoted entirely to the Davis Award ceremony the night before, she described all the glitz and glamour of the event, with names of attendees in bold print. My eyes, however, were drawn to the single picture, dead center in the column. A publicity shot Bass insisted upon. Dan and I posed together, he holding the coveted award, me looking like it didn't matter that he'd won it. At the time the photographer flashed the shot, I remember shooting a glance Dan's direction, thinking that I'd like to take the award and shove it up his pompous ass.

My eyes caught the caption: *Alex St. James gazes*

warmly at Davis Award recipient Dan Starck after his charming acceptance speech. The eyes say it all, don't you think, folks? Might there be romance blooming here, again?

My jaw dropped.

Jordan's voice was soft. "I thought I better show it to you before anybody else does."

Speechless, I looked up. While fury bubbled up from my chest, Jordan looked at me with sympathy.

"Goddamn it," I said, finally, slamming the article onto her credenza. "Can't I catch a goddamn break? Ever?"

"Sorry, Alex."

I shook my head, taking a deep breath to calm myself. "Not your fault."

TEN MINUTES LATER William appeared at my door. "Hi," he said. "Got a minute?"

"Of course." I jammed a file into the open drawer I'd been working in, then hit it shut with my hip.

William closed the door behind him. At the sound of the click, I turned, puzzled.

With a shrug, he smiled. "Nothing bad. Just too many prying ears out there."

I tossed the files onto my desk, but rather than head behind it, I took the seat next to him. I sighed. "I've got so much to tell you."

His face brightened. "Good."

"No," I said, waving my hands in front of me. "Not good."

"What is it?"

I opened my mouth, about to start with the events of late last night, but I stopped myself. He had such a pleasant expression on his face that I didn't want to wipe it away with terrible news.

"You know what? I'd really rather you go first," I said.

He didn't need me to prompt twice. "Okay." He took a breath, and I noticed again the color of his eyes. Like the lake in the afternoon. "I know that watching Dan Starck win that award at the Davis dinner was tough for you last night. It had to be. But," he touched the back of my hand for the briefest moment, surprising me with the gesture, "you handled the ordeal so well. Better than anyone else would have."

I shook my head to brush away that notion, but he continued, "No, really. You came across with real class."

That made me smile. "Well, it's just like you said in the parking lot. We'll get 'em next time, right?"

A flash of something I couldn't describe crossed his face, and he said, "Yeah," with what seemed like regret. "That's part of what I wanted to talk with you about. Last night…"

I opened my mouth, about to say that all things considered, the night had been a whole lot less painful than I'd expected it to be. That once I'd gotten over Dan's acceptance speech, I'd been okay. I wanted to focus on that part of the evening so that William wouldn't have any clue that I'd been disappointed when the night ended and we were still just as platonic as ever.

I stopped myself. Better to hear what he had to say first.

Taking his time, he set his mouth in a line and stared at me. I know it couldn't have been longer than fifteen seconds, but it felt long and drawn out. Like I was about to hear some really bad news. It dawned on me, however, that he didn't have any idea how to phrase whatever it was he wanted me to know.

"I wasn't exactly there for you," he said finally.

Confused, I shook my head. "Don't worry about it. I was fine."

William touched the back of my right hand again. It sent a tingle up my arm. "Be that as it may, I'd like to get a chance to talk about last night with you."

"Sure." I shrugged my shoulders, in a "go ahead" move.

"No," he said. "Outside the office."

I kept my face neutral.

"What I'm trying to say is," he said, with raised eyebrows, "would you like to go out...maybe tomorrow?"

Before I had a chance to answer, he added, "It being a Saturday, I thought we might find something we'd like to do..."

He let the sentence trail off, leaving the rest to my imagination, perhaps.

He and I had gone out a few times before, but it had always been for lunch during work, or for coffee after hours. We'd usually taken an hour or two, purportedly to discuss the day's business, but often we'd find ourselves sharing tidbits of personal information. The time flew, for me at least, and if I had to take a stand on it, I'd have to say William enjoyed our times together, too.

This, however, was a first.

"That'd be nice," I said.

He smiled. Not a big one, but a gentle one. "Great. It'll give us a chance to talk. How about if I pick you up around one?"

We decided to start with lunch and progress from there. He wanted to know what sort of things I'd like to do. At the moment, I couldn't think of a one. I'd hoped to have some time alone with William, almost from the first day he started. Now presented with the opportunity, I couldn't come up with any options. But I wasn't worried; I'm sure we'd make do.

"Now, your turn," he said.

Momentarily perplexed, I furrowed my brows. "My turn?"

"You had something to tell me about yesterday. Something 'not good.'"

In a rush, the night's events and Evelyn Vicks' murder tumbled to the forefront of my brain. I felt my shoulders drop ever so slightly, as though weighted down with the knowledge that I'd been able to forget when the chance of going out with William popped in front of me.

"Oh," I said, "that."

I told him as much as I knew and about my discussion with the detective last night. "I have to head over to the police station to provide a set of fingerprints, since I was there yesterday." I suppressed a shiver of apprehension. "I just can't get over it. I mean, I've had people die before. I've had people closer to me than Evelyn Vicks die. This death seems to be hitting me harder."

He leaned forward, reached for my hand. This time, not with his fingertips, careful-fashion, but by taking it in his own, gently. "Would you prefer we go out a different time? Maybe wait till things settle down?"

"No," I said, touched by his concern. "I'll be fine. I can handle it. I'm tough."

"That's right, you are." He shot me a smile, and stood up. "Okay, I'll stop by later. But, let me know if anything changes."

"Sure," I said, thinking that there was no way I would let anything change tomorrow's plans. "Oh," I said, stopping him before he left. "There's an article in the paper—" I began.

"Sandra Stanek's?"

"You saw it?"

"Don't give it a thought. No one's going to pay any attention."

I let myself smile too. "Thanks."

As he left, I moved to sit behind my desk. Jordan came around the open doorway. "You have a phone call," she said.

The tone of her voice coupled with the puzzled look on her face made me ask, "What's wrong?"

She bit the insides of her cheeks, cocked her head and asked, "Exactly who is David Dewars?"

"He's on the line?" I asked, reaching for the phone.

Just as my hand lifted the receiver, Jordan headed back out the door. "Must have been some party last night," she said.

I didn't understand her comment, but answered the phone in my business-like voice. "Alex St. James."

"Good morning!"

My first reaction was that he sounded far too happy. Or maybe it was just me, transferring my grief over Mrs. Vicks to everyone else. I managed to answer, "Good morning," more out of habit than feeling, before he jumped in to take charge of the conversation.

"I'm sitting here, in my corner office, overlooking beautiful Lake Michigan. The sunlight is dancing on the water, catching the tips of the waves like glints of morning joy. The variegations of the water produce the most spectacular collection of blues in one place."

I didn't say anything. I had no idea what an appropriate response would be to such poetic observations.

"In other words, it's a beautiful morning. One of the best ever." He paused for a beat. "Wouldn't you agree?"

"To tell you the truth, I've had better."

His tone changed immediately. "I'm sorry to hear that. Is there something I can do to help?"

"I doubt that," I said, deciding whether or not to burden him with my lousy news.

"Have you given thought to my offer?"

"What offer was that?"

His tone dropped even lower, slowed. "Dinner, Alex," he said, his voice softening as he said my name. He had a smooth way of saying it, and it made me immediately annoyed with myself for wanting him to say it again. "I was thinking maybe tomorrow night. I know of a wonderful place not far from here that has the perfect ambiance for quiet discussion."

"To tell you the truth…" I began.

"Or a place of your choosing. Whatever would make you most comfortable."

I'd been hoping for a handsome man to ask me out one of these days, and here, in the course of five minutes I had two. Feast or famine, I thought. "Actually," I said, hearing the smile in my voice as I spoke, "I have plans for tomorrow."

"I'm disappointed," he said. "Please don't break my heart and tell me you're refusing me because you have a date."

A date. With William. I felt a thrill of excitement at the use of the word. "Well…" I said. Truth be told, it was none of his business whether I had a date or not. "A colleague and I are getting together to get a few things done for a story here. It'll take all day."

"Remember Alex, all work and no play…" He paused just a half beat. "How about Sunday?"

He was one of those folks who calls a person by name at every opportunity. "David," I said, trying out his name myself, "there is something else I think you should know."

"Uh-oh, here it comes," he said. He waited a beat before continuing. "You're not married, are you?"

"No, no. Nothing like that."

"Good," he said. "Then I anticipate we'll get together some other time. Soon. You're an intriguing woman, Alex St. James."

Okay, I was flattered. Here he was, a bright, handsome, albeit older man, who was interested and who came at me with a directness sorely lacking in most of the male species. Still, I thought, time to return to the business at hand. "I'm afraid I have some personal business that might keep me occupied for a few days."

"Oh?"

I told him about Evelyn Vicks.

"What?" His voice, filled with incredulity, boomed loud over the phone. I heard a hollow seashell sound, as though he'd cupped his hand over the mouthpiece. When he spoke again, it wasn't to me, but I could make it out. "Donna, get Owen in here. Tell him it's urgent."

Geez, I thought, dialogue right out of a suspense film. I couldn't imagine why he was getting so worked up.

The seashell-against-the-ear sound disappeared and he returned to talking with me. "Oh, Alex," he said, his voice soft, like butter. "Not Evelyn Vicks."

"You know her?" I asked.

"She works…worked for me."

"You work at Banner Bank?"

"Well, I suppose you could say that." He cleared his throat. "I…own the bank."

"Oh," I said, astonished to speechlessness.

David chimed in to help. "She was a friend of yours?"

"Yeah," I said, suddenly finding it hard to talk. "I've known her all my life."

I'd not had a chance to fully appreciate the situation.

Instead I'd been hit in small, unexpected moments. This was one. A friend of mine. I wouldn't have described her in those words. I would have said she was my parents' friend, or my neighbor, or the elderly lady whose house was one of the best for trick-or-treating when I was a kid.

Remembering the casserole she brought over when my grandmother died, and the scarves she'd knitted for me and Lucy, and even last night, the fact that she knew the whole story about how Dan had stolen my feature and had taken all the credit—she suddenly felt more real to me than she ever had, and the fact that she was gone, murdered, felt like I was being sliced from the inside.

"It's hard to lose someone we care about," David said.

"It is," I answered, not knowing what else to say.

"Alex," he said, "if there is anything I can do, you'll tell me, won't you?"

"Of course," I said. It was a remote, automatic response.

"I'll call you another time," he said.

"Sure. Thanks."

I hung up, thoughtful, both hands resting on the receiver for a long moment. I was supposed to go visit that detective again today, and maybe, if I played my cards just right, I'd get some information out of him. Unlikely, since he seemed circumspect, to say the least. Still. I hadn't become one of the top researchers in my field by waiting around for details to fall into my lap.

Jordan popped around the corner again. "So?" she said, affecting a sassy air as she meandered into my office and pulled up a chair. "You want to tell me about this Dewars fellow?"

I brushed my hand in front of me, like shooing a pesky fly. "Nobody important."

"Uh-huh," she said in a flat, "I don't believe you for a

minute" voice, her brown eyes widening in amused affectation. "Girl, you are holding out on me."

"Why all the interest? I met him at the dinner last night."

Her lips set into a smug smile. "Don't you tell me that he's nobody important." She lowered her voice in an imitation of his, "'May I be connected to the lovely Alexandrine St. James, please?'"

"He didn't say that."

She wiggled her head and shot me a pursed-lip smile. "You bet he did." She grinned bigger, then asked, "There was something else you wanted to talk with me about?"

"Yeah."

I had an immediate crazy desire to pull everyone I knew into my office so I could tell them about Evelyn Vicks' murder all at one time. I'd never had such difficult and weighty information to impart to so many people, and I hated the thought of explaining it yet again.

I went through the whole scenario, trying my best to keep it light, and angry at myself for doing so. Somehow each time it got easier to tell and I didn't like that. As if Mrs. Vicks' murder somehow got lessened with each telling. That's how murderers get away, I decided. Enough people tell the story enough times till everyone is desensitized and the crime no longer holds the capacity to horrify. By the time the criminal makes it into court, the facts have been rehashed so often that it becomes simply words on a page, or facts stated aloud. The victim, the person whose life has been cruelly stolen from the rest of us, has turned into a mere statistic.

I managed to get through the ordeal of telling her without as many guilt pangs and without feeling like my throat was closing up. Dragging my purse onto my lap, I switched into business mode.

"I have to go down to provide my fingerprints today,"

I said, pulling Detective Lulinski's card from my wallet. "Here." I handed it to her. "Would you mind calling him and asking if there's a good time for me to show up? I'd hate to spend the afternoon sitting there, if they're busy."

"Sure," she said, standing. "You sure you're okay?"

I wrinkled my nose. "I will be. Thanks."

After she left, I remembered the phone message from Lucy's school. Dialing it, I got a sudden tingle of fear. What if they were calling me because something had happened to her? I berated myself for not phoning them the minute I'd gotten in.

The receptionist connected me with Lester Raymond almost before I'd finished giving her my name.

"Good morning, Les," I said.

"Alex."

Thirty seconds into our conversation, I was relieved to realize that things were fine with Lucy, but that the institution was in the midst of an upheaval. Inspectors had discovered asbestos in a high-traffic area, and plans were in place to effect its removal.

I knew the man on the other end of the phone, Lester Raymond. A slight fellow, with dark hair and deep brown eyes that stayed alert behind dark-rimmed glasses like a studious bird, he spoke with a bit of a speech impediment that caused him to slur his words. In person, I could tell that he was an intelligent, caring man. Over the phone he sounded like a drunken Elmer Fudd.

"We are sorry," he said, and I felt myself cringing at the hollow sound of his "r's." "But we require all the residents to be relocated."

"I understand," I said. "When will this take place?"

"Well," he said, and I realized that his "L's" were lost, too, "we were planning to have them all resettled by this weekend."

"Oh," I said.

My mind raced. This weekend. That was pretty short notice. He must have read my mind because he added, with a bit of apologetic haste, "I am very sorry, but we weren't aware that your parents were out of town. We left them two messages, but received no reply."

It took me a moment to decipher "awawe and pawents," but I understood a moment later. "My parents are in Europe."

"We discovered that this week. I'm afraid that we were so certain that Lucy would be picked up that she dropped through the cracks. You know, your family is very good at visiting. Most families are not."

"Thanks," I said, but my mind was still processing his comment about this weekend.

"We really need Lucy to be relocated," he said again. "We have made arrangements with another school, but the closest one that we feel comfortable with is on the far west side of Iowa, and I don't know if you would want your sister that far."

"No," I said, quickly, as though he was about to make an immediate decision and send her off that minute. "No, she can stay with me. Do you have any idea how long the asbestos removal will take?"

"We anticipate no longer than two weeks," he said. "What time can you be here tomorrow?"

I thought about William. "Can't I pick her up on Sunday?"

"I'm sorry, no. They'll be bringing in all the crew on Sunday, and taking over the area. We don't want any of our residents here at the time. We think it would be too stressful for them. Too difficult to see so many strangers here. Upsetting, you know."

"Tomorrow?"

"Yes, the earlier the better."

I sighed. "Fine. I'll be there as soon as I can."

Maybe, I thought. Maybe if I started out really early, I could have her back home by mid-afternoon, and still make my date with William. Maybe we could push it back a bit, but still...

I shook my head. Lucy would expect to spend time with me. I couldn't leave her alone—not with some kind of mad killer running loose in the neighborhood. I couldn't just drop her over at my aunt and uncle's house when I hadn't seen her in almost a month, either. They'd probably generously offer to have Lucy come visit while I was at work during the week, but to take advantage of their good nature by imposing on their weekend wasn't fair to them and it wasn't fair to her.

Even if I started out at eight in the morning, it was a three hour trip one-way, in good weather with no construction. Add in packing her things up for an extended stay, and the trip back, and the day was shot.

I stared out the window at the sunny day. Just as beautiful as David Dewars had described. I wished I could feel as good as the day looked.

SIX

I PULLED JORDAN in and brought her up to speed after my phone call with Lucy's school. I then stopped by Bass's office to tell him about Evelyn Vicks.

The team's offices lined the perimeter of the entire second floor of our building. Bass had a corner office facing north and west. My office was just a couple of doors away, and I overlooked the Chicago River, with a gorgeous view of the Wrigley Building and the Tribune Towers. Hank had the corner office that faced North and East, but William, tucked at the far end of the line of offices, faced south—right into the side of a marble building, so close he could touch it if the windows hadn't been welded shut.

His door was open, and the lights were on. Poor guy always had to have lamps and overhead lights on, seeing as how no natural sunlight ever pierced the narrow opening between the two buildings.

"Hi," I said, as I walked in.

He looked up and smiled. A genuine "glad to see you" smile. It both warmed my heart and made me feel immense disappointment at the same time.

He put his pen down and gestured for me to sit. "What's up?"

I shook my head. "Remember me telling you about my sister, Lucy?"

His head canted, ever so slightly. Concerned. "Yeah."

"Well," I sat across from him, "it looks like plans for

tomorrow have changed, after all." Explaining my need to make the long trek downstate in the morning, I kept my tone cheerful. I didn't want to make it seem like a chore—after all, Lucy meant the world to me—but I wanted him to know I was disappointed, too. "I'm sorry."

"Sounds like a full day," he said. His face had returned to that impassive look he was so good at. The look I had a hard time reading.

"Yeah," I said. "Very full."

We chatted a bit longer, and I lingered a few hopeful moments, but he didn't say anything that could even vaguely be construed as "Hey, don't worry, we'll just make it another time."

Pensive, I headed back to my office.

Jordan took one look at my face, and followed me in. "Looks like you're having a hell of a day."

"Tell me about it."

"I hate to make it worse, but..." She grinned.

"What?" I asked, frustrated by the tired sound in my voice. It wasn't even eleven in the morning, and I felt like I'd been through two weeks of boot camp.

"Bass wants you back in his office. He says something's come up. And," her brown eyes flicked up at me "that detective not only wants to fingerprint you, he wants to interview you again. He says to be there at three."

"Be there at three," I repeated. I made a mock salute to no one in particular. "Yes, sir." I stared out the window, trying really hard to soak in some of the good feelings the day was trying to deliver. No sense feeling sorry for myself.

"Do I need to call Detective Lulinski back?"

"Nope. He said he'll see you there."

"Of course," I said, and stood. I headed in to see Bass.

A HALF-HOUR later I caught William in the hub of the office, talking with his assistant. "Got a minute?"

"Sure," he said. He was back to his non-smiling persona.

He followed me into my office and I shut the door. "Guess what?" I asked, deadpan, my butt against the door, my hands behind by back.

"I give up."

"Bass has a new assignment for us."

William watched me as I wound around my desk and sat. His eyes narrowed. "Why do I get the feeling I'm not going to like this one?"

"I think you're going to love this one," I said, feeling yet another pang of disappointment. Bass had dropped opportunity in my lap not twenty minutes ago, but Lucy's imminent arrival could prevent my taking advantage. "You know that big media conference next weekend?"

"In San Francisco?"

"That's the one. Turns out there was some miscommunication. Bass thought Gabriela was going. One of the directors, too. Problem is, they had no idea, and now neither one can make it on such short notice." I watched a puffed-white cloud move across the otherwise clear sky. "Bass doesn't want to lose the hefty registration fee they paid."

"So he wants us to go."

"Yep. Both of us."

"I'll check, but I think I'm open," he said. "What about you?"

I shrugged, "Not sure," I said, thinking how if this had come at any other time...

"First you turn me down, then you send me away, huh?" He smiled, and I swore his eyes twinkled that time.

Returning the grin, I laughed. "Yeah, something like that."

Just as I said that, Jordan knocked then popped her

head in the door. "Here," she said. Pushing the door open with her back end, she came in smiling—carrying a long white box tied with a wide black ribbon. "This just came for you."

"For me?" I asked, standing. I flashed a hopeful glance William's direction, but he looked as surprised as I was.

"Uh-huh," Jordan said, sneaking a look at William too. She shrugged.

I'd seen enough old movies to know there were flowers inside the box; I'd just never received them presented this way before. "You sure?"

She laid the package on my desk with a sense of reverence. "I just signed for them. Came from one of those florists on Michigan Avenue. Open it up, already. I can't wait to see what's inside."

I didn't have to be coached. William took a half step back, allowing me room to maneuver the cumbersome box. It had to be at least two feet long, and I guessed about nine inches wide. Deep, too.

I undid the careful bow, my excited fingers fumbling at the knot.

Finally, with the ribbon removed, I lifted the lid off the white box to see—tissue paper. As I moved that aside, the scent rushed up. Roses. A dozen scarlet red roses exquisitely arranged. "They're beautiful," I said.

"Well, who are they from?" Jordan asked.

A small linen note with my name written in black sat at the middle of the arrangement, over yet another ribbon, this one shimmery gold. "I have no idea," I said.

Jordan grabbed the note, "Well, if you're not going to read this, I am."

I laughed, and let her. Mistake.

Her perfectly plucked eyebrows lifted and she shot me a knowing glance as she read the card aloud. "I am so sorry to hear of the loss of your friend and mine, Evelyn Vicks. Please accept these flowers as an expression of my condolence. And, if you are able to extricate yourself from your Saturday appointment with your colleague, please know that my offer for lunch and more remains open. Call me. With warmest regards, David Dewars."

I glanced at William. He held my gaze for an awkward moment, mumbled something about Dewars having good taste, then moved toward the door.

"I didn't..." I said, not knowing what to say, hoping to catch him, to explain. "I mean, I'm not..."

He didn't stop, but rather kept moving till he was in the doorway. Turning around, his hand came up, as though to stop me from talking. "Don't worry about it," he said.

I felt an immediate rush of embarrassment. How to explain that this was all a set of interlocked and unfortunate coincidences. "I *am* picking up Lucy tomorrow," I finally managed.

He nodded. "I never doubted that you were."

I watched the empty doorway for at least a half-minute after he left. Jordan stayed silent, watching me, then asked, "What was that all about?"

I dropped into my chair and rubbed my eyes. "Missed opportunity."

SEVEN

Bass CALLED A meeting for three-thirty, so I asked Jordan to reschedule my fingerprint appointment for one. I called my Aunt Lena to discuss Lucy's situation and was still on the phone when Jordan dropped a note on my desk. She shot me a look and rolled her eyes.

The pink paper gave me the police station's address with the message: "Two o'clock." She'd added the word, "Sharp," underlined four times.

"Hang on," I said into the handset. Scowling at the note, I put my hand over the mouthpiece and turned to Jordan. "Problem?"

She shrugged. "He wasn't too happy about changing the time, let me tell you. Two o'clock was the best I could do. I was trying to be real nice and I started to explain that you'd been called to a meeting but he didn't want to hear about that." She gave a little head wiggle. "He made some sort of comment too, I couldn't hear it all, but I thought he said something about you being 'high and mighty.' So I say 'What was that?' like I was being polite. He says, 'Nothing. But just tell her she better be on time,' and then he hangs up."

I glanced at my watch and nodded. "Sorry about that."

"I feel sorry for you," she said. "You're the one that's got to go over there."

Aunt Lena was talking again. "I need to let you go, honey. My bunco club is meeting in about a half hour and I still need to get my shoes on. But don't you worry. We'll be happy to have Lucy stay with us while you're at work. Okay? That's all settled."

I mouthed, "Thanks," to Jordan as she left, and turned my attention back to the phone conversation. In the midst of chaos it's always nice to know there are people you can depend on. Aunt Lena and Uncle Moose were just those people. "Thanks," I said again. "Lucy is going to love that, and it's going to make life a whole lot easier for me."

"Good. And you two should plan to come over for dinner tomorrow night. It'll be just the thing after that long drive."

"That," I said with enthusiasm, "sounds fabulous."

I ran behind schedule for the rest of the day but managed to leave the office for my appointment with Detective Lulinski right on time. An accident on the southbound Dan Ryan expressway slowed me down, and I watched the digital clock in my car turn to two just as traffic opened up at 35th Street.

Racing the rest of the way to the station at 51st and Wentworth, I got there about ten minutes late. Not too bad. I gave my name to the uniformed black woman at the reception desk. Sitting within a circular wall of chest-high brick, she took my name, phoned the detective, and then motioned me to a set of benches along the wall of windows to wait. Because the day was unseasonably warm, I'd left my coat in the car. Little did I know the station would be ten degrees cooler than the ambient air. Worse, the fabric of my skirt was so flimsy that the cold from the metal under my butt seeped into my body and made me shiver.

I crossed my legs to maintain body warmth and my airborne foot wiggled a nervous beat. I glanced at my watch: two-twenty. I didn't know how long the fingerprinting process took, but I reasoned that as long as Detective Lulinski didn't make me wait too much longer, I ought to be able to make the three-thirty meeting with a couple of minutes to spare.

The female officer shared the circular area with an older man, currently in conversation with two other officers. They flanked a handcuffed fellow dressed in baggy pink pants, a ripped orange down jacket, and a white knit hat pulled so low on his downcast head that I couldn't tell what he looked like.

I could tell that the officer standing behind the counter was a sergeant; he had three chevrons on his sleeve, a full head of white hair, bushy white eyebrows, and a jowl that hung, wobbling, over his snug collar. He kept both hands palms downward on the counter and leaned forward, giving instructions. An elderly black woman came through the glass doors, sending a rush of cold air my direction. Moving as fast as she could, using her three-footed cane to help her progress, she immediately started shouting at the female officer. "My boy is gone. My boy is gone. You got to help me find him."

Although the officer tried to keep her tone low, the elderly woman, her gray hair tight in pincurls, gesticulated with her free left hand and shouted over and over about her son having gone missing.

A flurry of activity expanded through the rest of the station, behind this small group. It reminded me of our hub, the only difference being that our people weren't in uniform.

Since the woman's son was an adult—thirty-eight years old—the officer behind the counter tried vainly to explain that he couldn't be considered missing unless there was evidence of foul play.

"But he's not smart," the woman insisted.

"He's handicapped?"

"No." She slammed her cane on the floor. "He's just not smart. He don't go out by himself. Never."

My heart went out to her and it dawned on me that I'd be in just that situation if Lucy ever decided to take off without telling me. I reminded myself to discuss safety issues with her when I picked her up tomorrow.

I eventually tuned out the shouting, choosing instead to stare over the parking lot beyond the tall windows. Trying not to think of the minutes ticking by.

"Ms. St. James?"

I jumped.

Detective Lulinski, looking even thinner and more haggard than he had the night of Mrs. Vicks' murder, stood before me, a bland expression on his face. Again he wore gray—a suit jacket and pants in a crisscross pattern, and a white shirt with a dark gray tie loosened and askew.

He motioned for me to follow him, and I did, walking past the round reception wall toward a pair of elevators. The building had only a basement and two floors. I eyed the wide-open adjacent staircase, but the detective pressed the "up" button before I could suggest we take the stairs.

"Have you ever been here before?" he asked as the elevator opened. I caught a whiff of just-finished cigarette as I walked past him into the boxy room.

I touched my nose in a dainty motion, as if that would help keep the smell at bay. "Not this station. I've been in a couple of others. I have a friend who's on the force on the north side."

He didn't ask me her name, where she'd been assigned, or anything. This guy wasn't going to win any Mr. Congeniality awards. When the doors slid open at the second floor he allowed me out first and gestured toward a long hall. Not knowing where I was headed, I stepped to the side. "Why don't you go first?"

"No, go ahead. Up there, on the right," he said.

I found it disconcerting to have him follow.

We wound up in a sizeable office, with more than a dozen desks. A busy place, more than half of them were occupied by detectives, with civilian guests seated next to each desk, apparently giving statements.

Detective Lulinski led me through the room and opened a far door. "We can do the fingerprinting in here," he said, by way of explanation.

When he set my first finger up for scanning on a glass plate, I turned to him, "I heard all kinds of horror stories about black ink that's so hard to wash off."

"Nope. We've moved to the twenty-first century here. We scan your prints nowadays."

He accomplished the fingerprinting task in a matter of moments, navigating my digits around with a smoothness that had to be borne of practice.

When complete, and once they'd been uploaded, he guided me back into the big room of busy desks and indicated where I should sit. We were nearly dead-center in the room, and I was amazed at the buzz of sound, with each detective busy on the phone or with the individuals seated at their desks. There were a handful of fellows Lulinski's age, but most of the detectives were hard-body young men, dressed in varying shades of black and dark blue.

One woman worked a desk in the far corner. I wondered about that.

Detective Lulinski's desk was a model of Spartan efficiency. Except for his computer monitor and a Rolodex, his workspace was empty. No pictures, no cutesy mugs, nothing that gave me any indication of his personality. All business, this fellow. But, to his defense, I imagined that he often interviewed less than ideal citizens at this desk, and the last thing he'd want to do is provide information they could possibly use against him.

The one out-of-place thing on his desk was his blotter. Evidently, Detective Lulinski was a scribbler and the entire white face of the calendar that covered the center of the blotter was awash in drawings and notes. He seemed particularly interested in drawing eyes—there must have been fifteen of them staring back at him, female eyes, male eyes, most of which had been rendered in black ink, a few in blue. I had to admit, he was pretty good.

No emotion in any of the eyes, however, and I wondered what that said about the man.

As soon as he sat, he pulled up a file from his computer, and concentrated on it, leaving me to my lonesome.

"Why…" I cleared my throat. "Why did a funeral home van come to take Mrs. Vicks away? I thought that this would be something for the coroner to do."

His eyebrows, dark with bits of gray hairs that went their springy different ways, raised up—not pleased. But he didn't make eye contact. He simply kept clicking at the form on the screen, even as he answered me.

"First of all, here in Cook County, we say 'medical examiner'—not 'coroner.' The difference is mainly semantics, but due to the overwhelming number of incidents every year, we're sending funeral homes to shuttle the bodies to the morgue."

That surprised me. I'd been about to follow up with another question regarding Mrs. Vicks' autopsy, when he interrupted my thoughts.

"You believe you last saw the victim at about six-twenty-five, correct?"

"Yes," I answered. The time reference reminded me about the meeting I still had to get to this afternoon. I sneaked a surreptitious glance at my watch.

Detective Lulinski caught me checking. One wiry eyebrow raised and his lips pursed.

"Okay, tell me again about the night of the murder. I'm going to transcribe it into this report and then you'll read it, sign it and you can be on your way."

Well wasn't he warm and fuzzy?

"I don't mind being here," I said. "I mean, I want to do whatever I can to help find out who did this."

He glanced at my wristwatch. "Uh-huh," he said in a flat voice. "Now, let's start at the beginning."

Within a few minutes he'd taken down every detail of my interaction with Mrs. Vicks, moment by moment. He had me repeat some of it several times and despite the fact that I knew I wasn't a suspect, I felt odd about it. As though I was holding back information. I knew better, of course, but I still felt guilty—like not having all the answers to who killed her was my fault. Like somehow I held the key to it all.

Lulinski clicked the controls and sent the file to a nearby laser printer. He got up, snatched it from the printer and perused it as he walked back to the desk.

"Okay," he said, keeping his attention on the report before him. Without making eye contact, he handed me the document. "Here, read it over, sign it if you agree with everything. I'll be right back."

Before he'd made it out the door, he pulled out a pack of cigarettes from his shirt pocket and a lighter from his pants. I watched him leave, then began verifying everything he recorded.

The guy was meticulous, I had to give him that. Both with recording details and with drawing eyes, and I wondered if that's why he came across as taciturn as he did. Hard to connect those attributes with friendliness, I supposed.

Just as I finished reading, he was back. Perfect timing. My guess is that it wasn't coincidence.

"Looks fine," I said. I reached for a pen in the holder across his desk.

He beat me to it, held it for a moment before handing it over, finally making eye contact. "You're sure?"

I felt the gears in my mind start to churn. "Yeah," I said, slowly. "I think this is pretty much word for word what I said."

He sat. "Then go ahead and sign."

I did.

Detective Lulinski watched me till I finished my name with my customary flourish. "You do know that this becomes part of the permanent record."

"I assumed as much."

"You're not going to be able to deny any of this."

"Why would I want to?"

"Well," he said, pulling a cigarette out from the pack and fingering it for a moment before tucking it over his ear, "I know sometimes you media types think that you can say one thing and mean another."

"What?"

"The night of the murder, you came traipsing over to let me know you'd been with the decedent earlier in the day."

"That's right."

"You were pretty forthcoming." He shrugged, staring at me with those dark eyes. "But not so forthcoming to let me know you worked for a television news station."

"What would that have to do with anything?"

He looked at me as though I were stupid. "You just happened to have been in contact with the victim hours before she was murdered. Murdered in a neighborhood known for being quiet and gang-free. Sweet innocent lady gets killed, it's big news. And guess what? You were there."

"You're not thinking that I had anything to do with it?" Stunned, I could hear the indignation and disgust in my voice.

"No," he said, slowly. "But I do find it interesting that you barged in, yet never said a word about what you did for a living."

"Why would that have mattered? It has nothing to do with the fact that she was murdered, and it can't possibly help you catch the guy."

"But it can help you get ratings, can't it?" His face tightened—not an attractive look. As if furious with me, his cheeks sucked in, giving added shadow to the burgeoning beard at his jawline. The long creases that bracketed his mouth deepened.

"What are you talking about?"

The background buzz in the office had quieted enough for me to realize that the otherwise unoccupied detectives nearby were listening in.

"You come in here, purportedly to provide a statement."

It was a prompt, and I nodded.

"What's the first thing out of your mouth? You start questioning why a funeral home picked up the body instead of the medical examiner."

"I was curious," I said, feeling defensive.

"Curious." His voice dripped sarcasm. "That's what you people call it nowadays, huh? Come on, Ms. St. James, we both know you media guys have a reputation for taking small incidents and turning them into heart-breaking feature stories with the requisite inept police investigators." He smirked. "By 'guys' I mean reporters, you understand. Non-gender specific."

This character was getting to me. I told myself to keep calm.

"I don't understand the basis for your anger, Detective."

"Never mind."

A swell of resentment gathered in my chest, and even as my voice rose, I wrestled with tamping down my frustration. "I will not 'never mind.' You obviously have something you want me to know. So, consider this your big chance." I sat back, folded my arms, and stared at him.

Despite the fact that I felt like a rotten little kid pitching a fit in the grocery store, I held tight for an excruciatingly long thirty seconds. He stared me down.

"I think we're about finished here," he said. Just as he propped his hands on the arms of his chair to stand, I stopped him.

"Listen," I said, my voice softer now, quiet enough to keep out of the reach of curious ears, "I don't know why, but we've gotten off to a bad start. If my occupation was important to your investigation, then I apologize for not mentioning it sooner. I didn't think it would make a difference." I cringed a bit inside. I'd held back on that tidbit of information for just that very reason. We in the media often were regarded with suspicion and I'd wanted to avoid that.

Fingers splayed on the desk before him, he took a breath. Whatever was bugging this guy, it was more than just my job at *Midwest Focus*. "Where can I reach you for follow-up, if I have any further questions?" he asked.

I pulled a business card from my purse. "Here," I said, standing.

He took one look at the card, then stood, stepping sideways to block my departure. "Wait."

Left without much choice, I waited.

"*Midwest Focus Newsmagazine*?" he asked, sounding surprised.

"Yeah," I said, the same way people say, "Duh!"

For the first time all afternoon, the detective appeared nonplussed. "I thought that you worked for *Up Close Issues.*"

I shook my head. "Nope."

"So you don't work with Dan Starck?"

I offered a thin-lipped smile. "Not if I can help it."

He opened his middle drawer and pulled out a clipping from the newspaper. Sandra Stanek's article. "What about this?"

Fed up, I rolled my eyes. "Don't believe everything you read, Detective."

"Hmm," he said. He stepped aside, allowing me passage. "I'll call you if I need anything further, is that all right?" His voice had softened enough to sound almost conversational. As though we'd just met and he hadn't decided to hate me, yet.

"Sure," I said.

I left, wondering what that had all been about.

EIGHT

"ALEX!"

Lucy ran at me, all arms and smiles, and threw herself into a bear hug.

As I pulled her close, I thought again about how I felt so much like her older sister, not three years her junior. She had bright blond curly hair, cut about shoulder length, and as I ran my hand across the back of her head, I felt a rough patch of knots. Lucy always twisted the back of her hair when she was nervous.

She was only five-foot-two; I was a good four inches taller. They say Williams Syndrome gives its victims a pixie look, and for Lucy, at least, it was true. She had bright blue eyes that tilted just enough to give her that "different" appearance, and her chin was narrow, coming almost to a point. The fact that she was tiny, both in stature, and in bone structure, made the pixie-illusion even stronger. She liked to wear dresses, as did I, but where I'd relax at home in a pair of worn blue jeans and a sweatshirt, she'd grab a cotton dress to pull over her head, and feel just as comfortable. It stemmed, I believed, from the fact that throwing a dress over her head and slipping on loafers took a lot less concentration than dealing with the zippers, buttons, and shoelaces.

She had a tendency to spill on herself, however, and my mom, in an effort to keep cleaning bills and replacement clothing costs down, started providing some of those elderly women housedresses for Lucy. I hated them. She was wearing one of them now, a blue checkered gingham.

She clung to me for a long time.

"What's wrong?" I asked, as we finally pulled away.

"Nothing," she said, smoothing the back of her head with her left hand. "I was just waiting and waiting for you to come."

"I told Mr. Raymond I'd be here by ten," I said, with a glance at my watch. "It's not even nine-thirty, yet."

Giggling, she bounced up on the balls of her feet. "I know. I just was so excited to see you."

I took another look at the housedress. As long as she was staying with me, I'd see that she had some slightly more stylish clothes to wear. "It's cold outside," I said. "Don't you have anything heavier?"

"I'm hot."

"It's cold in the car. Let's go see what else you've got."

Lucy was better than anyone I knew at reading people and pinpointing when someone was unhappy, or troubled. She herself was in a perennially cheerful mood, and in addition to her favorite activity—socializing—she loved to read, listen to music, and play the piano.

It hadn't been till she was eleven and I was eight that I started to notice the differences between us. I'd memorized my multiplication tables over the course of an evening, and I asked her to test me on them while we were grocery shopping with Mom.

Within a couple of minutes it was apparent to me that she had no idea what I was doing. It was then that I began to notice our mother taking her aside and explaining how much the bill should be, how much cash she should offer and how much she should expect back in return.

I was wearing my favorite pink top that day—the one with three puppies in hula skirts that were sewn on special so they moved in the wind, and a pair of matching pink shorts. "Here," I said, trying to inject some lightness into the conversation. I pointed to my shirt. "Think of it like this. How many puppies do I have here?"

I waited.

Mom waited.

Lucy bit her lip and looked down at her feet. She held her fingers out, low, and snuck a glance back up at my shirt, trying to match the number of fingers to the number of puppies.

I felt my heart break. Reality rushed at me, making me feel like I should have been more aware, should have been more sensitive, and at the same time knowing that I'd never look at her the same again.

"Don't worry about it, honey," Mom said. She turned to the closest grocery shelf and I watched her eyes scan over the boxes and cans, with frantic eagerness. "Here!" she said, in discovery, moving halfway down the aisle to reach. "You two love fruit cocktail." She held the bright-colored can up for both of us to see. Lucy's face rose enough to catch a glimpse. "We haven't had fruit cocktail for dessert in a long time, have we?"

Just as eager to change the subject, I said, "Could we buy some?"

"We'll get two cans," Mom said.

Somehow that night, the perennial favorite family dessert didn't taste so great.

Now, in Lucy's room, I sorted through her clothes and pulled out her suitcase to start packing. For an assisted living facility, this place was pretty nice. Each resident was treated as an important member of the team, each person had a job, and was responsible for his or her own living space. Lucy had a roommate, a young girl about fourteen with a mild case of Down Syndrome. Lauralee had gone home already, Lucy said. She'd left over a week ago.

"I'm really lonely here now."

She was standing behind me, trying futilely to see over my shoulder when she said that. I turned and saw the sadness in her pale blue eyes. "Well, no need to feel lonely any more. You're coming home with me and we're going to have a great time together."

"You won't have to go to work, right?"

I hedged, turning back into the closet and pulling out a deep blue T-shirt dress. It still wasn't warm enough for the weather, but it had long sleeves. "How's this?"

She grabbed it and made her way to the bathroom in the corner to put it on as I dug out her winter coat. She kept the door open, and peered around the opening. "You won't have to work, right?"

I hated the hopeful sound in her voice. From the time I got out of high school, and went away to college, Lucy constantly asked me when I'd be home again. Even if we didn't do anything together specifically, she always seemed happiest when the whole family was in the house at the same time.

I thought about the new story Bass had dropped into our laps. And that trip to San Francisco.

How the heck was I going to make it all right?

"Well, I was thinking about that," I said. "I do have a few projects I have to work on, but Aunt Lena and Uncle Moose are going to want you to come visit while you're home, you know."

She came out of the bathroom with a grimace. "Yeah."

"Come on," I said, hoping to coax her into a good mood. "They haven't seen you in such a long time, they miss you."

She nodded, unimpressed.

I turned on a classical music station on the ride back,

and watched Lucy's mood improve with every mile we traveled. By the time we were thirty miles out, she was fast asleep.

I gently switched stations to classic rock and let my mind wander. At the staff meeting yesterday, Bass had dropped another bombshell. If I couldn't make the trip to San Francisco, he'd offer the opportunity to someone on the film crew. He was certain one of them would take him up on the offer, and made mention that one of the women there had expressed interest in going.

I'd kept my voice neutral as I asked who it was.

Bass shrugged, "What's-her-name—the one who used to be a smoke jumper—"

"Caroline?" William asked.

"Yeah, that's the one. She says she's ready to pack up and go as soon as I give her the word."

"Great," I said, trying to sound enthusiastic. A beautiful girl, Caroline Bliss had a cheerful disposition and an adventurous spirit. She also had a tendency to hang around William and make small talk whenever we attended a filming. Bugged me. Big time. The thought of William and Miss Bliss jetting off for San Francisco together made me regret the timing of Lucy's visit, once again.

I tried to shake off those feelings as I backed into the garage. We made good time, it wasn't even three o'clock yet. The car's jerky back-up movement must have registered with Lucy, because she woke, sitting up fast, wearing a blank-eyed, "Where am I?" look. A half-second later, her face relaxed into a smile of contentment when she realized we were home.

With a pang I remembered Evelyn Vicks. I'd have to tell her about that. Sooner, rather than later.

I pressed the remote on my garage door opener, and to my surprise, it responded on the first try.

"There is some bad news, Lucy," I said, my words stopping her from opening the passenger door.

Her eyes, light blue, with a lacy pattern of white in the iris that made her gaze especially compelling, looked at me with fearful awareness and trust. "Did something happen to Mom and Dad?" she asked.

I shook my head.

The garage had dimmed, with the closing of the big door, and the only light in the area was the single 100 watt bulb attached to the opener above us. I hesitated, then switched on the car's interior lights. Lucy shot me a quizzical look.

I pulled in a breath.

"Somebody…" I didn't quite know how to phrase it. Lucy was the most sensitive person I'd ever met. How to tell her that a woman she'd known since birth had been brutally murdered?

"It's really bad, isn't it?" she asked, her voice high and childlike.

"Yeah."

We were silent for a long moment and I heard Lucy's breathing. Shallow. She was nervous.

"Mrs. Vicks," I said, finally.

"What about her?"

"She's…"

I hesitated again.

"She died?" Lucy asked.

"Yeah."

"When?"

I told her that it had been just two days ago, and that they hadn't even had the wake yet. That was scheduled for tomorrow night, with the funeral on Monday morning.

"We're going to go to that, right?"

I leaned my head back. When had we not gone to a wake

or funeral of someone we knew? Our parents toted us along from the time we were young, so the ceremony that accompanied death became, for us, a part of life. So many of my friends avoided the rituals, claiming that they hated wakes and funerals. Yeah, I always wanted to say…like I like them? "Of course," I said. "But there's a bit more."

Lucy shook her head, in a "tell me" motion.

"Somebody came into her house and…I'm sorry to tell you this, Lucy. Somebody killed her."

Lucy's eyes went wide, shifting suddenly around the desolate garage as though the person who murdered Evelyn Vicks might be waiting in the corner ready to pounce on us.

"It's okay," I said quickly. I had no idea whether it was okay or not, but I knew I needed to allay her fears. "The police are looking for him now. I talked to them yesterday." Switching gears, I said, "Guess what Aunt Lena made us for dinner tonight?"

Lucy shook her head, shrugged, and said. "I don't know," all at once. Her eyes still held fear that hadn't been there before.

I pushed myself to smile, waited for her to grin back. "Your favorite."

She bounced in the car's seat. "Mom's meatloaf?"

"Yep."

She lurched forward, and grabbed me into a full-body hug. "Oh, Alex," she said, "It's so great to be home."

NINE

Sunday evening, we stood outside the funeral home's glass doors. Inside, past the vestibule and second set of doors, I saw people walking by, all dressed in muted shades of blue, black, and brown. I wished I were somewhere else.

Lucy tugged at my arm, eager to see the neighbors, eager to talk to people she hadn't seen in almost a year. I held firm, wanting just a moment longer to quell the small trembling I always fought right before walking in to a wake.

"Hang on," I said.

Lucy looked at me and squinted. "You okay?"

"I'm fine."

The tile floor inside lent a homey air to the central lobby. A low fireplace to our right burned brightly, and a group of people occupied the easy chairs surrounding it, perhaps attracted by its cheeriness in these otherwise dismal surroundings.

A black fuzzy sign, with white letters pressed into its horizontal lines, directed us to the chapel at the far right of the building. Lucy nearly skipped down the hallway.

Just outside the chapel, Uncle Moose nodded to us, murmuring to me that Aunt Lena was inside waiting, keeping an eye on Diana. Mrs. Vicks' roommate had refused to return to live in the house, and with no family nearby, she'd begun taking turns staying at each of the neighbors' homes over the past several days. She returned to Mrs.

Vicks' home only to pick up necessities, and only when accompanied by someone else.

As soon as we cleared the double-door entryway to the chapel, Lucy let out a tiny squeal of excitement. She'd spied Mrs. McGillicuddy, another elderly neighbor who always invited her over to help with chores and baking. Lucy adored her.

I caught her as she was about to sprint, reminding her that we needed to pay our respects first. I knelt at the side of the casket and did that "pretend to pray" thing.

Lucy looked at Mrs. Vicks with curiosity.

"She doesn't look like anybody killed her." Lucy's stage whisper was loud enough for everyone to hear. "She just looks like a regular dead person."

She did. I knew from neighborhood scuttlebutt that she'd been stabbed. The rumor mill, however, came up short on accuracy. Diana had sworn she'd seen a slice in Mrs. Vicks' neck, but according to our local police-contact, Russ Bednarski, who said he heard it on the QT, she'd been run through the heart, multiple times. I had to put my money on old Russ, since there was no indication of mortician work done around her throat area.

As it was, she seemed, as most dead people do, to be a heavily made up sleeping person whose cheeks have gone slack at the sides. She had that pinkish tone to her skin, both from the caked on makeup and the spotlights directed from above the casket. Her hands were folded, looking puffed, like two blown-up latex gloves, one atop the other. A wine-colored rosary, strategically placed to look natural, reflected the light in tiny glitters.

I patted Lucy's hand, and stood. "Mrs. Vicks' son, Bart, is here. We have to say hello."

She sidled close. "Do I know him?"

I whispered, "Yeah, we met him at Mr. Vicks' funeral.

He came in for that." Lucy shook her head, clearly unsure. I continued. "I think he moved away when we were kids. He probably won't remember us." I made our way toward a large middle-aged blond man in a black suit standing two floral arrangements away from the head of the casket. He stared at a far wall, swaying. All I knew about him nowadays was that he lived up north in a small Wisconsin town, but beyond that, Mrs. Vicks hadn't often spoken of him. He finished talking with other neighbors and turned to us, the next participants in the receiving line of grief.

I held out my hand, "Accept my sympathies," I began.

He took my hand, but I got the impression my words hadn't registered. He stared at me for a couple of beats without saying anything and I wondered if the odor emanating from him was bad cologne, or if he'd been hitting the bottle. His small eyes shifted back and forth between Lucy and me, as if deciding something.

I put him in his early fifties. His head was shaped like a wide cylinder, his flat crew-cut hair exacerbating the image. He would have benefited from a chiseled jawline, but his second and third chins sagged and covered most of the collar of his gray shirt.

"You're Alex." His eyes took me in, head-to-toe. "Grew up some, huh?"

I tugged my hand back, with some resistance, and once free, used it to propel Lucy forward. "And this is my sister Lucy. We're very sorry about your mother," I began again.

"Yeah." He lifted his chin and stepped forward in an almost confrontational move. "I heard you were there right before it happened."

Bart's small eyes squinted at me, the deep folds of wrinkles in the extra fat of his face making them look piggyish. I couldn't make out their color. Light blue. More gray, maybe. Very pale. I decided he was a mouth-breather, since it remained open, his lower lip hanging sausage-like and wet as he waited for my reply.

"I was there—"

"Yeah, and you work for the newspaper, right?"

"No—"

"Diana, there, told me you did." His eyes flicked over to the sofa where Mrs. Vicks' roommate and my Aunt Lena huddled. "Hey," he said, louder, lifting his chin Diana's direction now. "She don't work for the newspaper. What are you trying to pull?"

In a reflexive gesture, to correct things before they got out of hand, which they looked about to do, I placed my hand on his arm. Mistake.

He jumped at my touch.

"I work for television," I said, pulling my hand away.

His expression shifted. "You do?" A quick look at Diana, possibly meant as apology, and then he was back to me. "Good. Then maybe you can pull some strings."

I felt my own mouth go slack. I shut it immediately.

He attempted a smile. "What I mean is, we're old friends, right?" As he said that, his glance raked over me again. "And I'm thinking that if you have some 'in' with bigwigs downtown, maybe you can help me out how I can get everything settled here."

Lucy whispered that she was going to talk to Mrs. McGillicuddy and scampered off, leaving me alone with Big Bart.

"It's not like I have an 'in' with investigations—" I began again.

"I'm not talking about the cops," he said, chopping the word short in a laugh. "Like they're really going to try to find out who did this. I know better. I know these big city types. Just another one for the books."

I thought about Detective Lulinski, and despite the fact

that he and I hadn't hit it off, I'd gotten a clear impression that he had every intention to get this one solved as expeditiously as possible. "To be honest—"

"I'm talking about this probate sh—" He glanced around, lowered his voice. "Crap. You know what I mean. I know my ma had a will. She and my dad took care of that way back when I was a kid. And I tried to get in her safe deposit box where she worked, to go get it, and they wouldn't let me. Said it was sealed because she was dead. And wouldn't even tell me how to get around that."

I was getting tired of being interrupted at every comment. I said nothing.

Not that he noticed.

"And you have to know lawyers and big shots, if you're in television." He pointed a fat finger a hair too close to my chest. I backed up. About to start talking again, his tongue darted out to catch the little bubbles of spit that had gathered at the corners of his mouth. "Get one of them to look into this for me, okay? I don't know anybody down here and I'm kind of in a hurry to get it all done, you know?" His eyes glanced around as though just remembering where we were. "I mean, losing your mother is real hard." His expression strove for earnest; his voice lowered. "I'm just looking to put this behind me. You understand."

I opened my mouth to say something—something like how I knew that his grief had to be all-consuming right now but that there was nothing I could do to help him, but he stared at me and moved a half-step forward.

"Right?"

From over my right shoulder a deep voice said, "Barton Vicks? I'm so very sorry to hear about your mother. She was a wonderful woman."

David Dewars stepped up, reaching to shake hands with Bart as his left hand reached out sidewise to skim my back.

It was a protective move, and I had no doubt he saw himself as my knight in shining armor come to rescue me. He shot me a conspiratorial wink that Bart didn't catch and I stepped away from both of them, happy to extricate myself from the situation, but knowing I could have handled things myself just fine, thank you very much.

Aunt Lena was escorting Diana to the ladies' room and Lucy happily trailed after them. There was nothing like a women's restroom to provide a bit of sanctuary. I decided to join the little group.

Inside the tiny, three-stall room, I was startled when I caught a look at Diana's face under the harsh fluorescent lights. Her flaccid face had gone red in patches and what little mascara she'd put on today had pooled beneath her eyes, making them look small and grotesque. Despite her relative youth, her ensemble of mismatched blacks with telltale deodorant streaks adorning each side of her shirt served only to emphasize her frumpiness.

"How are you holding up?" I asked.

Mistake again.

She opened her mouth to speak, but hiccupped instead, heralding a high-pitched profusion of sobs. Lucy, ever insistent on trying to help people not be sad, put her skinny arms around Diana's dark-clothed back and said, "She's in heaven, now. She's happy and watching over you."

Diana seemed to take comfort in Lucy's words and they both sat on a small divan near the door.

Aunt Lena had busied herself with wetting some hand towels and began to wipe at Diana's face to clear away some of the mascara-mud.

I've never been good at consoling people in situations such as these. I know that no matter what I say or do, that person's loved one is dead. Gone. There is never anything that can be said to make that better. When I try the old familiar line about the deceased being "in a better place," I feel like a hypocrite. So, mostly I just say I'm sorry and that's it.

Right now, I stood staring at Lucy and at my aunt. Both, without any prompting, seemed to know precisely what would help Diana. I felt inept and useless. "Anything I can do?" I asked.

My aunt smiled at me from the sink area, almost as though she understood my discomfort. "I made cookies," she said. "They're in the coffee room. How about you make sure they're all put out properly?"

Thankful for a job, and even more thankful that I didn't have to stay here and help in this claustrophobic room amid Diana's wails and sobs, I headed out.

The coffee room. I'd been to this place enough times that I knew exactly where it was. As a kid, I'd called it the cookie room. Tucked into the building's back corner, the area was set apart from the mourning chapels by both style and sound. In here the stuffy furnishings gave way to real comfort.

Round tables were set in three of the four corners. Designated cookie areas for each of the occupied chapel guests, apparently. There was a long bar-type configuration along one wall, complete with microwave, refrigerator and two sinks. The cabinets held all sorts of supplies, from Styrofoam cups and sugar packets, to a bag of suckers for little kids here under duress.

The sofas lining the walls were occupied by talkative folks, no longer worried about keeping their voices down, or their demeanor subdued. People chatted and poured coffee from the gurgling coffeemakers.

I caught a glimpse of a Tupperware container I knew to be Aunt Lena's. Full of her specialty, shortbread cookies, it hadn't yet been opened. I took a look at the plentiful offerings on the table assigned to Mrs. Vicks' visitors, and moved some of them around, as though I knew what I was doing.

I hadn't known how to comfort Diana, I didn't even think to bring goodies for the wake tonight, and right now, I stood here looking down at assorted cakes, cookies, brownies and lunch meats interspersed with condiments, and I knew there was some order, or setup that I should put them into. Something that escaped me entirely.

Mrs. McGillicuddy came in. We spoke briefly and exchanged comments regarding the brutality of Mrs. Vicks murder. All the while she talked, she futzed with the table and totally rearranged it all. Right before my eyes, it became appealing, clean and efficient.

"Wow," I said.

She looked at me surprised. "What?" Heading to the counter top, she started to wash her hands.

"The way you did that."

As if the whole arrangement business had been done without a second thought, she glanced over at the table, shrugged. "Did what?"

Just then David Dewars walked into the cookie room—and I didn't think he was looking for pecan clusters. He blinked from behind his small round glasses, his head turning this way and that, till he spied me.

"Alex," his voice boomed above the chatty din.

I moved toward him just to keep him quiet.

"I'm pleased to see you again," he said. His right hand gestured around the room. "I just wish it were under different circumstances."

"It's nice to see you, too" I said, in a low voice.

Mimicking my tone, he asked, "Have you been here long?"

He'd moved even closer—the man smelled great. "Not really," I said. "I see you met Bart."

His mouth twisted sideways and he gave what could have been a small snort. "That guy."

"What's wrong with him?"

Glancing both directions, just like in a suspense film, he brought his face closer to mine. Mrs. McGillicuddy had moved to a group of white-haired women chatting in the corner. "I heard him badgering you as I walked in."

"You mean about helping him with the probate problems?"

"Yeah. I find it just a little bit transparent, don't you?"

Transparent? Since I had no idea what David was talking about, I said, "Well—" hoping he'd take the ball and run with it.

He didn't let me down.

"I mean, come on." Settling so that his backside rested against the long counter, I recognized the move for what it was. He liked being able to watch the comings and goings of those around him. He folded his arms across his chest. Dressed in a dark suit rather than a tux this time, he cut no less of an impressive figure. I wondered if he folded his own navy blue handkerchiefs, or if they came that way. An identical match to his navy blue tie, he was the picture of the perfect mourner.

He settled himself a little more, and he brought his head a little closer to mine. "Mrs. Vicks didn't have an enemy in the world. She was truly one of the worthy souls I'd ever encountered."

Worthy? Interesting choice of words, I thought.

He smiled at me, and added, "Present company excepted, of course."

I made a murmur-like sound, hoping he'd take it as whatever response he expected, since I had no idea how to reply to that. I was having that problem a lot with Mr. David Dewars. He confused me. I decided to direct the conversation, at least to feel a bit more in control again. I got the feeling I knew where he was going anyway.

"Are you implying something?"

His eyes flicked around the room—wary—before settling on mine. I couldn't read him. He always seemed to have a glint of humor lurking behind those deep brown eyes. "Who else had the means, the motive, and the opportunity?"

"You think her son did it?" I asked. "What possible motive?"

I leaned my left hip against the counter, and he moved closer. Too close for such a warm environment, but a second whiff of his cologne I caught was very nice. Man, did this guy ever do anything wrong? He was Mr. GQ, or, owing to his age, Mr. GQ's…uncle. In either case, I wanted to find fault with him, but other than his imposing nature, which no doubt served him well in the business world, I couldn't.

He leaned in and spoke softly into my left ear, his eyes keeping watch on the rest of the folks in the room. "I shouldn't tell you this, but Mrs. Vicks had a trust fund accumulated."

I leaned away far enough to make eye contact with him.

He shot me a meaningful glance, then bent closer to tell me more. His breath was warm and minty as it brushed past my cheek. "Payable on her death, in full, to…guess who?"

I felt my eyebrows shoot up. "Barton Vicks?"

He nodded, but he wasn't finished. His right arm reached around my shoulders, pulling me a bit closer. "The fund is in excess of fifty thousand dollars."

I shot him a quizzical look. "Fifty thousand is hardly worth killing a person for," I said.

"Not much to you, maybe," he said, "But our friend Bart…" He came so close he could have kissed me. For half a second, I wondered how I would react if he tried, "has a gambling problem. Evelyn told me that in confidence."

"Still," I said.

His eyes scoped the room, but he still stayed so near I could feel his breath tickling past my ear. I had a feeling he did that on purpose. "The guy's always in trouble…he owes money…To a man like that fifty thousand can look like salvation." He leaned back finally, and as he did so, his hand skimmed the back of my arm. "This is all off the record, of course."

"Of course," I said, automatically. Then, as I processed the information, I shook my head, "You should tell the police about it."

"I have told them," he said. "But I thought you ought to know, too. Just keep it to yourself, okay?"

"Why tell me?"

"I heard Barton ask you to look into things. I figured that's what you'd be doing anyway—am I right?"

"Honestly? No."

He didn't try to hide his surprise, as a matter of fact, he seemed to amplify his feelings, but whatever he'd been about to say was interrupted by Mrs. Wozniak who reached an arthritic hand between us for a grab at the coffeepot. In her late eighties, she'd come to this country as a teenager but had never quite embraced the English language.

"*Co to jest?*" she asked me, indicating the powdered cream.

I explained, in Polish, what the flour-like substance was used for, and took small pleasure in noting David's reaction to my speaking the language.

Mrs. Wozniak made a sound, "Hmmph," that transcended any language, and hobbled over to the refrigerator where she scavenged till she came up with a carton of half and half, that she held up to me in triumph.

"You speak Polish?" David said.

I nodded.

"But you…" he faltered and I was glad to see it. "I mean, I don't want to sound indelicate, but your last name certainly isn't Eastern European. And, to be honest, you've got the look of the dark Irish about you."

"I know," I said. "A story for another time." I made no secret of the fact that I was adopted, nor of the fact that my father had had our last name changed from Szatjemski to St. James when I was little, but it wasn't David's business, and this wasn't the time nor the place for such divulgences.

"Good," he said. "I will look forward to hearing it."

Subject closed, I nodded.

"Back to Mrs. Vicks." He removed his glasses, and pulled a white cotton handkerchief out of his right pants pocket to clean them. One of his eyes narrowed and a slow smile spread across his features. He winked. "You mean to tell me that you're not the least bit curious—that you're not considering poking around to find out what you can from your contacts?"

I realized that if I had half the contacts people thought I did, I'd be able to write my own ticket in the world of network television. "Of course I'm curious. I'd love to be able to nail the bastard who did this. But I know my limitations."

"Uh-huh," he said without conviction. His glasses back in place, he turned himself to give his full attention to me, bringing his face close again. "You can tell me, Alex. Off the record."

I shook my head, but that seemed to further convince him of my involvement.

"Alex," he said in a voice that could have been termed sexy if we weren't in the coffee room of a funeral home, "Is Barton Vicks living at the house?"

"No. He said he'd prefer to keep his hotel room while he was in town."

"And the police, Alex? What are they up to?"

I opened my mouth to answer when I realized the trap he'd baited. I closed my mouth and stared at him. "Just because I know what's going on doesn't mean I'm investigating."

He grinned, as though about to argue the point, but at that moment, his attention suddenly shifted to something behind me. As his hand raised in greeting, his expression relaxed, not quite into a smile, but his mouth set. Whoever he saw, he'd expected to see.

I turned.

The man who ambled in through the open double doors of the cookie room wore a dark suit and navy blue tie similar to David's. I wondered if they'd intentionally color-coordinated.

He and David shook hands, then I was introduced. "Alex," David said, "this is my senior vice president, Owen Riordan."

I was taken with the difference in the two men. Owen had a pasty look to him, with bloodshot blue eyes that sagged downward at the corners, forming long lines running the length of his cheeks. Late forties, possibly early fifties, he had prematurely gray hair combed into a thin pompadour that sat like the Florida peninsula between the deep receding sides of his hairline. His facial bones were pronounced, giving him a sucked-in look, with bright red blood vessels that laced the tops of his cheeks. His broad, yet saggy frame said, "aging athlete."

Owen nodded. "Pleased to meet you."

I nodded. For my benefit, David added, "Evelyn worked for Owen in the loan department."

Owen shook his head. "It's a damn shame," he said. "What kind of a world is it when a nice old lady can't be safe in her own house?" He turned to me, adding, "The whole department's supposed to stop by tonight. I made sure that everybody knew."

"That's nice."

Owen turned toward the countertop and poured a cup of coffee. David raised his voice, just loud enough to get Owen's attention. "Did you finish the paperwork on the Marple account today?"

"Yeah, but I still need your signature on a couple of documents."

"Did you bring them?"

Owen looked around, his droopy eyes widening. "To a wake?"

David stared at the ceiling and let out a long hiss from between clenched teeth. "Where are the papers now?"

"I left them with Nina."

Lasering his gaze back toward Owen, David's tone was sharp as he said, "They were supposed to be Fed Ex-ed today."

I wasn't about to let this opportunity pass me by. Time to escape. "If you'll excuse me," I began.

"Alex." His voice had returned to its soothing cadence. "My apologies. We shouldn't be talking business here. Forgive me."

"Nothing to forgive," I lied. "But I should get back in there."

"I'll follow in a moment. I'm sorry to bring business

here, but we have a loan closing tomorrow morning, and our client is very particular." He smiled, but it didn't reach his eyes. "As a matter of fact, I wanted very much to attend the services tomorrow, but this closing demands my attention. I fear I can never escape the tentacles of the workplace."

"If you need to leave, I can let Barton know—" I began.

The relief on his face was palpable. "I do have to get back downtown to sign off on those papers."

"Not a problem," I said.

As I inched away, he grabbed my hand. "Thank you, Alex."

I WANDERED BACK into the long room. With its upscale, de-signed-to-be-soothing furnishings, it could have been con-fused with a very large living room if it hadn't been for the casket at the far end. Suffused under pink spotlights and flanked by tall floral arrangements, Mrs. Vicks, in death, held the crowd's gaze like a compelling puzzle crying out for a solution. Elderly folks who'd gathered early had ar-ranged the hard chairs in circles where they could converse and keep their canes and walkers out of the aisle. The line of mourners who'd come to pay their respects had grown, and as I breezed past them to talk to Bart, I caught the whiff of roses and carnations. Wake smells.

A quick grip to my arm stopped me mid-tracks. My first thought was that David Dewars had come back after all. I turned, instead, to see my Aunt Lena.

"Honey, can you do me a big favor?"

"Of course."

Her eyes had watered up again. "It's Diana," she said, twisting her head toward the exit. "She's still in the bath-room. She won't come out. This has been too traumatic for her and I was wondering if you could take her home."

"Sure."

Aunt Lena scrunched her nose, wrinkling up her slightly pudgy face. She took a hesitant breath before continuing. "Do you think maybe you can take a look around while you're there? You know, before the prodigal son gets his paws on everything."

"I thought she was staying at your house?"

"Yes, but if you wouldn't mind stopping back at Evelyn's first," she sighed with a glance toward the coffin up front. Her lips twisted and her eyes raked over Barton. "I guess I should call it his house now." Aunt Lena had her arms folded. Her eyes focused on Bart, but she leaned in my direction and kept her voice low. "I think he had something to do with his mother's death."

Involuntarily, my eyes shot up.

At that moment, across the room, Bart looked my direction and our eyes locked. I felt an immediate flush of discomfort and turned away. "He was in Wisconsin at the time of the murder," I whispered.

"Do we know that for sure?"

I shrugged.

Aunt Lena clucked a sound of her disappointment. "I know I don't. But maybe you could find out." She gave me as motherly a glare as I'd ever seen from her. "All I'm saying is, Evelyn told me that there were problems with her accounts. It really bothered her and," she said with effect, "she didn't want Barton to know about it."

I thought about what David Dewars had told me about her holdings. "What kind of problems?"

"She didn't say, exactly. She just told me that she wasn't sure that things were being handled quite right, and she needed someone she could trust to look into it."

I remembered our last conversation. "She mentioned that when I helped her get into her house."

"See?"

I saw nothing.

Aunt Lena continued, "I mean—she trusted you. She probably was going to ask you to look into that anyway. I sort of suggested she talk to you, you know."

"Why did you do that?"

"Well, I did suggest Barton at first. I mean, really, if you can't trust your kids, who can you trust? But she said no, Barton would try to 'take advantage.' Those were the exact words she used."

I shook my head, but my curiosity was piqued. "Did she say anything else?"

"She was pretty close-mouthed about her financial stuff, but she's been alone in that paid-off house for years. She's got her husband's pension, she held the job at Banner Bank, and she took in Diana, who I'm sure must have paid her some rent. I'm thinking Evelyn might have socked away quite a few dollars. And she wasn't all that old, you know. Barton might have not wanted to wait for his inheritance."

Bart was looking at me again, so I held off speaking till he shifted his gaze. "That's pretty thin. Unless I knew what problems she was talking about..."

"You see? Here's your opportunity to find out." She patted my arm. "You take Diana to pick up a few things— she's running low on clothing, and some of her incidentals—and while you're there you have a look around."

Pleased with herself, her voice had risen just enough to make me uncomfortable that others had heard our conversation, but I reasoned that taking Diana home would give me a valid excuse to get away from this place, and if I took a quick look around, I'd keep Aunt Lena happy, too. Win-win situation. Those don't come by all that often.

"Sure," I said. "Just let me get Lucy."

Quick shake of her head. "No, leave Lucy here. She's

good for everyone. She's cheerful and she reminds us of better times. Moose and I will bring her home when we leave."

"How late are you staying?"

She shrugged. "Until I know everyone's been greeted and thanked. That's what Evelyn would have wanted." Her eyes flashed up again. "Lot of good he's doing."

Bart still stood at the left side of the casket, his large body swaying side to side as he faced an elderly couple who'd begun to offer their condolences. His face registered nothing beyond boredom, staring at the exit door, as more and more people walked in.

I waited to approach him, standing just out of his line of vision. He nodded at the two people in front of him, saying, "Uh-huh," twice, clearly with no interest in their gracious comments about his mother.

Since the next set of people were still at the kneeler, I decided to make my move. Get in, get out, be done.

Barton, apparently, had the exact same idea at the precise time I did. As soon as the couple in front of them turned toward the waiting chairs, he stepped around them and stormed to the entryway. Before anyone knew it, he was gone.

I followed. Striding out the door myself, I heard a woman whisper, "Maybe he has to go visit the little boy's room."

Past the fireplace, over the wool rugs, he headed straight for the outside doors, pushing the right-hand-door with his open palm against the glass, his left grabbing for something in his back pocket. I expected him to dig out a pack of cigarettes, but instead he came up with a silver hipflask, and in a move so smooth that it had to be habit, he hoisted it to his lips as the door swung open, banging the back wall. A second later, I heard a swoop of air as he banged out the second door.

For a long moment there was no sound except the popping of wood in the lobby fireplace. Mr. Skulina, the funeral director, a squat fellow with salt and pepper hair, caught my eye and sidled over. Shrugging, he broke the heavy silence. "Had a snootful when he came in yesterday, too."

"Yesterday?"

Mr. Skulina shook his head. "Mrs. Vicks took advantage of our personal pre-need plan."

I shuddered. Pre-need. No matter how polite the term, the idea of planning your own funeral felt squirmy.

Mr. Skulina had to look up to meet my eyes. His were pale brown, rheumy, set deep in his creased, graying face. He blinked repeatedly, as if to clear them. I wondered who would meet his needs when the time came. "It's a good thing she did, too," he said, with earnest, "and that I got her decisions in writing. Barton came in here yesterday, demanding...and I do mean demanding." He rose up on his toes, making his point, "...all her money back. He didn't even want her to have a wake. Said it was a waste of money. No wake, no funeral. No flowers. What kind of son is that?"

The short speech had taken all his energy. He dabbed now at the corners of his mouth. "Get every detail in writing." He shook a wet finger up toward me. "Mrs. Vicks, God bless her soul, got the sendoff she wanted because I got her signature on my forms."

Aunt Lena bustled into the lobby, half-carrying Diana, who shuffled alongside, already bundled and ready to go. My aunt pressed Mrs. Vicks' house keys into my hand. "She'll perk up when you get outside." A half-hearted look out the dark doors, "Lord knows it's cold enough. She needs to rest up. Tomorrow's going to be a long day."

Diana moaned.

Pulling me closer, my aunt whispered in my ear, "She's terrified to go back there, especially when it's dark out. But I don't want her to get too comfortable at our house, if you know what I mean." A glance back at Diana, still totally out of it. "I'm sure it's safe now. You'll convince her, won't you?"

"Sure," I said, "No problem."

She then turned to Diana, with a more soothing voice, "You just pick up what you need, honey, and Alex will get you settled, okay? You'll see how safe it is. Before you know it, you'll be able to go back there all by yourself."

TEN

FIVE MINUTES LATER I pulled up in front of Mrs. Vicks' house. Up the block, one after another, solid brick bungalows hunkered down—their stalwart lines broken only by the occasional smaller, wood-porch cottage. No movement, no sound this night; it was brisk with the cold quiet of fading winter. Just like a ghost town, I thought. Mrs. Vicks' ghost had drawn all her loved ones just two miles down the road, to gather where her empty body lay.

Streetlights dropped undersized pools of light here and there—just enough to create long eerie shadows between the narrow gangways that separated homes. Almost as though Mrs. Vicks' ghost were truly here, I felt the pall that had settled over this neighborhood. My neighborhood. I'd never been afraid before.

My childhood sanctuaries were now tainted. The murderer had no doubt stood in one of these patches, waiting to move in on Mrs. Vicks, who wanted nothing more than to prepare a good dinner that night. And to talk to me.

Guilt spread its manipulative fingers through my mind and heart as I sat there. No matter what anyone said, no matter how much I tried to convince myself with logical arguments, I felt as though I should have been able to prevent her murder that night. I sighed both in regret, and with the realization that I could've been a victim, too. My aunt's request that I look into the murder suddenly seemed like the only possible course of action. And where better to start than here?

I didn't know much about the young woman curled in on herself in my passenger seat. I knew she'd attended college in Minnesota a few years back, but that it hadn't gone well. Her freshman year she'd met a much older man, who'd seduced her in more ways than one. She'd succumbed to the allure of the highs he provided, both in drugs and in danger. It got sketchy at that point, but despite interventions, and lots of futile tries, she'd drifted deep under the man's spell, and had begun to prostitute herself for drug money.

It had taken its toll on her. She was bloated—wasted, and now, at twenty-six, she was starting over—this time at a small Chicagoland community college, under Mrs. Vicks' motherly guidance. I worried for Diana, with no one to watch over her any longer. I imagined she'd move back with her family, wherever they were.

Just this past summer, after extracting a promise from me not to mention it to anyone, Mrs. Vicks showed me Diana's high school graduation picture. Back then she'd been slim, with shiny, poker-straight dark hair. Large expressive eyes, lined in black, stared back at me. Despite the bold makeup and the diamond stud in her left nostril, the girl was gorgeous. I'd said, "That's Diana?" without tempering my disbelief. She'd nearly doubled her weight since that photo was taken.

Being the curious sort, I'd asked how Diana came to live here. As she tucked the picture away into a china cabinet drawer, Mrs. Vicks gave a little sigh, and messed with other paperwork in the drawer as she spoke. "Diana's mother is a good woman," she said. "We've known one another for a long time."

I waited.

Looking almost as though she wished she hadn't broached the subject, Mrs. Vicks shook her head. "Diana's not that much younger than you, Alex. Her mother has had a hard time raising her alone. I almost wish…" She looked up at me with a sad smile. "Well, that's neither here nor there. I'm helping her out, is all. It's the least I can do."

As I left her house that day, Mrs. Vicks placed a warm hand on my arm. "You've been blessed to be adopted by such a wonderful family. Always remember that."

"I do," I said.

Halfway across her backyard, she called out to me again. "And they're just as blessed to have you, too, honey."

Now, parked in front of Mrs. Vicks' house, I gave Diana a moment. She seemed to need it.

She uncurled slow-motion, her face scrunched up as she stared at the house, more than wariness in her expression, I thought. Terror. I wondered again what her story was. The deep breath she took came out ragged and uneven, as though she was fighting tears again. Deep brown eyes turned my direction.

"You're coming in with me?"

"If you want," I said. I'd planned to; after all, that's what my Aunt Lena had asked me to do. "But if you prefer I'll wait here…" I let the thought hang.

"No, please," she said, startled, grabbing my arm. "Please come in."

Moments later we stood inside Mrs. Vicks small entrance hallway, the ribbed rubber mat still right inside, Mrs. Vicks' shoes exactly where she'd left them the day I'd helped her break into her own home. Two worn white gym shoes, their laces loosened, one of them knocked on its side, probably by the many people who trampled through the night of the murder.

I shut the front door, and heard a dull rattle from far across the house.

"What was that?" Diana asked. Even though she whispered, panic shot through her words.

"Air pressure," I said. "Probably the back windows vibrating. Happens at my house all the time when I open and close the door."

"You sure?"

I wasn't, but I knew better than to admit it. "Yeah. Same sound. Exactly." I turned on a nearby lamp, and smiled when light dispelled the creepy emptiness of the room. "See?" I said. "Nobody's here."

We took off our coats right inside, and draped them over one of the fat green swivel chairs that flanked the front windows. "Come on," I said, my voice a little loud, "we'll take a look around and you'll see it's fine."

Diana wasn't holding onto me, but she might just as well have been. She hovered so close behind that I could smell her stale, musty body odor. Mixed with the tang of sweat from her fear, it caused me to lean away. I kept my mouth closed, moving toward the kitchen, hoping to put some airspace between us.

Diana's bedroom stood just off the living room, and she broke away from me, toward it, looking every direction at once, peering around the doorway, the upper half of her body stretching to allow her to scan the small room, as she flicked on the lights before stepping foot inside. I pitied her, but this was exactly the way she'd have to do it. Small steps.

A half-second later, her voice rang out. "Where are you going?"

"Just right here," I said, inching down the dark hall, swinging my arm to gesture. Just like my house, Mrs. Vicks didn't have a dining room. Her bedroom was in back, just off the kitchen, and I wanted to take a look.

Diana spoke again, her panic so clear that her voice hurt my ears. "But she was murdered in the kitchen."

"I know."

"You don't want to go in there," she said.

"Actually," I said, in my best calming voice, "I do. I'll just take a look around while you gather your things, okay?"

I was curious in a morbid way, to see where Mrs. Vicks had been slain, but even more than that, I wanted to distance myself from Diana. Her closeness and her need to cling were smothering; I had to fight the urge to shove her away.

I knew my aunt wanted Diana to move back in here, the sooner the better. If her behavior thus far was any indication, however, Diana was never coming back.

Other than the occasional snuffle and sounds of moving about from the front end of the house, letting me know that Diana stayed busy in her room, the house was quiet.

Dark, too.

Whoever had been the last person out hadn't left on any lights. I crawled my left hand against the long wall, in search of the light switch I knew was about halfway down. Just before I reached it, I heard a muffled bump.

"You okay?" I asked.

No answer from Diana, so I raised my voice and called out again.

"Yeah, why?"

The last thing I wanted to tell her was that I'd heard an unexplained noise. My house was full of them. Everyone's house was full of them. But right now, in Diana's fragile state, it might be enough to send her screaming out the front door.

"No reason," I lied. "Just checking."

I flipped up the light, and the room flooded with artificial brightness. The cheerful yellow kitchen seemed less so today. The steaming scent of pork roast had given way to a chemical odor, and the warmth I'd felt that night was nowhere to be found. As if its life, along with Mrs. Vicks', had been taken away that day.

I made a slow tour of the room, documenting every detail that might or might never prove important. The police evidence technicians had been through the house, and black fingerprint powder clung to every surface. I couldn't imagine that I'd find anything material that they missed. I certainly had nowhere near their capability for obtaining and analyzing left-behind hairs, fingerprints, DNA.

But, as my mind warmed to the idea of analysis, I might be more likely to pick up on something out of the ordinary for Mrs. Vicks, that might seem commonplace for anyone else.

The kitchen table looked a lot like it had when I'd left the house Thursday night. Files and paperwork scattered across the Formica top, though rather than in precise piles, the papers were strewn about, having slid out from their neat manila folders. A few had hit the floor, some lying open and face-down.

I thought about David's tidbit of information regarding Mrs. Vicks' financial affairs and I picked through them, looking for her name as account-holder at the top of them.

Another bump. This time I cocked my head. I could have sworn it came from below me. "Diana?" I asked, raising my voice to be heard. "Did you knock something over?"

She didn't answer, so I ignored it.

The crime scene had been cleaned up. By whom I had no idea. Even though they'd done an admirable job of removing what must have been a stomach-wrenching mess, I could tell, by a few stray marks, where Mrs. Vicks had fallen. The evidence technicians who'd been through here had no doubt taken everything they needed. Now I had free rein to search for what I needed.

Too bad I had no idea what that was.

I knew just from standing there that I'd find nothing in the kitchen. Mrs. Vicks bedroom was steps away. The heavy oak door, four horizontal panels polished to a high sheen, stood slightly ajar and I pushed it open, wincing at the long creaking noise as the hinges protested my entrance.

Heavy draperies shut out even the pale moonlight. The room was dark as a cave and almost as cold. I fingered the wall, looking for a switch, even as my eyes became accustomed to the dimness. Flicking it up, I squinted at the same moment in anticipation of bright light, and felt my eyes widen in surprise when nothing happened.

From her room, Diana screamed. "Alex!"

I froze in place. "What?"

"My lights!"

Turning fast to return to the still-bright kitchen, I opened my mouth to answer her as Diana lumbered in. I caught sight of her panicked face for one half-moment.

Then, those lights went out.

Diana's high-octave scream coincided with the plunge of my stomach. Lights generally went out at once, not one room at a time. Not without help. The fuse box was in the basement, which meant whoever had killed the lights was still down there, too.

We weren't alone in the house.

"Alex," she cried again.

"Shush," I said, my voice sharp, my senses on frenzied alert. "Move," I said. Positioned dead-center in the narrow hall, she blocked our way out.

She ignored my imperative, her chilled fingers finding me in the dark. Clamping onto my right arm, she pulled me toward her, her breath coming in hot shallow beats against the side of my face. I shook her off, with an involuntary brusqueness that meant that my flight or fight reflexes had fully engaged.

Diana tried reaching again, her fingertips skimming me as she emitted little whimpers of terror. I sidestepped her in the dark, and issued a whispered order for her to run—to get help.

She didn't move.

More shallow sobs and even as I worried she'd hyperventilate, my mind raced through all possible scenarios, all possible outcomes. If the killer had come back, we needed help and we needed it now.

"Go," I said, shoving hard at Diana, fully intending to follow her out the front door. As my eyes started to become accustomed to the darkness, I flinched at the blankness I saw in her expression. The girl was in shock.

"Diana—" shaking her, "Go, already."

She sat, her body dropping against the wall, sliding down with a whump.

I grabbed for her arm; it was like pulling at a sandbag. Her bulky body didn't move.

I uttered an expletive under my breath. "Goddamn it, Diana—move! Or I will goddamn leave you here."

My words had no effect. Whether she knew I didn't mean it, or she just hadn't heard, I couldn't tell.

It didn't matter.

Dropping her arm, I lunged for the phone, just steps away.

Banging against one of the aluminum chairs, then banging into the kitchen table, I reached the receiver and grabbed the portable phone. Blinking, I tried to make out which was the "on" switch as I moved back to stand near Diana.

Two buttons looked promising and I pressed each, in turn, waiting for the welcome sound of a dial tone.

Nothing.

I shook the phone, then heard the heavy wooden basement door open below, realizing too late that the lack of electricity rendered a portable phone useless.

"Shoot."

My cell phone sat at the bottom of my purse fifteen steps behind me in the living room. Turned off.

Warning came with a sickening squeak from the basement stairs and as the back door flew open, I heard myself react—a gasp-scream silenced by fear.

Terror and indecision rendered my feet immobile. Before I could decide my best move, he was on us, his huge silhouette looming behind a piercing flashlight beam.

My head exploded in a flash of brightness and I heard, rather than felt, the sound of it hitting the kitchen wall. I had a moment of awareness, noting the skin-against-plastic sound of my face skimming downward as my legs gave out and I crumpled to the floor. I may have gone out then, I couldn't be sure, but I became aware of Diana crying— it was as though hearing her sobs through a fog. Curled into a fetal position on the floor next to me, she was making small mewling hiccups of pain. I tasted metal that I knew had to be blood.

Lying on my side, the cold linoleum against my left cheek giving me reassurance I was still alive, I tried to shout that I'd already called the police, but my brain couldn't make the connections to force my lips to make the right sounds.

At my indecipherable mumbles, I heard a grunt, which I took as surprise. A moment later, I suffered a solid kick to the stomach. Vomit, hot in my throat, nearly choked me, till it chugged outward from my mouth and nose, forming a warm puddle beneath the left side of my face. The flashlight's beam cut across my eyes.

I no longer heard Diana. A man's voice addressed me, or so it seemed. Whatever words he uttered were punctuated by further kicks, mercifully less intense. Or maybe I was less aware. My mind worked enough to convince me I ought to feign unconsciousness.

It wasn't hard. My body had had enough. I felt it shut-down. All I wanted to do was close my eyes make the pain of breathing go away.

I heaved.

Another bubble of hot bile shot from my mouth. I took a ragged slice of breath and finally, sweet darkness carried me away.

ELEVEN

My HEAD POUNDED with the kind of headache that makes sound fade in and out with every throb. Loud, soft, loud, soft.

It took a full minute of this see-saw wailing before I realized it probably wasn't a European police car giving chase. I sat up gingerly, every movement causing head-pound flashes behind my eyes.

Cool moonlight draped the area in blue, and I listened, hard, as I blinked my eyes to clear my vision. A soft rush of heat poured from a vent near my face. I listened for a long time, waiting for some indication that our attacker was still in the house.

Nothing.

I hadn't lost consciousness—the part of my brain that maintained my life support had also kept me awake, though barely—tucking away small memories as I lay there. The man had been saying, "Not here," repeatedly, and I'd heard the drag of the uneven back door scraping against the cement landing. He must have pulled the door shut when he left.

Now, my tongue felt huge, and the right side of it burned as though it were on fire. I wiped my chin, my fingers coming back sticky-warm with my own blood. I blinked, trying to see, still trying to determine the source of the uneven noise.

Diana lay on her back, her left arm bent mid-forearm at an angle so gruesome that seeing it nearly churned my stomach upward again. Her pained eyes were clamped shut, and her long, high-pitched moans rose to the ceiling. My European siren.

Bracing myself on all fours, I tried to balance, holding my breath against the searing pain in my abdomen. My left knee must have twisted as I fell; moving it shot long streams of heat up my leg. I braced myself on my right knee and was about to stand, when my foot caught the edge of a slippery puddle and gave way.

My head, already hammering with the shushing sound of pain, bounced against the linoleum. I rested for several shallow breaths before trying again.

When I finally made it to my feet, the down-rush of blood helped the headache subside. I looked down at Diana's twisted arm and hoped for her sake she was unconscious.

Extending my right arm, I winced at the unexpected pain there, too. I pressed my hand flat against the wall and cautiously stepped over Diana's supine form. I knew I'd forever remember the interminable half-walk, half-crawl to the living room to dig my cell phone out of my purse.

When my fingers finally curled around its cool metal exterior, I whispered a small prayer of thanks, and hoped I wouldn't lose consciousness before help came.

DETECTIVE LULINSKI SHOWED up moments after the paramedics arrived.

Part of me wanted the efficient medical personnel to be more careful, to be sure they weren't trampling over clues that might point the finger at the guilty party, but more than that I wanted them to stop the pain in my head.

"You might have a mild concussion." The clean-cut young man who said this to me stared so hard into my face that I was mesmerized.

He continued to stare into my eyes, aided by the beam of a small handheld lamp. The house lights had come back on at some point, but I didn't know who'd taken care of that. "Did you lose consciousness at all?"

"No," I said, knowing that any other response would land me in the hospital for sure.

He asked me several other questions, which I answered as precisely as I could, feeling as though I were talking with a clothespin clipped to my tongue.

Time had no meaning for me. I watched as Detective Lulinski took reports from both paramedics and from uniformed officers. He strode back and forth through the room several times as the young medic ministered to my wounds.

I made out the name stitched above his pocket: Chet. With effort, he helped me over to the long beige couch. I sat there and he knelt on the floor in front of me, taking readings, reporting in via radio, and marking notes on a clipboard. We'd moved to one side of the room to allow passage of the stretcher that would eventually carry Diana out to a waiting ambulance and off to the emergency room.

Chet reached into his case to pull out gauze packages, when Detective Lulinski crouched in front of me. "Can I talk with her a moment?" he asked.

Chet nodded, still concentrating on his task at hand. "Yeah," he said. "I want to keep her alert and awake. As long as she's up for it."

Catch this bastard, I wanted to say. I nodded with as much eagerness as I could muster, then was immediately sorry. It felt like rocks banging against the inside of my skull.

"Miss St. James," Lulinski began.

"Call me Alex," I said, the end of my name coming out in a lisp. I tried to smile, but it hurt.

Detective Lulinski wasn't wearing his customary gray suit. Instead he had on a blue flannel shirt and jeans, no jacket. When I looked into his gray eyes, I didn't see the hardness I was used to. Instead, his expression was filled with sympathy and that caught me off-guard. He reached out and, lightly, took my right hand in his left. "Don't worry," he said. "You're strong."

The warmth of his hand, the sense of relief knowing how lucky I was to be feeling it, sent hot stings to my eyes. "I look that bad, huh?"

He gave me an avuncular pat. "Nah," he said. "Just a little frazzled around the edges."

Even though Chet had made a valiant effort to clean me up, I couldn't ignore the surrounding sourness of remaining upchuck. My face felt sticky from the antiseptic pads he'd used to wipe it, and when I tried to tuck my hair behind my ear, my fingers got stuck in a gummy mess.

I still felt as though I'd been shot in the tongue with an extra-strong dose of Novocain. "How's Diana?"

Lulinski's gray eyes clouded for a split-second before he managed to settle an impassive expression onto his face. "She'll live, if that's what you mean. Her arm's been broken in several places and the paramedics think she's in shock. That's what's really worrying them now. She's totally out of it. She doesn't seem to have the spirit to rally."

"But I do?" I asked, pulling my mouth around my tongue, trying to control my words better.

"I'm counting on it," he said. "Now tell me everything."

DESPITE DETECTIVE LULINSKI'S insistence that I go for an MRI, I signed a waiver declining a night in the hospital, and promised that I'd have my aunt come stay with me till morning. Overcome with guilt for sending me back to the house with Diana, Aunt Lena insisted on staying up the entire night, checking on me every twenty minutes.

Lucy wanted to help, and between the two of them I spent restless hours, dozing off for short moments only to be awakened by a cool touch of fingers to my wrist, my cheeks, my forehead. I must have cried out once, because I sat up instinctively to see both Lucy and Aunt Lena there, twin frightened looks on their pale faces.

"I'm okay," I said, and lowered myself, with effort, back to a reclining position.

My mother had always said that the mouth heals quickly because saliva helps speed the process. So, when morning light snuck through the mini-blinds in my room, I worked my jaw, and practiced a couple of words aloud, surprised at how much clearer my speech was compared to the night before. My tongue had even shrunk back to its normal size, although there was a small patch on the right that I still couldn't feel.

I vaguely remembered washing up the night before and then crawling into my oversized T-shirt. Now, as I sat up, I tugged at its hem, feeling a chill on my legs as I inched the covers from them, grimacing with each movement.

Now, wincing, I eased my legs over the side of the bed and considered my options. Too raw to brush my teeth last night, I'd rinsed my mouth with warm salt water instead, hoping to wash out as much blood as I could. At the time I thought I'd done a decent job, but right now it felt like my teeth were wearing sweaters.

Steadying my feet on the cool wooden floor, I started to boost myself upward.

"Don't try to stand up by yourself." My aunt's sudden appearance at the doorway startled me. "Lucy," she called behind her. "Come here and help your sister."

"I'm fine," I said, then as though to prove it, I took

several steps forward, trusty fake smile in place. Aunt Lena didn't have to know I'd sucked in a whoop of breath at the first step. I felt like I'd done about a thousand sit-ups, and was now wearing hundred-pound weights on my arms and legs.

I got to my doorway, and braced myself against the wall with my left hand. "I have to get into work today."

For a half-second I thought Aunt Lena would laugh, but her face sobered and she shook her head. "I'm making breakfast. Why don't we try starting with that, first?"

Over my aunt's protests that I'd slip and crack my head open, I took a long, hot shower. Raking my damp hair backward off my face as I toweled off, I leaned toward the mirror, trying to see how bad the bump above my right temple looked. Not too bad, I decided. The steam from the shower softened my reflection, blurred the bruising, but I just knew I was going to have a shiner.

I felt much stronger after showering. Energized, I shuffled into the kitchen, to be greeted by the warm waft of bacon, eggs, and coffee.

"I feel like I've died and gone to heaven," I said with a smile, meaning it as a compliment to my aunt's cooking.

She snapped at me. "Bite your tongue."

Lucy, seated at the table, watched us both through wide worried eyes. Aunt Lena glanced her direction, then smiled at me, softening her rebuke. "I just mean that last night was too close, Alex. I'm sorry I asked you to look around at Mrs. Vicks'. If I hadn't been so eager to have Diana move back—" Her voice cracked.

"Everyone's fine," I started to say, then noticed brightness streaming in from my back porch. I glanced that direction, out the window, then up at the kitchen clock. "It's after eleven," I said with alarm. I'd told Bass that I planned to be in extra early this morning for a meeting about the

San Francisco trip. I could only imagine his fury when I hadn't shown up. And then I realized something else. "You missed the funeral."

Aunt Lena pulled out my chair and thunked a steaming plate of food in front of me. "Some things are more important, dear," she said. "Anyhow, Moose is at the services. He came by to check on you this morning before heading out."

I sat, nodded and turned to Lucy. "Can you grab me the phone?"

Aunt Lena placed a mug of coffee on the table, accompanied by a little ceramic pitcher of cream. "I already called in for you."

"What?" I said, a bit rattled. Nobody had "called in for me" since high school. "But I need to talk to Bass about the trip on Friday."

"Oh, yes, he mentioned that."

That sent me off-kilter. I sputtered before I spoke. "You talked to him?"

Placing a matching platter of food before Lucy, Aunt Lena rested a hand on my shoulder. "Of course. I asked for your boss, Philip Bassett. I told him everything that happened last night. He was quite sorry to hear about it. Very concerned about you. Such a nice man."

Bass? I thought.

She continued. "He wanted to know when you'd be up and around again—when he could expect you back in."

Okay, that was more like the Bass we all knew and didn't love.

"I told him you were going to see your doctor this afternoon, but I definitely let him know how badly you were hurt. He asked me if I thought you'd be able to make some business trip to San Francisco this Friday, and well, I told him no, of course."

"But," I said, then stopped. The aches and soreness suddenly seemed ten times worse.

"Don't worry, honey. Mr. Bassett said he would find somebody to take your place."

Yeah, I thought. That's exactly what I was afraid of.

TWELVE

LATE THAT AFTERNOON, when the long white box arrived, I knew who it was from even before I opened it.

"Good news travels fast, apparently," I said to Lucy as she carried the gift into the kitchen for me to open. An envelope, tied to the large black ribbon in the center, read: "Get Well," in gold-embossed script.

"What do you mean?" she asked.

I shook my head, and Lucy didn't push it. Aunt Lena had just left for the hospital to check on Diana, after extracting a promise from me and from Lucy that we'd call if even the smallest thing went wrong.

I opened the card, half-hoping the flowers were from William, knowing better. "My Dear Alex," it read. "Had I known your plan to revisit the site of that brutal murder, I should have accompanied you, of course. I am devastated by the news that you've been hurt. Please call me and let me know if there is anything I can possibly do to speed your recovery. Yours, David."

Oh, so now it was just "David."

I untied the wide satin bow and lifted the lid. Rather than roses this time, he'd chosen a variety of flowers. A rainbow of roses, lilies, daisies, tulips, and a few I didn't recognize. Picking up the box, I took a deep whiff of their scent and tried to be cheered by the gift.

"What's wrong?" Lucy asked. "Don't you think they're pretty?"

"Yeah," I said, unsure. "But something about them… I don't know."

She leaned over my shoulder to look into the box for a moment then up at me, bright realization in her eyes. "I know why you don't like them. They smell like the wake yesterday."

I dropped the box onto the kitchen table. She was right.

Lucy canted her head at me, twisting at the back of her hair as she spoke. "You seem really sad today. Can I do something for you to make you feel better?"

I pretended to think hard. "You know," I said, "I haven't heard you play the piano since you've been home."

Her face lit up with such sudden happiness it broke my heart. She'd been worried about me, I knew, but up until this moment I'd lost sight of her needs in this whole mess.

Sprinting toward the living room, she shot a question over her shoulder. "What do you want to hear?"

"Surprise me," I said.

Seconds later the house filled with the syncopated sound of Scott Joplin's "Solace." It fit my mood perfectly, and, sitting at the kitchen table, I pushed the box of flowers to the far edge, hoping the distance would help. I wrinkled my nose again. David Dewars had probably paid a lot for this arrangement, but the smell of them turned my stomach.

When the phone rang, Lucy was just ending her first song. "Do you want me to stop?" she asked.

"No."

Standing, I took the few small steps to the phone, and wondered if my stomach muscles would ever feel normal again. "Hello?"

"Hey, bruiser."

William's voice sent a warm wash of pleasure over me. "Hi," I said.

"I tried calling you earlier. They said you were at the doctor's."

"Lucy told me someone called." I said, hearing the cheer in my voice. "That was you, huh?"

"Had to check on you myself," he said. "How are you feeling?"

I gave him a quick rundown. "I guess Lulinski doesn't suspect me anymore," I said with a short laugh.

A couple of beats went by as strains of "Rhapsody in Blue" trickled in from the living room. Lucy would never be able to balance a checkbook, but she played her music with tender emotion. When William spoke again, his voice was quiet, and I had to push my ear close to the receiver to hear. "I was worried about you."

"I'm okay," I said. "Plan to be back at work tomorrow."

"That's my girl."

The sentiment made me grin, which hurt, but not so badly this time. "So," I began, broaching the subject that weighed on my mind. "You and Caroline are headed to Frisco Friday, huh?"

"Actually…" I heard the discomfort in his pause. "One of our sister stations out there invited us out a couple days early."

"Early?"

"We're taking off Wednesday morning and spending two days in Napa before we head down to San Francisco for the seminar."

"Napa?" Wine country. Featured in the travel sections of upscale magazines. Known for its romance. "Sounds like fun."

"Ever been there?"

"No."

"Well, I'm sure I'll have lots to tell you when I get back, then," he said.

I forced fake cheer into my voice. "I'll look forward to that."

"Me too," he said. A voice in the background called to him. "Hey, gotta run. Don't push yourself, okay? Take tomorrow off too, if it'll do you some good."

"Sure," I said, thinking: The hell I will.

THE FOLLOWING MORNING, unwilling to subject myself to the double set of stairs from the building's gilt lobby, I'd ridden the elevator up one level to the second floor. It might have been my imagination but the elevator's other occupants, having pushed numbers fourteen and twenty-three, sighed dramatically and said "tsk" when I got off at two.

Good lesson, I thought. If I had a set of crutches, no one would think twice. Reminded me not to be quick to cast judgment. Things are not always what they seem.

I let loose a sigh of my own at the prospect of dragging open our station's heavy glass entrance doors. I pulled, feeling pressure in my sore abs, wishing a magic sensor would have whooshed the doors open for me.

I'd gotten in extra early because I wanted to avoid the heavy commuter rush. I hadn't taken a bus downtown to work since my car had to be impounded after having been doused with gasoline six months ago.

My doctor wanted me to wait a couple of days before driving again. In fact, he'd strongly advised me against coming back to work so soon, but since he admitted I was merely battered and bruised, not broken, I decided to push myself. The bus ride had been jarring, but getting an early start at least guaranteed me a seat.

Bass was in early, too.

"What the hell are you doing here?" he asked.

Oh, the support I got from this man. "I work here, remember?"

He perched his fists onto his hips, regarding me. "You don't look too bad."

"Thanks," I said. From Bass, that was a high compliment.

With his small hands tucked into the sides of his steel-blue suit coat, he reminded me again of a little boy playing grown-up. One eyebrow lifted, and he gestured with his chin. "In my office."

He circled around to the black leather chair behind his desk as I braced myself on the arms of the chairs in front of it, lowering myself slowly, trying to feign smooth movement. If Bass noticed, he graciously pretended not to.

He'd pulled the window's sheers across the expanse of blue that overlooked the Chicago River behind him. They'd predicted more snow, but the sky seemed way too clear for that.

"You could have waited to talk to me," I said.

Hazel eyes shot a look of disbelief across the desk. "You can't mean the trip to San Francisco."

"Of course that's what I mean. You knew I wanted to go."

"Your aunt said you'd be out for at least a week."

Frustrated, my hands shot up. "I'm here, aren't I?"

"You shouldn't be."

"The point is, I am. And the further point is that you should have at least waited to talk with me before making a decision to send someone else."

He held up a hand. "Hey, I made the best decision I could, given the circumstances. I thought you were out for a week. I even gave Gonzales the stories you were working on." Anger crowded his features for a moment which I then read as indecision as to whether to get them back from Gonzales or not. "Besides," he said, his voice weary with having to bother explaining things to me, "they're leaving tomorrow now instead of Friday. You're in no shape to travel—even I can see that. As far as I'm concerned, the subject is closed." He looked at me with an expression that dared me to argue, then added, without feeling, "Better luck next time."

I wanted to let him know just how pissed off I was, but the fact remained that he had, indeed, made the best decision he could at the time. For the station, that is. I shook my head and looked away. Things happen for a reason, they say. All of this. I blew out a breath, then worked to get my face into a semblance of calm. "Okay, so I'm here now. What have you got for me?"

He tapped a pencil's eraser against his blotter, and spent a long moment watching the action.

Oh, this is promising, I thought. "What's up?"

Tilting his head to acknowledge my question, his attention remained on the center of his desk. "You realize we have an opportunity here."

"For?"

"For…" he let it hang, with a stare at me as though I should finish the sentence.

I didn't.

"Our chance to trounce *Up Close Issues* and Dan Starck on a very big human-interest story."

"You lost me, Bass. What story?"

He gestured, indicating my face, my aching body. "Your story."

I shook my head, wagging a finger at him. "No," I said. "Not my story."

"You're trying to tell me you aren't planning to follow this through? To find out exactly what's going on?" Bass shot me a skeptical look. "I think I know you better than that."

I set my mouth in a line, and formed my next words in

my mind before saying them. "I don't know who killed Mrs. Vicks and I don't know who attacked me Sunday night. I don't even know if the two incidents are related. The police don't think they are."

"That's what they say." He lifted one eyebrow.

"Bass," I said, in my serious voice, "you know as well as I do that when an obituary runs in the paper, thieves see the deceased's unoccupied home as an easy target. That's what the police think happened."

"Uh-huh." He smiled. "And why were you there, anyway?"

"I drove Diana there to pick up a few things." I shrugged. "No big deal. Just bad timing."

"Uh-huh," he said again. "So you weren't there to have a look around yourself at all? Not the least bit curious about the murder? Not trying to see if there was something in the house that the police might have missed? Something to point to the murderer?"

I fixed my gaze out the window. A gray front appeared to be moving in. Maybe we would get the big snow all the newspapers were predicting. "You've been watching too much TV. I have no intention of getting involved in this one."

"That's not what your aunt said on the phone."

My gaze snapped back to meet his. Smug amusement there. He waited me out.

"She asked me to look into it," I admitted. "But if you talked to her, then you know how sorry she is. She wants me out of this one. Pronto."

"But you're not going to let it go, are you?"

Goddamn it, the man knew me too well. "Of course I'm letting it go," I lied. "Look at me, I'm getting a black eye. It could've been a whole lot worse. I don't plan to tempt the fates again."

The truth was, Detective Lulinski's accusation that I would use my connection with Mrs. Vicks to further my own feature story aspirations, still rankled. Of course I wanted to know who killed my neighbor. And I wanted to know who assaulted us at her house. But I'd felt the beginnings of rapport between myself and the good detective after the attack. The truth was important—but for its own sake, not for the station's. Not this time.

Tilting his head, Bass examined my right temple for a moment. "Nah. No black eye. You might get a little bruising—some green, some yellow, maybe."

"Doesn't matter. I'm backing out of this one. Let the police handle it."

As if I hadn't said a word, he continued, "And since you're going to look into this, why not do it with the station's sanction? We can give you lots of backup, lots of help and we'll come out with a kick-ass story. Homegrown, you know? Sweet old lady killed in her house as she's fixing dinner. Ace reporter Alex St. James gets attacked when she starts looking into it. This is lightning, and we can catch it."

I shook my head again. "Didn't you hear me?"

"I see a Davis award in this one," he said in a sing-song voice. "Wouldn't it be nice to show up your former boyfriend with a trophy of your own?"

I boosted myself from the chair, with a look toward Bass that was meant to be withering but no doubt fell shy of the mark when I winced in pain. "You're dreaming, bub," I said, heading for the door.

"And in case you forgot, we're a news organization, not an investigative service. We *report* what happened, we don't take part in it."

"You did. Last time. And Dan Starck got the award you deserved."

That hurt, but I refused to react.

He spoke to my back. "So what are you here for any-way? I gave Gonzales all your stories. You got nothing else to work on. So why not? I'm giving you all the time you need to bring this one home."

The worst part was that this was a silver-platter offer. I had every intention of following through this one on my own, but the station's resources were a compelling temp-tation.

Facing him again, I wondered if this was how so many trusting folks sold their souls to the devil.

I held my hand up, but even I could see that he knew I'd acquiesce. "Let me start looking. See where it goes. No guarantees, okay?"

He grinned with such evil cheer that I half-expected horns and a tail to sprout out as he sat there. "It's a deal."

FIFTEEN MINUTES LATER, the hub began to populate as the support staff wandered in, one at a time. Jordan caught me on my way back from refilling my water at the dispenser. Still wearing her red wool coat, sprinkled with white snow on the shoulders, she blocked my path, one hand perched on her cocked hip.

"And what are you doing here?"

"Don't you start."

"Don't you be telling me what to start and what not to start. I know why you're in today."

"Oh you do?"

"Uh-huh," she said, pulling her coat off. I couldn't mis-take the concern in her brown eyes as she checked me out from head to toe. "How you feeling?"

"Not bad," I said. And it was the truth. Moving felt good. It was only after sitting for a long time that my abs stiffened up again and caused me pain when I got up again.

I followed her to the closet.

She shook her head when I told her about Diana, still in intensive care. Jordan's super short hair barely registered the movement, and I wished I could carry off that carefree look with the snazzy she did. "You were lucky, girl. Damn lucky."

I made a face. That was a mistake. I winced again.

"I know what you're thinking," she said. "You get that thought out of your head. You just ought to be grateful that the only thing you're missing is a trip to Frisco. You could be missing a whole lot more."

"You're right," I said, humoring her.

Her voice shot up an octave and she wiggled her head at me. "I know I'm right. I'm always right." She grinned, and as we walked back to my office she added, "So when Bass tells you about the phone call from David Dewars, and he asks you to investigate this lady's murder, you're going to tell him no."

She sat down at her desk, leaving me to lean against the side of her cubicle. "Hang on a minute," I said. "What phone call?"

Jordan's face communicated her delight at having a delicious secret to impart. "Yesterday while you were out, your flower-buddy Mr. Dewars called Bass."

"About what?"

Raising her hand, she twisted her index finger in a side-to-side motion indicating for me to hold all questions till she was done.

"Frances took the call, of course," she began, her eyes lighting up in the telling. "But Bass was in talking with Hank, so she asks if she could take a message. I told her about those flowers you got the other day, so when she heard the name Dewars she wondered what was up with that."

I could see it. Frances was a stately woman, almost two decades older than me, with spiky maroon hair. She carried herself with a sense of self-possession that I hoped some day to acquire. She was tough, she was nosy. And if she wanted to know what was up, she'd find out.

"And?"

"And," she continued, "Dewars wants to meet with Bass to discuss the station's involvement in the murder investigation. He said that he'd be willing to be real cooperative with us if we portray his bank in a, quote, 'favorable light' unquote."

Shutting my eyes, I pinched the bridge of my nose. In a ridiculous way, this made sense. David's information about Mrs. Vicks' investments would become part of the investigation, and when it hit the news, Banner Bank would, no doubt, be mentioned. As owner of the bank, David had to be worried about the negative publicity associated with murder. I nodded. "The big bank that cares about you," I said, quoting their slogan.

"Yep."

I pushed myself away from the wall of her cubicle, and headed into my office. "Let me know if you hear anything else, okay?"

"You got it."

I OPENED UP a new document on my computer and labeled it "Vicks Investigation." In it I started to record everything from the moment Mrs. Vicks came to my garage asking for help. I hadn't gotten very far when I noticed William walking by, on the way to his office. A glance at the clock on my computer told me it was just after nine. A bit late for him.

I decided to give him a few minutes to get settled before I went over there to talk. I'd pushed myself to get into work today just to have a chance to connect before he took off for the trip to San Francisco, but now I had second thoughts. The bruised state of my face made me reconsider the wisdom of my decision. He'd seen me at my worst before, but still. I pulled out my compact mirror and lowered my head down to desktop height to examine my face more closely.

Still trying to decide whether I was presentable or not, I heard a knock at my door. I sat up fast. William stood there, waiting to be invited in. I tried to mask my surprise.

"Hey," I said.

"Hey yourself." He moved toward my desk, a big smile on his face. "Got a few minutes?"

"Sure."

He sat across from me. "Good to see you up and about. I was hoping you'd make it in today."

"You were?" The words popped out, complete with their blatantly hopeful tone, before I could catch myself.

He nodded, and what I could only describe as a fond look came over his face. "I wanted to see you before I left. Make sure you're really okay."

"I got this." I pointed to the bruising over my right temple.

He made a so-so motion with his right hand. "Not too bad. You're feeling all right?"

"Little bit sore. But yeah, okay." I nodded an end to that line of conversation. I found I was quickly becoming tired of discussing my well-being with everyone. "What about you? You all ready to take off tomorrow?"

"Just about. As a matter of fact, I'm heading down to the studio now to go through some of our tapes that we're taking with us." He shook his head. "I wish we would've had more time to prepare. This is going to take all day."

"Will you have time for lunch?" I asked. "I thought we might get a chance to talk before you leave."

He shook his head, then glanced out the big picture window that looked north over the Chicago River. Big white flakes of snow drifted downward, angling right to left, to drop on the pavement below. "I doubt it. As soon as we get this project complete, I need to get home. I still haven't packed."

"Oh," I said, disappointed.

Almost as though he hadn't heard me, he added, "As long as our flight isn't cancelled."

"They're predicting six inches."

Disappointment clouded his face. "Yeah. We have to hope it holds off."

He'd said, 'we.' Jumping on that I prompted: "Caroline's got to be happy about this."

I couldn't tell if it was my imagination or if his face flushed momentarily. "Yeah, she lived out there for a while. She promised to show me some sights."

"Great," I said, with forced enthusiasm.

"Not that we'll have a lot of time," he said quickly. "I think they're going to keep us busy all day at this seminar, and at the sister station event."

"I wish I was going."

"Eh," he said, with affected disinterest as he boosted himself from the chair. "I'm sure it'll be a bunch of bor- ing speakers and dull dinners."

Maybe my brain was still affected from being bashed in the head, but I couldn't stop myself from saying, "So I guess I won't talk with you till Monday, huh?"

His dimples deepened to match the smile in his eyes. "I'll call you while I'm out there," he said. "In a way, it'll be like you're part of it, too."

"Sounds good," I said.

Before his movement had a chance to register, he came

around the side of my desk. "You going to miss me?" he asked.

"I will," I said.

"Good." Cupping my chin, he leaned down and touched his lips to mine in a quiet little kiss. Breaking away, he winked. "See you soon."

I watched him head out my office door and for the first time since I knew he was going away with Caroline I felt my mood lighten.

TAKING A BREAK from my first pass at the chronology of events, I leaned back in my chair, watching a blustery Chicago from my second floor perch. A little snow had begun to accumulate in the corners, giving my view a Christmassy feel. Too late, I thought. I needed spring, and I needed it in a hurry. The unending chill served to make my soreness increase, and for the first time I understood what older folks meant when they said that the cold had settled in their bones.

Frances showed up in my doorway. With a look that spoke of amusement, she pursed her lips and wiggled her eyebrows. Most fifty-something women wouldn't be able to carry off her trendsetter style, but Frances did.

"Bass needs you in his office right now."

I shot her a skeptical look. "What's so funny?"

Bright red grin. "He's not alone. Your faithful admirer is in there with him."

"David Dewars?"

Bigger grin. "They're waiting for you."

On the short trek to Bass' office I caught sight of William, shrugging into his charcoal gray wool coat, headed for the exit. He paused long enough to fix the coat's collar that had flipped inward on itself. I bit my lip, hoping he'd glance back.

"C'mon," I said to myself. "Turn around." Like a silly teenager, I made one of those "if he likes me" deals. "Turn around," I whispered.

Just before pushing through the glass doors, he stopped. I waited.

His hands patted the outside of his coat up near the chest and down around his hips, searching. In what felt like slow-motion, he reached into his left breast pocket, and pulled out a thick envelope that looked to be his plane tickets and itinerary. Thus reassured, he shoved the glass doors open with his shoulder, and walked away.

Bass poked his head out of his office—looked at me—then at William's departing figure. He shook his head and grinned. "Back to business, kid."

I shot him a lips-only smile.

David stood as I entered, his face breaking into a long, slow smile of appreciation. "Alex," he said, his voice booming.

"Mr. Dewars."

His eyes widened behind the round lenses of his glasses. "Oh please, call me David. But I'm surprised to see you back to work so soon. How are you? Really?"

I waved my hand in dismissal and lowered myself into one of the seats in front of Bass' desk since it appeared that David wasn't going to sit until I did. "I'm fine."

He squinted as he watched my ginger movements. "You received my note?"

Classy move, I thought. He didn't mention the flowers. "Yes, they were lovely," I said, enjoying the confused look on Bass' face. "I mailed you a return message, thanking you, this morning."

As he sat to my left, he pulled his chair close enough to mine that our knees nearly touched. "No need for thanks," he said. "As long as you suffered no long-term effects."

Clearing his throat, he continued. "As a matter of fact your little escapade is part of the reason I'm here today."

I shot a quizzical look at Bass, but got nothing. He sat in rapt attention, waiting for the other man to continue.

Adopting a serious, businesslike demeanor, David launched into a smooth monologue.

"Evelyn Vicks, God rest her soul," he began, "was one of our own. She'd been an institution at Banner Bank, having started working there back in the late seventies. When I took over about five years ago, I pledged to protect the employees. When I promised that, I'd intended it to mean that their jobs were safe. Today, I mean it in an entirely different way."

Sturdy words, I thought.

"But." He stared upward, at the ceiling, and his eyes squinted for half-a-second. "I need to protect the bank now, too. Our reputation is on the line. I don't want our good name sullied because some prodigal son decided to make an early withdrawal on his inheritance."

Just because Mrs. Vicks worked for Banner Bank didn't mean that anyone was about to blame them. I thought he was reaching, overestimating the bad publicity. Not only that, but at this point, all we had on Barton was conjecture. I said as much.

"I know, Alex," he said, his gaze returning to encompass both me and Bass. "You're right. But I didn't get to be owner and chairman of Banner by letting things go. I follow my hunches. Some are stronger than others. This time I know. I know deep in my bones that Barton did this. And I mean to collect all the evidence I can to bring the bastard to justice." He glanced at me, worried. "Sorry for my language."

I waved away his apology. I'd used those words myself.

"I also want to be sure that Banner Bank is, shall we

say, protected in all feature stories about the murder." He gave me a meaningful look. "I know you'll be fair—I can sense that about you."

He waited for my cursory thanks. I simply nodded.

With a nod himself, he went on. "I'm willing to put my bank's resources in your capable hands. I have it on good authority—" He glanced at Bass. "...that you will be investigating the murder."

No sense in beating about the bush. "I plan to look into it," I began. I held up a hand when he looked about to interrupt. "I don't pretend to be a criminal investigator. And anything I find will have to be shared with the police."

"Of course," he said. The huge smile on his face stretched wide. "But if we collaborate, then I can rest easy, knowing Banner Bank will come out smelling like a rose when the story breaks."

I shrugged.

He wagged a finger at me in playful fashion. "The story will break. Barton will be found to be guilty."

Bass had taken to jittering in his chair, looking eager to jump into the conversation, but unwilling to stop David before the entire offer was on the table. At the short lull in the conversation, he piped in. "So, you'll allow some of our staff to take a look at your files?"

David held up his hands. Large hands.

"I'd prefer only one set of eyes on our files. Discreet eyes." He glanced at me with meaning. "I can get into trouble if I allow broad access to our records. Allowing one investigator, sanctioned by yours truly, to help launch the bank's own research into the matter, will be understandable."

"Alex here can do it," Bass said without so much as a glance in my direction to consult me.

"That's precisely who I had in mind," David said.

I wanted to say something sarcastic, like "Surprise, surprise," but then he smiled again. I expected a leer or some snarky look, but his expression was devoid of guile.

I had no idea what either of them expected me to uncover, but I knew that I often found information in the least likely places, so I nodded. "You'll arrange to have the files sent over?"

David blinked. The small lenses of his glasses served to make his eyes appear bigger. "Oh, no, we can't let our records out of the bank. At this very moment, I have my staff setting up a work area for you."

The question popped out of my mouth, sharp and indignant. "You were that sure of me?"

"Well…" His voice took on a soothing tone, I got the feeling David viewed me as he would a rambunctious kitten. Avoid the claws and the tiny teeth. Maybe they can't do any real damage, but they sure can smart. "Alex," he said, in gentle chastisement. He seemed to like saying my name. "When I heard how you and that other woman had been brutalized, I knew we had to do something. I'm afraid for you. If Barton stays on the loose, there's no telling what kind of danger you're in. This solution is best for all of us."

"I'm not convinced it's Barton," I said, my own voice straining for patience.

"Of course," Bass said, jumping in. "That's why you're investigating. So you can find out for yourself."

David stood, and in a gentle motion, took my right hand in his. "I have several pressing engagements this afternoon. But perhaps tomorrow we could get started?"

"That's perfect," Bass said.

I shot him an annoyed glance, which he missed.

David, apparently picking up on my displeasure, squeezed my hand, ever so slightly. Surprisingly it didn't hurt. "Alex? Is that all right with you?"

I nodded. "Sure. What time?"

"Let's do breakfast tomorrow. I'm an early riser, but you let me know whatever time is best."

I looked into the sparkling brown eyes smiling at me. The man had been nothing but the picture of consideration since I'd met him. I found him a bit overbearing, but no different than any hundred other successful businessmen out there. Breakfast might be nice.

"I'm up early too. Where would you like to meet?"

As though I'd given him a precious gift, he smiled. Letting go of my hand he thought for a moment. "I'll pick you up here, say seven o'clock?"

"Sure."

"I know a great little place," he said. "We'll have plenty of privacy to discuss the investigation."

Momentary panic made me blurt, "It is a restaurant, right?"

I must have caught him unawares, because he laughed out loud. "Yes, Alex, it's a restaurant. I don't have any ulterior motives here." He winked, then spoke just loud enough for me to hear. "Not yet, at least."

DEEP INTO CREATING my Vicks file, I jumped when my desk phone rang a half-hour later.

Without preamble, Detective Lulinski asked, "You up for a cup of coffee?"

"Sure," I said.

"I'll meet you at the Emperor's Roost in fifteen minutes, okay?"

The Emperor's Roost, a small restaurant that had seen better days, sat at ground level between my building and the one next door. Everything about the place was dark. Umber-paneled walls were broken up with the occasional yellowed painting. Every one depicted Emperor Napoleon in a battle pose. Booths lined the crescent-shaped seating area along the perimeter. Downstairs from my office, the restaurant was convenient for me. Not so much for the good detective. Something was up. "Sounds great," I said. "I'll grab a table, so look for me."

The phone clicked in my ear without him saying anything more.

Fifteen minutes later, almost on the dot, I watched him walk in from the restaurant's north entrance. He brought in a gust of cold air, or so it seemed from the reaction of the woman manning the to-go counter adjacent to the door.

His eyes scanned and found me in seconds, and five strides later he was at my table, a semi-circular booth in the bar area of the place. Smoking section. As he took off his coat and then sat, he eyed the clear glass ashtray between us, then up at me with a quizzical look.

"It was the only open table," I said.

A quick smile, gone as fast as it came. He pulled a box of cigarettes out of his suit coat and laid it on the table. But he didn't light up. Instead he looked at me for a couple of beats, and I watched him take in the bruises, and the shadow that promised a black eye despite Bass's predictions that I'd skate on that one.

A gum-cracking waitress showed up with a pot of coffee. We both turned our cups over for filling. "You hungry?" he asked.

"I am, actually," I answered, surprised. I hadn't taken any menus since he'd said "just coffee," but when Lulinski ordered a Monte Cristo sandwich with fries, I decided on a bowl of broccoli soup.

"Thanks for meeting me," he said. Nothing about my looks, no chastisement about my being back to work so soon. Rather than being disappointed, I was relieved not to have to go down that path with yet another person.

"Not a problem," I said, "I take it something's going on?"

Gray eyes, gray hair, and wearing his gray suit again. I wondered about this fellow, and tried again to decide his age. Somewhere between late forties or early fifties, I thought. He nodded, fixing his gaze on the cigarette box again. He started sliding it back and forth between his hands. "Could be."

Despite the fact that his face was slim, his cheeks sagged a bit below the jawline. Coupled with gray stubble that told me he hadn't shaved in a while, I wondered if he'd been up all night. "You okay?" I asked.

His eyes jumped up at me, as though I'd brought him out of a reverie. The man was tired, all right.

"Yeah. Lot on my mind." He chanced another smile, just as brief as the first one. "Here's the problem. Diana's still unable to speak. I can't get anything from her."

I didn't think Diana would be much of a witness, to be honest. She'd panicked so quickly that I doubted she'd even remember anything from that night. But I kept quiet.

Lulinski took a breath. "I ran a check on her. She did time; I don't know if you knew that."

"I knew she had problems."

"Yeah," he said. "I'll say." He didn't expand, but changed direction. "She was involved with a guy some years back. He went away; did some hard time."

"I heard something about that."

"Well, seems like he just got out." He held my gaze, watching me as the import of his words took hold. "Parole."

Following his lead, I asked, "And you think he might be the guy who attacked us?"

"I'm looking into it."

I took a sip of coffee and considered it. "And Mrs. Vicks? What would be his motive for killing her?"

His long fingers wrapped around his own coffee cup,

Lulinski shook his head. "That's part of the problem. He's a good suspect—he's had drug convictions, he's done time for home invasion and for armed robbery—but we need to know what it is he wants. What he was looking for."

"Looking for?" I asked.

"Both times the house was entered, it was searched. For what, is anyone's guess at this point."

"What's the guy's name?"

Lulinski hesitated. "Grady," he said, with a sigh of resignation. "Larry Grady. First name Laurence with a 'u'."

"Grady? That's Diana's last name."

He nodded. "We think they got married. Either that, or she took his name as part of a common-law arrangement."

"You don't know for sure?"

Shrugging, he took a long sip of coffee before he spoke again. "Not worth my effort at this point. We know they had a relationship. If I need to, I'll trace down any evidence of a legal arrangement later."

My conversation with Bass and David this morning sat at the back of my brain like a headache waiting to happen. I'd agreed to investigate this story for my station. Right now the question was, should I share that information with the detective here?

He interrupted my thoughts. "What?"

I shook my head, not understanding.

"You were miles away there for a second. What's on your mind?"

I deflected. "Diana would have some idea, but—" I let it hang.

"Exactly," he finished. "There's no way we're going to be able to talk to her anytime soon. Even if she's up and around in the next couple days, she's apparently so fragile that to interrogate her could be traumatic."

The waitress brought our food. I took a big spoonful and

blew on it, seconds later realizing that the word of the day was: tepid. I preferred my food hot; this wasn't. I glanced at the waitress, now fetching orders halfway across the restaurant. When my eyes returned to the table, I saw that Lulinski had almost completely downed the first half of his sandwich, shoveling it in with a gusto that surprised me for such a thin guy.

By the time they would get my soup warmed up, he'd have the rest of his meal scarfed down. With a sigh, I took another big spoonful and pretended it was gazpacho.

Lulinski pushed the mouthful of food into his left cheek as he finished his thought. "Diana was seeing a therapist," he said, chewing now. "I talked to the man today."

Still chewing, he started in on the second half of the sandwich, then dug into his jacket pocket, pulling out his notebook. He flipped it to a page in the middle and read the information to me. "Dr. Thomas Hooker, psychiatrist, located not far from here, just off Madison and State."

"Hooker?"

"Yeah, I know. Bad name." He shrugged.

"Why are you telling me?"

"Dr. Hooker won't talk to me. He can't. Bound by those damn privacy laws." He said that last part with a heavy dose of sarcasm, then held a hand out to stave off commentary. "I know, I know. I understand the need for them, but…"

I waited for him to finish the thought.

"He wants to talk to you."

No way, I thought, and I said so. "He won't talk to a cop, but he'll talk to someone from the media?"

Two big bites and the rest of Lulinski's Monte Cristo was history. I resisted the urge to comment.

He shrugged. Grabbing the bottle of mustard, he covered the thick-cut French fries with layers of yellow, taking a moment to salt them liberally before shoving three into his still-masticating mouth.

"Mustard? On fries?" I asked, then added, "Eeyoo."

Gray eyes shot up and he grinned through his chewing. "Old habit. My first partner made me try it on a long stakeout once. Been hooked ever since." He took in a breath and shrugged us back to the topic. "Dr. Hooker won't give up any information on Diana because of patient confidentiality," he continued. "But when I advised him of Diana's condition, and of the incident that transpired, he wanted more information. He says that the more he knows about the attack, the better he's going to be able to help Diana get back on her feet." Still chewing, Lulinski averted his eyes. "I mentioned you, and he thought that it would be helpful to Diana if you made some time to talk with him."

I'd gotten about halfway through my soup, and now I held an empty spoon above the bowl. "And you think if he talks to me, I'll uncover information about Diana's old boyfriend that can help you."

He rolled his tongue around his teeth, clearing food. "The thought had crossed my mind."

My disbelief came out in an almost-laugh.

"What so funny?"

"Didn't you accuse me of using my relationship with Mrs. Vicks to further my own investigation?"

One side of his mouth curled up. An abbreviated nod. "Yeah, but that was before I knew we shared a mutual distaste for Dan Starck."

Ooh…interesting comment. I tucked that little tidbit away for later. "But now you want me to use my relationship with Diana to further *your* interests."

"Something like that."

I put my spoon down, and stared at him. "You gotta be

kidding," I said. "Confidentiality is confidentiality. What makes you think he'll say anything that can be useful?"

"You're a sharp girl," he said. "And you're good at what you do—getting information out of people. Am I right?"

Careful nod.

"I'm not even sure what the shrink knows. Maybe nothing. But if we get you in there checking it out, I'll feel better."

There was a compliment in there somewhere, but I chose to ignore it.

The waitress took that moment to ask if there was anything else we needed. We both demurred, not looking at her. She dropped the check on the table. Lulinski grabbed it. "I got it this time," he said.

Yeah, like I was going to arm wrestle him for it.

He stared at the bill for a long moment, before answering my question. "He might not give us anything, but I can't afford to overlook a single possibility. Even though we know about Diana's record, and we have information on Laurence Grady. Despite the fact that we know he's in the area, we don't know if she's been in contact with him, or what her relationship was with Mrs. Vicks."

I gave him a look that said, 'duh.' "She was Mrs. Vicks roommate."

"Yeah," he said with enough hesitation that my mind made a quick leap to deduce what he was getting at.

"You think Diana had something to do with Mrs. Vicks' murder?" My skeptical voice had gone up just a little, and I lowered it before continuing. "There's no way."

Lulinski's eyebrows arched in a resigned way. "I don't assume anything. I follow where the information leads. And the more information, the better." Pushing his plate forward, he leaned on the table, crossing his arms. "Will you talk with Dr. Hooker? Yes or no?"

I pressed my fingers against my temples and took a long breath. "Okay."

"You'll do it?"

"That surprises you?"

"Frankly, it does."

I held off saying anything further for a long moment. This would be the perfect opportunity to let Detective Lulinski know that I'd agreed to investigate the story for both Banner Bank and for Midwest Focus. Instead, I bit the inside of my cheek and shot him a lips-only smile. "I want this guy caught. And if you think my talking to Diana's shrink will help, then I'm all for it."

His mission accomplished, Lulinski pulled the napkin from his lap, wiped his mouth, and scooted out the side of the booth. He handed me Dr. Hooker's business card. "Here. He'll see you tomorrow afternoon at two."

THIRTEEN

LUCY SHOULD HAVE been home fifteen minutes ago. Pulling on my leather jacket, I headed down my front steps to look for her. Fat snowflakes, heavy in the predicted late-season blizzard, came down so hard, it made me squint as I stepped outside.

The days were getting longer, but it was dark now. I'd worked late and the falling snow slowed traffic with the not-so-subtle reminder that winter wasn't over yet. Drivers made careful progress over the late-season slick, knowing better than to push their luck. Lucy waited for me to come home every night, and on the slow crawl through traffic, I'd tapped impatient fingers on my steering wheel, knowing I'd let her down, again. The minute I got in, I called Aunt Lena to let her know I'd made it and she could send Lucy home. Only after that did I peel off my work clothes and snuggle into my comfy jeans, sweatshirt and gym shoes.

The snow, accumulating on the ground, and in tiny mounds perched between tree branches, brightened the neighborhood with its fresh sparkle. If I hadn't been concerned with Lucy's tardiness, I would have stopped to enjoy the sight.

Every night Aunt Lena watched Lucy make her way on the three-house trek home. There was no danger of her getting lost; she'd grown up in this neighborhood and it was as familiar to her as her music was, but what with Mrs. Vicks' murder and the subsequent attack on our street, my aunt and I felt better not letting her walk home unsupervised.

The sky poured white from its inky depths, its intensity evident in the flakes rushing through the pink streetlights' glow. I wondered, briefly, if they'd cancel all flights out of O'Hare tomorrow, leaving William and Caroline snow-bound in Chicago. I tamped down a grin. That'd be a nice surprise, I thought, then berated myself for wishing rain, or in this case snow, on someone else's parade.

Right in front of my aunt's house I saw her.

"Lucy."

She turned, and reflection from the ambient light caught the smile in her face even before she said my name. "Alex!"

In the moment that she turned, I noticed that she wasn't alone.

She was talking with someone. A short man, slim, wearing dark clothing, and a bright yellow knit cap. "Hey!" I said, sprinting forward.

"Thanks, Lucy," he said, then he raised his voice to add, "Catch you later." I watched him take off, but the thick snowfall kept me from getting seeing who it was.

"You! Wait!" I said again. Then to Lucy. "Go in the house."

I charged, passing her at a full run, glad I'd changed into blue jeans and Reeboks when I'd gotten home. "Stop," I called, louder now.

He didn't stop, but he did turn at my shout, and for an instant in the light, I caught a good look at him. In the quiet of the drifting snow I could hear my pounding breath and his crunching footfalls ahead, far quicker than mine. I winced at the pain the running shot through my still-aching bones. Even as I pushed my speed, I watched the soles of his snow-covered shoes get smaller and smaller. I listened hard, trying to follow the sound of rubber hitting snow until that noise faded into the sounds of the street.

I'd run for no more than twenty seconds, but I'd lost him

already. I kept going, another half-block, knowing it was futile but unwilling to give up until I saw him turn a far corner and disappear. I slowed, watching my breath curl out of my mouth in big spinning clouds. "Damn," I said.

Glancing back, I saw that Lucy hadn't listened. She stood outside our house, watching me. I waved, then stuck my bare hands in my jacket pockets and made my way back.

"Who was that?" I asked, out of breath.

Lucy opened her mouth, but no words came out. I saw the confusion on her face. She wore navy blue earmuffs and her right hand drifted behind her head in a nervous gesture, twisting her hair. "He didn't tell me his name."

A strange man had been conversing with my sister, but he'd obviously learned her name. I had more questions than I could get out of my mouth at once. "Where's Aunt Lena? Doesn't she usually watch until you get home?"

Lucy smiled, eager and willing to tell me everything. "She did. I got all the way up the steps when the man…" she gestured in the direction he'd run "…came up and said 'hi.' So I walked over to say 'hi' to him, too."

"Who was he?" I asked again. "Why didn't Aunt Lena do anything?"

"I don't know," she said. A tiny crease formed between her eyebrows as she searched for the right answer. "I think maybe she went back into her house before he came by." When she shrugged, the small collection of snow that had dropped onto her shoulders shook off. Lucy's confused expression told me that she didn't understand my concerns. "He was nice, Alex," she said. "He just asked my name. Can we go in now? I'm cold."

"And you told him?" I asked, striving to keep the anger out of my voice. "Don't you know you aren't supposed to talk to strangers?"

She looked at me with the most solemn expression. "Alex," she said. "I'm older than you are. You can't treat me like a baby just because I'm 'special.' I've been learning how to take care of myself, you know."

The last part of her little speech came out just shaky enough that I knew she worried how I'd take it. I sucked in a breath to keep myself from exploding. A man had attacked me, had put Diana in the hospital, and someone, possibly the same guy, had killed Mrs. Vicks. What I wanted to do was chew out Lucy for being careless, for forgetting she was no longer safe within the protected confines of the assisted living facility.

Instead I chose more neutral ground. "What did he want?"

"I don't know. He didn't say he wanted anything."

"What did you tell him?"

"I told him that I lived here with you and that you would be worried if I wasn't home soon, and he asked why and I started to tell him about what happened to Mrs. Vicks."

"What did he say?" Bursts of light shot through my head as a thousand questions ripped through my brain at once. Panic and fear made me sick—thinking that the murderer might have been standing in front of my house with Lucy within his grasp. "Did he seem surprised about the murder? I mean…" I tried to slow myself down, "…a murder is a big deal, Lucy. A very scary, very important event. Was he shocked when you told him? Or did it seem like he knew about it already?"

"I don't know," Lucy said. "That's when you came out and he ran off."

Inside, I called Aunt Lena, trying to balance my concerns without sounding like I blamed her for not being more conscientious. No matter. She apologized repeatedly, promising never to let Lucy out of her sight again. A prickle of guilt wormed its way through my brain. "Aunt Lena," I said finally, "Lucy is my responsibility. I'm just so very grateful that you're willing to keep an eye on her during the day. If it was any other time, I think she'd be fine, even alone here. But with all that's been going on...." I took a deep breath. "I should probably take some vacation time and stay here with her myself."

"No, honey, no." I couldn't see Aunt Lena shaking her head, but I knew she was. "You do this investigation and you find out all you can. Lucy will be safe here. I promise you that. You trust us, right?"

What could I say? "Of course."

"Then that's settled."

Once Lucy had gone to bed, I felt comfortable enough to put in a call to Detective Lulinski. I dialed the cell phone number he'd given me and was surprised when he answered.

"What's up?"

"Don't you ever sleep?" I asked.

I didn't know the man well, and I wasn't even sure I liked him yet, but I liked his answer. "Not when there's work to be done."

"Listen," I said, feeling suddenly stupid for calling him so late. "This might not be anything, but..."

I gave him a quick rundown Lucy's encounter and my lame chase. "Why didn't you call me sooner?"

I hedged. Decided to go with the truth. "I didn't think of it. Not till about fifteen minutes afterward. I was just so afraid for my sister." I stopped myself from over-explaining. "By then he was long gone. So I waited till she went to sleep to call you. It was after hours and I thought I'd get your voicemail anyway."

"No such thing as after hours," he said. "Next time, call me first. Got that?"

I nodded. "Yeah. Sorry."

"And, hey, give me a call when you have some time tomorrow. We can go through mug shots. Maybe you'll recognize the guy."

"Sure. What time's good?"

"Anytime," he said. "I'll be here."

Near midnight, I checked on Lucy before I went to bed. She slept curled up on her left side, covers pulled close to her chin, her mouth open, lips twitching as though she wanted to whisper secrets in the quiet night. Standing there in her doorway, with my arms folded, and fear crawling around in my brain, I wondered if this was how mothers felt late at night, when the cold wind howled and the only thing keeping their children safe from the bad things outside were the flimsy walls around them and their own careful diligence.

DAVID PICKED ME up precisely at seven the next morning. I'd expected him to be late because of the snow, but he called and suggested we meet underground on Lower Wacker. A silver Rolls Royce, with the distinctive double-R hubcaps pulled up in front of the service entrance beneath my office building. The driver got out, came around, and opened the back door with a gray-gloved hand. David Dewars smiled out at me, patting the gray leather seat. "Good morning, Alex," he said.

Coupling this chauffeur business with David's description of the breakfast restaurant as a place where we'd have plenty of privacy, I'd conjured up a vision of something hushed and intimate, with an attentive but unobtrusive wait staff bearing silver platters of eggs benedict to our tiny table for two.

We emerged from Lower Michigan at Grand and traveled about two blocks to a corner restaurant with a small hand-painted sign that proclaimed it "The Outland Café." It couldn't have been more different than I'd expected.

David placed a restraining hand on my arm as I started to reach for the door handle, his bright eyes squinting in amusement behind the tiny rimless lenses. "Roger will get it."

Of course. Not only did Roger open the door, but he efficiently cleared a neat pathway for us to walk up to the establishment's front door, first. That meant I didn't have to wade through foot-high drifts in my shiny navy pumps. Chalk one up for David here. I was impressed.

Boisterous conversation, sizzling eggs, clanging pans, and constant movement took me aback as he pulled open the door to the busy restaurant, allowing me to enter. Tall yellow walls, covered in black-framed Warhol-like lithographs, rose up to meet the metal-beamed ceiling that did little to ease the cacophony below.

A small sign immediately inside the door suggested that we seat ourselves, but it looked to be quite a wait.

Every fifties-era Formica table was occupied with clusters of chatting, coffee-drinking people in various stages of eating. A woman wearing a T-shirt two sizes too small for her voluptuous frame, held a handful of curly red hair up out of her face as she made a point to an unimpressed, bulky woman wearing a baggy denim jacket across from her. At the table adjacent to them, four white-shirted young men leaned forward, with identical looks of clean-cut intensity, as one of them held up a Bible and spoke with an earnestness I could see even from my position by the door. Next to them, two young mothers juggled coffee and toddlers who stared mesmerized out the wall-size picture window at the buses and cars that plodded by through the still-falling snow outside. A March blizzard in Chicago didn't slow down its natives.

With its tables tight against one another, without one extra inch of navigation space, the restaurant should have felt claustrophobic, but the soaring open ceilings, and white-painted heating vents kept the place airy, though so noisy, it felt like the very air clacked.

"Mr. Dewars." A young woman carrying menus broke into a winning smile, her perfect teeth matching her perfect features. Petite, with shiny brown eyes to match her straight dark hair, she raised inquisitive eyebrows at my companion, then shifted her gaze to me in a once-over, skimming politely over my black eye as though she didn't notice it. "Two?"

"Good morning, Linda," he said, as he placed a proprietary hand on the small of my back. "Is my table ready?"

"Of course," she said. "Follow me."

She wound through the bustling dining room, into a small silent passage that opened into yet another part of the restaurant. These walls were muted shades, and this room's tables were spaced much farther apart, and the clientele all business folks, talking in low-tones, so engrossed in their dealing that not one pair of eyes looked up as we entered.

Linda held my chair out and placed a tall plastic-covered menu in my hand. Having seated us at a table for four in the windowed corner, she attempted to guide David into the chair opposite mine, but he chose to sit cornered to me instead. "Cozy," he said, not noticing Linda's surprised smile.

"Enjoy your breakfast," she said, with just the right measure of perkiness.

"They know you here." I said when she'd gone. "You must come by a lot."

"Good place, great people."

A young, jeans-clad waitress wearing a tight white

T-shirt, poured coffee for both of us and left a good-sized thermal carafe on the table for us to help ourselves.

After we'd ordered, I folded my arms and leaned forward. With all the busy-ness going around us there was no need to worry about eavesdroppers, but I kept my voice low anyway. As far as I was concerned this was a business breakfast, and I was ready to get down to it. "You're pretty convinced that Barton killed his mother."

David nodded. "Absolutely. The proof is there."

"It isn't unusual for a woman to designate her account for her son. And, like I said before, fifty-thousand dollars isn't that much money."

"This is why I wanted you to come inspect the files for yourself." He put down the mug he'd been sipping from and brought his voice low to dovetail mine. "Evelyn Vicks made some unusual changes to her account—regarding her beneficiaries—over the past several months."

"What kinds of changes?"

"Up until three months ago, all of Evelyn's retirement-planning accounts were handled outside our offices. She had a couple of trust funds, too, and she had her will."

"What happened three months ago?"

"She came to us and asked if we could take over her investment portfolio."

"Do you know why?"

"I asked her that myself." David picked up his coffee cup again, pondered it. "She seemed to have difficulty explaining her actions. I assured her that I would take care of it." Alert eyes captured mine. "To be frank, her accounts are so small that it doesn't affect our bottom line at all. But I was worried for her because she's one of my people, and there are unscrupulous folks out there who would take advantage of elderly women. I wondered if that's what was going on."

"So you don't know why she made the change."

"Not precisely. At the same time, she told Owen Riordan—the loan officer you met at the wake Sunday night…" he raised his eyebrows in question until I nodded my acknowledgement that I remembered him, "that she needed to update her will." Weighty gaze. This part was going to be important, it seemed. "Owen had his own law practice before coming to the bank. Mind you, he's not our corporate attorney. We refer all our legal matters to O'Shea Associates."

"Why would she have approached Owen with any of this?"

"Mostly because Evelyn liked Owen," he said with a shrug. "She confided in him, often. To her, he was more than just a boss. On top of that, Owen writes up wills for bank employees for free. It keeps my people happy since they don't have to drop a few hundred bucks on legal work, and it keeps Owen happy, because I figure that goodwill into his annual bonus. Win-win situation. Anyway, she told him she had changes that she wanted to make, and he wrote it up for her."

"Nothing suspicious about that."

"Except," he leaned even closer and his voice dropped to a whisper, "she made Barton the sole beneficiary."

I didn't understand. "Wasn't he always the beneficiary?"

"We have no way of knowing that. But consider this: why would she need a new will if that hadn't changed? According to Owen, she seemed extremely unwilling to offer explanation."

"That doesn't sound like Mrs. Vicks." I said.

"Exactly." The brown eyes lit up and David pointed a triumphant finger at me.

The waitress arrived bearing our steaming breakfast platters. I'd chosen a ham, green pepper and mushroom skillet with scrambled eggs over the top and David decided on a butterflied filet mignon, done medium rare, with eggs over-easy on the side.

It was delicious. Already I was gauging how much I could finish. The platter was huge; if I had three hours, I might be able to make a dent in it.

"You think it wasn't Mrs. Vicks' idea to change her will?" I prompted, to start the subject again.

"No, I don't. I think she was acting on Barton's direction."

"You think. You don't know."

Chewing, he acknowledged my point with a nod.

"That's pretty sketchy," I said. "And you don't even know what the terms of the prior will were."

He shook his head as he chewed.

"Who drew up the prior will?" I asked.

He shrugged.

"Any way to find out?" I asked. I poured coffee for myself, then realized that his cup was empty too. I raised the carafe in question.

"Thank you," he said, pushing his mug forward. "I'm not a lawyer, so I don't have the answer to that. But what difference would it make now? The new will is in effect, and has been for several months. Barton gets it all."

I nodded, thoughtful. I'd love to get a look at the old will. Maybe Mrs. Vicks had a copy at home somewhere. Or maybe in that safe deposit box that Barton couldn't access.

As I refilled David's cup, he smiled. "Business aside, I'm very much enjoying our breakfast this morning," he said.

Surprised to find that I was enjoying myself too, I smiled. "Cream?"

When the waitress finally came to clear our plates, I resisted the overwhelming urge to ask for a doggie bag for the remainder of my food. If I'd been going back to my own office, I would have jumped at the chance to save some of the platter for tomorrow, but seeing as how my next stop was Banner Bank, and I was getting there in a chauffeur-driven car, I decided, this time, to let my more ladylike tendencies win out.

"YOUR HOME AWAY from home," David said with a sweeping arm gesture that made the small office seem even smaller. He followed me in, his solid presence making the cramped quarters immediately claustrophobic. "I'm sorry it isn't more luxurious, but we're undergoing an audit from the FDIC and they claimed all the decent free space we had."

My ears perked up. "Audit?"

The look of annoyance he wore when he'd first mentioned the Federal Deposit Insurance Corporation smoothed to one of reassurance toward me. "Scheduled audit. Nothing unusual."

I nodded, in absent-minded fashion, taking the two steps into the room that brought me to the far corner. Ten-by-ten at best, with a table and a chair, it was windowless, pictureless, and the walls were a shiny russet color that clashed with the flattened orange carpet. An uneven hum droning above me promised air movement, but provided none. From its stale smell, I guessed that no one had used this space in a very long time.

It had been designed as a privacy room for patrons to open their safe deposit boxes in seclusion. Four other similar rooms lined the vault area, but this one, the farthest down the dark corridor, and the largest, evidently got the least amount of use.

"Right now," David continued, pointing to a scarred wooden table snug up against the west wall, "that's the best we can do for a desk." Two small cardboard boxes sat atop it, my name scribbled on them. "But the chair should be comfortable."

"Thanks," I said, putting my hand on its black leather backrest and giving it a twirl. He stood close enough that his chest skimmed the side of my left arm. Leaning past me, he indicated a call button I hadn't seen earlier.

"This will summon Lorna, our vault clerk. You need anything, she'll contact me or Owen. One of us will take care of you."

I'd assumed I would have free access to the entire bank. Horrified at the thought of spending long hours in this cheerless enclave, I blurted my disappointment before I formed polite phrasing. "You mean I'll be stuck back here the whole time?"

"I am sorry, Alex. There were twice as many auditors this time as we expected, but I'd be happy to share my office with you," he said. "Of course there may be some instances where I'd need you to step out if—"

"No." I stopped him. Sharing an office with a bank president—not my idea of comfort.

He looked around the room again. "The auditors should be gone by Monday. We can find you a better space then."

Monday? I couldn't imagine Mrs. Vicks' records would take that long to pore through. "Well," I said clapping my hands together in a gesture of dismissal. "Let me get started then."

The moment he left, I took off my hem-length suit jacket, draping it over the back of the chair, and fanned the neckline of my sleeveless dress, hoping to create a little breeze. The room wasn't hot exactly, but the static feel coupled with the fusty smell made me want to bolt outside and breathe in some of the snowy air.

I'd given the boxes a once-over and had been about to sit down with the first one when I realized I had no pen and paper. I probably should've brought them myself, but the breakfast meeting had taken me out of investigative mode. I hit the call button.

An older woman came around the corner moments later. Dark-haired and large, possibly of Romanian descent, she smiled through blood-red lips. "You must be Miss St. James," she said, with a smile and crusty smoker's voice. "I'm Lorna. You and Mr. Dewars passed me on the way in, but I was busy with a customer. What can I do for you?"

I explained what I needed.

Lorna had the biggest eyes I'd ever seen. They bulged in such a way that I could see the white all the way around her dark irises. She shook her head, making a clucking sound. "I can't believe they're sticking you back here."

"I heard about the audit."

"Yeah." She rolled those big eyes. "I say, stick one of those pests down here. Maybe they'd be out of my hair sooner, then."

"They're pests?"

"Every year it's the same thing. 'Get me this file,' 'Get me records for the past ten years on that,' 'Write up your procedures for me.' Yadda, yadda, yadda. It's a safe deposit vault, for crissakes. My procedures are just the same as last year's."

Her delivery made me grin.

Casting a glance around my little room again she said, "Let me see what I can do for you."

"Did you know Mrs. Vicks?"

Nod. "A little. She worked up on twelve, in the loan's bookkeeping department. I saw her once in a while if we had break at the same time. When we did, we talked some. Nice lady. Real nice." Lorna tightened her lips and looked away. "It's a damn shame."

"Her son told me he can't get into the safe deposit box."

"He's an ass," she said. "Excuse my language. Came in here demanding to get into his mother's safe. Guess what? She didn't have one."

"She didn't?"

"Nope. She never came down here."

"Are you sure?" I asked.

Bulging eyes hardened at my question. "I know all my customers. Every one. I been doing this job for fifteen years here, and Evelyn Vicks never once stopped in."

"I'm sure you're right," I said, trying to soothe her quick anger. Despite Barton's overindulgence in his liquor the other night, he'd been clear on the fact that there'd been a safe deposit box here under his mother's name, and I doubted he had the imagination to come up with that on his own. "But, don't you ever get relieved? I mean, could she have come in when you were at lunch?"

I'd done it now. She rolled those big eyes, clearly annoyed. "Well, of course, I go on lunch, but that doesn't mean I don't know who has a safe deposit box and who doesn't." She thrust an angry chin the direction she'd come. "Follow me, I'll show you."

Back at the desk, she moved toward two desktop filing cabinets that had about twenty skinny drawers, each. The safe deposit area was separated from the rest of the bank by the building's lobby, an enormous, twenty-story atrium. The tellers and customer service representatives were located in the northwestern corner of the building. Here, facing a huge window-wall that opened to streaming skylight, we were in the far southeast corner of the building.

"See," she said. "These are our signature cards. She pulled out one of those long skinny drawers. Inside were at least fifty four-by-six orange index cards. She flipped up the top one and the rest followed suit, like dominoes in reverse. "Everyone with a box has a card like this. Evelyn Vicks isn't in here."

I noticed from the drawer tags, that the cards were filed numerically. Over fifteen hundred boxes. "Do you keep an alphabetical file?"

Her look told me she thought I was stupid. "Of course," she said.

Moving to the desk, she flung two fingers toward another set of drawers, these holding vertical three-by-five cards. "Here."

I nodded, smiled.

Rolling her eyes again, she yanked open the last drawer, and flipped to the Vs. "Vaci, Vandenberg, Vanekis, Versale, V—" She stopped, then looked up at me. When she pulled the card up, it was as though she needed to prove it to herself. "Vicks. Evelyn Vicks."

I waited while she stared.

"When did she open this?" Lorna asked rhetorically. Turning the card over, she read the date, April sixth, twenty years earlier. "How did I not know this?" she asked again.

I scratched my head. Her confusion didn't help me right now. The only things that interested me were Mrs. Vicks' accounts and her will. "Barton is pretty sure the will is in the box," I said. "But I guess that's not possible."

Her chin came up. I could tell the mistake she'd made about Mrs. Vicks' safe deposit box had thrown her, but her face brightened at my question as though she was relieved to have recaptured her expertise.

She shook her head. "Common mistake. Never keep a will in a safe deposit box. Causes too much hassle. Sonny-boy needs to work with the attorney who wrote it up. Whoever that is, is bound to have a copy."

"I guess he needs to talk with Owen then."

"Owen? You mean Mr. Riordan?"

I nodded. "Mr. Dewars said he wrote up Mrs. Vicks' will, not that long ago."

"Makes sense I guess," she said with a shrug. "That'd be where I'd start if I was the son."

"But she probably didn't put in the box," I said. "If she hasn't been down here."

"I'll check." Lorna shook her head after pawing through more files. "Must have been when I was on break, like you said." Her eyes were clouded with self-doubt when she pulled out the file. "She was in here just last week."

She followed me back to the tiny cave of a room, still muttering about her error. I wasn't quite sure how to shake her, but a buzz from the front jerked her attention that way.

"Customer," she said. "I have to run. I'll get ahold of Mr. Riordan for you now. Let's see what we can do about finding you a better space to work."

Not ten minutes later, a woman breezed into my dank cave. "Hi," she said in a breathless way, as though she'd just run in from an adventure and couldn't wait to tell someone about it, "I'm Maya." Her perfect teeth flashed brilliant white against the ebony of her face as she dropped three legal pads of paper and an assortment of pens on the table in front of me. I could tell from her glance and slight hesitation that she'd noticed my black eye, but she didn't comment. "Maya Richardson." Tall and thin, her black hair was pulled back from her nearly poreless face, and though the effect was severe, it was also quite elegant. She wore small thick-banded gold hoop earrings and a cross pendant gold necklace. Her taste in clothes was superb. I recognized the pink and navy block suit from a display at Neiman Marcus that I had to pass on after seeing the sticker price. She thrust out a perfectly manicured hand and we shook. Firm grip. "Lorna called Owen, but he's out at a client's, so I'm here to help you."

"I'm Alex St. James," I said.

"You know, you'd think they'd tell me that you were here. Not a word." Maya maintained eye contact while she spoke, whirlwind-fashion. "Lorna told me why you're here. Thank God they're finally doing something. It's been what? A week already?"

"One week tomorrow."

"The longer it takes, the less chance of catching the monster who did that to poor Evelyn."

"You knew her?"

"Very well. She was one of my clerks." Apparently realizing that I wasn't familiar with the bank's reporting structure, she continued. "Owen and I run the loan department. He handles all the corporate and foreign transactions— you know all the important stuff." She emphasized the word and grimace-grinned conspiratorially. I could only guess that there was a male-female competition involved. "I handle the personal accounts. Lines of credit, home-equity, things like that."

"Mrs. Vicks worked for you?"

"Ten years," she said. "The old management hired me straight out of grad school and within two years I was running this end of the department," she said with pride. "If you have any questions about anything, you go ahead and ask. If I can't help you, I'll find somebody who can."

"I thought she worked for Mr. Riordan."

Her brows furrowed over dark eyes. "That what they told you?"

I nodded.

"I guess technically that's true." She grimaced again, less good-naturedly. "Two months ago I got promoted to Senior Vice President. I still report to Owen, because he's Executive VP. That means that my employees are still his employees, too, but Evelyn and I worked together every day. She helped Owen occasionally, but not nearly as much."

She stopped herself, taking a quick glance around the room. "Lorna was right," she said. "This is miserable. I can at least help out with this. Come on." She grabbed the box closest to her, and canted her head toward the hall-way. "Follow me."

I scrambled to throw the paper and pens in the other box before picking it up and heading out.

On the way, Maya chatted like we were old girlfriends. The lunchroom apparently had an abundance of unused space and she figured I'd be happier there. I followed her, keeping up the brisk pace even though I still felt vague aches from my recent tussle with the intruder at Mrs. Vicks'.

"It might be noisy in there sometimes," she said, apologetically over her shoulder as she led the way, "but it can't be worse than that room downstairs."

Getting to the lunchroom meant an elevator ride up to twelve, then wading through half-a-dozen offices where busy people, mostly women, glanced up with curiosity as we passed. One after another, like a wave of surprised eye-balls, their gazes followed us on our path to the far reaches of the twelfth floor.

"Wow," I said, pleased, when we walked in. One wall boasted floor-to-ceiling windows and though it offered only a bird's-eye-view of Clark Street, the room practically shimmered with cheer when compared to the ground-floor vault area. Snow clustered in one corner of the windows and stretched out icy patterns across half the expanse as though Jack Frost had come by and been interrupted mid-task.

"You like this better?" she asked with a hopeful tone.

"Much better," I said.

"Good." She dropped her box on one of the many empty tables. "Take your pick."

I glanced at my watch. Nearly eleven o'clock. "This is great," I said, meaning it. "Thanks."

"Not a problem." She glanced at her watch, too. It was one of those black-faced ones with no numbers, but with a sparkling diamond where the twelve should be. "I have to run," she said. "Busy day today."

"I have an appointment at two this afternoon. Can I just leave these records here when I take off?"

Maya thought for a moment. She raised an index finger. "Hang on." Within a minute she'd left the room and come back again with a contagious sort of triumph. "Hand me a piece of paper, okay?"

I did.

Maya wrote a quick note, and I was surprised at her little-girl penmanship. Tiny proper letters in an almost back-slant handwriting. Had I encountered the note before meeting the woman, I would have come to the erroneous conclusion that Maya Richardson was timid and introverted.

"There," she said, "Nina Takami in bookkeeping will lock them up for you every day, I'll leave this on her desk to let her know. She's right in the next room."

"Got it," I said.

"Great." She started toward the door and turned just as she cleared the threshold again. "Listen, I mean it. You have any questions on anything, you see me. Owen didn't know Evelyn as well as I did."

AN HOUR LATER I knew nothing more than I'd known before. I couldn't imagine why David considered anything in either box important. Mrs. Vicks had opened her accounts with Banner Bank twenty-three years earlier, a few years after Barton had left home. Flipping through the old documents, I found a pattern of sorts. Paychecks automatically deposited every two weeks, and a series of small dollar amount checks, some of which were written with such precise repetition that I gathered Mrs. Vicks had been on the budget plan for all her utilities. Every month, however, she wrote one even-dollar amount check. No payee listed on the statements. If I wanted to know who they were written to, I imagined I'd have to look them up on antique microfilm machines.

Interesting pattern. The checks were for two hundred dollars for the first three years, then moved to two-hundred-fifty. They stayed there for just over five years before inching up to three hundred for about four years. They zoomed to five hundred then and stayed at that amount for three more years until ceasing completely.

Could be a savings plan. Retirement account. Investment. David had told me that she'd accumulated over fifty-thousand dollars. I made a note to research the checks' payees as soon as possible. It was probably nothing, but if I was going to be here anyway, what the heck.

Right now, though, it would have to wait. Almost one o'clock. I wanted to get back to my office to check on a few things before my meeting with Dr. Hooker at two. I boxed everything back up and looked for Nina Takami.

WHEN I WALKED through the glass doors of our office, everyone looked up. Not used to such attention all at once, I stopped in my tracks. Across the expanse of the hub, where the entire support staff worked in low-rise cubicles, I saw Jordan spring from her chair and make her way in my direction.

"What?" I asked.

Her dark eyes scanned the corridor I'd just left. "Come

on," she said, with a tug at my arm, "I'll tell you all about it in your office. We have to get you out of sight."

I stood my ground. "Why? What happened?"

"Nothing, yet," she said. "But Barton Vicks came by this morning. Early. Like eight-thirty. Wanted to see you. Nobody else." She spoke quickly, her eyes over my shoulder as though he'd barge in any moment.

"What about?"

She shook her head. "He wouldn't talk to any of us," she said again, with asperity. With a glance to the side and another shake of her head, she added, "No, that's not true. He talked to us plenty. Complained the whole time that we were hiding you and that we were lying about you not being in. Wouldn't talk to Bass, wouldn't talk to Gonzales. I told him I'd be happy to make an appointment, but he said he'd just sit and wait till you showed up."

"Where is he now?"

"About a half hour ago he started screaming about being made to wait, about how his mother was murdered, and how you were part of the conspiracy against him." She gave me one of her meaningful looks. "We called security and had him escorted out, but I know he's coming back. I'm afraid of that dude, Alex. He's creepy. And he knows where you live. Remember that."

"Okay, listen," I said. "If he comes back, give him my cell phone."

"What are you, nuts?"

"The best way to handle this is to make him believe I'm trying to help. Give him my cell number and get his. Tell him I'll try to give him a call as soon as I can."

Her mouth twisted, skeptical. "You sure?"

We started moving toward my office. "I'm out for the rest of the afternoon anyway. I have that meeting at two and I told Detective Lulinski I'd try to stop by today. Let me just grab a couple things, and I'll be out of here."

"The sooner you're out, away from that guy, the better I'm going to feel," she said with a backward glance. Then, "Holy crap."

FOURTEEN

I TURNED TO see Barton Vicks exit the elevator at our second floor landing. He moved with heavy-man deliberation toward the glass doors, his lips moving in an angry conversation with no one. Intent on the door, he didn't notice me until he'd pulled it open.

"Hey!"

He immediately picked up his pace and made his way toward us, looking for all intents like a linebacker about to go for a tackle. I pulled my arm out of Jordan's grasp and decided to meet him head on, closing the gap in three strides. "Barton?" I said.

"What the hell is going on?"

I feigned ignorance. "What do you mean?"

"You're avoiding me, that's what the hell I mean. I sat out here in your lobby for over three hours this morning, waiting for you. You said you were going to help me. This is how you help my mother? The old lady's dead, and this is how you treat her son?"

"Barton—"

He interrupted me, again. The man was apparently never interested in what anyone else had to say. "Don't you give me no lies about how you've been working on this and that's why you weren't here. I know that's the kind of crap you business people hand each other, but I'm not going to fall for it."

"In all honesty, Barton," I said, my voice coming up

enough to go over his. I was sick of him taking the floor with his speeches, "I went out to breakfast this morning."

Jordan had moved out of my line of vision. I caught sight of her again, behind Barton. She picked up the nearest phone and spoke into it, her left hand cupping the receiver as she watched us with wary eyes.

Barton took a step forward, his voice rising. "Out to breakfast, huh? My mother isn't even cold in the ground yet and you're out on a date with the rich bastard she used to work for."

"How the hell do you know who I went out with?"

His fat face broke into a smile that made me cringe. "My mother told me she was talking to you. She told me that the day she died. Said you were going to help her through some of her problems. Money problems. Well, let me tell you, Miss Prissy-pants, whatever she told you, you better tell me."

"I think it's time you leave, Barton."

"I'm not going nowhere until you spill it all." He took another half-step forward, planting his feet shoulder-width apart, his hands balled into fists at his sides. I took a reflexive step back, and as my field of vision expanded, I noticed that Bass had joined the wide-eyed audience. He stood directly outside his office, balancing on the balls of his feet as though ready to step forward to help, then stopping himself with a jerk and a look of confusion.

Oh yeah, I had a lot of help here.

Bart wasn't finished talking. "I tried making this easy for you." He shifted his weight. To say he towered over me would be an understatement. He leaned forward—menacingly, and the only thing that kept me from leaning away was pure stubbornness on my part. "I tried asking nice for your help the day of the wake. And what did I get from you? You ain't done squat for me. Nothing. Where's your loyalty to my mother?" His jaw thrust forward and he worked it. I could feel the tremble in his body—his need to lash out—to hit something or someone. And since I was the closest, I figured he would aim at me. His voice dropped to a growl. "I ain't going nowhere," he said again.

"No, really," I said in my calmest voice, as I watched Jordan meet the security team at the glass doors—three men in beige uniforms, one of them carrying something yellow and ribbon-like. "I insist. It's time you left."

They grabbed him from behind, pinning his arms back. Two of the men held Barton as he thrashed, issuing a scream so primal it made my ears clench and the hair stand up on my arms. The third uniformed guard wrapped the yellow ribbon around Bart's wrists and I saw now it was some sort of plastic tie-wrap.

They had him out the doors in less than thirty seconds, but I'd hardly say he'd been subdued.

"Holy crap." Jordan repeated.

I watched him go, quelling my frantic heart pounding and blowing out breaths to regain some calm. "You can say that again."

"WHO YOU LOOKING for?"

The elderly security guard behind the semi-circular desk interrupted me as I consulted the building directory. Skinny, with a ring of sparse gray hair rimming his bald pate, he scrunched up half his face as he addressed me again, his voice weary with impatience. "Just tell me who you're looking for. I got it all here." He tapped his forehead.

Walking over to him, I smiled. "Dr. Thomas Hooker," I said.

He leaned backward, eyes wide, giving me a once-over with undisguised confusion. "Dr. Hooker?" He scratched the side of his head. "You're not one of his regulars."

"No."

He waited several beats. Maybe he expected an explanation for my visit, but I remained silent, smiling, wishing I'd just gotten the suite number off the directory.

"Four-oh-one," he said, finally. "You sure he's expecting you?"

I ignored the question, and murmured, "Thank you," as I turned toward the two elevators standing open to my left. Three others juggled passengers somewhere between the ground and fortieth floors.

Four-oh-one proved to be a small office at the far end of the corridor. A heavy wood door with the suite number and "Health Partners, Office of Medicine and Mind," let me know I'd found the right place.

There was no receptionist. A tiny, hand-lettered note tacked to the center of three inner doors addressed me: "Alex St. James," it read, "be with you shortly. Please help yourself to something to drink. Thank you."

I assumed coffee and water awaited me beyond the closed door, but I opted to pass. Just as I was about to sit, the leftmost door opened and a man stepped out, looking surprised.

He was beautiful. He sported blond hair, cut Robert Redford style, but he didn't have the famous actor's rough complexion. I guessed him to be just about my age, but with the smoothest, purest skin I'd ever seen on anyone older than a toddler. "Dr. Hooker?" I asked, extending my hand.

"Yes," he said, as we shook.

"Alex St. James."

Blue eyes. Bright blue eyes, they clouded in uncertainty. "I'm just leaving now. Do we have an appointment?"

"Yes," I said, my turn to be puzzled. I pointed to the note. "Two o'clock."

I watched understanding clear the tight expression off his gorgeous face. "Oh, I'm sorry. You must mean my uncle."

"Oh," I said, trying to mask my disappointment. "I didn't realize…"

"I know," he said with a smile that knocked me for a loop, "it happens a lot around here." He pointed back toward the seat I'd almost taken. "I'm late for an appointment, but I'm sure he'll be with you in a moment." He glanced at his watch, as did I. Five before two. "Don't worry, he's very prompt."

"Thanks," I said to his departing figure.

Darn. That could've been fun.

I sat with a fishing magazine on my lap, turning pages, reading nothing. At two o'clock Chicago time, it was noon out in California. As far as I knew the snow hadn't cancelled any flights, so William and Miss Caroline were out there now, until Sunday. I knew I should put him out of my mind, but I couldn't.

When I turned the page, a large mouth bass made me think of Bass at work, and I flipped the magazine shut with a sigh.

The hallway door opened with a quick click-bump that startled me; I jumped at the noise. A balding man, with a gray-streaked black beard, wearing blue jeans and a thick down coat blew in, grinning. He was about six-foot-two, at least forty pounds overweight and he smelled of smoke. Not like he'd just finished a cigarette, rather as if he'd just walked in from a bonfire.

Like David, his voice boomed. "Alex St. James?" he asked as I stood. "I'm Dr. Hooker."

We shook hands and I noticed that beneath the shaggy black eyebrows twinkled eyes of bright blue. He had ruddy cheeks, and I couldn't tell if he'd just run a mara-

thon through snow-covered streets, or if they were that
color naturally. He stripped off the jacket that made him
look like the Michelin Man, and I was surprised to see that
he wore a ratty yellow sweatshirt underneath.

"Nice to meet you, Dr. Hooker," I said.

He nodded and smiled bright teeth at me. The front two
were slightly crooked, just enough to give the appearance
of them coming to a point. Slight imperfection, but a nice
one, it made his smile all the more winsome. "But please,
call me Tom."

He watched me as we talked, and he'd moved to take
my hand in both of his. Friendly, warm, I put immediate
trust in this man, and then shook off the feeling, since we
both knew we were here to find out information from one
another. But I couldn't repress it entirely. The big man with
the booming voice emanated the enchantment of a well-
worn teddy bear, warm, safe, and always willing to listen.

From his youthful demeanor, I would have put him in
his mid-forties, but since I'd met his thirty-ish nephew, he
might have been older. Fifty, maybe. But no more.

"You found my note," he said, leading the way into the
door on the far right. "Good. Now, come on in, we have
lots to discuss."

FIFTEEN MINUTES LATER, holding a mug of warm tea up near
my face, I interrupted him. We'd discussed everything
from the wicked March snowstorm to his office's impend-
ing redecoration when he mentioned he'd just come from
visiting Diana in the hospital.

"Any change?"

Wide smile there. "Big change. She's talking."

"That's wonderful," Flooded with an immediate sense
of relief, I was jarred when the good feelings washed back
far enough for me to realize that if Diana was now awake

and talking, then he didn't really need me. My chances of getting information from him were slim to none.

But since he didn't seem ready to kick me out at the moment, I thought I'd stay a while and see where things led. We waded through a few more safe subjects, each of us assessing the other as we did so, when Tom started to mention that he shared the practice with his nephew.

"I met him," I said.

"Good kid," he said. "Needs a few more years under his belt and he'll be great."

Lowering the mug to my lap, I realized how relaxed I felt. My ankles were crossed in front of me and my butt was slightly forward on the seat putting me into an oh-so-slight reclining position. I scooched back.

He grinned and took a loud slurp of the tea from his own mug. He'd fixed us both some in the tiny kitchen adjacent to his office. The mystery center door.

"That was nice of you to come all the way down from the hospital to meet me. Do you live nearby?" I asked.

"Hyde Park," he said with a shrug. "I didn't mind. I looked forward to talking with you. I've heard your name several times during my sessions with Diana, and after what happened to you both, I knew we needed to meet."

"She talked about me?"

"Several times," he repeated. "Even before today." I started to notice the fact that his eyes squinted almost imperceptibly when he was gauging my reaction to something.

"Care to share?"

The corners of his mouth curled up. I could tell by the way his mustache spread, just a bit. "As a matter of fact…" He'd leaned back in his armchair, his body taking on a relaxed pose as well. Warming up to talk, it seemed, he leaned forward, gripping his mug, resting his elbows on the scuffed-denim knees. "I think we're in a position to help one another."

"How's that?"

He captured me with intent blue eyes. "Detective Lulinski wants to solve his case. I know that. I respect that." He tapped a palm against the side of his mug, like a catcher fisting his glove. "And as much as I hate the idea of a killer running loose, as much as I want this crime solved—if you and I had met yesterday, I would have claimed confidentiality when you tried to get information about Diana out of me. I mean," he lifted a shoulder, "even if you asked whether she's right or left-handed—I wouldn't have told you."

Digesting his little speech, I canted my head. "Do I sense a 'but'?"

Smiling, he nodded, never breaking eye contact. "But." He took another long drink of his tea, and I sipped mine. Starting to get cool. "Today, I told Diana that you and I were scheduled to meet. She's open to sharing information."

The best news I'd heard all day. "Excellent," I said, placing my mug on a nearby table. Time to get down to it. "Then tell me about Laurence Grady."

Dr. Tom Hooker was a man who reacted with small movements. A job requirement, I supposed. One black eyebrow twitched as though it had been about to fly upward but caught before it could move.

"Well, aren't you direct?" he said with amusement.

"Part of my job."

"I imagine it is."

We sat for a few beats as the second-hand on the clock over the doorway took silent steps past two and three.

"First," he said. "Tell me about the night you were attacked."

I hesitated. Not because I was reluctant to relive the

experience, but more because I didn't have much recollection of Diana's state of mind during the encounter. And except for her refusal to get her ass out of the house when we had the chance, I didn't have much to add about her participation. How was that going to sound to a shrink? Placing blame. All her fault.

Then again, I rationalized that he was the expert and we were here today in the spirit of 'one hand washes the other.' And so I began with my aunt's request to take Diana home and finished with the arrival of the paramedics. Through it all, he nodded. He took no notes.

"I'm wondering if Laurence Grady might have been the man who attacked us," I said, finally.

He nodded, his face solemn, open—encouraging further explanation.

"According to Detective Lulinski this Grady fellow and Diana have a history together."

The doctor nodded. "Go on."

"And," I strove to put weight into my words, "Grady is out on parole. He could've been the person who murdered Mrs. Vicks. He could be coming back for Diana."

I waited, but the good doctor effectively waited me out.

"That's why I want to know about him. What Diana can tell us that might shed some light on the situation. There might be more here going on than she realizes."

"I don't think Grady is your man."

"Why not?"

He pursed his lips then—thoughtful fashion, but remembering the magazine from the lobby, I thought he looked like a fish pressing up against a glass bowl. Not a pretty sight. He sucked in a breath through his puckers. "I'm not at liberty to say at the moment."

My "Oh?" came out in a skeptical tone—which was exactly how I meant it. "How convenient."

"Diana gave me authorization to tell you anything you want to know—as long as it relates to the murder."

I felt my brow furrow. "Who makes the distinction?"

"I do."

I shook my head, concealing my growing frustration. "What if something's germane and you don't know it?"

He spread his hands before him. "It's a risk you'll have to accept. I'll be in contact with Diana, myself. Regularly. I'll monitor all of this. She's suffered a trauma, and I'm not telling you anything new, I believe, when I say that she's a fragile soul."

Fragile soul. Exactly how I'd describe her. "I certainly don't want to jeopardize her recovery," I began.

"Good," he said. "And everything you've told me about the night you two were attacked is immensely helpful. I'm very glad we've connected."

"Doctor," I said, to finish the thought I'd begun, "Diana may be the key to all this. Even though you might not think that her friend Grady is involved, I hope you'll not withhold potentially important information."

His eyes bored into mine. "Diana is giving you more than most patients would. I think you need to be cognizant of what she's risking by doing so."

I took a deep breath at his gentle admonishment before responding. No sense in alienating him. Not yet at least. But I'd still gotten very little bang for my buck. "Of course," I said. "And if I have specific questions—more than you're willing to answer—I can always just talk with her directly." I wasn't exactly asking his permission, but I wanted him to know I'd be working every angle open to me.

"I'd prefer you don't."

He'd prefer. My knee-jerk reaction was to tell him that I didn't care a whit what his preferences were, but I found, to my surprise, that I actually did care. The man engendered trust. I knew I could trust him and I wanted him to trust me. It scared me. But I had a job to do.

"Sorry, no promises," I said, smiling to take the warning out of my words.

He grinned as we stood, and he took my right hand again in both of his. "It was wonderful meeting you, Alex. We will be in touch. I have time Friday afternoon if you want to come by. We can discuss this further."

I'd gotten precious little information from him, but he'd gotten plenty from me. I wondered how much he charged per hour. Whatever it was, this guy's clients were getting off cheap.

FIFTEEN

I DIDN'T GET to Detective Lulinski's station till the following morning.

"You met with Hooker?" he asked by way of greeting when he came down to get me from the reception area. He waved for me to follow him.

"Yesterday. Two o'clock. As ordered."

He turned at my verbal jab, and I thought I caught a smile on the laconic detective's face. "And?" he asked.

I double-stepped to catch up with him by the elevator. "Don't you want to walk up? It's just one flight."

He was saved from reply as the elevator dinged its arrival and the doors slid open and he made the universal arm movement of "after you."

"Truth is," I began as we made our way to the interview room, surprisingly vacant, "I got nothing out of him except for the fact that he doesn't believe it was Laurence Grady who attacked us."

"Let him stick to his shrink business, and let me take care of the police work," Lulinski said as he rolled weary eyes. "Everybody's a detective." He sat at his desk and gestured for me to take the chair I'd occupied last time. "So?" he said, leaning backward, lacing his fingers behind his head. "What else?"

I hesitated. "Not much."

One eyebrow rose. "Uh-huh." His mouth twisted to the side as if cradling an imaginary cigarette. "You don't sound very convincing."

I waved away importance and took a deep breath. "Barton Vicks came to see me."

Lulinski sat up. "When?"

"Yesterday, at work." I launched into a quick narrative and included the fact that Bart had apparently known my comings and goings, as evidenced by his comment on my breakfast meeting. Lulinski's face remained impassive, but I watched his eyes flick as key points registered.

"What happened when they took him away?"

I started to laugh as I remembered Bass's sudden spurt of courage as they dragged Big Bart out the doors. My diminutive boss had trotted after them, face red, finger-shaking, issuing warnings against bothering his employees ever again. He'd built up such a head of steam that when the security staff stopped to readjust their unwilling captive, Bass's momentum had nearly made him stumble against the big man's ample gut.

The detective's stern expression stopped my amused reverie and we both looked up when the room's back door opened and an older-gent janitor walked in, dragging his wheeled cart of cleaning supplies behind him. He nodded to us, and set to his work, emptying trash cans and mopping around the chairs and desks with a heavy rag mop.

"So," I continued, "my boss, Bass, decided to file a complaint against Barton. Beside a restraining order, keeping him away from the station and all its employees, he had Barton arrested for criminal trespass and disorderly conduct."

Both eyebrows shot up this time. Lulinski reached for the phone. "Hang on, I'll find out what happened from there."

He held the phone snugged between ear and shoulder as he flipped through a file of pages, searching for something. Answering with one-word affirmations, he sent me a look of boredom and mouthed something I didn't catch. A half-minute later he nodded, said, "Sure," and told me he was on hold.

"By the way," I said, "any information from the autopsy or from forensics that you can share with me?"

"Nope."

"Nope, you have no information, or nope, you can't share?"

He grinned. "While we wait," he said, pulling a single sheet of paper from the stack, "let me have you look at a few pictures. See if any of these guys look familiar. Maybe we'll find out who it was that accosted your sister yesterday."

As he slid the laser-printed sheet my direction, I had my doubts that any face on it would ring a bell. After all, it'd been dark, and my glimpse had been fleeting, at best. Plus the fellow had worn a knit cap which meant I couldn't depend on style of hair to help me. I blew out a breath and glanced downward. My hand flew up. I pointed. "That's him!" I said, surprising myself. "Oh my God, that's really him." I never would have guessed it. Five black and white, none-too-flattering mugshots graced the top third of the white sheet of paper. All five men were white, dark-haired, and had a frightening expression of malevolence leaching from their eyes. But only one was familiar.

My jaw had dropped when I saw his picture and I shut it, amazed at the recognition. No mistake. I couldn't say for sure how I knew, I just knew it was the man. The shape of his nose, perhaps—it was long with a ball-shaped tip and it looked as though it might have been broken once. His slightly wide-set eyes, maybe. I didn't know specifically what feature of his made me certain, but I knew it was the same man the moment his angry gaze stared up at me.

The person on the other end of Lulinski's line came

back to talk. Grabbing a pen and paper, he started to jot down information, but then relaxed his hand as he fell back into the rhythm of grunting affirmation. The detective was nothing if not terse. After a brief conversation with the arresting district, he dropped the receiver back in place and leaned forward on his elbows as he turned my direction. "Barton Vicks is back out. Got released this morning on an I-bond." Lulinski fixed me with a stare. "If he spent a night locked up, he's going to be one angry son-of-a-bitch today. I'd keep as far away from him as possible. We don't know what he's capable of."

"Is he your primary suspect?"

"I can tell you we're looking at him." Lulinski shook his head. "Guy's gotta be hard up for cash. He could've bonded out last night with a hundred bucks, but I guess he didn't have it on him."

I shrugged. "I wouldn't have either."

"You don't carry at least a hundred dollars on you at all times?"

"Not even close. Twenty. Maybe."

He shook a finger at me. "You should. What happens if you get arrested? If you didn't carry enough cash, you'd have to spend the night in lock-up just like your friend Big Bart did yesterday."

"I don't plan on getting arrested anytime soon," I said.

"Nobody ever does."

I was spared further admonishment by Lulinski circling the mugshot I'd indicated.

"Who is it?" I asked.

"Who do you think?"

"Laurence Grady?"

Lulinski didn't even have to answer. For a slim man, he sure could make himself look imposing. I suppressed a shudder. Grady had been talking to Lucy. The scumbag had been talking to my sister.

Lulinski said, "I'm going to follow up from this end—check with his parole officer—see what I can dig up. You have my cell phone number?"

"Yeah."

"You see him again, you call me. Right away."

"I will," I said.

He smiled then, as if to reassure me, but the forced look served only to remind me of the very real danger that surrounded us all: Mrs. Vicks' murder, my own encounter, and now definitive proof that Laurence Grady had been talking with Lucy. As though a drain suddenly pulled all life from me, my mind shut out all sound, all feeling, all sight for an extended moment.

Detective Lulinski leaned forward. "Are you okay? You're not going to faint, are you?"

"No." I tried a reassuring smile of my own. "I'm fine."

He placed a restraining hand on mine, like he thought I might bolt that minute, and he turned to speak to the only other person in the room. The janitor's head popped up, as did mine, when Lulinski addressed him in Polish.

As the man scurried back out the way he came, Lulinski turned to me. "Stan's going to get you a glass of water," he said.

"I know, I heard you ask him," I said. "You speak Polish?"

"Do you?"

Stan came from behind me this time, and handed me a paper cup of cold water, his calloused fingers grazing mine as he did so, a concerned look on his face. Feeling myself again, I thanked him in Polish and was gratified to see my use of his native tongue brought a smile to his face. He cautioned me to take it easy and then set back to work, picking up the mop from the floor where he'd dropped it in his haste to get moving.

Lulinski shook his head. "Well, aren't you full of surprises?" He twisted his mouth off to the side again. "Your color is back," he said. "You went pale on me for a minute there."

I sipped my water, raising it slightly in Stan's direction as thanks. He smiled again. Nodded again.

Lulinski's eyebrows lifted. "So why don't you tell me how a girl with Irish looks and a last name of St. James, can speak Polish like a native daughter."

ON THE DRIVE from the police station to Banner Bank, I turned my phone on to check for messages. Other than noting that my battery was getting low, there was nothing. Not that I'd expected any messages, of course. Bass knew I wouldn't be in till after lunch and Lucy was out shopping with Aunt Lena at the mall all day. I didn't really expect anyone to call me. Not really.

I wondered what the weather was like out in San Francisco today. And what sorts of plans the sister station had come up with that required William and Miss Bliss to get there so many days early. I decided that they must be very busy.

When I found myself grimacing out the windshield at nothing at all, I decided it was time for some music.

I flipped the radio on, and sighed with pleasure as the opening chord of one of my all-time favorite Train songs reverberated through my tiny Ford Escort's interior. I cranked the volume up and sang along with gusto, musical talent be damned.

When I got caught thus emoting at a red light by an old

man in the car next to me, I shrugged. He laughed, and I did too. When the light changed, I was still smiling.

Maybe things were beginning to look up.

I READ THE nameplate before I introduced myself. "You're Nina?" I asked, extending my hand with a smile. "I'm Alex St. James."

Nina Takami raised her head with an insouciant swing of her jet black hair. Her chin jutted high and I got the feeling she labored to maintain such a studious bored look in her eyes. "So?" she said, ignoring my outstretched hand.

I dropped my fingers to grip the edge of her desk, feeling my smile fade. Leaning forward slightly I blinked, twice. "So..." I said, drawing the word out, "Maya Richardson told me that you'd take care of handling my files for me while I'm here."

Nina Takami stared. Worked at it.

Instantly tired of her, I sighed an explanation. "When I left yesterday, you weren't around. I talked to Beth instead." I gestured toward the empty desk next to Nina's. "She put the records into one of your drawers." Swinging my hand, I indicated the file cabinet behind her. "Bottom one."

"So talk to Beth."

My patience waning, I said, "Beth isn't here."

"Well then you're out of luck."

"What is your problem?" I asked, not caring that my voice rose. "I'm here doing a favor for Mr. Dewars, and all I'm asking for is a little cooperation."

"Trust me," she said, jutting a defiant jaw as she spoke, "you're not doing anyone a favor by being here."

Her attitude floored me. "Fine," I said, "I'll get them myself."

Resisting the urge to mutter under my breath, I headed

for the cabinet, crouching to retrieve the file from the bottom drawer.

Part of me was disappointed that she turned aside, thereby granting me *de facto* access to the cabinet. I'd have welcomed the chance to toss her on her size two ass. I began to pull the papers out of the drawer when I realized above the office din that my buddy Nina was on the phone, talking about me.

"So, what do you want me to do?" she asked, eyeing me with distaste.

I ignored her.

When I stood, arms full, heading for the lunchroom, Nina Takami stood too, effectively blocking my path. Jaw set, she fought a smirk. Failed. "You have to wait here."

Giving a weary headshake, I moved to get past her. She stepped in front of me again, this time folding her arms.

What was this, a playground skirmish? We were both adults here. Yet I couldn't stop myself from saying, "Says who?"

Staccato answer. "Mr. Riordan. He's on his way."

David was going to get an earful, that was for sure. "Fine," I said, dropping the files on her desk. "When he gets here, say hello to him for me."

This time when I moved, she let me. Around us, all chattering conversation, keyboard sounds, and calculator noises ceased as every pair of eyes in the place fixed on the two of us. Had I been required to bulldoze my way out, she might have been able to coerce witnesses to say I assaulted her. Five minutes I'd known Nina Takami and already she made my skin crawl.

No matter how hard it is to keep one's head up after an altercation in front of an audience, it's a thousand times harder to keep from going red in the face. One of those autonomic reflexes, it accosted me now, and even as I walked the long row past the arrangement of desks, I could feel my cheeks throb with heat.

I hadn't gotten halfway out when who should appear at the far end of the throughway, but Owen Riordan himself. He took five long strides and less than two seconds to close the distance between us. "Ms. St. James," he said, with a smile that pushed his cheeks sideways, but didn't quite reach his eyes. "How nice to see you again. How are you today?"

I flashed a glance behind me to see Nina Takami still standing before her desk, glaring in our direction. Back to Owen, I said, "Why don't you tell me?"

I've seen people arrange their faces before. Never works to make them look innocent; rather it serves to point up their complicity in whatever the sordid situation. Baffled, because I truly had no idea what agendas were playing out just beneath my level of comprehension, I waited for Owen to arrange his soft-dough face into feigned confusion. I could have spoken his words with him, he was so predictable. "Why, whatever do you mean?"

I clasped my hands together, almost prayerfully, pressing my fingers hard against one another to keep myself from blasting. "Owen," I said, calm as can be, remembering how I'd had to maintain composure the day before when I talked with Barton. I had new respect for Mrs. Vicks; she'd been stuck dealing with these two clowns on a regular basis. "Mr. Dewars asked me to look into Mrs. Vicks' bank accounts." I kept my voice low, my manner soft, like I was addressing a kindergartner. "To be honest, Owen," I said, using his name again, condescendingly, "I don't know what he thinks I might find. But you know what?"

His eyes had hardened. He didn't like this at all. I knew it. I could feel it. I loved it. "What?" he asked.

I nodded my head to accompany my nearly sing-song words. "This is my story, Owen. This is what I do for a living. If you have a problem with my investigation, why don't you take it up with Mr. Dewars?" I smiled then. "I know I plan to."

"There's no need to be angry," he began. "Nina?" he called, walking past me toward the girl, still standing at her desk like some sort of toughie. He waved his fingers for me to follow.

I stood my ground.

He rested a protective hand on the account information I'd dropped on Nina's desk, and turned to me again. "We've just gotten started on the wrong foot here. I have no problem with your investigation. Of course not. None whatsoever. I do have a problem with these files being removed from the vault area. Nina knew that. That's why she called me. Right, Nina?"

Arms still folded, her glare never wavered from me. "That's right, Mr. Riordan."

I stared at Owen's homely face, but said nothing. His flaccid facial muscles under pasty skin, combined with his "let me try to fake a pompadour" hair, and gaggable cologne screamed "has-been playboy" to me. The fact that twenty-something Nina here looked at him with something akin to hero-worship made me wonder what these two might be doing behind vault doors.

"All I'm saying," he continued, easily, "is that we have to keep these files protected. That's why David set you up downstairs in the first place. Maya didn't know better, but I've gotten things squared away with her now too. So," he attempted a conciliatory smile, "let's get you settled back down there."

I had no intention of getting settled back into that hole. "I'll pass," I said, then turned to walk away.

"Wait."

Owen trotted after me, caught me by the arm. I shook his hand free, about to say something utterly impolite when he surprised me. "Please," he said. "Walk with me. I'll explain."

He grabbed both boxes of files, and I didn't offer to help. I led the way out through the busy offices to the bank of elevators.

"So?" I said as we walked. "Explain."

"I'm sorry about the difficulty in there," he began. His voice grunted as he shifted the weight in his arms.

"Difficulty?" I said, my voice filled with incredulous outrage. "You and that Nina person treated me like a two-year-old. I don't have time for that."

"No, no, of course not," he said, his voice attempting to take on the same sort of soothing tone I'd noticed from David, but I could tell the heavy boxes were getting to him. "There are a few things you don't know."

"Enlighten me."

"Don't," he said, as I reached to press the 'down' button. He glanced back the way we came.

I raised an eyebrow.

"You heard about this audit?" he asked, lifting a knee to bolster the boxes in his arms.

I nodded. "David told me that it was scheduled. Nothing out of the ordinary."

Owen shook his head, his breath labored. "No. There's more to it this time. We're afraid that we have an embezzler in the bank. Maybe several. No idea which department, or who or how many are involved. And no one knows about this but me and David." He winced, readjusting the boxes yet again.

"And this affects me, how?"

His pasty face reddened as he struggled. "Can you grab one of these?"

I slid the top box off his load and held it in both arms. Then I waited.

"Thanks." He blew out a breath. "It could be anyone. It could even be Maya, or Nina." He jerked his chin back toward the offices we'd just left. "We've instituted a new rule that the auditors can't take files out of their temporary offices. We're doing that to protect our own interests. If I let you waltz around with Mrs. Vicks' accounts, and keep the auditors behind closed doors, it's going to look suspicious."

"You gotta be kidding," I said. "Mrs. Vicks' accounts are a completely different issue."

He shrugged, sneaking out a finger to press the down button. "I'm sorry. That's just the way it is."

Before I let Owen leave me alone in the vault cave, I made him stand there and wait while I dug out statement after statement from the boxes, and while I marked off each and every one of those even-dollar amount checks written on Mrs. Vicks' account over the years.

"Hang on," I said, when I caught him checking his watch for the third time. "Almost done."

Stepping up to watch over my shoulder he asked, "You want a copy of every one of those?" not bothering to disguise the whine in his voice.

"Yep," I answered. "Every one." Truth was, I would have been happy with a random sample of copies of the checks in question, but I didn't feel like being especially gracious at the moment. "I know Mr. Dewars wants me to be thorough."

"Fine," he said, just as I'd begun to copy down the check numbers from year two. He rubbed his temples as he turned to leave. "Give the list to Lorna. I'll get to it later."

I MADE IT back to my office close to four o'clock.

"Nice of you to grace us with your presence," Bass said. Judging from the constipated look on his face, I gathered he had news, and it wasn't good. He dropped into one of the chairs opposite my desk. "Why isn't anything easy?"

I didn't have time for his complaints. "The problem isn't things going wrong, Bass," I said, deadpan. "The problem is you expecting otherwise."

"I'll try to remember that," he said rolling his eyes, leaning forward to rest his arms on my desk. "Barton Vicks came back."

"I thought—"

"Yeah," he said, interrupting me. "We all thought the restraining order would keep him out of here. But he showed up today, hat in hand, apologizing for his behavior the other afternoon. Wants to talk to you."

"Me? About what?"

"He says he wants to apologize to you personally."

Now, I rolled my eyes.

"Yeah," Bass said, "I know. He's up to something. But that's not what I'm here to talk to you about."

"Oh?"

"Hank Mulhall wants this story finished. He did some checking and he believes that *Up Close Issues* isn't covering this one at all. He thinks, what with your connection, that we can really make this story sing. That we can get the top spot with this feature."

"You told him I'm working on it?"

Bass bit his lip. "He wants it filmed Monday."

"Monday?" As the word burst from my mouth, I stood up. "What is he, nuts?" I started to pace past the picture window that overlooked the Chicago River, stopping to stare, while I collected my thoughts. Where for a brief few hours, the city had been covered in pure-white snow, the mounds lining the streets were now decorated with dark speckles, like dirty polka-dots. Why couldn't things that were beautiful just stay the way they were? The once-pure snow had turned into so much filth.

"The further we get away from the date of the murder, the less gripping the story," he said to my back. "It's already been a week. How much more time do you want?"

I spun. "As long as it takes, Bass." I advanced on him then, taking small satisfaction in the fact that he gripped the arms and leaned back in the chair, as if trying to get away from me. "And if you go airing this next week, you're going to screw up the entire investigation. For crying out loud," I muttered, pacing. The frustrations of getting nowhere, no matter where I turned, suddenly blossomed upward in my chest like a silent explosion.

I ranted, unable to stop myself if my life depended on it. Grabbing each of my fingers, in turn, I enumerated my problems. "Despite the fact that David Dewars is convinced I'll find incriminating evidence against Barton Vicks, I get nothing from Banner Bank but aggravation," I said, my voice rising. "And then Big Bart comes here to intimidate me. At the same time…" I took a breath, winding up, "I find out that there's this lowlife, Laurence Grady, who's involved with Mrs. Vicks' roommate. Now, this guy's hanging around my neighborhood, and I caught him talking to my sister. How do you think that makes me feel?"

Bass shook his head, for once in his life, wisely remaining quiet.

Still indicating my frustrations on my fingers, I stopped long enough to point. "The detective, Lulinski, doesn't trust me. And with good reason. If we're planning on running this story without all the facts we're going to totally screw up his efforts."

"He doesn't trust you?"

I'd stopped long enough to allow my thoughts to catch up with my mouth. "Well," I hedged, "I think he's beginning to. He asked me to talk with Diana's psychiatrist to find out what I can from him."

Bass's little hazel eyes lit up. "And?"

Anger flaring again, I snapped. "And nothing. The guy got more out of me than I got out of him, okay?"

"If the detective's starting to trust you, then use it. Get what you can out of him."

"Have you met the man?" I asked.

"No."

"Well, let me tell you, it ain't that easy. He doesn't trust any media people. He hates Dan Starck in particular." I mumbled that I'd like to know what that was all about, then blew out a breath. "This Lulinski guy plays his cards close to his chest. Real close. I get nothing from him. Nothing from him—nothing from anybody."

"What's with you anyway?" Bass asked. "This story hit too close to home?"

I glanced up at that, expecting to see understanding in his eyes.

Instead, he glared at me. "Is this too much for you, little girl?" he asked. "Maybe you just can't handle it."

"I'm handling it perfectly," I lied. "I just need more time."

"Uh-huh," Bass said without conviction. He squirmed forward in the chair till his feet hit the ground, then stood, staring at me. "We pay you based on results. A half–story is the same as no story. Get it?"

We stared at one another till he finally broke eye contact.

"Monday," he said. As he walked out my office door, he threw a parting comment over his dandruff-covered shoulder. "That's plenty of time."

SIXTEEN

Right before pulling out of our underground parking lot, I remembered to call my aunt to let her know I'd be late getting back tonight. I wanted to stop by the hospital and talk with Diana myself, no matter what Dr. Hooker preferred. I decided it was time to get the information straight from the horse's mouth. Apologies to Diana.

While I updated Aunt Lena on my plans, and she assured me that Lucy was fine and I needn't rush, the cell phone's low-battery-sound signaled in my ear. "Gotta go," I said, after it blipped a second time. One more and I'd be incommunicado.

I shut down the phone and turned my mind toward navigating traffic. One nice thing about working late was avoiding the rush-hour.

The hospital, a massive multi-winged structure built in the early part of the twentieth century, spread itself over four city blocks like a giant petrified spider. It was the sort of place that imposed itself, taking up my entire field of vision as I pulled into the multi-storied open-air visitors' garage.

As I followed signs that led me from my twelfth-floor parking spot through two antiseptic-smelling hallways, I had time to gather my thoughts and decide how to approach Diana.

Aunt Lena had told me which building, which room, but as I arrived in the hospital's lobby, I caught the tail end of an argument between a heavily pierced young man with shaggy hair and the prim forty-something woman behind the desk. He held a cellophane wrapped bouquet of pink roses down at his left side, while his right hand trembled with frustration.

The woman shook her head, making tiny touches to her upper lip with her tongue, just waiting for her moment to jump in. Another head shake. "I'm sorry," she said with a gleeful lilt. "There's nothing I can do. Visiting hours are over."

I veered off to the far left alcove that housed a bank of in-hospital phones. Leaning against the wall with my back toward the reception desk, I hoped it looked like I was a person who belonged there, making some important phone call. Keeping my movements slow, I dug through my cavernous purse and pulled out my trusty notebook.

They were still arguing as I emerged from the alcove, and I'd arranged my face into my best imitation of bored worker bee. I draped my down coat over my arm, knowing that my business-suit attire wasn't going to hurt me either. The woman gave me no more than a passing glance before she returned her attention to the young man, and I turned the corner away from them just as an elevator opened, as if waiting for me.

Once I made it to her floor, I was fine. No one seemed to question my being there; no one seemed to have any care that it was past eight. Encouraged, I strode into her room full of purpose.

But when I saw her, all my carefully nuanced questions went out the window. They'd moved her out of intensive care into a ward of four women. Diana had the left-hand bed closest to the window and as I made my way toward her, I nodded hello to the three other ladies who dragged their eyes away from the television to watch me with patent curiosity. I couldn't begin to guess at their individual ailments.

"Diana?"

She'd been staring out the wall of windows at the eastern sky which winked with starlight. Her eyes fluttered in a way that I knew she'd heard me, but as she turned, she grit her teeth, and the tendons in her neck stood out in bas-relief. Her mouth curved in a peculiar way as she croaked out my name.

Pulling a heavy wooden chair to her bedside, looking around at the barrenness of her surroundings compared to those of her roommates, I realized I should have brought something. Flowers, maybe. One of the other women had a bouquet next to her bed, carnations and roses. The scent of them reminded me again of Mrs. Vicks' funeral, and I reassessed the flower idea. Get well balloons, maybe.

So consumed with getting answers, I'd come empty-handed and I apologized for that. Diana waved the free fingers of her left hand, as if to dismiss my concerns. She wore a cast on that arm which encompassed everything from the knuckles to her shoulder and whenever she moved, even slightly to adjust herself, she winced and used her free arm to bolster herself.

"How's it feeling?" I asked, indicating her arm.

"Not terrible," she said in a rusty voice. "But it figures that I broke this one."

"You're left-handed?" I said. "I didn't know that."

"Yeah." Her mouth turned downward in an exaggerated frown. "Left-handed people are supposed to be cursed, you know. My mom used to tell me I had to work harder to beat the curse."

I was about to respond to that with some reassuring remark, but she interrupted.

"You look pretty good."

"I was lucky, I guess."

She coughed out a laugh and her dark eyes clouded. "No," she said. "I watched you go down. You got hit worse than me."

I pointed to her arm. "But—"

"Cursed." She gave what might have been a shrug. "Don't even remember this happening. All I remember is that you didn't leave me, Alex." Shaky tears gathered just below her eyes, catching the vaguely bright reflection of the fluorescent lights above. "He would've killed me."

"*Who* would've?"

As she blinked, the trembling pools released, dripping sideways across her face to fall in fat splashes onto the pillow beneath her cheek. She stared out the windows again. "The guy who was in the house."

Sotto voce, I said, "You know who it was."

Avoiding my eyes, she bit her upper lip and shook her head.

"We both know who it was."

More blinks, more tears, and she now sucked in her upper lip so hard that it pulled her nose downward. Long full-bodied sniff.

"Diana," I tried again, "It was Laurence Grady, wasn't it?"

This time her eyes snapped my direction, widening and tearing up with an immediacy that took me by surprise. Her right hand shot toward me, grabbed my arm. "It wasn't him. He swears it wasn't him."

Her words stunned me. "He's been here?"

"He's got his life back together, Alex. This time he really does. And he wants me back."

The catch in her voice spoke volumes, and I looked away, needing to gather my thoughts. I noticed the three other women in the room had turned their attention from the ceiling-braced TV, to watch us. They'd even turned down the volume. Lately, it seemed I was forever on display.

I spoke in a whisper. "I talked with Dr. Hooker."

Her pained expression relaxed. "You did? Good. Because he'll tell you, too. It wasn't Larry who hurt us. Larry wouldn't hurt anyone."

"That's part of what I want to talk with you about. Dr. Hooker won't tell me much about Laurence." I couldn't quite bring myself to refer to him as Larry. "He says he'll only tell me what I need to know."

Diana's dull expression told me that she didn't see the problem.

Tamping down my exasperation, I tried to soften my words with a smile. "Dr. Hooker might not realize something's important. Maybe if you give him permission to talk to me about Larry…" I let the thought hang, and take hold.

She bit her lip, and seemed to ponder that.

"I know Larry didn't hurt us, and I know he didn't hurt Mrs. Vicks," she said, finally. "So, okay, when I talk with Dr. Hooker next, I'll tell him he can tell you anything. Would you like me to do that?"

I patted her hand, just as a black nurse came in with a tiny paper cup of pills for Diana to take. "Visiting hours were over at eight," she said with more than a little annoyance. She grabbed at the privacy curtains and tugged. The ceiling-mounted hooks slid with set-your-teeth-on-edge-scraping, till Diana's bed was completely blocked from view of anyone else in the room. "And it's time for her to sleep."

THE HOSPITAL SMELLS seemed to have shifted in the short time I'd spent with Diana. On the way out, through the labyrinthine corridors, I caught the scent of fresh-brewed coffee and microwave popcorn. It was after nine o'clock, and my guess was the night shift needed to gear up for the long lonely hours ahead with snacks and solid jolts of caffeine.

I probably shouldn't have stayed so late, I mused, as I exited the final corridor and headed for the parking garage elevator. I'd missed the herd that must have departed just as I'd arrived, and it left the area quiet except for a few stragglers.

Two men, one elderly, one young, obviously together, but not talking with one another, both looking deep in thought, made me wonder who they'd been visiting. The young man's mother, perhaps? They waited with me and we took the same elevator. They got off at two, and I continued the climb to my level, stepping out of the bright box at eleven.

The door sliding shut behind me—the accompanying whirr from the electric box that operated the elevator systems—these were lonely sounds in the dark.

I started up the gentle ramp to my Escort. The only car on the entire level now, it caught the reflection of lights from the city surrounding the open-air lot. I heard my footsteps echo, making tiny clip-clops so loud in my ears that it drowned out all thought.

Maybe it was the lack of direct lighting, or the distant train whistle that sounded, but I shivered, suddenly vulnerable as the weight of all that had happened resurfaced in my memory.

Jitters. Too much going on, too quickly, I thought.

Like a dream where I run but can't move, I felt as though every step I took toward my goal fought against an unseen current, making my movements slow and heavy. Even as I tried to pick up my pace, the car didn't get closer. My clipping steps annoyed me. Too noisy, they broadcast my location, my alone-ness. I wished I'd worn my Reeboks.

An out-of-place sound stopped me in my tracks. A whishing, scraping noise, like fabric against concrete.

I turned my head in short twists, trying to catch the source.

Nothing.

There were two main pillars at each end of my section of ramp. Both were fat columns of cement, and the one I'd passed had had a bright red metal call box, with a huge white sign above: "If you need assistance, please call security."

My car sat thirty feet to my left; the call box forty feet to my right. And my imagination sat closest of all, in super-high gear.

The noise again.

It came from the pillar just past my Escort. If someone stood behind it, no way would I beat him to the car, get my keys out and get safely inside before he got me.

But, was anybody there, or was I just being foolish? Right about now, I knew I'd rather be safe and feel a fool, than be brave and find trouble. I inched closer toward the call box, trying to keep my shoes from making tell-tale noises, while digging my right hand into my purse, searching for my pepper spray, hoping my shallow breaths and pounding heart wouldn't give me away.

Tiptoeing, I kept my eyes trained on the far pillar. Nothing. No movement, no sound. Small backward steps, slow steps, they brought me closer to the call box, and took me farther from my car.

My fingers finally wrapped around the black plastic handle of the pepper spray, and I used my thumb to release the sliding safety device. "Okay," I whispered, more to affirm my bravery than anything. "Almost there."

Still keeping close watch on that far pillar, I switched the pepper spray to my left hand and reached around with my right to grab the phone. When I encountered nothing but cold metal, I looked over in fear. "Shoot," I said, louder than I intended. The phone had been ripped out of the box, leaving a mass of multi-colored wires extending out into the dark like so many helpless arms.

The elevator was no more than fifteen steps away. The stairs—adjacent. And maybe, just maybe, I'd simply imagined these noises. My hand back in my purse once again, I had a fleeting giddy thought that my purse was like Batman's utility belt, and all I needed to do was reach the right tool. My cell phone, this time. I hit the power button as I moved toward the scant light of the elevator waiting area, still walking on tiptoe, still watching that far, far pillar.

For the first time all night, something went right. My phone came on and registered in-service, much more quickly than it ever had before. "Thank God," I muttered, as I dialed *911. I heard the tiny beeps as each digit sounded.

"Emergency 9-1-1," a flat voice answered.

As I pulled in a breath to answer, the phone gave an extended beep and powered down. "Shoot," I said again. The damn battery.

From behind me, movement. Breathing. Someone shifting their weight. Someone waiting. For me.

"Who's there?" I shouted, bolting for the stairs.

The clip-clop sound of my shoes blurred as I sprinted. God, please don't let him follow me. Visions of the night Diana and I were attacked rushed through the pounding blood in my head, and through the red lights of panic flashing before me. I could barely make out the yellow metal door that would be my salvation.

His gloved hand grabbed me, stopping me cold, the

yank on my upper arm strong enough, even through the thickness of my down coat, to make me wince.

Panicked, I spun.

"C'mere, bitch."

Laurence Grady stared back at me, his eyes glittering with anger and something more. Hatred? I felt the fear in my stomach drop as my heart rate skyrocketed—all the power to my legs, to my feet, dissolved.

"Where do you get off reporting me to the cops?" He pulled me so close that his hot beer breath steamed against my face.

He had me up on my toes, and as I opened my mouth to scream, he jammed his other hand over it, gagging me.

I flailed against him, trying to bite down, but the leather of his glove was too thick. My left hand strove for leverage to push away, when I suddenly remembered the pepper spray. Feeling triumphant and stupid at the same time, I rushed my hand up toward his face, pressing the trigger as I clenched my eyes and held my breath.

He'd been saying something about the police when the orange-yellow spray hit with a wet hissing sound of splatters on skin. He grunted in pain, the attack startling him. For the briefest second he froze. But it was enough for me to wrench free. Giving his shin a quick kick, I ran, coughing, my eyes teary-eyed and stinging, to the sanctuary of my car. I'd caught some of the spray, but Grady had taken it full in the face. Judging from the intense smarting I felt, he had to be in excruciating pain.

As if I'd willed them to do so, the keys leaped into my hands. Vowing that my next car would have remote entry, I jammed the right one into the lock, yanked the door open, jumped in and locked myself inside before I chanced a look back.

He was gone.

Twisting my body within the confines of the seat, my
puffy coat making the effort ever more difficult, I tried
to see where he'd gone. My right hand had found the ig-
nition, and I started up the car, still coughing, a sharp
vile taste in my mouth, and my eyes feeling as though
I'd stood downwind of a raging fire. I didn't care that the
world blurred before me and I could barely see to drive; I
was getting out of there.

SEVENTEEN

DETECTIVE LULINSKI'S VOICE was thick with anger when I called him from home. "Why didn't you get ahold of me sooner?"

I started to say tell him that my cell phone had gone dead, when he interrupted.

"And why the hell were you alone in a deserted parking garage at night?"

In my mind's eye, I could see red-hot frustration work its way over his face. I suddenly realized that I was a trial to this man. Here he was, trying to clear a murder, stuck working with a member of the media he so despised, and at every turn, I made huge mistakes and gross errors in judgment.

Knowing, however, that the best defense is a good offense, I snarled right back at him. "I was trying to get information for you, in case you forgot."

He muttered something I didn't catch.

"What was that, Detective?"

"Nothing you need to hear." I could tell he took a deep drag of a cigarette, taking his time to blow it out before continuing, much toned down: "All right. We talked with Grady's parole officer this morning and made it clear that he's supposed to stay away from you, Diana, the neighborhood. He's obviously not cooperating, so I'll put out a pickup order on him. Aside from him grabbing you…and the battery charge I'll nail him with, what else?"

"I blasted him with my pepper spray."

I could almost see his terse nod. "Good girl," he said. "I've requested extra coverage past your house for the next few days. And yes," he added, answering my question before I spoke it, "I'm covering your aunt's house too. As long as nobody's in Mrs. Vicks' house, I'm not too worried about that one, but they'll keep their eyes peeled."

"Thanks."

"Part of the job. And Alex…"

"Yeah?"

"Keep the goddamn phone charged."

LUCY HAD BEEN listening from the tiny hallway that separated our bedrooms. She hung on the corner, like a little kid caught doing something wrong, her expression half-curious, half-frightened.

"Is Grady that the same man who talked to me yesterday?"

I nodded.

"Did he hurt you tonight?"

I shook my head, but as I moved to sit at the kitchen table, I winced.

"He did hurt you!" Lucy said with alarm, as she pushed off the wall to help me.

"No, it's just leftover aches and pains." I forced a smile. "Too much excitement today and I forgot about them. Now they're all back. With a vengeance." Grady's appearance tonight had shaken me up more than I cared to admit. "Listen, Lucy, if you see the guy again, or even if you just think you see him, you let me or Aunt Lena know, okay?"

Her right hand reached behind and she twisted her hair. "I don't think he's a bad guy. He was nice to me."

"Until we know what he wants, we can't be sure," I said. Torn between wanting to come down hard on Lucy, to make her understand the stakes, and keeping her from being too terrified to step outside the house, I treaded a fine line and my reasoning sounded lame, even to my ears. "Just stay with someone. Me, Aunt Lena, Uncle Moose. Someone we know, okay?"

"Okay." She dropped the twisted piece of blond hair as she nodded.

"By the way," I asked, "any phone messages? Anybody call?"

"Yeah." Concentration crossed her face as she struggled to remember. "Somebody for you. A man."

"Really?"

"Yeah, he said something about wishing you were there."

My mood brightened with a suddenness that surprised me. I glanced up at the clock. Ten. That made it about eight o' clock in San Francisco. I could still call him back and maybe we'd have a chance to catch up. I'd love to be able to bounce some of this stuff around with William.

"You didn't erase it?"

"No."

I hit the button on my answering machine and the mechanical voice announced that there was one saved message. I smiled at Lucy, who was grinning back, trying hard to understand my sudden attitude change.

"Hello, Alex."

The instant I heard David's voice, my exuberance plunged with the impact of a gut-punch. His words drifted past me, but the room had closed in and I missed the entire message.

"Is that the guy you were hoping to hear from?" Lucy asked.

"No," I said, stringing the word out. I turned my back to her as I pressed the repeat button. She was the most perceptive soul I'd ever encountered and I didn't want her to see my disappointment. Injecting false cheer into my voice, I said, "My mind wandered. Let me hear that again."

David, his voice warm, soothing, had expressed regret at my leaving the bank before he'd arrived that day. He wished I'd been there. He said we needed to talk.

"Who was that?" Lucy asked when the machine beeped off.

Without getting too far into an explanation, I gave Lucy a basic idea of David's role in Mrs. Vicks' murder investigation. I shrugged. "He and I are working together on this and we need to talk tomorrow."

She nodded, a solemn look on her face. "So if he called, he must have something important to tell you."

"Probably," I lied.

Lucy's face lit up. In a burst of emotion, she threw her arms around me. "You see?" she said. "Something finally went right for you today. I knew it would."

"Yeah." I cleared my throat. "Finally."

FRIDAY MORNING, I turned on my fully charged cell phone and checked for messages just in case someone had happened to call overnight. My in-box came up empty, yet again, so I shut it down. Keeping it on all day, even while accessible at work, was a luxury I could no longer afford.

When I pulled into my regular parking spot in the garage beneath our building, I gathered my coat, purse, and briefcase, to step out of the car.

"Alex?"

I screamed as I spun.

Barton Vicks stepped back, alarmed. "I'm sorry," he said, his wide face turning this way and that, as though expecting security to come and cart him away again. "I didn't mean to scare you."

"What are you doing here?"

More than anything else, the panic in my voice made me angry; I hated feeling so out of control. This wasn't the way I liked to handle things. I called the shots; I was used to it. Mrs. Vicks murder and subsequent events had sent all my self-confidence into a frustrating tailspin and I wanted everything the way it used to be.

"Back off," I said.

To my surprise, he did. A sheepish look came over his face as his little eyes blinked a couple of times and he gave a short shrug. "I just need to talk with you, Alex. I'm really sorry about the other day. I..." As his words trailed off, his eyes sought answers in the cement ceiling above us.

I became aware of others parking their cars and heading toward the elevators. Lots of footsteps, chatter, and clunking of doors. A few people glanced our way. I waved to one of the assistants from out station. Despite the fact that I wasn't alone this time, I still moved around my car, keeping a safe distance between us, reaching in my purse for the familiar comfort of the pepper spray.

"You think popping out of the shadows in a dark garage is going to make me want to talk with you?"

He dropped his head, nodding toward his big, brown loafers. "I know. I was going to come by your house last night, but every time I drove by, there was another cop car." Still looking down, he swayed a bit from side to side, making a funny noise, as though he didn't quite know what to say next. He reminded me of Diana, at Mrs. Vicks' wake—swaying instead of talking. It made them look dithering and dull. Finally, he added, "And I know that your boss has a thing set up so I can't come visit you at work."

"Can you blame him?"

I still fingered the pepper spray, hoping I hadn't used the full contents last night. Geez, that little tool was getting quite a workout.

"No," he said. "I was…I mean…"

He shifted his weight and chanced a look up at me.

The anger and determination I'd seen on his face when he'd accosted me in the office was gone, replaced by chagrin, maybe. I didn't think Big Bart had it in him to pull off such an effective ruse, but I still didn't like the man.

"Spit it out, Bart."

He took a deep breath and stared up at the cement beams again. "I have a problem," he said. Then, with what appeared to take every ounce of his courage, he bit the side of his lip, tightened his face and then said, while exhaling: "I'm an alcoholic."

Okay, so that wasn't exactly the surprise of the day. I waited.

"I was out of control when I came to see you. I just don't have any answers. I don't know what to do…" He watched himself shuffle, then looked directly at me. "I was doing good until Ma died. I mean, I wasn't perfect or nothing, but I was going to meetings and all. And today, I been good all morning. But I don't think I can get back in the program until I get some answers. You can do that for me."

"I don't have any answers," I said, in as calm a voice as I could muster.

"I know that," he said quickly, his hands coming up to stop me from leaving, even though I hadn't made a move. "I know I screwed up here, but I know you're trying to find out who killed Ma and I'm getting desperate."

"Desperate? How so?" I prompted.

"Okay, listen," he said. "Let me level with you. I should've done that right at the start, huh?" He shook his massive head, a wincing expression on his down-turned face. "I should've told you the truth."

Apparently, a sober Bart was a somber Bart.

"Tell me now," I said.

His left hand twitched, making a movement as if to grab the hip flask, suddenly stopped by some unseen power. I waited, shivered. "You cold?" he asked.

I was. With only a thirty-second walk separating my car from the elevator, I'd chosen to drape my coat over my arm, rather than wear it. "Yeah," I said. "Come on, we can talk in my office."

As we walked through the hub of busy workers to my office, I felt like a zoo trainer leading a well-behaved gorilla through their midst. Resisting the urge to reassure them with "It's okay," I simply smiled and, when we got to my office door, gestured him in. Jordan stared at me with her, "What the hell are you thinking, girl?" look on her face.

As Barton got himself settled, I turned to her. "Would you mind holding my calls for a while?"

Her eyes flicked toward my open door, then back to me. "You're not going in there alone with him, are you?"

Frances had apparently alerted Bass, and now he came toward us, his little legs bustling our direction as fast as they could. "He's here?" Bass asked, not bothering to keep his voice down. Leaning backward slightly to look into my office, he held out his hands. "What's he want?"

"I plan to find out," I said. I didn't want to leave Barton alone for very long. Not until after I'd had a chance to talk with him. There was no telling when his self-control would falter and he'd reach for that flask again.

"I'm coming with you," Bass said, little hazel eyes glinting with bravado. "You never know if he gets out of hand; you might need protection again."

I opened my mouth to make a caustic remark, then thought better of it. "Fine."

Barton stood as we entered. Mrs. Vicks would have been proud to know he occasionally had manners. When he spied Bass, Barton's face colored. He stammered. "She said it was okay to come up here," he said, pointing at me.

Bass shook a warning finger up toward Barton's face. "You just better not try anything this time."

"I won't, sir."

Sir? The absurdity of the situation seemed to be lost on everyone but me. Barton Vicks could probably bench press Bass without breaking a sweat. When Big Bart had said he was desperate, he evidently wasn't kidding.

"Look," I said, taking control of the conversation as we sat. "I'm willing to listen to what you have to say, Bart, but let's just get one thing straight. I don't have to tell you anything." I said, gauging his reaction, "Nada."

He nodded, blank-eyed, eager to please. "I know that."

When under the influence, this man, to my mind, easily possessed the capacity to murder someone. But now, in this listless, sober state, I couldn't picture this sloth-like creature hurting a soul, least of all his own mother.

"Then what brings you here?"

Barton shifted in his seat, his girth prevented from escape by the chair's wooden arms. "I have another problem too," he said, staring at the floor. He sucked on his droopy bottom lip for a long moment. "It's not just the drinking. I'm in deep for some big money. I like to go to the track sometimes, and I've been having some bad luck the past few months."

The gambling problem. Score another point for David.

He lifted his eyebrows, still facing downward. "I don't see a way out of it this time. I owe a crapload of cash and I don't got enough to pay it off. I don't make big bucks the way some people do." He'd lifted his head at that comment, and I saw a remnant of the anger he'd had the other day.

"How much are we talking?" Bass asked.

Barton's shoulders heaved. "Twenty-five."

"Twenty-five thousand?" Bass repeated.

Barton's eyes widened as though saying the words aloud made them more real. "Yeah," he said, giving a panicked nod of his head.

I thought Bass's mouth would drop; I know mine did. We exchanged glances. All of a sudden David's admonishment that fifty grand would be a shot in the arm to Barton screamed out at me.

"And you don't have that kind of money?" I asked.

"Hell, no," Barton said. "But I sure know that my ma did. She told me she was socking it away for me. Matter of fact, she told me that she put a bundle away every month."

That tidbit tap-danced through my brain as Bart plodded onward about his mother's plans for him. Mrs. Vicks had written those even-amount checks every month for about fifteen years. It reminded me that Owen Riordan hadn't gotten back to me on that issue yet.

I tuned back in.

"She must've said it a hundred times," Barton continued, "she said that she was looking to take care of my future. She said even if I didn't see it so clear myself—that she was taking care of everything for me. So you see, she must've got everything set up. All's I'm asking for is that somebody gives me my due. And I don't think I should have to wait, no matter what that guy at the bank told me."

"Which guy?" I asked.

"The guy with the fruity name. Owen." Barton strung the name out, sing-song. "He told me that he went and filed the will, or some bullcrap like that." He opened big hands in a gesture of frustration. "And now I can't get any action on it till he gets it back."

"I know that they have to file a will within thirty days of the person's death," I said, "but doesn't he have a copy on file?"

I could almost see the proverbial lightbulb go on over Barton's head. "Hey…" he said, with dawning realization. "Yeah. Why do I have to wait till he gets it back? All I want is to see what she had."

Despite the fact that my stomach churned at the thought of this big lug benefiting from Mrs. Vicks' death, I knew that if he was indeed the sole beneficiary, he had every right to pursue his interests in that regard. I, however, had no obligation to help him. I'd done enough.

"Well, then," I said, "Looks like you have your work cut out for you."

"Maybe you could get it for me?" The corners of his mouth tugged into something akin to a smile, his fleshy dollop of double-chin sagging lugubriously.

"Not a chance."

Bass had angled his chair so that he could observe our conversation more than actually participate himself, though in the world of body language, his positioning was anchored to me. Now, his head twisted back and forth between us, like he was watching an old-fashioned game of pong.

"Maybe," Barton said, looking helpless as he shrugged, "maybe you could loan it to me and when I help you solve it and get that reward, I could pay you back?"

"Reward?" Bass and I repeated the word together.

"Yeah. You didn't know about it?" Dark eyes sought reassurance.

"No," we answered together, again. I could hear the surprise in Bass's voice and I sure the heck felt it in mine.

"What reward?" I asked.

"That bank guy is offering a fifty-thousand dollar reward for anyone who comes up with information to find who murdered my mother."

"The bank guy?" I asked. But I knew. David's phone call. That must've been what he wanted to tell me.

As the man with the answers all of a sudden, Barton affected a swaggering tone. "Well, yeah," he said, as though it were common knowledge. "She worked there for over twenty years. They oughta do something—don't you think?"

Bass ran a hand down his face, rubbing his chin. "When did they tell you this?" He shot a questioning look my direction.

I shook my head. This was the first I'd heard of it.

Barton shifted in the chair again. "When I went over there yesterday. I wanted to talk to them about the will and that's when they told me they sent it out for some kinda legal reason." He licked fat lips till they glistened. "They didn't want me being there. Said that it was bad for business and that I should go home. Said they would get ahold of me when the will came back."

"Who did you talk to?" I asked.

"Fruity guy."

"Owen?"

"Yep," he said. "He told me he'd call me back at Ma's house. I'm going to be moving in there now, you know— it's a hell of a lot cheaper than staying in a hotel."

I didn't know that, and I said so.

"Yeah, well, when I first came down I thought it'd be quick, you know…" He had the decency to look away. "That I'd be walking away with enough that I could afford a hotel for a couple of nights. I guess not, huh?" Making a see-saw motion with his head, forgiving himself his mercenary tendencies, I supposed, he continued. "So anyway, Owen tells me that if anybody can come up with evidence to get somebody convicted, then the bank will give them this reward. He said that the cops think the murderer was looking for something. I figured I'd look around myself, maybe I'll solve it and then I can collect, right? What the heck?"

"No wait," I said. "I'll do it."

Detective Lulinski had said that the intruder had been looking for something in Mrs. Vicks' house. Maybe Barton was guilty, maybe he wasn't. But truth would be better served by my poking around in there, than by his.

He squinted at me. "Uh-uh," he said with a solemn shake of his head. "I'm not sharing this money with nobody."

"I don't want the reward," I said. "Honest. I just think that…" my mind raced, trying to come up with a plausible reason to let me look around without Big Bart breathing over my shoulder. "I think that I might be in a better position to recognize…clues," I said.

Lame, very lame. But this guy was no rocket scientist.

He appeared to consider it and I could almost see relief wash over his features at the prospect of having the work done without having to do it himself. Eyes narrowed in my direction. "You ain't kidding me about not wanting the reward?"

"No, swear to God," I said, doing a funny little cross-my-heart movement.

It was enough for him. "Okay," he said, sucking on his lower lip again. "But maybe I should move back in anyway. I mean…" He didn't finish, but I knew where he was going.

"What do you say, Bass?" I turned to him. "Think the station can pick up the tab for Barton's hotel for a couple days?"

Hazel eyes hardened in my direction. Bass kept a grip on the station's money like it was his own. I knew he wanted this story, but the question now was whether or not he was willing to cough up some cash to help it along.

I smiled, all innocence. I had him in a touchy spot, where he had to make a decision that twisted his tender parts. One of my favorite parts of the job.

"Sure," he said. "Send me copies of your bill. We'll reimburse you."

This was fun. Getting money out of Bass was like getting the Pope to start handing out birth control pills.

To Barton, I said, "I have your permission to look around the house," without phrasing it as a question. "We're clear on that, right?"

He nodded. "Yeah," he said. "Clear. And I get the money."

"*If* there's money," I said with weight. "And now," I said, with a dismissive handclap, "why don't we all get started on what we need to do."

Barton left amid much thanking and groveling. When he tried to shake my hand for a third time, I pretended to be busy at the computer. Bass stood in my doorway and watched until Barton cleared the office doors and had stepped into one of the hallway elevators.

"What's with you?" he asked as he sat back in the chair he'd recently vacated.

"Something the detective said," I said, shrugging. "Don't know that I'll find anything of interest, but I feel like I have to try."

"Aren't you the one who told me off the other day? 'I'm not getting involved.'" He made little bird wing gestures and spoke in a falsetto voice, "'Let the police handle it.'"

"I thought you'd be thrilled."

"Thrilled? Hardly. I don't get thrilled much anymore at my age." He stared out over the city of Chicago from my bright window, shook his head. "Nope. Never try to bullshit a bullshitter." He stood up then, made his way to the doorway. "I knew you'd never let this one go, no matter what you told me." He gave an exaggerated wink. "And you knew it, too."

OWEN SANG A "poor me" song when I called him to ask if he'd had those checks looked up yet. When he started to rehash all the things had gone wrong today for him I cut him off, letting him know that I was busy and that, as soon as I hung up, I still needed to return a phone call to David.

Instant change of tune.

Owen fell over himself at that, promising me he'd have the information collected and ready to go by mid-afternoon. "Good," I'd said, in a false-encouraging voice. I provided my fax number, and if that little stutter on the other end of the phone meant that he was reluctant to send the records to my office, then he wisely chose to keep his hesitation to himself.

Time to call David.

I identified myself to his secretary and her efficient tone switched immediately to one of warmth. "Thanks for calling him back, Ms. St. James. He's out of the office right now but he left a message for you."

"Oh?"

She didn't fiddle with papers, not that I could tell at least, so she must have had this one memorized. I could hear a smile in her voice.

"Mr. Dewars is out for the day at a seminar in Mundelein where he'd prefer not to be disturbed. He will be calling in periodically, however, and he wanted me to ask you if you'd be free this evening. He has two tickets to the opening of *The Merry Wives of Windsor* at Navy Pier. And possibly dinner beforehand?"

Taken aback, I hedged. "Tonight?"

"Mm-hmm," she answered. "If you're free, the play begins at eight."

I had an impish urge to ask what time the play began if I wasn't free. I didn't chime in, however, so she continued. "He thought you'd like to choose the restaurant, since he picked last time. Would you like me to e-mail you a list of what's available?"

"No," I said, too quickly.

"No, you can't make it?" she asked, slowly. Damn, damn, damn. I needed to talk with David.

I wanted to talk with him about Owen, and about Barton's problems. Not to mention this reward issue. Lots to cover. And Bass's Monday deadline loomed. That man made me scream, sometimes.

But again, here it was. A silver platter. I'd been salivating to see Chicago Shakespeare Theater at Navy Pier since it opened there in 1999. No time, no one to go with…name the reason—I hadn't made it there, yet.

"No, I don't need a list," I said. I'd been to the pier itself a hundred times and I knew the restaurant offerings. Everything from a paper cup full of sugared almonds to McDonald's to Riva, the white linen, skyline-view restaurant that boasted celebrity clientele. "I have to check," I said. "Can I get back to you?"

"Sure," she said. The smile-voice was back. "He said he'd call again at two-thirty. Why don't you let me know by then?"

After we hung up, I started talking to myself, making "if this, then that" deals.

"Okay," I said, picking the receiver up again. "If Aunt Lena can't keep Lucy tonight, I'll tell David no."

Five minutes later, I spoke with a giddy aunt Lena. "A date, Alex?" she asked. "As long as it isn't Dan, I'll keep Lucy for you all weekend." She laughed at her own bawdiness.

"It's not like that," I protested.

"Don't worry, honey, she'll be fine here. I'll fix up Diana's room and Lucy can stay the night. By the way, the doctors think Diana might be ready to be released Monday, isn't that good news?"

"Fabulous," I said, meaning it. "But you'll only have to keep Lucy if I go. I still might not."

"You should go, dear. You deserve a night out. You just have fun, and don't you worry about a thing."

I hung up, and headed over to talk to Jordan.

"William didn't call," she said, when I sat at her desk.

"I wasn't going to ask," I said.

"Sure you were." Her brown eyes fixed me with a stare that told me Bass wasn't the only bullshitter I shouldn't try to bullshit.

"So," I said, opening my hands in a gesture of defeat, "Why?"

She shrugged. "Don't know why you let it bug you the way it does. Not like he's the only fish in the water, you know."

"I know. I just thought…"

"I *know* what you thought."

I wrinkled my nose, looked away. "David asked me out for tonight. Dinner and a play."

"He ain't bad-looking for an old guy," she said with a grin.

"He isn't old," I said, far too quickly, wondering whyI felt the sudden need to defend him. I took a deep breath, looked away again. "But that doesn't answer the other question. Why no word? It's Friday, and if he hasn't called by now, I doubt he'll call over the weekend."

I'd said the words, half-hoping Jordan would pooh-pooh that thought, and reassure me that the weekend would afford William plenty of time to call. But she didn't."

"You never know," she said in a humoring-me voice,

"maybe he can't get service on his cell phone. And there's that whole time difference *thang* too."

"Thought of that," I said, frowning at nothing. "So then why doesn't he call me from his hotel room late at night? He could leave a message on my cell and I'd get it first thing in the morning, you know." I stared at her. "I mean, really, what's a couple of minutes before he goes to bed?"

Jordan lifted an eyebrow at me.

"What?" I asked.

"Maybe when he goes to bed, he's not alone."

"Shit," I said. That thought hadn't even occurred to me.

"Sorry," she said. "I'm just thinking that it's best you don't keep hoping there's something where there's not."

I nodded, stood, tried to smile. "Thanks," I said to Jordan, who stared up at me with concern. "You're right. I guess I just needed to hear it."

"Hey," she said to my back. I turned.

"Tonight…" she said with a mischievous smile, "Don't be all worked up about stuff you can't control. This Mr. Dewars is a good-looking guy—and he's a rich guy. Not to mention the man is crazy about you, woman. Don't be thinking you gotta love the dude. Just go out and have some fun."

I CALLED DAVID'S office around one, fully intending to decline. More in the mood to wallow, I decided that a night in front of the television in warm flannel pajamas and an endless supply of snacks might be the best option after all.

"Ms. St. James," his secretary said. If it were possible, she sounded even more cheered to hear from me this time around. "I have good news for you."

Her version of good news and mine might be at odds, but I let her continue.

"Mr. Riordan found all the information you were look-

ing for. I don't quite know what it is." Papers shuffled; she
was looking for something. "I assume you know what he's
talking about."

"Yeah."

"Well, as it turns out, Mr. Riordan says it's far too much
to send by fax and so he just made a set of copies for you.
He's heading over to that meeting with Mr. Dewars right
now and taking everything with him. So this way, Mr.
Dewars can give you the whole file when you see him
tonight." She ended her little spiel on a triumphant note.
"Isn't that perfect?"

"Yeah," I said. "Great."

Cornered again. *Damn*, I thought.

Truth was, I wasn't nearly as disappointed at this turn of
events as I should have been. As a matter of fact, I liked the
idea that the decision had been practically taken out of my
hands. I could use distraction—a night out. And it wasn't
as though David was poor company. I found him intelligent, witty, attentive. Handsome. What more could I want?

I bit my lip. Maybe that was a question better left unasked.

EIGHTEEN

WHEN I TOLD Dr. Hooker about my encounter with Laurence Grady, his blue eyes made the switch from small talk to down-to-business in a heartbeat. He'd been sprawled back in the same upholstered chair he'd occupied last time, and as I progressed through the tale of my terror-meeting in the dark, he shifted body, eyes, demeanor, all at once. Sitting forward, elbows on knees, his right hand came up to stroke his gray-streaked beard in a gesture that I assumed indicated concern.

The expression fit the man today. Wearing a muted blue sweater with collared shirt and snug tie underneath, he looked a lot more like a psychiatrist-professor type than when we'd first met.

"Are you all right?" He did that back-and-forth-stare thing that people do, when they're trying hard to decide if someone's telling the truth.

"I'm fine," I said, straight on.

"You're sure it was Laurence Grady?"

"No question."

Disappointment clouded those expressive eyes. Or maybe it was defeat. In either case the twinkle I'd seen there moments before fell away as though a protective curtain had dropped, and the show was over. As though he now chose to turn his view inward, to weigh and study and consider, alone.

"So," he said, after a moment's break. "You went to see Diana, after all."

"As a matter of fact, I did."

"I had a feeling you might." Shoving himself upward he moved into the adjacent kitchen-room, still talking. "What did she tell you?"

His bulky frame disappeared from my view and I followed him, rather than shout from my chair.

"Not too much." He turned to look at me and I shrugged. "She swears it wasn't Grady who attacked us at the house, and she says he wouldn't have hurt Mrs. Vicks either."

"Tea?" Dr. Hooker asked, holding up two mugs.

I nodded, leaning against the doorjamb. "But what else was she going to say?" I asked, rhetorically. "I mean, it's obvious she's still in love with the guy."

He looked at me again, his eyes giving a peculiar glint. "Is it?"

I moved into the room when he turned his back to make the tea. Leaning against the counter top, facing outward, next to him, I asked, "What do you know?"

Our two mugs turned slowly in the microwave. He waited for the ding to pull them out and drop teabags in. "I know that you want Grady to be guilty."

"No, I don't."

He raised an eyebrow.

"I want to know Grady's involvement, sure," I said, "but I don't *want* him to be guilty. What I care about is that whoever did it is found. And brought to justice."

I'd pushed off the wall, and now reached for the mug he handed me.

"No," he said. "You want Grady to have been the murderer because he fits. He's an ex-con, out on parole. He's got a history of drug use, a long rap sheet." Hooker took a sip of his tea before returning to the chair, dropping his hindquarters onto the cushion, while concentrating on his outstretched arms to keep the tea from spilling. He raised his head, and shot those baby blues straight on. "He fits."

I resumed my position in the chair opposite. "Okay, you got me. He fits. Why shouldn't that make him a likely suspect?"

Hooker shook his head, and the silver-streaked black waves that surrounded his shiny head loosened enough that he ran a hand to push them back into place. "I didn't say he isn't a likely suspect, I just said that you're dwelling on him because you want him to be guilty."

"What's wrong with that?"

"The truth?"

"Please."

"I believe your efforts are better directed elsewhere."

I pressed my lips together to keep from an outburst I'd be sorry for, later. Resisting the urge to address him as Mr. Know-it-all, I demurely inquired, "Why don't you tell me who *is* guilty, then?"

His face split into a wide pleased-with-himself grin. "Are you angry with me, Alex?"

"Of course not," I lied. "But it comes down to this: Diana is giving me carte blanche where your records are concerned. Rather than help me…in a murder investigation, I might add…you're dancing around the subject and parrying with me like we were fencing, for crying out loud." I pulled my lips in tight after that, realizing how agitated my voice had become.

"You are angry."

"Damn right, I am."

The grin widened further. "What do you want to know?" He spread his hands out before him. "I'm an open book."

"Fine," I said, setting my mug down on the table between us with a clunk. "How are you so sure it wasn't Grady who killed Mrs. Vicks and who attacked us?"

Like a slow-motion, silent mirror, he gently set his mug down near mine. Working his tongue around his teeth he stared down at the brew for moment, then up at me, eyes all serious now. "Since Diana is my patient, and Larry is not, I am allowed to tell you this, but I'm treading carefully here..." He held up a finger. "I've been counseling Diana now for about two years."

"Larry?" I asked, surprised. "You called him Larry."

Hooker opened his mouth. Closed it again before speaking. "Good catch."

"You've *met* him?" I asked. "Has he come here for counseling?"

I'd have to classify Hooker's reaction as a wince. "No. Not exactly. Here's where my dilemma lies. If Larry were a patient, I couldn't tell you that. I can tell you that he's accompanied Diana occasionally since his parole release."

"But you're not treating him."

Hooker smiled, canted his head, answered slowly. "No."

"You mean, not officially."

He spread his hands. "I can only reiterate that he is not a patient of mine."

Pressing fingers into my brow bone, I hissed out a breath from between clenched teeth. "Okay..." I said. "So why does he come?"

"We make it worth his while. And, I think he likes the idea that he's helping Diana in some way."

"I don't buy that," I said. Granted, I'd only met the scumbag once, but in that darkened garage, with one hand clamped around my arm and the other over my mouth, he came across touchy-feely all right, but not in any cerebral sort of way. "That man has issues. He was angry. Two more minutes with him, and they would've been rushing me to the hospital's emergency room."

Hooker had stubby fingers—hairy ones that now

stroked his shiny head as if remembering days of his hirsute youth. "Alex," he began, straining so far forward at the
edge of his chair that I thought he might jump out at me if
I tried to interrupt, "I can't tell you how sorry I am that so
much has happened to you. And in so short a time." The
lower lids of his eyes crinkled up, his stare immobilizing
me in my seat. "I am so sorry. More sorry than you can
even know. But…" He licked his lips as words failed him.

"But?"

Working his fists and looking away, his face made a
contortion that telegraphed pain. He nodded to himself,
several times before meeting my gaze once again.

"But," he said, "you're a strong young woman. Stronger than most would be in such circumstances. And you
have to believe me when I tell you that Larry—Grady—
isn't your man."

"I believe he's capable of killing."

Hooker shook his head. "I don't think so."

"God, you're smug," I said, not even trying to keep the
thought from blurting out.

"Not smug, but I know people. That's my job. That's
yours too, isn't it?"

"Yeah, and I know you're toying with me. Why won't
you just tell me what you do know? Make it easy on both
of us."

He gave me a look like a teacher might give to a student
who'd failed an important exam. I half-expected him to
wag a finger at me. Instead, he scratched his beard. "You
know I can't do that, Alex. Even if Diana has given you
permission to talk with me, it goes against everything I
stand for to put her life on display for you to tear apart."

A thought that had occurred to me earlier, bubbled back
up. "Diana is not a wealthy girl."

He sat back, folded fingers across his ample stomach. "No, she's not."

With a show of looking around his office, I pressed on. "You've got a Loop address. That means high rent, doesn't it?"

He acknowledged my point with a nod.

"So how does Diana afford your prices?"

He didn't answer.

"Who's paying the bills?" I asked.

"That, I won't tell you."

The hell with being polite anymore. We were wasting my time. I had a goddamn date tonight and I wasn't about to spend my night with Buddha here. I glanced at my watch. Five-fifteen. I was supposed to meet David at his bank in fifteen minutes. It'd take me ten minutes to walk, but I could always call and be picked up here, if need be. David's secretary had helpfully provided me his cell phone number.

"Listen, Dr. Hooker—"

"Really, Alex, I'd prefer you call me Tom."

I ignored that. "Forget everything else. Just answer this, and explain it to me like I'm a four-year-old because I'm about to ask you the same question for the third time. How can you possibly know that Grady didn't kill Mrs. Vicks?"

"I don't know. We can never know. But from what I've come to understand of the man, he's hardened all right, and he's angry, but he's no killer. I'd stake my professional career on that."

I stood up, bit the insides of my cheeks. "I'll try to remember that," I said. "The next time he grabs me in some dark parking garage."

BY THE TIME I got to Banner Bank, I'd exorcised the bulk of my anger by making the ten-minute walk in just under seven minutes. Grateful that the recent forty degree warm spell had puddled the icy sidewalk that would have otherwise set me on my ass, I'd pounded out a tempo brisk enough to soothe my frazzled nerves.

Chilly gusts whipped my hair at each intersection where the tall buildings couldn't offer protection and I tried to picture my tension taking flight out of my head and into the atmosphere where it wouldn't grate on me at every turn. Visualize, I told myself, and I took a deep, cleansing breath.

Maybe everyone else was right. Maybe I needed this night out.

David's office was on the building's eighth floor. My first visit to this part of the bank, it smelled richer than the other areas I'd encountered. Lots of glossy wood trim, sage-colored walls, and carpet so thick I couldn't hear my own footsteps.

The woman at the nearer desk was most likely the assistant I'd spoken to earlier. I took a cue from the look on her face. "I guess I need to take a minute," I said, running an embarrassed hand through my hair. "Is there a washroom nearby?"

David waved away my concerns. "You look wonderful," he said. "Like a spirit that just blew in from above."

I sent his assistant a girl-to-girl look. She stood. "Hi, I'm Linda Farrell," she said as we shook hands. "We spoke on the phone."

"Good to meet you," I said.

Her face matched the smooth, cheerful voice. With wavy red hair cropped close to her head and a petite build, this forty-something woman meshed efficiency with warmth in a tidy little package. "Come on," she said. Gesturing to David that he should wait, she walked briskly back toward the elevator corridor. "I'll show you the way."

"Whoa," I said as we stepped inside. This wasn't a washroom, it was a women's lounge, much like the ones in the fancy Michigan Avenue stores like Nordstrom and Lord & Taylor with inviting couches, pale wallpaper, and all sorts of female doo-dads like hairspray and deodorant aligned neatly on the granite counter.

"Yeah, it's nice," she said, watching me as I tried to settle my hair back into decent shape. "You have no idea how glad I am that Mr. Dewars is taking you out tonight."

Puzzled by the non-sequitur, I met her eyes in the mirror. "Really? Why's that?"

She made a face. "It's none of my business, of course," she began.

My ears perked up.

"It's just that he's been under a lot of stress lately. He's such a sweet man, and so easygoing—he doesn't usually flip out over small things, you know?" she asked.

"Mm-hmm," I said, to keep her talking.

"Maybe I'm wrong, but since Mrs. Vicks got killed, God rest her soul," Linda laid a hand across her chest, "he's been impossible to deal with. Not only is he broken-hearted about her death, he's also very worried about the bank surviving this."

I turned to her. "That's what I don't understand. Why would any of this reflect badly on the bank? It doesn't make sense to me."

She pulled her lips in tight for a moment, considering this. "You're in the media, aren't you?"

"Yes."

"But you're going out with Mr. Dewars socially, right? You're not covering any kind of investigation of the bank, are you?"

Here was a woman who wanted to spill the goods, all right. I just needed to appease her protective instincts.

"I'm sure we'll talk about Mrs. Vicks tonight," I said. "And I know he has those records you mentioned for me…"

I let the thought hang, but she didn't pick it up.

"Beyond that," I added, "I don't think the bank is any of my concern."

"Good, that's what I thought," she said. In a belated move, she poked her head around the wall that separated the gathering area from the stalls. Glancing back at me, she grinned. "Nobody here."

I smiled encouragement.

"It's this audit," she said.

"I thought it was scheduled, right? A routine audit."

Her expression said, so-so. "It was definitely 'scheduled,' but only because the FDIC started coming down hard on us. Wanted us to explain a bunch of discrepancies that they thought they found." A roll of her eyes told me exactly what she thought of these requests. "They threatened us with big penalties if we didn't comply with their request for a full audit. So…here we are. But, technically, we scheduled it. Allowed them to come in as of last Monday."

When she looked backward to lean against the countertop, I shot a surreptitious glance at my watch. Five-forty. David said he wanted to be out the door by quarter to six. I pictured him staring down the hall where we'd disappeared into this female haven, tapping a foot. Probably muttering.

Oh well.

"Same day as Mrs. Vicks' funeral," I said, just to prod Linda along.

"As a matter of fact, that became a very big deal, too." She held up quote-fingers at the words "very big," and her eyes widened as she spoke. "Mr. Dewars was very upset that he had to miss it. If it weren't for this damn audit, we'd all sleep a little better at night. Anyway," she continued,

"It's looking like somebody was messing with accounts. We're not sure who, just yet."

"But you have a guess."

"I shouldn't tell you this but..." she said. "A woman in the loan department that Evelyn Vicks worked for. And if we find out that it's true, and there's the kind of money missing that it looks like..." She shook her head, a dire look on her face. "It's going to look real bad for the bank that Mrs. Vicks was killed just then."

A woman in the loan department. A woman Mrs. Vicks worked for.

"I don't know," I said, feeling her out. "I know I've only met Maya a couple of times—"

"I didn't say it was Maya," Linda said quickly, nearly jumping from her perch against the granite. "I never said her name."

"It's okay," I said, raising a hand to calm her. "I'm not going to say anything. I promise. I just guessed." Turning back to the mirror, I strove for nonchalant. As if that bit of information didn't faze me at all. But I could feel the prickle of something growing in my busy little brain. This was worth examining later.

The startled panic in her eyes began to dissolve as she leaned back again. "Wow. Good guess. But now you understand where Mr. Dewars is coming from?"

"I do," I assured her, smiling. "And I'm really glad you told me. Maybe tonight will take his mind off his troubles."

I'd said the right thing, apparently. She pushed forward again as I finished my makeup and hair ministrations. "That's what I'm hoping for," she said, smiling like we were old girlfriends now. "I swear, the only time he's in a good mood lately is when he's talking about you."

NINETEEN

"You look great," he said, when we emerged from the washroom. "Let's go, we're running behind."

"Sorry," I said.

He touched his hand to my right shoulder blade, guiding me toward the back of the building, through a dark utility corridor. He pulled at a gray painted metal door, sending a hot whoosh of air at us from the vent above, mixed with the cold from the outside. David's car, the SUV, idled in the alley with Roger at the wheel.

When we appeared, the chauffeur stepped out of the car, held the passenger door open for me, and I shot David a surprised glance when he climbed into the driver's seat.

As if he read my thoughts. "This is a date, Alex; I prefer to drive myself." He winked. "It's not like we need a chaperone."

Roger tipped his hat to us in an informal salute as we took off through the alley, headed for Navy Pier.

David shared moments from the day's off-campus seminar. The man certainly had a talent for making dry situations sparkle. He talked, maintaining control of the road even as he conversed, totally at ease.

"So," he said, his voice as relaxed as his demeanor. "You and Linda were in the washroom for a long time. Should I be concerned about her spilling all my deep dark secrets?" He shot a high-wattage smile my direction.

"Your secrets are safe," I answered.

"Mysterious, aren't we?" he said with a playful lilt.

"So, do I take it that you mean she didn't tell you my sordid life story, or that you are a woman who can be trusted with the information?"

My turn to smile. "Isn't this where we turn?"

David pursed his lips, amused, as he completed the right turn onto Illinois Street. A few minutes later the big bulbs of Navy Pier's carnival-like entrance came into view. "I love it here," I said with a sigh, as we joined the queue of cars waiting to be waved into the parking area.

"Then I'm glad that we could make this work tonight," he said. Glancing at the clock on the dashboard, as he dug into his jacket pocket, then reached into the back seat where his cell phone sat atop his briefcase. "Here," he said, pulling it up front. "The last number I dialed is the restaurant. Why don't you give them a call and make sure they hold the table."

Before dialing, I glanced back there. "That information Owen was getting for me…" I began.

"Got it," he said. "It's in the briefcase. You don't want it now, do you?"

I did, but politeness won this round. "No."

"Remind me to give it to you later."

I noticed the name of David's cellular service. Same as mine. That meant we could call each other any time of the day or night for free.

The woman who answered told me not to hurry, that the evening's rush for dinner hadn't yet kicked into gear. In one of my many phone calls to Linda over the course of the day, I'd given her my decision on where we'd eat. I'd chosen the very casual, very busy, Bubba Gump's rather than the ritzy Riva. We parked in the pier's garage and as we headed in and the hostess led us to our booth, he asked why I hadn't gone for the glam.

"I've been there," I said, with a shrug. "Wasn't terribly impressed."

As we slid into scuffed wooden benches on either side of a clutter-decorated table, he leaned forward, more to be heard over the din than anything. "What does impress you, Alex?"

Our waitress, a raven-haired girl with a heavy Irish brogue, interrupted then, greeting us with an explanation of the nifty gimmick that sat atop the table. Two license plates hung from a stand. The entire restaurant's theme based itself on the movie *Forrest Gump* and the top license plate, green, said "Run, Forrest, Run."

Pointing to it, she said in a slightly raised voice to be heard over the music and the laughter from tables nearby, "If y'have everything y'need, and you won't be needing to be bothered, you keep this one hanging."

Flipping the contraption, to the plate behind it, she pointed. This one was red, with the words. "Stop, Forrest, Stop."

"Now," she said with emphasis, "if you be wanting anything, or if you be needing me to stop and check on you, you put this one out and I'll be here in two shakes." She smiled at us both, canting her head. "What'll you be wanting to drink?"

She departed, leaving us to study our menus. Lots of seafood, and plenty of other choices as well. As I debated ordering a steak, I shot a look up at David. To my surprise, I caught him watching me.

"You've decided?" I asked, nodding toward the menu face-down on the table.

"I always know what I want right away," he said. A smile played at his lips. "And I generally have the means to get it."

The dangerous sparkle in his eyes made mine shoot

back to the list of offerings. I felt the weight of his gaze on me as I tried to decide if I had a taste for the "Bucket of Boat Trash" combination.

"So, I'll ask you again, Alex. What impresses you?"

I considered the question. Looked up at him. "Sometimes I don't know till I find it."

"Fair enough," he said.

Colleen, the waitress, came back bearing my iced tea and David's Vodka twist, setting them down, and taking our orders with cheerful efficiency. I settled for crab-stuffed shrimp, one of Bubba Gump's specialties.

"How is the investigation going?" David asked.

I wiggled my hand in front of me to say so-so. "The detective in charge doesn't tell me squat," I said with a roll of my eyes, "and even though I'm doing my best to find answers, all I come up with are more questions."

"What kind of questions?"

"There's another suspect," I began.

His dark eyebrows lifted, till I saw them over the tops of his glasses. "Oh?"

I gave a quick and sketchy explanation of the connection between Diana and Laurence Grady, ending with: "And this psychiatrist fellow is convinced I'm barking up the wrong tree where Grady's concerned."

David speared into his salad with a crunch, and held the fork aloft as he spoke. "What do you think?"

I moved my lettuce around. "I'm not sure."

He waited.

I shrugged, looked up and out the nearby windows. The view from my vantage point was limited, but just beyond the edge of the pier, I could see a small slice of water, ever darkening as evening settled on the city. Quick glints from the moving water as it caught the remaining light, coupled with the smell of the place, sizzling shrimp, beer, and the burgeoning spring, gave me a wistful feeling of vacation. Of getting away.

And of Fisherman's Wharf in San Francisco.

I should have been on that trip. I should be out there right now.

I sighed.

"Alex." David touched my hand, bringing me out of my reverie.

I couldn't decide if that was genuine concern in his eyes, or if he was simply annoyed that I'd checked out of the conversation, however momentarily. But David, with his theater tickets and dinner on the pier—David, attentive date extraordinaire—was here, and William was not. It wasn't fair for me to let my mind drift.

"Sorry," I said.

"You were a thousand miles away."

"A little more than that," I said. "What were we talking about?"

"I asked you what your assessment was of all this."

"If I could only get into that detective's mind," I answered, stirring my iced tea with the straw. "But as much as he wants my cooperation, he's not very forthcoming with information. Not to mention, he has a deep-seated hatred of media people."

"I met him," David said. "Lulinski."

Colleen set our steaming platters of food on the table before us, with a reminder to change the hanging license plate if there was anything we needed. She encompassed us both with her comments, saying, "That way I won't be disturbing you if you'd rather be keeping to yourselves."

"What did you think of him?" I asked David when Colleen left.

"Not much," he said, with a slow shake of his head, surveying the New Orleans shrimp entrée before him. "I mean, come on. How does the man keep his job? It's been over a week and they haven't arrested anyone." He met my eyes. "What do *you* think of him?"

"I get the impression that he's methodical. Tenacious, even."

"Yes, well, if he had any brains he'd haul Barton Vicks in for questioning."

I'd been about to repeat that I wasn't yet convinced Barton did the killing when David interrupted.

"But I do know why your meticulous detective hates the media."

"Oh?" I popped a small bite of stuffed shrimp into my mouth and nearly groaned with delight as the garlic and crab tastes dissolved on my tongue. "This," I said, pointing down at my plate, "is fabulous."

David smiled. "Want to hear the story?"

Great food, pleasant company, and the potential for enlightenment on the good detective? I was in.

"How well do you know Dan Starck?" David asked.

I searched his eyes for some sense of guile, wondering if he knew that Dan and I had a history together and was just playing me here.

I answered slowly. "He and I went out for a while."

David's subtle body shift told me that had come as a surprise. "Then you must know about the bad blood between them."

I enjoyed another bite of shrimp. "No," I said, thinking hard. "I don't think Dan ever mentioned Lulinski's name."

David drained his drink, then switched the table sign to get Colleen's attention. Half-a-minute later our capable waitress appeared up at the table, asking what she could do for us, then switching the sign back. "Another one, please." David said, holding up his glass.

Colleen grabbed my half-finished tea. "I'll refill yours too, while I'm at it."

David adjusted his glasses, and the pink glint from a neon sign over the windows reflected there, momentarily obscuring his eyes. "That doesn't surprise me," he said. "I would figure Starck would want to keep this one buried."

Colleen set our drinks before us, and, hands on hips, cast an appraising look at the progress we'd made on our meals. "I'll check on you again in a bit," she said as she left.

"That bad?" I asked.

"You know Dan," he said "He's only happy when he's on top."

I resisted further comment in that direction. "In any case," I said, trying to segue back into the story, "what happened?"

David chewed, sending his gaze up near the ceiling before bringing it back to me. "Had to be seven years ago. Maybe ten."

A gear clicked into place as I tried to remember where I would have been back then. I waited to hear more.

"Starck was doing a series of stories on a guy that Lulinski had arrested for murder. A real low-life. Lulinski had a history with this guy, having arrested him before, and Starck broadcast a slew of fan-the-flames interviews with the gangbanger's family and friends. They accused the detective of bias. It was a hot story, I can't believe you don't remember it."

"Ten years ago I was in grad school in Florida, and seven years ago I was interning at a small station out there."

David's face broke into a smile. "Yes, of course," he said, with evident pleasure. "You are so young."

"Back to the investigation."

He smiled. "Starck had a screaming headline for his

supposed exposé. 'Good Police Work or Set-up?' was the title. On top of that, Starck came up with witnesses who swore that their buddy couldn't have committed the murder. Had them milking the camera every chance they could. They provided enough of an alibi that the gang-banger's attorney got the judge to reduce the bond and the guy got sprung from County." David looked across the table at me.

I raised an eyebrow. "So what happened?"

"Day after he gets out, he murders the young girl who testified against him at the Grand Jury," David said, with a sad shake of his head.

Nothing gets ratings like the portrait of an innocent man, wrongly accused. I remembered Dan saying that one time. I thought he was speaking in generalities.

I winced. "No wonder Lulinski hates him."

"Most everyone does," David said, and I knew he was right. Dan had that effect on people and it made me wonder again why I'd willingly given up almost a year of my life to be with him.

"You know a lot."

"It's my business to know what goes on in Chicago."

Truth be told, I seemed to remember the story, in a vague way. But, as a student, twelve-hundred miles from home, with papers due and a social life, I'd paid less attention than I should have. And back then, I hadn't yet met Dan.

Without being summoned, Colleen cleared away our plates, inquired about dessert and left a leather binder with the bill on the table near David's hand. He pulled out a credit card and set it back at the edge of the table for her to grab on the next go-round.

"Moving ahead…" I said, resting my elbows on the table's edge.

"Yes," he said, with a soft look in his eyes. "Moving ahead…" He reached across the table and ran his index finger over the back of my hand. It was a small, tender gesture, and I should have enjoyed the tingle of pleasure that shivered up my arm. Instead, I felt detachment, as my logical left brain tried to convince an eager jury of hormones that I hadn't sent my heart to San Francisco.

Colleen picked up the payment, giving me a reason to move. I sat back, pulled my hands to my lap and asked, "So, what brought you to banking?"

Mimicking my position, David sat back in his chair, a smile on his face that I'd have characterized as amused. "I inherited the financial gene from my father's side. He owned several small banks. When he passed on, I sold them to a holding company and when I decided to strike out on my own, I realized banking was what I knew best."

Colleen left us with the credit card receipt, along with her thanks and wishes for our pleasant evening. He signed the small form with bold flourish. "Why do you ask?"

"Just curious," I said. "You and I have had a lot going on over this past week—"

"And very little of that has been pleasant," he interrupted. "Until tonight."

I acknowledged his observation with a nod. "But I really don't know you at all."

"Would you like to, Alex?" His voice was like butter, and an alert feminine part of me reacted. From the change in his dark eyes, I could see he knew it had.

I made a show of glancing at my watch. Just after seven o'clock. The performance started at eight.

"Would you like to walk around?" he asked.

Teeming with tourists and browsers, the busy center of the pier boasted an eclectic mix of indoor shops. Although David asked me several times if there were any I'd like to explore, I just wasn't in the mood to fight the knots of busy customers who crowded the tiny boutiques full of plastic souvenirs. I much preferred empty places during off hours, and antique stores, with creaky floors and memory-smells.

We headed up the escalators and through the glass-topped arboretum. I pulled my coat on as we stepped out the doors and took a deep breath. "You know," I said, surveying the relative silence outside, "even though there are still piles of dirty snow hanging around, I can smell that spring is coming."

David took a deep breath, pressing his hands to his chest. "I smell mostly dead fish," he said.

I gave his upper arm a playful slap, which he evidently took as that as an opening. He took my hand and asked, "Would you like to go for a ride?"

Before I could answer, he canted his head toward the giant Ferris Wheel, its long spokes aglow with thousands of lights, turning slowly in the crisp night air.

"Oh," I said, happy to have caught his meaning. "Do we have time?"

The ticket seller informed us that one complete circuit around took just over seven minutes. But the line looked like it would take at least twenty. Our meandering through the promenade of shops had unfortunately taken too long.

"Next time," David said, still holding my hand.

"Next time."

"Promise?" He gave my hand a squeeze.

I smiled up at him and remembered Jordan's directive to just have fun.

"Sure," I answered. "I promise."

As THE PLAY ended, and the curtain calls began, I applauded with gusto. I had a smile on my face and a lightness of heart that I hadn't felt in a long time. Everybody had been right. I needed a night out. Shakespeare's comedy, *The Merry Wives of Windsor*, had been just the right touch. I'd been captivated by the character Falstaff, and had had to look twice when he first strode onstage. With his dark-haired bulk and his blustering, imposing personality I thought for sure it was Dr. Hooker up there. We occupied seats very near to the thrust stage of this cozy theater and even up close, the resemblance was so strong, that I checked the program to see if perhaps the psychiatrist had a younger brother actor.

David leaned to read over my shoulder. "Who are you so interested in?"

"All of them, actually," I said. It was the truth. "But this guy," I pointed to Jason Noble's picture in the *Stagebill* program, "looks just like Diana's psychiatrist."

"The one who won't tell you anything?"

"Yep."

After the last bows, David pressed his hand against the small of my back to guide me out of the theater, headed back toward the parking garage. Along the way, he pulled me from the mass of departing Shakespearean patrons to look out the full-length windows to the south. "It's a beautiful night," he said.

It was.

"Come on," he said. He had my coat draped over his arm and now he held it for me to slip into. We stepped outside into the chilly air, and I blew out a breath in front of me, watching it curl and dissipate in the darkness. There were lights along the perimeter, but the lake was black, and as uneven waves slapped against the walls, sometimes splashing over the edges, I wanted to close my eyes and fall asleep to the sound.

"Walk with me?"

We headed east along the path in silence, taking our

time to get to the far end of the pier. Even though the night was cold and my feet were in heels, I enjoyed the freedom night air always seemed to provide.

We rounded the far end and I leaned against the railing, looking out into the lake and sky, realizing I could barely tell where one ended and the other began. A far off structure blinked a single red light, but otherwise I faced an expanse of blackness, hearing only the steady hits of water against the sides near my feet, cooing pigeons wandering nearby, and city background noises, faded to near quiet.

The freshness of the late night felt wonderful, and I smiled up at David, grateful for the evening's enjoyment. "Thanks," I said. "I had a wonderful time."

A breeze off the lake twisted my hair around my head and I smiled even as I shivered.

"You're cold," he said. He stood behind me and wrapped his arms around mine, pulling me close—his chest against my back—sharing his warmth. Pressing his cheek against the side of my head, he whispered, next to my ear, "It doesn't have to end this early."

I'd learned the hard way that the body can respond even when the heart does not. Trouble came when the two were confused. David pulled me closer, and dipped his head to place a kiss on the side of my head. I took a deep breath, and steeled myself against the pleasant feel of the gentle stubble of his cheek, soft on my own. He smelled so good.

"I should go," I said.

"Alex," he said, and being so close, I not only heard my name, but I felt the reverberations of his voice in my head, "why don't you be a little selfish, just for one night?" Still tight behind me, he trailed a finger down the left side of my face, and along my collarbone.

I brought my base needs under control enough to shake

my head. "No, really," I said. "Thank you, it's been a lovely evening, but I think it's best I head home. Busy day tomorrow."

I pulled away to face him but couldn't read his eyes in the dark. "Of course," he said, with a nod.

Taking my hand again, we started back the way we'd come, and he asked, "So what does busy day on a Saturday mean to a beautiful girl? Do you have a date?"

I grinned at him. "No. No date."

"Good," he said with an accompanying hand squeeze. "So, what do you have going?"

I told him about my plans to search through Mrs. Vicks house, now that I had Barton's permission to do so.

"What do you think you'll find?"

"Honestly," I said, "I have no idea. Something out of place, I guess."

"Be careful."

"I will."

"Don't let Barton accompany you."

I glanced up, but still couldn't read those eyes. "He won't. I convinced him that I do my best work alone. And," I added, "I have those files that Owen put together for me. I don't know what I expect to find in that information, either, but it's a place to start."

"What exactly is in those files?"

"Didn't you look at them?"

David shook his head. "No, the envelope was sealed. I didn't open it."

"I'm expecting that it's simply copies of checks. Mrs. Vicks wrote even-dollar-amount checks every month for years. It's probably nothing. Maybe it's money she sent to Bart. Or her savings plan. Or a retirement account. But I don't like to leave loose ends, so I'm following up."

"You're tenacious," he said.

"I take that as a compliment."

"Exactly how it was meant," he said. Tugging me close, David leaned down to whisper in my ear, "When I spoke with Owen today, I asked him if he could get me a copy of Mrs. Vicks' will for us to look at. He should have that for me by Monday."

"Is that legal?" I asked.

"You're consulting for us. I could put you on the payroll temporarily, if need be. I think it's a gray enough area that there'd be no problem. Plus," he added, "it isn't as though you're going to broadcast the information before it's released to Barton, right?"

I knew that big business often exploited these gray areas to their own benefit. And the truth was, I wouldn't use the information for anything more than my own investigation, which was, at best, amateur. Still, something didn't feel right.

"I'd feel better if I got Barton's permission on that." I said.

"As you wish."

He held the car door open, but stopped me just before I slid into the seat. Under the fluorescent lights of the deserted parking garage, I could read his eyes this time, very well. Too well. The raw desire I saw flickering there made my heart beat faster, till I could almost hear it bang outside my chest. "Thank you for tonight, Alex," he said. He leaned in to kiss me, cupping my face with his free left hand.

And I kissed back.

TWENTY

I RIPPED OPEN the fat envelope the moment I got home.

Quick glance at the kitchen clock. Already after one in the morning. David had dropped me off back at my building so that I could pick up my car and drive home—which I did, as fast as the laws allowed. I couldn't wait to see what Owen's department had prepared for me.

I thought about how I wanted to get an early start in the morning, and I promised myself I wouldn't go past one-thirty. Reaching into the oversized envelope, I grabbed the manila file folder; I needed to curl its thickness in order to ease it out.

Whoever had put this package together had done a thorough job. Savings and checking account statements for every month over the past twenty-three years were paper-clipped together, month-at-a-time, with copies of all the even-dollar-amount checks over one hundred dollars, that I'd requested. All set up in chronological fashion. All neat and easily surveyed.

I started from the beginning.

The first questionable check, for two-hundred dollars, had been made payable to cash. Fair enough. Maybe Mrs. Vicks needed spending money. Or maybe she added regularly to her savings account. I checked that statement, but found no corresponding deposit.

The conscientious person who'd provided this folder had also provided me copies of the back of each check. I examined that now, expecting to see Mrs. Vicks' signature, but instead was surprised to find a stamped endorsement: "For Deposit Only," followed by an account number.

I dropped my high-heeled shoes to the floor with a clatter, and tucked my left ankle under me as I tilted the photocopy to read it better. Another stamp sat in the center of the check, this from the bank that had accepted it. Judging from the blurry copy, the deposit had taken place about five days after the check had been written. I could barely make out the bank's name.

Five checks later, all with identical endorsements and following nearly identical patterns of written and deposit dates, I was able to finally decipher in which bank these checks had been deposited. Second Federal Bank of Dubuque.

Iowa?

It could be an investment account, I surmised. But that didn't feel right. I didn't know what would persuade Mrs. Vicks to send regular checks to an out-of-state account, but I intended to find out. Most of the elderly women in my neighborhood, particularly those who had been widowed, were exceptionally savvy in terms of investments, but almost without exception, they preferred to keep their interests close to home. Iowa made no sense.

There was no way that Second Federal of Dubuque would give me the account-holder's name on this, no matter what ruse I could come up with, but—I thought as I slapped a stack of copies against my hand—perhaps David could find out.

In the meantime, I still had a stack of this to get through.

By three in the morning, I'd changed into my typical sleepwear of ratty T-shirt and shorts, brushed my teeth, and scrubbed my face till it felt as pink as it looked. I'd tried three times to get to sleep, but the fact that I hadn't gotten through all the months' information bugged me and made me return to the solitude of the kitchen table, with only the buzz from the overhead light and the click-step motion of my wall clock to keep me company.

Mrs. Vicks pattern changed only occasionally. Every few years, the dollar amount of the Iowa checks went up, and every so often an individual hundred-dollar check would surface. At Christmas and Easter, she wrote checks to the church, and every March fifteenth, she wrote one out to Barton, with "Happy Birthday, Son," noted in the memo.

Eight years ago, the Iowa payments stopped, though the church donations and birthday gifts continued. I continued my scrutiny of her statements and was surprised to find something I'd missed. Regular even-amount checks started up again two years ago.

"Hmmph," I said aloud.

I scanned the statements for a pattern before pulling out the backup information. Monthly checks, in the amount of two-hundred dollars, written with the same regularity as before. When I pulled the copies out, I expected to see that they'd also been made out to cash. When I saw the payee on these checks, however, I couldn't believe it.

Dr. Thomas Hooker.

I sat back in my chair, hearing the accompanying squeak of the metal legs protesting my fidget. I asked myself why in the world Mrs. Vicks would be writing checks to Dr. Hooker. The answer, of course, was that she'd been paying for Diana's therapy, but for the life of me, I couldn't imagine why.

Standing, I stretched out my back, humming with pleasure as built-up tension dissolved in a scale of cracking noises. I walked into the darkness of my back porch to gaze out at the tiny yard and look up at the sky through the heavy double-hung windows that rattled oh-so-softly in the early morning breeze.

Despite the fact that it was a real room that opened to the rest of the house, the porch was always cold in winter, hot in summer. Frosty air surrounded it on three sides now, and the linoleum was nippy under my stocking feet. Rather than seek out the warmth of my bed, I stood there, perversely enjoying the chill. My body craved sleep, but my mind kept leaping from Mrs. Vicks accounts, to Barton's talk of reward, to my night out with David.

And then, to William.

They say that absence makes the heart grow fonder. On me, it was having the opposite effect. The longer he was gone, with no word, the more I questioned what it was I expected from him, and the more I questioned why I did.

Leaning my fingertips on the sill, I pressed my forehead against the cool pane of glass and stared for a long while at nothing. I thought about what Jordan had said about seeing something that wasn't there.

With the kind of clarity that can only come when one is alone and staring at nothing at four in the morning, emptiness washed over me, mixed with an unexpected sense of relief.

In that moment, I knew Jordan was right.

Birds in the nearby trees chirped to one another, back and forth, their high-pitched cries both lonely and hopeful, as we all waited together for the sun to rise.

Glancing around the empty room, I suddenly wished I had a pet. A cat, a dog. Maybe both. Lucy would like that. Lucy loved animals.

With an ache, I realized that she'd be headed back to school in another week and I hadn't yet made any effort for the two of us to spend time together. I vowed to rectify that tomorrow.

I PICKED UP Lucy on my way to Mrs. Vicks house when I finally got myself moving at ten in the morning. So much for that early start.

Aunt Lena placed a tin of still-warm oatmeal raisin cookies in Lucy's hands before we left. "So you'll have something to snack on," she said. "And come back here when you're done; I'll put together some sandwiches or something."

I'd been about to say she needn't bother, when it dawned on me that this was Aunt Lena's way to contribute to the investigation. "That'd be great, thanks."

"And here," she said, thrusting a rubber-banded bundle in my arms. It must have weighed seven pounds. "I've been taking in the mail." Her careworn face tightened, and she shook her head. "Always looks bad to have mail piling up at a house. Tells the world that nobody's home. In Evelyn's case, though…" she let the thought trail off.

Uncle Moose accompanied us, to make sure it was safe before letting his two nieces have the run of the place. "Your folks called again last night," he said on the short walk between houses. "They thought maybe they should come back, but I told them everything was okay and they should try to enjoy their trip." He gave me a man-look, the unsure, "did I handle that right?" look that guys get sometimes when presented with confusing matters of family and protocol.

I patted his arm and could feel the strength of it, even beneath the spring jacket he'd put on. "I'm glad you did," I said. "Good job." I meant it. They'd been looking forward to this trip for over a year. Nothing would be served by having them rush home from Luxembourg.

At Mrs. Vicks', we used my Aunt Lena's keys and I swallowed a peculiar combination of tight gut and dry throat that buzzed its way up from my feet when we first pushed open the front door. The last time I was here I'd been brutally attacked, and although I knew in my heart there was nothing to fear today, I still felt shaken enough to be grateful for Uncle Moose's burly presence.

He pounded his steps through the small house, moving his head from side to side, stopping to check out all rooms, all corners, before pounding again.

"Why are you stomping?" Lucy asked.

"If somebody's here, I want to make sure they know it," he said, without turning toward us. "Like cockroaches. You make enough noise, they hightail it outta there."

Lucy eyed Mrs. Vicks' piano in the living room, and I put a restraining hand on her arm. "Let's wait till we know everything's clear."

Moments later, Uncle Moose returned from his full-house examination and pronounced it empty. "You want me to stay?"

I'd pushed past my initial trepidation. "No, I think we'll be okay," I said.

He pointed at me. "If not, you call."

"I will."

DELIGHTED TO HAVE an in-tune piano to play, Lucy started in immediately on a Bach Minuet. Perfect music, I thought, as I started toward Mrs. Vicks' bedroom. The energetic tempo was just what I needed to fuel my search.

After my wee-hour discoveries in Mrs. Vicks' accounts, I knew just what I was looking for. I wanted to find her reasons for subsidizing Diana's visits to Dr. Hooker.

Standing in the center of Mrs. Vicks' bedroom, I was caught again by the sadness of it all. A fine layer of dark fingerprint dust covered her dresser tops. Judging from the reading glasses, left upside-down atop a pile of books on her nightstand, I assumed that the intruder who'd been searching her home hadn't gotten very far.

What he *had* done was pull out almost every drawer in Mrs. Vicks' two dressers. The drawers had all been left open, and from the looks of things, the killer had rushed through a search of each one. Her underwear was bunched into a pastel-colored jumble of cotton, and I could see in my mind's eye how it must have gone down. Open the drawer, run hands through, come up empty, move onto the next.

That told me something right there.

The murderer had been looking for an item of bulk. Had he been searching for a tiny thing, like a ring, or a key, then Mrs. Vicks' underthings would have been shaken out one at a time. I found it unlikely that the searcher would have cared enough to replace the items into the drawer. No, this spoke of quick movement and a cursory search.

Still standing in the room's center, trying my best to get a feel for what I needed to do, I played around with another thought. This could also be the work of an amateur in a hurry.

Not sure. Nothing was sure.

Although the overhead light was adequate, I pulled at the hem of the vinyl window shade to raise it. It snapped up, scaring me, whipping out of sight behind the blue-green valance that matched Mrs. Vicks' comforter.

Where would I keep important information if I were Mrs. Vicks?

With Lucy's musical accompaniment, I began my own search. Under the bed I found only spare sheet sets and an extra pillow. For a moment, in her closet, I thought I hit pay dirt. On the floor, tucked into the corner, she had a large fireproof filing box with a lid that opened upward. A silver key sat in the lock, its mate dangled off the beaded metal chain that connected them.

I struggled to pull it out of the closet. This thing was heavy. The fact that it wasn't locked didn't really surprise me. My parents had a box similar to this one. I'd asked them why they never locked the thing and my mother had laughed at my question. "Nobody's going to steal my old papers," she'd said. "But I want them protected in case of fire. And if I lock it, then I have to worry about losing the key."

To some extent, I understood the reasoning. The problem was, there'd been two intruders in this house before me. Maybe the same guy both times, maybe not. If there had been anything of value in here, it was probably gone.

Sitting on the floor cross-legged, I flipped through the files. She kept the current year's bank statements in separate hanging files. I gave it all a quick look. Brown bank statements, blue bank statements, a file full of personal things. I pulled that one out, my heart racing with possibility, but after I'd gone through it twice I shoved it back in the box with a sigh. Other than her voter's and social security cards and a few other standard items, I came up empty. The rest of the files were related to her utility and medical bills. Nothing else.

Returning to the drawers, I felt the wood beneath each and every one, knowing how many people tape their secrets in such a place where they believe no one will look. Nothing.

Shaking my head, I blew my bangs out of my face in frustration. I'd begun to work up a sweat, despite the fact that my T-shirt was loose and light. Think, I told myself. Where would my parents keep important documents?

After an hour of futile searching, I called to Lucy to sit with me at the kitchen table while we shared some of the cookies. Puzzled by the excitement in her eyes when we sat down, I asked her about it.

"I want to talk to you about something really important," she said, her smile bright.

I had no idea what was up.

"Sure," I said.

"Somebody likes me," she said.

I laughed. "Everybody likes you, Lucy."

With a prim look of exasperation, she explained, "I mean somebody at the residence. A guy I know." Turning red, she added, "He says he loves me."

Words dropped away, rendering me speechless. From Lucy's reaction, a sudden apprehensive look that rushed to her face, I could only imagine what mine looked like. A hundred scenarios, none of them good, raced through my brain in the course of the three seconds it took me to come up with a response innocuous enough not to alarm her. "Really? What's his name?"

"You don't seem very happy."

"You just took me by surprise, Lucy, that's all," I lied.

"Uh-huh." She twisted her mouth to one side. "Maybe I shouldn't have told you."

"No, no," I said, too quickly. "I'm glad you did, really glad. What's his name?"

"Bobby."

"That's great," I said. "I can't wait to meet him."

Lucy had been unlucky in love ever since she'd hit puberty. She'd developed a series of crushes on her male teachers and, once, just before she turned thirty, she'd "dated" a young man in her special-ed music class who'd broken her heart when he got caught fondling another other girl in class, and then lied about it when she confronted him. She'd been confused, angry, and wanting to forgive him all at once. My appalled parents had consulted with

Lucy's doctors and teachers and they'd come to the unanimous conclusion to change her class schedule, so that she'd never see old Romeo again.

While it'd been an efficient way to handle the situation, I'd always wondered how Lucy had perceived it. As hard as the male/female thing was, how much harder it had to be to have such personal issues decided by committee—decisions lifted out of your hands because those who know best believed you incapable.

I worried for her, always.

"Maybe when you drive me back down next week his parents will bring him back too, and we can all meet."

"That would be wonderful," I said. But all I could think of was "Oh, my God."

"We didn't get a lot of time to talk this week," she said. "I know you've been very busy with all the work about finding the person who killed Mrs. Vicks, but I remembered you said we were going to go to lunch or maybe downtown or something."

"That's right," I said with a forced smile, berating myself for forgetting I'd even said that. She'd been waiting for me and I'd let her down, again. "When do you want to go?"

"Downtown?" she said, in an almost-squeak.

"Yeah, just you and me."

"How about tomorrow?"

Tomorrow. God, I so needed to make headway on this story. I needed to get some answers fast. Bass was on my butt and I felt the pressure of time from him, as well as knowing that the longer this stretched out, the less likely we'd find Mrs. Vicks' murderer.

Lucy started to reach behind her head, ready to twist her hair into knots at the delay in my answer.

"Sure," I said with a profound feeling that this was the

right thing to do, even if it would cost me a fight with my boss. "Let's plan to just have fun tomorrow."

My cell phone buzzed in the back pocket of my jeans, and I jumped at the vibration.

Detective Lulinski's voice barked at me over the wireless connection. "Where are you?"

I told him. "Why?"

"Good," he said. "Stay there."

He hung up before I could say another word. I shrugged at Lucy, shoved the last bit of oatmeal-raisin cookie into my mouth and said, "I think we're going to have company. How about a little Mozart?"

Smiling, she jumped up from her seat and headed back to the piano while I resumed my task of trying to get into the mind of an elderly woman with secrets.

By the time the detective showed up at the front door, I'd about exhausted every idea. I remembered a writer friend who had her protagonist hide a valuable item in the fridge, tucked into a carved-out head of lettuce. I tugged open the white metal door and turned my head at the ten-day-old smell of rotting food. When I found myself braving the stench in order to search through Mrs. Vicks' vegetable crisper, I knew I was starting to lose it.

Fortunately, I was saved by the doorbell.

"Any luck?" Lulinski asked me, by way of greeting when I opened the door.

"Any luck what?"

"Solving my case for me." He grinned as we moved into the living room where I introduced him to Lucy. She was unaccustomed to strangers offering a hand to shake, but she smiled as she took it.

"Hi," she said.

Detective Lulinski sent a quick glance to me before

addressing my sister again. "So you met Laurence Grady, didn't you?"

"Out front," she said, pointing.

"Can I ask you about it?"

Lucy looked to me and I gave her a nod of encouragement.

"Sure."

"Did he hurt you?"

"Oh, no," Lucy said. "He was really nice. He was surprised about Diana and wanted to know which hospital she was at."

"And you told him, right?"

The way Lulinski phrased it, with such a natural inquisitiveness, Lucy didn't think before she answered. "Oh, yeah. He wanted to know that right away." She seemed to consider that. "But I shouldn't have told him, should I? That's where he tried to hurt Alex."

To his credit, Lulinski didn't drop the friendly smile from his face. "It's okay, Lucy. Nothing bad happened. And it helps me to know everything I can about when you talked with him. Did you see where he came from?"

Lucy shook her head.

"Do you remember which direction he came from?"

"Yeah, I do," Lucy said with eagerness. "He was walking from here, I think. Yeah. I think so."

Damn, I thought. Why hadn't I asked her that?

"Was he carrying anything?"

Lucy stared up at the ceiling for several beats. "Just his keys."

After a few more questions, Lulinski thanked my sister and I sent her back to playing music as he and I headed to the kitchen.

"What was that all about?" I asked.

Dropping into a squeaky chair, Lulinski craned his neck

around, stopping when he spied the coffeemaker. He shot it a look of contempt, then turned to me.

"I can make some." I said.

His eyes lit up.

"Your sister is really talented," he said as I stood.

"Thanks." Pouring water into the appliance's reservoir, I added, "She plays several other instruments, too."

"I thought you told me she was mentally handicapped," he said in a low voice. "She seems pretty sharp."

I smiled, and as I moved around the small kitchen, I explained the vagaries of Williams Syndrome and how my well-read, articulate sister could still not possess the faculties to live on her own. Carrying on a conversation felt strange; I was making coffee in the same house where Mrs. Vicks had been murdered. Detective Lulinski, fingering the cigarette package he'd pulled from his pocket, seemed far more at ease, and he turned his body to watch me as I worked.

"They did a good job cleaning this place up," he said.

I glanced around and shuddered. I hadn't seen this room directly after the murder, nor did I want to. A service took care of the worst of it, then my aunt and several other women from the neighborhood had come in to finish up. Now nothing visible remained of the vicious attack.

"There," I said. "Couple of minutes."

The coffeemaker issued a water-hits-heating-element hiss, followed up by the almost immediate stream of coffee dripping into the glass carafe. When the warm brew smell seeped my way I felt myself relax. Normal smells, normal sounds. It made this abnormal process of finding a killer just a little more bearable.

"So, to what do I owe the honor of this visit?" I asked.

Arms on the table, Lulinski leaned forward. "Grady's

gone. No sign of him, no word. I talked to his parole officer and told him I to wanted call Grady in. The folks at the halfway house where he was staying haven't seen him, and his place has been cleaned out."

"Okay," I said, in a prompting tone.

"I don't know what that means, yet," he said, spreading his hands out in a gesture of unsupported explanation, "but despite this latest development, I have to tell you, my gut tells me Grady isn't our guy."

Our guy.

"Why not?" Standing, I guessed at which cabinet held Mrs. Vicks' mugs, grabbing two and pouring coffee for us both. I cast an uncertain glance at the refrigerator. "I don't think there's any cream," I said. "At least not any that's safe for human consumption."

He gestured for me to hand him the mug, which I did. I didn't particularly care for black coffee, but without much choice in the matter, I sipped the bitter brew.

"Our evidence technicians were backlogged, but I got their report this afternoon. Unidentified fingerprints, blood, and hair samples all over the kitchen and in the bedrooms and basement. Just where our guy was."

"Barton?" I asked.

"Nope. We printed him. We have Grady's on file and we've got yours, and Diana's in addition to the victim's. All accounted for. But there are clear prints that don't match up to any we have on file."

He pulled out a small notebook before continuing. "Blood type issues, too. What are you?" he asked.

"B-positive," I said.

"Good." He nodded, still consulting his notes. "We speculate that the killer was type AB. Looks like Evelyn

Vicks, her son Barton, and the roommate Diana all had the same blood type—'O'—the most common, you know."

I did know. "Why are you telling me all this? I thought you didn't trust the media."

He met my questioning eyes straight on. "You could find out any of this if you wanted to. We both know that. But I figure that if I tell you the things I can tell you, you won't go behind my back, and maybe you'll share what you know with me."

I didn't know why that stung, but it did. I deflected. "So you're saying you found type AB here, too?"

"Not a lot, some."

"What's Grady's blood type?"

"B-positive, same as yours."

"Then it isn't his," I said, thinking about that. "So, where did it come from?"

"Isn't that the sixty-four thousand dollar question." He set his mug down on the table and rolled its sides against his palms, back and forth, almost hypnotically. He played with it like I'd seen him play with his cigarette package and I wondered if it helped him concentrate.

"Speaking of which…" I met his eyes over the rim of my coffee cup, "did you hear about the reward?"

His rubbed his face so hard that for the first time, a pink tinge crept up from beneath his saggy gray stubble. "Did I? Every lunatic in the city of Chicago has been calling the station trying to get the fifty G's this David Dewars offered."

"How'd they hear about it?"

He tilted his head my direction, gazing at me over the tips of his fingers. "You're kidding, right?"

I shook my head.

"The idiot took out a goddamn ad in the goddamn *Sun-Times*," he said. "Goddamn full-page ad."

"Must have missed it," I said. "I read the *Trib*."

With a baleful glare, he went back to massaging his coffee mug, staring down at it for a long moment until one gray eyebrow lifted in my direction. "So, how did *you* hear about it?"

"At first, Barton told me," I said, "but then last night I asked David about it and he—"

"David?"

"Dewars," I said, feeling my face color. "He and I were talking about all this."

The other eyebrow joined its mate. "Last night." He didn't phrase it as a question.

"As a matter of fact, yes."

"At the bank?"

"Well," I said, hating the hedging tone to my voice. "We met at the bank." I didn't like where this conversation was going. "Why do you want to know?"

He sat back, with a funny look on his face.

"Did you go on a date with him?" he asked.

I opened my mouth, closed it, then shrugged. "Kinda."

"Well now," he said in as close to a drawl as a native Chicagoan can get, "I find that a little bit odd."

"Oh you do."

He nodded, leaning forward again. "He's got what?" Lulinski's eyes flicked up toward the ceiling for a split-second, "twenty-four years on you? Don't you think that's a bit much?"

He hadn't said, "around twenty," not "twenty some-odd," but "twenty-four."

"How do you know our ages?"

"I make it a point to know my suspects. All of them."

"I'm a suspect?" My voice squeaked.

"No," he said. And then, with a comedian's sense of timing, he waited till my shoulders relaxed and I breathed out a sigh before adding, "Not anymore."

"I was?" I asked, aghast.

"Everyone involved is a suspect until it's proven they're innocent."

"I thought it was supposed to be the other way around."

The corners of his mouth curled upward. "Why did you go out with David Dewars?"

"Is this an interrogation?" I asked.

"Why, do you have something to hide?"

I felt like we were playing the "Questions" game from the *Whose Line Is it Anyway* television show.

"No," I said, putting an end to the silliness. "I went out with David Dewars because he asked me. I've been looking into Mrs. Vicks' bank records—at David's invitation—and he wanted to touch base with me about all that." Punctuating my sentence with a look that said, "I hope you're satisfied," I continued. "Last night was really the first opportunity we had to connect."

I couldn't read Lulinski's expression. "What are you hoping to find in the victim's bank records?"

"Honestly, I have no idea," I sighed.

"But the bank president is letting you have free rein over her accounts, and he took you out on a date."

I was beginning to wonder why he seemed so interested in my social life. He certainly had no romantic interest in me, and my perplexity came out snappish.

"We went to a play, and that was it," I finished, feeling foolish at my attempt to say "nothing happened" without actually saying the words.

He seemed to get it, but his expression was still off-kilter as he focused on the empty space between my left shoulder and the wall behind me. "Okay."

"That's it? Okay?"

I'd gotten an impression from the very start that Lulinski was the sort of man who didn't answer when he didn't want to. Nothing in his manner contradicted that notion now. "So what exactly are you looking for?" he asked. "I mean, I can't imagine why the victim's bank records would be of interest. But," he interrupted himself, "I'm no ace reporter, so what do I know?" He tempered the sarcasm with a smile. Glancing over to my left, lifted his chin. "What have you got there?"

"Mrs. Vicks' mail. My aunt took it in all week."

"You haven't opened it, have you?"

"That's actually next on my exploration agenda," I said. Responding to the look in his eyes, I added, "I'm sure Barton's okay with this."

Lulinski pulled out his cell phone and flipped a few pages in his notebook. Moments later he'd connected with Barton and identified himself. "We'd like your permission to take a look at your mother's mail." I couldn't gauge Barton's answer from the look on Lulinski's face, so I waited till he spoke again. "No, really, you don't have to," he said. After repeating himself, he rolled his eyes my direction. "Sure, okay. We'll see you then."

"He's coming here?" I asked as he snapped his phone shut.

"Wants to help."

"Only if it means he gets the reward."

Lulinski sat back again and scratched at his left eyebrow. I got the feeling that, for a few moments, he forgot I was there. "Something doesn't add up."

"Care to share?"

Like a camera lens he blinked, and suddenly his focus was back to me. "Not particularly," he said with a grin.

"Where was he?" I asked.

"He's staying at the Tuck Inn Motel," he started to say, stopping when he caught my expression. "What?"

"I didn't know that place rented for longer than four-hour increments."

He snorted what could have been a laugh. "And how would a nice girl like you know about places like that?"

"I grew up here, remember? That's the neighborhood skank place. Everybody knows about it." Lucy moved into playing an off-beat version of "Chopsticks." I stood up, smiling. "I hope he asked for a second floor room."

"Why is that?"

Smiling to myself, I recalled some of the rumors that I'd heard over the years. "The owners supposedly rent out the rooms in numerical order," I said, then amending. "And so, if you want half a chance at something clean, you have to ask for the rooms that have seen the least action. Second floor."

Lulinski shook his head, wearing a grimace that matched my own reaction. "Well, Big Bart must not have gotten the scoop," he said. "He's in one-thirteen."

"Lucky number," I said. "And he's a gambler?"

I'd forewarned Lucy, but when Barton showed up, minutes later, he threw open the front door with the force of a gale wind. Simultaneously, I heard the concomitant dissonance of a misplayed chord coupled with Lucy's squeak of terror. I jumped up, meeting her halfway between the rooms. She grabbed my arm.

"Barton," I said in a sharp voice.

"What?" his insolent tone led me to believe he'd shared company with a warm bottle of booze in that hotel room. I wanted to tell him he should have knocked, but we were in his house now and that would have come out child-ish, not to mention stupid. So, all I said was, "Settle down."

"Sorry," he said, then looked at me, as though seeking for an atta-boy.

Lucy stayed close, whispering in my ear that she wanted to go home now and could we please leave. I could feel her entire body tremble next to mine and I could only imagine how frightening a big lout like Bart was to my tender sister. "Sure," I said. I gestured Bart into the kitchen and pulled out my cell phone to call Aunt Lena.

Within five minutes, our aunt had zipped over to spirit Lucy back to her house. As she did, she handed me a bag, and plate full of food for those of us remaining to work. "Just a little something," she said with a wink. "It'll give you strength to deal with Barton."

The two men's eyes lit up when I uncovered the tray of sandwiches. My aunt had included chips, cans of pop and some side items in the bag. She'd made ten half-sandwiches in turkey, beef, and ham. Since the two fellows seemed to be waiting for me, I grabbed one of the roast beef sections and then watched them dig in too.

Ten minutes later, I'd eaten my single half-sandwich and a handful of chips, but all that was left on the plate was a slice of tomato and some crumbs. I eyed the tomato, and when it looked safe enough for me to take it without having one of the two guys mistake my arm for another sandwich, I grabbed.

"So, down to business?"

I took charge of the mail, and sorted it into three piles, trying not to make it look too obvious that I was handing Barton mostly sale paper and credit card offers. I split the personal correspondence, banking stuff, and anything that looked official between myself and Detective Lulinski. For a good five minutes, we worked in silence.

"This is stupid," Barton said, flinging a shiny flyer across the table—it landed, tented, so that the zero-percentage rate faced us in bold red and blue. Immediately after his pronouncement, he belched, and the stench of lunch mixed with sweet alcohol that bubbled my way nearly curdled my stomach. "What do you think we're going to find in this crap, anyway?"

"Probably nothing," Lulinski said, without looking at him.

"Shit," he said again. He began ripping envelopes open with uncontained fury. "This is a waste of time."

I'd seen Barton fight off those security guards; I knew he could be a formidable adversary when he was in a snit, especially when tanked to the gills the way he was now. Lulinski placed one piece of mail to his left, and picked up another, still apparently unconcerned. Still paying no attention to Barton.

Seated at the head of the table, to Barton's immediate right, I could see the big guy's hands spasm, even as I tried to concentrate on the handwritten envelope in front of me. Barton moved his neck and jaw at once, like his shirt was too tight. Unlikely, since he wore a torn polo with an open collar. A few dark chest hairs sprouted from its "v" and I reassessed whether Barton was a natural blond or not.

Eeyoo.

He looked from Lulinski to me, then at the mail. His mouth twisted downward. "You think I don't know what's going on?" he said, standing. "You two gave me all the junk mail because you both really just want to get that damn reward for yourselves. What do you think, I'm some kind of idiot that I don't see that?" With one angry sweep of his arm, Barton scattered his pile of mail across the table and onto the floor.

Faster than I could say, "smooth move," Lulinski was

out of his seat and up in Barton's face. I hadn't realized until I saw the two men nose-to-nose that Lulinski was taller, by several inches. Barton just always seemed so much bigger to me.

"Listen, fat-ass," Lulinski said, and I could see tension in his body fighting the urge to grab Barton by those wayward chest hairs and twist, tight. "Your mother was murdered. Or did you forget that?" As Lulinski advanced, Barton backed up. "She was murdered, here, in her own goddamn kitchen— a place where she should have felt safe."

The red-rimmed bottoms of Barton's eyes twitched. "Yeah," he said, bluster fading, "and all I want—"

"All you want is walk away from this with the goddamned reward money in your pocket so you can pay off your bookie."

Barton's color drained. He shot an accusatory look in my direction.

"Don't look at her. It's my job to know these things. And it's my job to find out who killed your mother. For all I know, you did it."

Barton's attitude swung from anger to simpering fear in the time it took for me to switch my glance from Lulinski to him. "I didn't do it, I swear." His hands came up in a gesture of surrender. "I swear it," he said again.

Lulinski turned his back on Barton, making his way back to the table. "She was your mother, jerkhead. When did you forget that?"

Suddenly it was too much for the big guy. Too much liquor, too much tension, too much confrontation. Barton's face crumpled and tears leaked down his pudgy cheeks as he started to blubber right in front of us.

Embarrassed for him, I looked back down at the square envelope in my lap. Hand-addressed on plain pink stationery in a woman's hand, it felt weighty, as though there were several sheets inside. I'd been about to add it to Barton's pile of to-be-reads when I noticed the return address.

Iowa.

Standing so close now that he could have read over my shoulder if he wanted to, Barton gripped the back of his chair, leaning hard. I kept the letter on my lap, wanting to read it, but wanting even more to keep it from Barton, at least for now. I didn't know why, but I knew I wanted to digest its contents alone. I could feel its importance tingle along the tips of my consciousness.

I hated waiting.

Standing, turning, I grabbed my purse which I'd slung over the back of my chair. "Excuse me," I said, and I pressed the envelope against the back of my bag, hoping Barton wouldn't notice the awkwardness of my movements.

Lulinski gave me a look that asked what was up.

"Washroom," I said.

His skeptical gray eyes shot from the purse, clasped at my midsection, to my face, but he said nothing. I held tight, letting the long shoulder strap dangle, feeling as though any idiot could see that I was hiding something. I counted on the fact that Barton wasn't just any idiot.

Five steps away, the bathroom door stood open. I was just about to cross its threshold when I glanced back.

"Hang on a minute there," Barton said, his voice cracked and impatient.

Without meaning to, I pulled my purse tighter into my gut.

"What's up?" Lulinski asked, moving between us.

The big lug pushed past the detective. "Let me get in there first, okay?" he asked. "Just want to splash some water on my face, is all."

"Sure," I managed.

When I heard the small lock click, I blew my bangs out of my face in relief.

"All right," Lulinski said in a low voice, sidling up to me as I moved back to the table, "what's going on?"

I gave him a sheepish half-shrug as I set my purse on my chair and pulled the pale pink envelope from behind it. "I don't know. Maybe nothing."

"But you think it might be something."

Knowing Barton might emerge any moment, I moved as fast as I could, sliding my finger into the corner where the envelope glue hadn't stuck, loosening it. The letter, three pages folded in half, had been sent two days before Mrs. Vicks' murder, according to the handwritten date up top. Before reading it, I flipped to the last page to see who signed it.

"Theresa," I said, quietly.

"Mean anything to you?" Lulinski asked.

"No."

Turning back to the first sheet, I began to skim. Theresa's letter began "Dear Evelyn," and, in the way that friendly letters often do, asked if everything was going well in Chicago. I wondered, briefly, at Theresa's age. Beginning her letter by using Mrs. Vicks' first name might indicate that they were contemporaries.

Theresa then went on to mention a couple of recent events in her own life, including the fact that she'd apparently been out on "another date" with a farmer named Ned.

When I heard the toilet flush in the next room, I read faster, vaguely aware that Lulinski wasn't reading over my shoulder, but appeared ready to run interference the moment Barton stepped out.

Before the end of the first page of script, Theresa asked about Diana. She mentioned the fact that she hadn't gotten a call from her in over a month. She said that she knew that Laurence Grady had been released from prison, and that her concerns for Diana were mounting. The next page held another interesting tidbit. She wrote: "Dr. Hooker called me at home again today. I don't know if I'm going to be able to make the trip to Chicago, but he thinks it's important that I be there when the time comes. What do you think?"

The bathroom door clunked open and I slammed the letter to my chest in a "Look at me, I'm guilty!" move. Lulinski moved to intercept Bart and I shoved the pink sheets into my purse as the two did a narrow-hallway dance, buying me some time. I still didn't have any reason to hide the letter from Barton, beyond a sense of needing to sort things out in my own mind before sharing them.

With a neat little click, a piece of the puzzle fell into place. Remembering the day Mrs. Vicks had shown me Diana's school picture and spoken fondly of her, I knew, even before confirming it, that Theresa was the girl's mother. My eyes shot to the top drawer of the built-in china cabinet where Mrs. Vicks had stored the photo that day. I would bet there were more letters like this one, there and I'd bet some of them would explain why Mrs. Vicks had sent money out to them all these years.

Barton dropped into the squeaky kitchen chair with resigned lethargy. "I'm bored with this crap," he said.

I returned to the same chair I'd occupied earlier and fingered the next few pieces of mail in front of me while I waited for the detective to come back from the washroom. Nothing else looked promising at the moment, and I wanted to get into the little room myself to read the rest of Theresa's letter in peace.

"Hey," Barton said. "This isn't where Ma worked."

He held up a blue bank statement.

I'd seen several similar statements in the fire box in the closet, but I hadn't paid them much attention. I took a closer look. "May I?"

He handed it to me.

I had to give the big guy credit, this was indeed not issued by Banner Bank. According to this monthly statement, Mrs. Vicks maintained a savings account and two certificates of deposit at a neighborhood bank.

"This is the bank on Pulaski," I said aloud, "The one on the corner."

Maybe those bank statements I'd seen earlier this morning deserved a closer look. I grimaced. Yet another thing I'd rather do with Barton out of my hair.

Lulinski came back to our little group and after a few minutes of watching me fidget, asked Barton where he could get a pack of cigarettes in the area. As Barton started to give directions, Lulinski interrupted. "It'd be just as easy for you to show me. Come on, let's take a ride."

Not realizing he was being manipulated, Barton gave a so-so motion of his head and stood, with a little bit of interest in his eyes. I resisted the urge to ask Lulinski if he was going to let Barton play with the siren along the way.

The detective caught me as they headed out the door. "I expect you to share," he said with a wink.

TWENTY-ONE

THE MOMENT THEY were gone, I grabbed the old wooden buffet drawer with both hands and dragged it out from its recess. Cumbersome and heavy, it was almost a perfect square, about eighteen inches to a side, and a good six inches deep.

Crammed with a lifetime of miscellany, this was Mrs. Vicks' important junk drawer. Easy to recognize, since I had several of them, myself. My eye caught a thick envelope labeled "Photos" next to a four-inch ball of string, and I knew I'd struck gold.

Inside the envelope were pictures of Diana from the time she was a toddler. Each photograph, whether a candid, or a posed school portrait, had been carefully labeled with her name, her age, and the date.

Quite the cutie when she was little, Diana morphed from a sweet-faced little girl who wore every shade of pink into a sullen young woman who preferred deep browns and black. I came across the graduation picture Mrs. Vicks' had shown me last summer. Such drastic changes over the past eight years.

Pushing the pictures aside, I searched for more letters. I knew deep down from the insoles of my Reeboks that Mrs. Vicks had kept her correspondence from Theresa. Just as she'd kept all those pictures of Diana.

The biggest question in my mind, was why. To find out, I kept digging, through Christmas card lists, twenty-odd years' worth of pocket-date books, and about a dozen

keychains, each holding a single key. These had been labeled with all the neighbors' last names. Everyone on the
block apparently stored their keys with Mrs. Vicks', and
I shook off a shudder when I thought about how close the
murderer had been to getting to the rest of us.

With that in mind, I came to the realization that my parents had probably given up a set themselves. No time like
the present to take them back, I thought. I didn't much like
the idea of my keys in Barton's possession.

I scraped a handful of them along the inside of the
drawer and toppled them onto the table, using my finger
to poke among the litter, looking for either "Szatjemski"
or "St. James."

Nothing.

I grasped around the bottom of the drawer and pulled
out what I hoped were the rest of the keys. I found mine,
along with my aunt and uncle's keys. I moved them all into
a single-level pile and gave a little noise of surprise when
I came across a completely flat key, attached to nothing.
It was obviously a key to a safe deposit vault, but the number stamped on it, thirty-two, was not the number of Mrs.
Vicks' box at Banner Bank.

A car door slam broke into my thoughts, freezing me
in place, head up—listening. After what I thought was a
reasonable amount of time, I decided it wasn't Lulinski
returning with Bart, and I returned to the task at hand,
moving faster now.

I rooted around the drawer, opening envelopes and
small boxes for the letters I knew had to be there. I came
across a tiny red envelope that the safe deposit key had
fallen out of. No bank name. No identification, just bold
letters warning the owner not to lose the key because replacement costs were hefty. I pocketed that.

But not one more letter from Theresa.

When I heard yet another car door slam, I picked up the drawer and returned it to its niche, deciding that it was about time those bank statements from the closet got another look.

The front door opened, bringing with it a rush of fresh air that made it all the way to the kitchen, where I sat at the table, this time poring over the file full of blue bank statements. "You're right," I said to Bart as they came in, Lulinski's scent of just-finished cigarette following in his wake.

"I am? About what?"

I held up the bank statements. "Your mom had a few accounts down the street at Crawford Bank and Trust."

"I knew it. I betcha they're all in my name, too."

He caught the withering glances Lulinski and I sent his way, and tried to back-pedal. "I mean," he said. "Ma had me sign a bunch of signature cards a while ago. I'm just guessing that maybe these are the ones, since they tell me I'm not a signer on the Banner Bank accounts."

I started to page through the statements, realizing that the accounts had been opened even before those at Banner Bank had. "Hmm," I said, aloud.

"What?" Lulinski and Bart both looked up.

"Nothing." I felt as though all the information in my head needed to be arranged properly. That I was missing the big picture, somehow.

Barton picked up some of the statements I hadn't gotten through yet. I couldn't very well stop him from reading his mother's papers, but I hated the fact that they were now out of order. "Hang on," I said. Mrs. Vicks had kept a coffee mug full of pens near her phone. I pulled out two and handed one to Barton. "As I go over the statements, I'll initial them, like this." I demonstrated, writing "AS" in tiny letters on the upper right hand corner of the page.

"You do the same, in the same spot, so I know which ones we've each gone over, okay?"

He nodded, and grabbed the pen from me, looking like a little-boy-lost with no clue as how to sort through the records before him. Wrinkling his nose, he shifted the pen to his left hand, and scribbled on the statement in front of him.

"You're left-handed?" I asked.

The surliness was back. "Yeah. So?"

Swirling, facts swam around in my brain, doing tantalizing dances that made my heart race with possibility. I started to see what I'd missed, and the pieces of the puzzle dropped, one at a time, until they lined up with a precision that told me I had to be right about this. What it had to do with Mrs. Vicks' murder, I wasn't sure, but I needed to push to find out.

I fingered the safe deposit key in my pocket. I thought I might know where those letters were, and what information they held after all. "Barton," I said.

"Yeah?"

His eyes were clearer than they had been an hour before. I hoped to heaven he was sober and lucid enough to access the working parts of his brain. "How did Diana come to live with your mother?"

"Hell if I know." He shook his head, looking grateful for a reason to stop examining the bank statements. "One day Ma calls me and says she thinks maybe it's a good idea if she gets somebody to live with her, you know, to help around the house and drive her places. Next thing I know, she has this Diana here."

"You never met Diana before?"

"Not before that. One time, Ma asked me to come down because she said she had something important to talk about. Diana was living here by then."

"And?"

He made a face of annoyance, shrugging dramatically. "I take a day off of work to make the drive, and when I get here, she just says that she wanted to see me. What was so important about that?"

Lulinski watched our conversation with interest. He leaned back in his chair, nothing moving but his eyes, flicking back and forth between us as we spoke.

"What did you think of Diana?"

He gave me a look that told me he thought I was nuts for asking. "She was a kid. What is she, twenty? Twenty-five? If Ma wanted a roommate and the kid was willing to cough up some rent money and drive her around to her doctors' appointments, I had nothing to complain about."

All of a sudden, Dr. Hooker's voice came into my brain. He would have told me to stop here. He would have told me to butt out of something that was none of my business. But I couldn't let this drop. Not now.

"Who's Theresa?" I asked.

He looked at me with those small, piggish eyes. "Why?"

"Answer the question," Lulinski chimed in.

Bart looked at him, then back to me. "She's my cousin. What's that got to do with anything?"

His cousin, I thought. Oh, God. It took me a moment to figure out what to say next.

"I take it you and Theresa were…close?"

He squinted and his mouth dropped slightly. Like I'd opened the door and let out the dirty little secret that he'd been keeping all these years.

"When we were kids, yeah. So why?"

"Maybe the better question is, Barton, how close were you?"

I paused to let the full implication of the question sink

in, then said. "Diana's left-handed. Her mother always told her that it was a curse."

The big guy sat back in his chair, looking like he'd just come off of a spinning carnival ride that had left his brain jumbled and his stomach turned inside-out.

Behind me, the kitchen clock ticked a rhythmic beat. I didn't count, but it must have been at least thirty seconds before it all came together in the big guy's mind.

Leaning his head forward, he stared at me. "She was supposed to get that taken care of."

Taken care of, I thought. With a parent like this, no wonder Diana needed to sort things out with a shrink, though I doubted she knew that Bart was her father. I couldn't imagine what effect it would have on her self-esteem once she found out.

"Nicely put, Bart," I said, barely able to conceal the contempt in my voice. "But it looks like, for whatever reason she didn't. Happy Father's Day."

"She said she never wanted to see me again," he said. "I thought that was okay. I'd go back to my life and she'd go back to hers and I thought…"

I knew what he thought. He neither wanted to assume the financial obligations of fatherhood, nor the emotional burden that came as part of the package. How nice for him to have it all taken away with the promise by his former lover. But she hadn't followed through, and Mrs. Vicks had stepped in to provide what she could, when her son fell short.

The sadness weighing on my heart at the moment wasn't for Barton's lost years with his daughter, nor for his sudden comprehension of all that had gone on behind his back; what hurt was realizing that Diana had missed out on knowing that Mrs. Vicks was her grandmother.

Pulling the safe deposit key from my pocket, I held it up.

"I found this while you fellows were out," I said. "I have a feeling all the proof we want is sitting in a safe deposit box in the bank down the street."

Barton shook his head with wide-eyed disbelief. I knew he didn't need any proof, but I wanted to see what was in that box.

"Come on," I said, standing. "I'll drive."

Lulinski glanced at his watch, then sidled over. "I have to get back to the station. Couple of other things I need to follow up." His wary eyes raked over Bart, then returned to me. "You going to be okay with the big lug?"

The piss and vinegar attitude was gone, along with the scowl of distaste Barton had worn from the first. He'd paled a bit, looking to me for guidance. I nodded. "I'll be fine."

Lulinski leaned over and whispered, "Neat bit of detective work there, Nancy Drew."

I shot him a smile. "Doesn't do much to solve the murder, though," I said.

He made a so-so movement with his head. "Let's wait and see what other secrets Mrs. Vicks was keeping, shall we?"

AT THE BANK, I wasn't surprised to find Barton's name as signatory on the safe deposit access card. "Told you I signed one of these," he said, when the young black girl behind the desk smiled and led him into the vault area.

Barton and the girl came back around the corner; he carried a very large box. Ten-by-ten inches high and wide, it looked to be about thirty inches deep. The girl showed us to a minuscule examining room. Thank God it was cold in there, because otherwise it would have been unbearable with him in such close quarters. The box's lid hinged about three-quarters of the way down, and opened upward.

Inside, just as I'd expected, we found hundreds of letters, in all sorts of stationery, separated in rubber-banded bundles by year. I let Barton read through them, content with the knowledge that if something unexpected popped up, he'd let me know.

He flopped into the only chair in the room, and started reading, in stunned silence.

I pulled out piles of nine-by-twelve envelopes, each carefully lettered with descriptions of their contents. "Bank," "Questions," piqued my interest. I picked those up along with a few others. One, called "Nursing Home Residents" seemed out of place, but I grabbed that too.

Barton's fist came up out of the recesses of the box with a bundle of official-looking papers, unbound, but sitting snugly in one of those narrow cardboard legal wallets. While I continued to search, Barton picked through the documents it contained.

Since one set of hands in the jumble were better than two, I didn't comment on his lack of participation, but I did keep an eye on him.

A thick manila envelope, brick-like and adorned with at least a dozen multi-colored rubber bands sat in the back corner of the box. When I pulled it out, and moved aside enough of the tight bands to see what was inside, I gave a little gasp of surprise.

"What?" Barton asked, instantly on his feet.

I didn't have time to respond before he yanked the package out of my hands. "Holy sweet Jesus," he said. "Yes!" He pulled out the fat wad of cash with an expression of pure delight in his eyes. "Thank you Momma!" he said waving the bundled bills in the air.

"Barton," I warned through clenched teeth. "Put that away."

"Hell no. I'm counting it. Gotta find out how much I got here."

Afraid he'd react like a hungry and ferocious dog whose food was being snatched, I resisted the urge to grab the money from him. "Put it away," I said again. "Don't you know that you're not supposed to keep cash in a safe deposit vault?" Two beats later, I added. "If they find out that was in here, you'll have to pay tax. And maybe even a fine."

That got him. Staring at me like I was some sort of authority all of a sudden, he rewrapped the money and looked around for a place to hide it.

"Just...here." I found another, bigger manila envelope and, after emptying its contents, offered it to Barton and told him to stuff it.

He nodded a thanks, still looking skittish.

We jumped when a tap came at the door. "Excuse me," the vault girl said in a honey voice as she peered around the doorway. "The bank will be closing in a few minutes."

She'd missed seeing the cash by seconds. I threw Barton a look that said "I told you so," and then heaved a sigh. There was a lot I wanted to sort through, still. "Do you happen to have a big shopping bag?" I asked. "Maybe a couple?"

She smiled. "I'll see what I can do."

While she was gone we sorted through the rest of the box as quickly as we could, Barton keeping one eye on the envelope like he was afraid it might jump up and dance away. When he shouted, "Hey!" I stood straight up, startled.

"Look," he said, with a little catch of excitement in his voice, "it's Ma's will. It's right here."

I started to read over his shoulder, but he thrust the sheaf of papers into my hands. "What's it say?" he asked.

The vault girl returned and we started loading up as much as could be stuffed into the two bags she'd provided.

We shifted positions, and I got Barton to bag while I continued to read. With the running commentary keeping me vaguely aware of what he was choosing to take and what he chose to leave behind, I skimmed enough to get the gist of the disposition Mrs. Vicks intended.

"Hang on," I said.

He stopped.

"I want those," I said, pointing.

Without questioning me, Barton nodded, grabbing two more file folders, held together by thick crisscrossed rubber bands and paper-clipped sides. Mrs. Vicks had written "Maya, home phone" in pencil on the top folder. That struck me as odd enough that I wanted to know what was inside.

"What does the will say?" Barton asked, standing too close.

All of a sudden, a wave of claustrophobia hit me. Too tight. Whoever designed these dinky little rooms certainly didn't have the patrons' comfort in mind. "Let's get outside first, okay?" I said, brushing past him.

Back in the car, Barton started counting his money. I locked my doors with the master lock, worried that some carjacker might decide to target us and not only get away with my little car, but also Mrs. Vicks' windfall.

"How much?" I asked when he finally came up for air.

"Forty-two hundred," he said in a hushed, disbelieving voice. A big smile broke over his pudgy face and for a half-second I could see a shadow of the boy that Theresa might have found handsome all those years ago. Eyes wide with delight, he said the words again. "Forty-two hundred."

"Okay Bart, I got it. Now pay attention." Reading over the will, I summarized. "It looks to me that your mother had her will drawn up about twelve years ago. That'd be right after your father died, wouldn't it?"

Barton looked like he'd just buzzed in on *Jeopardy!* and had forgotten the answer. "Yeah, I think so," he said.

"I'm guessing," I continued. "But the timing seems about right."

"Come on," Barton said, his voice high with impatience and fists tight around the cash, "What's it say about her other money?"

I wondered again how such a perfectly lovely woman could have birthed such a deplorable son. "It's split between you and Diana. Evenly."

"What?"

"*Per stirpes*," I added.

"Speak English."

"What that means," I explained, "is that if you would have died before your mother did, and if you didn't have a will, then your share would have gone to Diana, too. And it means," I let my gaze float over till it landed on the cash sitting in his lap, "half of that belongs to Diana now, too."

"The hell it does."

I waved the will. "It says it right here. Half to you, half to Diana."

His face went red in the amount of time it took him to gather the bills into two fat fists. "This is *my* inheritance," he said, stuffing the cash into his pockets and spitting as he spoke. "She was my mother and this is mine. I ain't sharing it with nobody. Got that?"

"Barton, you're breaking the law."

I could tell it was too much information at once, and he was having difficulty processing it all. "Give me that," he said, ripping the will from my hands. He began to read it, and I could tell from the blank expression on his face that he didn't comprehend a word. "I don't understand," he said, in classic understatement.

I shook my head, not understanding a lot of this, myself.

"David Dewars told me that your mother wrote up a new will, and that you were the sole beneficiary."

Barton's eyes lit up. "Yeah?"

His face suffused with puppy-dog eagerness now, like I'd just held up a leash and offered him a walk. I gritted my teeth, but I would have much rather slapped that hopeful look off his face. "Barton," I said with a sharpness that got his attention, "that doesn't make sense. Why would your mother have suddenly excluded Diana after all these years?"

"Maybe because she was having problems. Didn't you say that low-life boyfriend of hers came back?"

He had a point.

"Maybe," I agreed. Letting loose a deep breath through pursed lips, I turned to regard the big bags in my back seat. "Let me take all this stuff home and go over it, okay?" Even as I said the words, I cringed, wondering when I'd have a chance to examine all this as fully as I needed to. Lucy was counting on a day out tomorrow, and I couldn't let her down.

"Why do you get it all?"

"I have the time to go over it," I lied.

"Uh-uh," he said, his mouth pushed downward in anger. "I don't trust you."

I pressed my fingers into my eye sockets, trying to force the building aggravation out of my head. There was no way I was going to give up this stash of information. Not to Big Bart, anyway, "Okay, how's this for a compromise?" I began, thinking it through as I spoke, "We'll go together to the copy place down the street. I'll make a duplicate of everything we picked up," shaking my head, I amended, "except for the letters." There were too many of them, and I doubted they held much more than an ongoing narrative of Diana's life, anyway.

"You can keep the letters." He swung his hand behind us. "It's the bank account statements I want to see."

Never accuse Bart of being a sentimentalist. Had our situations been reversed, I would have killed to read my mother's letters. "Okay, deal," I said. I'd put in an expense report for the cost of duplication, looking forward to the look on Bass's face when I presented it to him. This would be one hefty photocopy bill.

"But I'm keeping this," Barton said, ripping his mother's will from my grasp, with a look that dared me to object. "And the cash." As though to underscore his meaning, he held tight to the document with both hands, pressing it to his chest. With what seemed to be enormous relief, he closed his eyes and muttered, "This is just what I need to keep that loan shark off my back."

"Fine." I bit back both my disappointment and a more harsh retort. "Just don't lose it."

"I won't," he said.

I believed him, but he had a peculiar gleam in his eye that I didn't understand.

TWENTY-TWO

WHEN WE GOT back to his car, Barton took off with his photocopies right away, crawling back into his hole at the Tuck Inn to count his money again, I supposed. I watched him go, then dragged the two shopping bags full of papers into my house, only to be greeted by the telephone's shrill ring.

I picked it up in the kitchen without even checking Caller ID.

"Hello?"

David's smooth voice came over the line, asking how my day had gone.

"You sound like you've been running," he added.

Walking back to the living room, I took a deep breath to center myself. "I have been, in a way. I just came home. Haven't even closed the front door yet." Punctuating that remark, I pushed it shut with a slam. "There," I said, smiling. "Now I'm in."

"Where were you all day? I tried calling you twice."

I opened my mouth to tell him, then stopped myself. "I spent a little time with my sister," I said. It wasn't exactly a lie, and I embellished on the truthful parts. "I haven't spent nearly enough time with her since she's been home."

"Do anything special?"

The fact that David had told me Mrs. Vicks had left her entire estate to Barton still had me rattled. Until I could sort out the truth here, I didn't want to share what I knew with anyone other than Detective Lulinski. Making a mental note to call him next, I avoided David's question by deflection. "Not really. Tomorrow, though, she and I plan to spend the day together."

David made a regretful-sounding noise. "The whole day?"

Making my tone sounds just as regretful, I said, "Pretty much," then added, "She wants to go downtown. I'm there every day, but for her it's something exciting and new. We'll find plenty to keep us busy, I'm sure."

"She might enjoy Navy Pier," he suggested. "I know I did."

"Actually," I said, almost to myself. "She might. Thanks. That's a good idea."

"I could always meet you both there. For lunch, perhaps?"

I'd been about to reply that Lucy wanted time alone with me, but he interrupted.

"Tell you what," he said in a hopeful voice, "I'll call you tomorrow after I get a few things squared away. Don't rearrange any plans on my account, but let's keep our options open, okay?"

"Sure," I said, knowing I'd probably decline. Lucy needed one-on-one time.

"Wonderful," he said. "I'll look forward to seeing you."

I left a quick message on Lulinski's voicemail and then glanced at the kitchen clock. The lunch Aunt Lena had prepared was long gone and I was starting to feel hunger pangs again. No doubt I could stop by to pick up Lucy and scrounge some dinner over there, but the bagged files clawed at my consciousness. I couldn't ignore them.

After a quick phone call to my aunt, I pulled out the files and tried to make sense of the copies of bank records and handwritten notes Mrs. Vicks had seen fit to keep under lock and key.

Two hours later, the phone jarred me out of my concentration.

"What's up?" Lulinski asked.

I hadn't gone into deep detail in my phone message, but I did so now. I told him about the letters, the will, and now the files I was sorting through.

"What do you make of it?" Lulinski asked. "You haven't seen the more recent will, have you?"

"No," I admitted. "I'm going on David Dewars' recollections. I have no idea if he's got the story straight or not. Maybe she did change her will. My gut tells me she didn't. But…"

"But?"

"There's more here." I scratched my head, vaguely aware that it'd become dark outside. "What time is it?" I asked, even as my gaze strayed to my clock.

"Eight-thirty," Lulinski answered. "Why? What's on your mind?"

"Honestly," I said, hesitating. "I'm not sure."

"You found something else in the safe deposit box." He didn't phrase it as a question. "Want me to come by?"

"It's late. You've been at this all day."

"So have you."

"Yeah," I answered, acknowledging his point. "But Mrs. Vicks was a friend and I have a personal interest in finding answers here."

Lulinski was silent.

"You there?" I asked.

When he answered, he spoke in a low voice. "Don't you think I have a personal interest in solving all my homicides, too?"

I winced, grateful he couldn't see me. "Sorry."

"The offer still stands. You want me to come by to-night?"

"There's someone I really need to talk to first." I hedged telling him more, since all I had were questions, and only guesses at their answers. "How about I call you after that, and we'll go over everything."

"Okay. You have my number. Oh, and Alex…"

"Yeah?"

"We got a line on Grady. He's been spotted in Michigan."

"I thought you didn't suspect him in the murder."

"What I said was that we didn't find his blood type at the crime scene," Lulinski said. "There's the possibility he was working with an accomplice and that's whose blood we found." He grunted. "Keeping our options open."

David had used that exact phrase with me earlier in a totally different context and the echo of his words coming from Lulinski felt odd.

"Plus," Lulinski continued. "I'm planning to nail him for accosting you in the parking lot. The sooner we bring him in, the better."

FOR SOME REASON, I'd anticipated getting Maya Richardson's answering machine when I called her at home. I hesitated contacting her, particularly since I didn't want to do anything to upset the FDIC investigation currently going on at the bank, but the records in front of me appeared to deal with a different matter entirely. With her name penciled onto the top file by Mrs. Vicks, Maya seemed like my best bet.

The familiar phone prefix and exchange gave me the impression that she lived in the south suburbs, probably near Palos Hospital. She picked it up on the third ring.

"Maya, this is Alex St. James. We met the other day?"
I put it as a question, hoping she remembered.

"Alex, yes of course," she said.

"I'm sorry to bother you at home," I began.

"That's all right," she said with automatic politeness.
"What's up?"

"That's the thing," I said, "I'm not sure. I have some
files here—"

"Are you at the bank?"

"I'm at home."

I could hear wariness creep into her voice. "Owen let
you take bank files home with you?"

I took a deep breath. "No." I explained the circumstances that brought the files to my possession. She was
mostly silent during my narrative, offering up an uncertain, "Okay," that I knew meant more to prompt me along
than to agree with anything. I left out the fact that I'd made
copies that Barton now possessed.

"I have an idea of what some of this means," I said. All
of a sudden this phone call felt lame; my expectation that
she'd be able to sort through all my questions, without seeing the records, was the work of a pie-eyed idealist, not the
ace researcher I tried to be. Knowing it'd be a tough sell
to pull her out on a Saturday night, I forged ahead. "But
I'm not sure if the conclusions I'm coming to are solid, or
way off. If it wouldn't be too much of an inconvenience,
could I meet you somewhere to get your ideas?"

Her thoughtful silence over the phone made me believe
I'd lost her. "Tonight?" she asked.

"Well…yes." I'd been about to hedge, to suggest that we
get together Monday after work, but I knew that my questions couldn't wait, and I still had Bass on my back, waiting for me to cough up a story. "I realize it's a Saturday

night, and you've probably got a million things you'd rather do, but—"

She cut me off, her voice skeptical. "You think this has something to do with why Evelyn was murdered?"

"I honestly don't know. That's why I need help here."

Sensing that she was choosing the right words to decline, I clenched my eyes shut for a split second, worried about the chance I was about to take. "Listen," I said, "do you know why the bank is being audited by the FDIC?"

"Because we're due for an audit."

"That's not the whole story," I said. I took a deep breath, and decided to go for it. "They're investigating you."

"What? Me?"

"Please," I said. "I promise not to take much of your time. Is there a restaurant or something near you where we can talk?"

"What exactly do you have there? What kinds of files did you find?"

For a half-second, the antagonism in her voice made me wonder if she was, indeed, involved in some embezzling scheme at the bank, but my gut told me differently.

"I'm no banker—"

"What did you find?"

I took a deep breath. "Look, I don't know what some of this is. If I'm putting it together correctly, it looks like you've set up an elaborate scheme to siphon money out of the bank, but," I added that in before she could interrupt, "a couple of things don't fit that scenario. I think you're being set up. Let me show you, okay?"

I took her silence to mean she was considering my proposition. Wanting to tip the scales my direction, I added, "I could be out your direction in twenty minutes." Closer to thirty, I thought, but I'd push.

"Okay," she said at last. "But I have to tell you, I'm not

real happy to be thinking you're considering me a suspect here."

"I'm not," I said. "If I did, you're the last person I'd
talk to."

TWENTY-FIVE MINUTES later, having grabbed a cheeseburger
and iced tea at the fastest drive-thru I knew, I rang Maya's
doorbell. When she'd finally agreed to meet me, she suggested I come to her home rather than discuss bank business in a public place. I had an initial feeling of unease
about that, but I attributed my nervousness to the fact that
I might be on the verge of finally coming up with some
solid leads.

On the drive over, just to be safe, I phoned Detective
Lulinski to tell him my plans. I'd learned, the hard way,
not to put myself in compromising positions without a
backup plan. I got his voicemail, which was just as well. I
had no doubt he'd try to talk me out of my visit, or worse,
he'd want to accompany me. I knew in my gut that I'd get
a lot more information from Maya girl-to-girl, than with
a detective listening in.

Maya opened the door, not smiling, but the looseness
of her hair, released from its customary pulled-back style,
framed her dark face giving her a softer appearance. She
wore a belted silk robe in an African pattern, and her feet
were bare. I offered a smile, relieved at least, to see that
she wasn't in a hurry to go out.

Coffee-colored eyes bore into me, not with the furtive
apprehension of a guilty party, but with a pointed anger—
"kill the messenger" rang out loud and clear.

Her house was small, as Palos Park homes went, but it
was still at least twice the size of mine. An affluent sub-
urb of Chicago, Palos boasted sprawling mansions deep
in wooded cul-de-sacs. Maya's brick ranch must have cost

her a fortune, though it was certainly not out of the reach of a Loop bank vice-president's salary.

"Forgive the mess," she said, the way a woman always will when faced with a surprise guest, even if her house is pristine. "Just moved in a few months ago," she said, gesturing around the older home. "Didn't get much done, yet."

"I really am very sorry to bother you," I said again, taking in my surroundings as quickly as I could. Framed prints sat atop the back of her sofa, leaning against the wall, in preview of their placements. The musty smell of the home's past lives relaxed me. Not a pretentious house, it was sturdy, creaky with promise, and just waiting for its new owner's personal touch. "This is lovely," I said, meaning it.

"Let's sit in the dining room, the light's better," she said. She moved with wary impatience, as though she both wanted to know, yet was afraid to see what damaging evidence I held in the papers I carried close.

TWENTY-THREE

"THE BASTARD!"

Maya stood up from the chair she'd taken just over an hour ago. Her exclamation bellowed in the otherwise quiet room, where we'd been discussing the records in whispers, as though some unseen entity might overhear.

She paced the dining room, her bare feet making angry "whumps" as she strode over the creaky wooden floor, head down, her loosened hair shaking from side to side.

I waited.

"Damn, damn, damn," she said. Stealing a look up at me, she cringed, her eyes imploring, as though I could somehow make all this go away. She fingered the gold cross hanging from the chain around her neck. "Lord Jesus, help me in my time of need," she said, her voice cracking.

We'd just finished reading a letter written by Owen Riordan, addressed to the Banner Bank human resources manager, with copies to Maya's personnel file and to David Dewars. In the letter, Owen voiced his concerns about Maya's honesty and reliability, and stated that he suspected she was attempting to perpetrate a huge scam from her position in the loan department. The peculiar thing was that the letter was dated over three weeks in the future, but I'd found it in Mrs. Vicks' safe deposit box.

Maya nodded, a glint of anger making an appearance behind her wet eyes. "I'm not going to let him set me up—I swear."

"Good," I said. "That's exactly the attitude we need." I

picked up my pen and looked at her pointedly. "Now, talk. Let's go over what we've got here one more time."

Tugging her robe tighter around her slight frame, she nodded, her gaze already dancing over the papers on the table, stopping long enough for her to grab the hand-lettered page Mrs. Vicks had seen fit to create.

"I still can't believe all this," Maya said, holding onto a corner of the legal sheets, "Banner Bank opened 'Line of Affluence' accounts for dozens...no, more than that... hundreds of people who probably never knew they applied for the accounts."

"You're sure?"

"No," she said, "but it makes sense. Look," she said, digging to find the copy of a computer printout Mrs. Vicks had made with tiny blue ink checkmarks in the column adjacent to many of the names. "Here. Every one of the people Evelyn indicated on this list has a Chicago area PO Box as an address. That's the first clue that they're bogus. You always get a home address when you're issuing a loan. Always. It'd be stupid not to."

I took the copies from her as she continued.

"These people," she tapped the yellow sheets this time, "according to Evelyn's notes, are nursing home residents. From all across the country. Their names and socials match up to the files, but I doubt they'd apply for this kind of loan. We marketed this program to young, urban professionals. Retired seniors are far different from our target demographic. And yet," she sighed with quiet incredulity, "every one has my name on it as approving their application."

"But you didn't approve them, did you?"

Her eyes jumped, her voice shot out angry—defensive. "I've never even seen these before tonight—how could I have approved them?"

"Hey," I said, in a soothing voice, "I'm on your side."

Her expression shifted; she leaned forward, pulling tight at the front of the robe again, covering protectively. "That's what I don't understand. Why are you on my side? Why didn't you just take all this information and bring it to Owen?"

"Because…" I met her eyes, "I knew better."

I could almost see her brain working behind narrowed eyes, so I explained. "Remember that day you tried to rescue me from the bowels of the vault department?"

She nodded.

I held up the copy of the computer printout to show her the scrawled message: *Approved: M. Richardson—Please File.* "The note you wrote that day—completely different handwriting than this."

Canting her head, her voice went up a notch. "You can recognize peoples' handwriting? After one look?"

I smiled at that, and for the first time since I'd arrived, I felt a small amount of tension drift away. "No, but I do remember thinking that your handwriting didn't match your personality." I held out a hand in her direction. "You're energetic and outgoing. Your note looked like it was written—no offense—by a timid third-grader."

Leaning back in her chair she let go a short laugh. "Thank the nuns for that. They used to crack the rulers against my desk and scare the living daylights out of me if I didn't keep my letters small and legible." With a wistful smile, she added, "I guess I never realized I'd be so glad they were tough on me, huh?" She narrowed her eyes again. "That's it? You came out all this way, and took a chance because of some handwriting?"

"Of course not," I admitted. "When I went over all this stuff tonight at home, I could see something wasn't right. I had an idea, but I needed help figuring it all out." Shrugging my uncertainty, I continued. "I had to ask somebody…either you or Owen, and since Mrs. Vicks had your home phone number written on her notes, I took it to mean that she wanted to get in touch with you outside of work. She must have had faith in you. Plus," I added, "I've met you and I've met Owen. I asked myself which one of you I would trust." I shrugged. "And here I am."

She smiled at that, and a couple of quiet beats passed before we both sat forward, getting back to work. A gentle bubble of camaraderie had enveloped us, ready now to face the task of dismantling the scam together.

WHEN WE FINISHED sorting through it all, we were confident we had the details worked out. "Line of Affluence" accounts had been opened for the one hundred and seventy-three people Mrs. Vicks had listed on her ledger sheets, for varying amounts, all under ten thousand dollars. Compiled in chronological order, the first accounts had been opened six months earlier. I was sure hundreds more had been added to the list since then.

Maya explained that the "Line of Affluence" account was a pilot program. A brand-new idea to bring in customers, it had generated a buzz even more intense than they'd hoped. Professionals everywhere were clamoring to sign up. A checking account with credit privileges, it offered a super-low rate on overdrafts. Not ordinary overdrafts, these customers could, in essence, write themselves a loan up to their assigned credit limit with no collateral—nothing but a signature to guarantee future repayment.

I gave a low whistle when she'd first explained the program. "Nice setup. At least till the bills start."

"That's the thing." She sifted through the paperwork for several minutes while I watched, trying to read her expression. Tiny frown lines deepened between her dark brows and when she finally looked up again, her lips were pursed in thought. "This printout was dated three weeks ago," she said. "But it lists each individual approval date. Every single one of these accounts was funded on the very day they were approved."

"So every one of these people," I held up Mrs. Vicks' yellow sheets, "have the same address and opened identical accounts?"

"Yeah," she said with a wry look.

"And we can safely assume these people don't know one another."

Maya finished my thought. "Which means that it looks like one person is controlling all the accounts."

"But why?" I asked. "Why go to all the trouble? Wouldn't the pattern become apparent the minute the loans weren't paid back?"

She shook her head, staring upward in apparent disbelief.

"What?" I asked.

"This is perfect," she said. "This is beautiful. I get it." Sitting up and leaning forward as though the words might come out more quickly if she were closer, she explained. "I'm going to bet that not one of these people paid back a single penny."

"I'm not understanding."

Maya shook her head. "The world is a strange place and the world of banking is sometimes even stranger. Since none of these people borrowed more than ten thousand dollars, our loan department can choose to write the losses off rather than send them to collections."

"Oh, come on," I said, disbelieving.

Her eyes were bright. "It's true. We're having such success with this program that we've extended six-figure credit to most of our client base. Six-figures," she emphasized. "These," she indicated the list, "are small potatoes.

Very small. And, if I can guesstimate, even all put together, they don't make up more than three percent of our asset base. All of these are within tolerances, and definitely within a loan officer's limit to write them off without approval from David. And, the argument can be made that ten grand isn't worth the trouble to go after it."

"So what happens?"

"Whoever wrote these checks, knew that the bank wouldn't follow up, so Owen," she raised her eyebrow and pointed to his name on the paper before us, "came up with hundreds of fake borrowers. Not one of them is large enough to go after, but put together they total a real nice haul."

"But, who are they?" I asked.

Maya squinted, and I could tell she was thinking aloud as she continued. "We can't do anything without a person's social. As long as we have that and their name, we have enough to run a credit check." Her gaze on the ceiling, she spoke slowly. "My guess is that elderly folks in high-priced retirement homes…" she indicated a couple of the group home names that lined the top of the lists, "have money. So, when we ran a credit report on them, they came up as excellent prospects. Owen must have seen them as an untapped resource—he borrows money in their names, never pays it back, and when they go past due, he writes off their small balances as a loss."

"And if anyone ever questioned the accounts," I said, "like the FDIC doing this audit, Owen had you all set up to take the fall." Maya let loose a sigh that might have been a sob, and I bit my lip for a long moment, before putting the final bit of information together. "And it might have worked, except Mrs. Vicks' apparently recognized one of the account names."

Maya nodded. She fingered the letter we'd found from

Ursula Siewicz, a resident of one of the nursing homes heavy with Banner Bank customers. "I can't believe this," Maya said. "I'd like to go confront Owen right this minute with this. This is the thing that seals it."

I read it again.

Dear Evelyn,

I was pleased to receive your lovely letter yesterday. It is always wonderful to hear from old friends, particularly when I feel so far away from home. I was, however, puzzled by your question about a bank account in Chicago. I made certain to have all my accounts transferred to a local savings and loan when I moved here five years ago. The thing that worries me was that the social security number you wrote in your letter is definitely mine. I'm sure I didn't leave any accounts in Chicago. And even if I'd forgotten one, I never banked downtown, I always kept my business local, as you know. I'm very concerned about this. Unless Richard opened an account before he died and forgot to tell me about it, I can't imagine how my social security number could have gotten into a downtown bank's records. But then again, with all the bank name changes going on, I suppose anything is possible.

Would you be a dear and check into this for me? If there's any money in the account, you can have them mail me a check, and then I'll send you something for all your trouble. But honestly, I think it's really just some clerical mistake. My best to you—When are you going to retire to enjoy the sun?

I tapped the cream colored stationery. "Mrs. Vicks must have recognized Ursula's name and wondered why her old friend was applying for such a significant line of credit. But how would Mrs. Vicks have come across this information?"

Maya leaned back in the wooden chair and crossed her arms and legs. "Evelyn Vicks worked for me, you know," she began. "But things have been slow in my department lately and Owen's assistant Nina has been so busy with this new program that he asked if I'd mind if Evelyn would run credit reports in her spare time. I said that'd be fine."

"Do we think Nina is in on this?"

Maya scrunched up her face in thought. "I can't say for sure." Shaking her head, she shrugged. "But I wouldn't rule it out."

"Mrs. Vicks obviously recognized her friend Ursula's name," I said, picking up the thread. Maya nodded. "But, what? She started to investigate?" I tried out the scenario in my own mind. Maya understood my question.

"Yeah," she said. "Why wouldn't she have asked Owen about it directly? It seems more her personality to tell someone about her friend saying the application was fake."

We were both silent, staring without seeing, at opposite corners of the room.

When our eyes met again, I could read that she'd come to the same conclusion I had. Quietly, I said, "Maybe she did tell someone."

"Oh, God," she said.

"What?"

"If I wouldn't have let her take on the extra work, Evelyn might still be alive." Maya's dark eyes welled up and her mouth twisted as she looked away.

"You can't think like that," I said. "And we're talking about murder, here. Do you really believe Owen is capable of killing another person?"

Her face clouded as she shook her head. "I don't know

what to think anymore. I've always found him to be a little weasel, but you're right. I don't see him as violent." Heaving a weight-of-the-world sigh, she added, "But I never thought he'd embezzle either."

"You couldn't have known," I said, reaching across to place my hand on hers. She grabbed it, and squeezed, hard, before meeting my eyes again.

"Thank you for saying that," she said.

"We might be jumping to conclusions, you realize." I stood up and began to pace, tapping my lip with an index finger. "Mrs. Vicks was killed at home, and I distinctly remember bunches of Banner Bank statements on her kitchen table when I saw her that night, and I know they were still there when I went back the night I was attacked."

Maya shook her head, not understanding.

"If Owen killed her, wouldn't it stand to reason that he would've taken all the Banner Bank files with him when he left?" I asked.

She considered this. "Can you swear that every single paper was there? That none of the files were gone?"

"No," I admitted. "But still, why leave any?"

"Maybe somebody came before he could take them all. Maybe that's why he went back the night of the wake. You were there yesterday, right? Were the bank statements there, too?"

I didn't know. Feeling stupid for not thinking about that sooner, I knew I'd have to call Lulinski and see what he knew. I said as much.

Maya had that look of concentration again. "No matter what, we still need to be able to prove this is what's going on."

"So, we need to find out if these accounts are past due?" I asked.

"Exactly. I mean," she said, "what we need is a good long look at Owen's files."

"Can you do that?"

Both elbows on the table, she leaned forward, rubbing her temples. "That's going to be tough. This 'Line of Affluence' program is Owen's baby. He keeps everything on his side of the loan department. There's no way I could spend much time searching through them without somebody wondering what was up."

"If all this falls under his jurisdiction, then how could he claim you approved any of the applications?" I asked.

Her eyes were weary as she lifted one slim shoulder, resigned. "It'd be my word against his, I guess, and there are a couple of girls in that department who he'd easily be able to influence."

I thought about Nina Takami, and nodded.

Rubbing a thoughtful finger along her temple, she closed her eyes for a long moment. "What I need to do is to find out the status of these accounts. See if payments have been made on any of them." Opening her eyes again, she rubbed an eyebrow. "And if we could pull up the original application for Ursula Siewicz, we could compare handwriting." She flashed a weary grin. "I'd have to depend on your expertise for that."

"I don't see how I'm going to get a look at that anytime soon."

"Yeah," Maya said, letting the word drift. "Unless…"

"Unless?"

"We could go in tomorrow, when nobody else is there." Complicit eyes searched mine.

"On a Sunday?"

"I have keys, and as an officer of the bank, I have the alarm codes, too. This way nobody sees what we're up to, right? We could both go in, make copies of everything we need and then we'd be all set."

"Don't you guys have security cameras?" My hands splayed out in front of me, I tried to think. "And how will we explain about me being in the bank during off hours?"

"Cameras are set up only in the bank lobby and in the vault areas. You and I won't be going anywhere but the loan office. And anyway, I'll be there with you. I have a right to go in anytime I need to."

What Maya suggested sounded all perfectly legal, safe, above-board. But it sure the heck didn't feel that way. I took a deep breath.

"Okay," I said. "I'm in."

Lulinski had called me Nancy Drew. I remembered how cautious he'd been about Mrs. Vicks' mail. He'd probably tell me to back off until he got a warrant. But I didn't think we had enough here to get one. Not yet. A tight ball of exhilaration bounced around between my jittery stomach and my eager brain and I couldn't wait to get in there and find the answers.

"And no one will be there on Sunday night?" I asked.

"Nobody but us."

"Good."

Tomorrow, I thought. Tomorrow we'd have this all wrapped up.

"Oh," I said.

"What's wrong?"

"I'm taking my sister downtown tomorrow." Damn it all to hell.

"Well, maybe she can just meet you later, or something."

I shook my head. "She's handicapped." I hated using that expression when talking about Lucy, but it cut through an otherwise drawn-out explanation. "Can we do this maybe after four or five?"

"Sure," she said. "It's already late and I want to go to church tomorrow anyway." Her gaze swept over the table. "Lotta prayin' to do."

My cell phone buzzed, making me jump. I'd forgotten about the message I'd left Lulinski until I saw his number there. "Hi George," I said, using his name for the first time. I knew by the split-second delay in his response that I'd probably taken him aback, but I didn't think Maya knowing I had a detective on the phone would preserve the open lines of communication she and I had established.

"Got your message," he said. "Everything okay? I'm nearby. I can be there in five minutes."

"Just fine," I said, "but I don't think we'll be able to get together tonight." Maya continued to shake her head, staring down at the tabletop. I hoped Lulinski trusted me enough to cut me some slack here and not show up, badge in hand, at Maya's door. "But I'd really like to talk with you tomorrow about a couple of things. Do you think you'll have time?"

Too late I remembered my promise to Lucy. How could I keep forgetting about her? If they ever awarded a 'worst sister' trophy, I was a shoo-in.

"I'll make time," he said, then asked again. "You're sure everything's okay?"

"Yeah, absolutely. I'll talk with you tomorrow, then."

We both hung up and Maya tried to smile. "Boyfriend?"

"No," I said automatically, then wondered what excuse I'd come up with if she pressed me to know who "George" was.

"I didn't think so," she said, then shot me a quizzical look. "The scuttlebutt around the bank is that you're seeing David Dewars."

I held up my hand, staving off that idea. "We went out

twice, but it was definitely more business than pleasure," I said.

Maya's eyes teared up. "He's the one who hired me. Straight out of grad school. Said he saw that I had promise. What's he going to think if he sees all this?" She gestured over the paperwork strewn before us, and a raw, hiccupy sound jumped out of her throat. "What do I do?"

I didn't know how to answer that.

In this quiet dining room, near midnight, I tried to shake off a sudden vulnerable terror—as though Owen would have some omniscient knowledge of what we were doing and would burst through the door any moment, prepared to kill us both.

TWENTY-FOUR

THE NEXT MORNING, I called my aunt early, thanking her profusely for keeping Lucy overnight yet again.

"Anything to help," Aunt Lena said in her chipper voice. Bacon sizzled in the background and my stomach grumbled so forcefully that I was afraid she'd hear it over the phone line. "Were you able to find out anything at that girl's house?"

"A little." A bit of a fib. Although I'd told my aunt last night that I needed to follow up a lead by visiting someone from the bank, I didn't want to go into detail with too many people before I talked with Lulinski. "What time do you think Lucy will be ready to go?" I asked.

She laughed. "That girl likes to sleep late. I'll wake her up when breakfast is ready. She's really looking forward to spending time with you, Alex."

"I'm looking forward to it, too," I said. "How about I come by at ten? I still have to get ready myself, and call a couple of people."

"Better make it a little later," she said. "Moose wants to show her the dove's nest he found outside the garage last night. You know how Lucy is with animals."

I did. "Okay, I'll be by closer to eleven, then."

After showering, I sat at the kitchen table, my hands wrapped around my hot mug of coffee, watching the steam curl upward in mesmerizing grace. I'd left a message on Detective Lulinski's voicemail to call me as soon as he could.

Every sip of the searing coffee that traveled hot down the back of my throat felt like a catharsis of sorts. God, it felt good.

I shut my eyes for a restful moment, picturing Lulinski's face when I gave him the story. The fact that he hadn't answered meant he might still be asleep and I was glad for that. There hadn't been a moment over the past ten days that he hadn't been busy with some aspect of the case. He deserved a break.

So did I. And today, Lucy and I were going to get it.

They'd predicted a high of fifty-three degrees and the sun poured through my back porch windows. With a burst of feel-good anticipation, I cracked one open in order to smell spring in the air. Life was fun again, for the first time in a while. Things were definitely looking up.

Staring out the windows, feeling the light breeze twist past me into the house to chase away the winter mustiness, I took a deep breath to clear my head.

Everything Maya and I had gone over the night before added up. It added up with a precision that told me there'd be no surprises when we checked those accounts this afternoon. I knew they'd be delinquent and I knew we had Owen in our grasp. All that remained was bringing Lulinski up to date, and having him move in for the kill.

A couple of small details nagged at me. Why would Mrs. Vicks have asked Owen to draw up a new will? It made no sense, particularly if she suspected him of such enormous fraud. Maybe there was no other will. That left two possibilities. Either David was mistaken—when he told me about it he said he'd gotten the scoop from Owen, after all—or he and Owen were in collusion, somehow. I shook my head.

David had given me carte blanche at the bank; it'd been Owen and his faithful little helper Nina, who'd shortened my leash where investigating records was concerned. David had been nothing but generous with his time, and he'd even offered a reward for information leading to an arrest in Mrs. Vicks' murder. And, most importantly, I knew to follow the money. As a shareholder of Banner Bank, as well as its president, David involved in embezzling made little sense.

I hadn't kept a copy of the will Barton and I had found the day before, and now I wished I had. I'd love to know who Mrs. Vicks' lawyer was back then, and I felt like an idiot for not grabbing that information when I had the chance.

My watch told me it was just about nine-thirty. Plenty of time to swing by Barton and grab a quick look at that original will.

I was just about ready to go, giving myself a last-minute check in the bathroom mirror when my cell phone buzzed in my back pocket. Expecting Lulinski, I wiped my just-washed hands on my jeans and pulled the phone out to answer. The number on the display took me aback.

"Hello?" I said.

"Hi Alex, it's William," he said in an upbeat, lively tone. "Told you I'd call."

An enthusiastic flush worked its way upward from my chest, till I could feel it warm my cheeks. "Yeah," I said. "You did."

"How's everything going?" he asked.

"Actually, pretty great," I began. Suddenly energized by the thought of being able to share the news with him, I was about to launch into a quick explanation of everything I'd found out over the past week, when he interrupted.

"Good." He gave a dramatic sigh. "It's been really busy out here. They have us running constantly. I would have called sooner, but there just wasn't any time."

"I understand," I said, even though I really didn't. "Learning a lot?"

"It's too much. I can't wait to get back."

"Really?"

"Oh yeah," he said. "It'll be nice to be home."

Despite my best efforts to keep my eagerness down, I felt immensely cheered by that sentiment. "That will be nice," I said, meaning it.

"Well, hey," he said. "I need to get moving here to make the plane on time."

"What time's your flight?"

"Uh…three-ten."

I glanced at my watch. "Isn't it only about seven-thirty out by you?"

"Yeah," he said with a half-laugh I didn't understand. "But I have a bunch of stuff to get done, you know. Return the rental car and all. And get to the airport."

"Sure," I said, still thinking he was giving himself way more time than he needed. From what I knew of the station out there and the airport, it was about a twenty minute trip—tops.

"See you tomorrow," he said.

"Looking forward to it," I said.

We both hung up and I stared at the phone for a long moment. I'd waited all those days for that? Not much of a chat. As I felt my high color drift down to normal, I wondered again at what it was that made me light up when he was around.

Just as I tucked the phone back into my pocket, it buzzed again. This time it *had* to be Lulinski.

Nope. William again.

Suppressing a smile, I hit the button to answer, my mind making the hopeful leap that perhaps he'd realized he'd forgotten to ask about the investigation and he wanted me to bring him up to date. Or maybe ask me out to dinner next Saturday. It was amazing how fast my mind could cover all possibilities.

Hey, I thought, a girl could dream.

"Hello?" I said.

This time William's voice was low, warm with pleasure.

"Tricia," he said.

I felt my heart stutter; the happy flush that had graced my cheeks a moment ago, dropped straight through to the floor, leaving my feet prickling as though they'd both instantly fallen asleep. I opened my mouth, trying to jump-start my brain. "No," I finally managed, stringing the word into two syllables, "This is Alex again." Then I added, "Sorry to disappoint you."

"Oh," he said. He coughed out a nervous laugh.

"Guess you dialed wrong," I said, without inflection.

"No, I just…" I could practically hear his brain working as he stammered. He gave another embarrassed laugh. "Alex. Yeah."

After several very long, very silent, seconds, I said. "Well, I bet you have to get going."

"A bunch of us are getting together," he said. "For a meeting this morning."

I wanted to tell him I didn't really give a hoot. All I cared about right now was getting off the phone as fast as I could. But some perverted masochistic curiosity made me ask, "So, who's Tricia?"

"Oh, uh, just our driver," he said, talking faster now. "I'm supposed to call her to let her know what time to pick me up here. She's just the driver. The station hired her."

The moment he said that, we were cut off. My phone buzzed yet again, almost immediately. This time when I saw William's number, I hit the ignore button and waited a couple of minutes for the icon to pop up indicating that he'd left a message. He did.

"Hi, Alex," he said. "This is William again." Same cheery voice as the first time he'd called—when he'd actually meant to reach me—but I heard that chagrined, almost-laugh one more time. "Sorry I missed you, but I guess you're busy. I'll talk to you when I get back."

Deleting the message, I debated calling him back. Given the circumstances, I didn't want to, but if his plane went down in a fiery crash, I'd probably regret this being our last conversation. I rubbed my eye sockets with my free hand, and leaned my butt against the wall.

Just about a quarter to ten, Chicago time. Quarter to eight in San Francisco. I thought about the long hours before William's three-ten flight and the fact that he mentioned returning a rental car. And yet he'd told me that "Tricia" was a hired driver.

I made a face; it didn't take a rocket scientist to figure this one out.

There had been other notable moments in my life where what I believed soundly clashed with what was actually true. The fact that he'd lied to me told me all that I needed to know. As I stared at the floor, I wondered why these moments of realization never got easier to handle.

I pushed away from the wall and assured myself that airplane travel was very safe nowadays. Pocketing the phone for the last time, I decided the hell with it. I'd take my chances.

THE TUCK INN motel could have been worse, I supposed. Though I'd passed our infamous neighborhood dive hundreds of times over the years, I'd never gotten up close before. Hidden behind a six-foot wall, no doubt designed to keep passersby from recognizing cars in the lot, the

two-story brown brick structure was bookended by black
metal staircases. The surrounding wall sported two wide
openings, one entrance, one exit. I pulled in, and had my
choice of plum parking spots.

Barton's rusty white Buick sat in front of his room,
number one-thirteen, the vehicle's frame leaning low and
to the left. Pulling up next to it, I got out of my own little white car, hoping no one at the front desk could see
me right now. All of a sudden that big brick wall was my
friend. The last thing I needed was to be spotted at the
Tuck Inn by sharp-eyed neighbors heading out for a nice
breakfast after church.

When Barton didn't answer the door after I'd knocked
twice, I moved to the left and tried to see inside the adjacent window, ignoring the grunge of its dirt-encrusted
corners. There were wide oval streaks—whoever washed
the windows here must have swiped a wet rag around in
the middle. From my angle, with the morning sun hitting
it from the east, it looked like a giant had left three enormous thumbprints on the glass.

Cupping my eyes, I peered in.

Nothing but the back end of vinyl-lined drapes and my
own eyeballs' reflection. I rapped on the window, hard,
then leaned back, looking side-to-side, to see if anyone
might have heard me. I listened for movement, but heard
nothing.

Despite the brightness of the clear-sky morning, the air
was crisp and chilled. I pulled my jacket close and listened
harder, trying at the same time to decide what to do next.
Nearby, a cardinal chirped his distinctive call, and traffic
zoomed by on the busy street outside the walled fortress.
Otherwise all remained quiet.

Back at the white wooden door with its fake brass one-thirteen screwed on, I leaned forward and tried to see through the peephole, knowing it would be a futile attempt.

Disappointed, my hand reached for the scuffed knob and tried it, fully expecting resistance.

It turned.

My hand retracted, as if burnt. But now the door stood hairline-crack-open, though not enough for me to see anything in the dark room.

I took a step back, and another glance around, feeling for all intents and purposes like a thief ready to move in when the time was right. A gurgle startled me. It seemed to come from inside the room and I canted my head, waiting for it to repeat, but it didn't. Barton snoring, I decided. If I were any judge of character, and I liked to think I was, I had no doubt that he was sprawled out on his back, slack-mouthed, sleeping off a drunk.

I should turn around and come back later, when he was awake, I reasoned. But when? I had the day planned with Lucy, then another trip back to the Loop with Maya this evening. And although I knew that the information I needed could probably wait, I was here—now—and impatient.

Two fir trees served to obscure my view of the front desk and I hoped that meant it obscured their view of me.

When I heard another snore-like sound, I made my decision. Barton wouldn't even have to know I'd been here.

I pushed the door open and stepped quickly inside, hoping that no one noticed my furtive movements.

Just as I'd predicted, Bart was on his back, open-mouthed and huge. His fully clothed body lay diagonally across the still-made bed, his head tilted backward over the side so I couldn't see his face. I shook my head, feeling smug. So predictable. He'd left on a single lamp, far in the corner, its stained shade listing sideways, and though it helped me to navigate the small area, it did little to cast out the room's dreariness.

Determined to get in and out quickly, I eased forward. Circa 1970 shag carpet, its deep brown pile matted and worn in paths around the bed, looked to be the newest addition to the rummage-sale-reject décor. Avoiding Bart, I tried to decide where he might have stored the will. The smell of old cigarettes and booze, along with the odor of the big man's stale sweat, kept close company as I started for the suitcase in the back, just outside the bathroom. Another smell, something metallic, swirled by with an unpleasant tang, to join the collection of scents that surrounded me. I kept my mouth closed, wishing I could avoid breathing in the filthiness of the room. I couldn't wait to get out of the place.

Crouching, I brought my eyes to the level of the old-fashioned hardback suitcase, wondering why in the world a motel with the reputation of the Tuck Inn's would have invested in valet caddies. Most people staying here didn't bring luggage.

I released the lock, first on one side, and then the other, holding my thumb over the flip-up mechanisms to keep them quiet. Lifting the lid, and standing, as I did so, I moved slightly to my right to allow the meager light to help me in my quest.

It didn't look promising. Before me sat a jumble of dingy underwear, socks, and a couple of shirts. Barton's very personal belongings.

I'd been about to reach into the mess, when all of a sudden it felt wrong. Like I'd crossed a line, somehow. I'd been able to rationalize every step along the path so far, and here I was, ready to plunge my hands into Barton's privacy. It didn't feel right. I didn't like what I was doing. And I knew how I would feel if the situation were reversed.

With regret, I closed the suitcase, pressed shut the locks, and decided to come back another time.

With ginger steps, I made for the door. Barton hadn't moved. Giving his sleeping figure a final glance, I shuddered at my presence here, and wished I'd never come. Fortunately, he was totally unconscious, but as I slid past the bed on my way out, I noticed the abstract pattern on the coverlet.

I stepped closer. The shapeless expanse of deep red beneath Barton's supine body caught the light. It glistened.

Blood.

A lot of blood.

I heard my own gasp, instinctively moving in to get a closer look. My God, what had happened here? I felt like I was in a dream where I needed to run, but couldn't. I moved toward him in slow-motion, holding my left fist up to my nose; the unpleasant smells I'd detected at first were much more intense close up. He reeked of urine and fecal matter. Combined with the close dankness of the room, I felt my stomach clench, and threaten to shove upward. But I had to check if he was alive.

I came around the side of the bed that allowed me to get close to his face, every nerve in my body sending warning signals to an over-stimulated brain, trying to process all this at once. Whoever had done this to him could still be nearby, but I didn't think so. I couldn't think so. I had to check him. That was the only thing I allowed myself to focus on. I forced my mind to blank out thoughts of anything else.

His eyes were open, wide, and terrified.

As I reached my right hand out to search for a pulse in his neck, I saw the bullet wounds. Two, that I could tell. One near his heart, one in his stomach. Both bubbling out tiny fountains of blood.

Just as my fingers touched his extended neck, he let out a deep gurgle, and I jumped back, stifling a scream. My God, he was alive.

I automatically reached for the hotel phone, stopping myself just short of touching it, remembering that this was a crime scene. A crime scene I'd contaminated already. I dug my cell phone out of my back pocket and dialed Lulinski's number from memory.

"It's Bart," I said, thanking heaven when he answered. "He's been shot."

"Where are you?"

"At his hotel room. How quick can you get here?"

"Not long. Did you call 911?"

"No."

"Do it. Do it now."

The blood fountains had slowed, and I didn't know if that was good news or bad as I watched Bart's life ease out from the two wounds, looking like small mouths drooling red. Standing close to him as I spoke to the dispatcher, I maintained a close eye on Barton's chest, willing his respirations to continue, holding my own breath each time they hesitated. I knew I could do CPR if I needed to, but I hoped it wouldn't come to that. "Please hurry," I said.

I remained near him, not knowing what to do or to say. "Help is coming soon," I offered, feeling lame. "You hang in there."

Just as I heard sirens blazing into the parking lot, Barton's chest shuddered. His lips worked, but no sound came out. Two fingers of his left hand jerked, and then were still.

"CALL IT," THE LEAD paramedic said, stepping away from Bart's body. The burly, white-haired fellow had his back to me, but I read disappointment from the slump in his blue-uniform-shirted shoulders.

His younger colleague nodded, looked at his watch and said, "Ten-forty-one AM." When he stood, and began to scribble notes on a clipboard, I looked at him more closely.

A cop appeared at my left. "Over here, please," he said, gesturing me outside the hotel room door.

When he stopped and settled in to start talking, we were in front of the window of the next motel room. "Let me have your name," he said.

At that moment, I realized how violently I trembled. Deep breaths did nothing to slow my heart rate and my legs shook. "Can I sit down?" I asked.

He shot me a dark-eyed glare from a weathered face so reddened and lined, its texture resembled beef jerky. "Why?"

"I'm kind of shaky." I attempted to tuck some errant hair behind my right ear, but my fingers quivered and I couldn't get it to stay.

Fixing me with a grimace, he heaved a protracted sigh. "We can sit in the squad. Will that do?"

Finding it difficult to form words, I simply nodded.

He held open the back door and I slid in, unsurprised this time by the plastic-molded seat. Despite that, I must have looked shell-shocked because he asked, "First time in the back seat of a police car?"

I shook my head. How to explain everything that had gone on since Mrs. Vicks' murder?

"Name," he said, without preamble.

Answering him, I stared out the side window, searching the crowd of medics, officers, and assorted onlookers for Lulinski. One of the trench-coated officials, striding about with an air of authority, looked familiar, and I sat up straighter, fingertips of my right hand pressing against the window with hope.

"You his wife? Girlfriend?"

My hand dropped to my lap in defeat, when I realized the man I'd seen wasn't Lulinski after all.

"Whose?"

"The victim, Barton Vicks."

I believe the brain moves into auto-pilot during traumatic situations. Right now, even as my knees beat a frantic rhythm against one another and my eyes flitted back and forth between the confines of the car and the busyness outside, I knew I wore the look of guilt. My calm omniscient mind tried in vain to convince the rest of me that my trembling was unnecessary, that I had nothing to fear, that I should face this situation as I'd faced many others, with a cool sense of composure.

But then I remembered the small moth-like holes in Barton's body, releasing his lifeblood, murmuring death.

"My God," I said.

"Excuse me?"

My hands shook, my legs shook, and I could feel every one of my internal organs vibrate with a combined sense of fear and regret. "He was alive," I said. "When I got there, he was alive."

"Okay, Ms. St. James," the officer said. "Settle down."

For the first time, I noticed his name badge. "R. Mason." The part of my brain that could still process random thoughts decided he looked like a Richard.

"I am settled," I said with asperity, despite the fact that I was anything but.

"Good," he said with heavy sarcasm, his expression baleful and annoyed. "Then answer my question. How did you know the victim? Were you lovers?"

"No," I said, angry now. "Of course not."

It wasn't this officer's fault. I knew that. I knew he had every right to ask me anything he wanted…I understood that my presence here at the scene of a killing spotlighted me as the prime suspect. But the horror of what I'd seen, coupled with all that had happened over the past ten days made my words come out sharp. My body throbbed with impatience. I needed to talk to Lulinski.

"Listen, missy," the cop said. "Do you have any idea what kind of trouble you're in?"

Pressing my shaking fingertips to my eyebrows, I worked at them, striving to recapture some of that calm I prided myself on. "Yes," I said. "I do. Let me start from the beginning, okay? I can explain."

Turning toward him, I took a deep breath.

His sun-crinkled face expressed patent disdain, as his pen stood poised over his notebook. "I'm waiting."

Seconds later, a gray-suited body appeared in the doorway behind Officer Mason, and I heard Lulinski's voice. "I'll take it from here."

Relief rushed over me so quickly that I called him by his first name, "George!" I said, scooching sideways to get out. That must have startled Mason, because his chin came up in surprise, even as he'd started to slide out of my way.

"You're acquainted with her?" he asked Lulinski.

Nodding to Mason, he repeated, "I'll take it from here," then extended his hand to help me out of the car. Grateful for the strength I felt there, I let go with reluctance when I finally made it to my feet. "Tell me what happened, Alex," he said. His eyes narrowed. "You okay?"

The brisk fresh air with its promise of warmth made me remember my early morning thoughts of spring, and I wondered what happened to the girl who believed in herself so completely just hours before.

Still, I nodded. "Yeah."

He led me to his navy blue sedan, opened the door and helped me into the passenger seat. Inside the closed car, its ashtray full of cigarette butts, I could tell that he'd just finished one. For the first time in my life, leftover smoke smelled like heaven to me.

His gray eyes were intense. "What the hell were you doing here?"

"I wanted to get another look at the will. The one I told you we found in the safe deposit box," I said.

His anger evident, I watched him work his jaw. "What was so goddamn important about the will that you had to come here alone? What if you would've walked in on the killer in the middle of this? Then what? Then I'd have not one, but two more goddamn homicides on my hands, and one of them would have been you."

His fury broke through the barriers of my own, and even as I raised my voice, I was grateful. Anger was so much easier to handle than fear. "I called you," I said. "This morning. Why didn't you call me back?" I flung an accusatory hand in the direction of his coat pocket, where I knew he kept his phone. "You have it turned on. You must have gotten my message. If you would have called me back I wouldn't have come here by myself."

His body relaxed, almost imperceptibly and his eyes lost their unsympathetic gaze. "That was you?"

The gentle tone of his voice was contagious. "Yeah."

Hooking his left elbow over the top of his steering wheel, he nodded, staring out at the people still swarming outside. "I'd just gotten out of bed and turned on the phone when you called me just now. As soon as you told me where you were, I came out. Didn't shower, didn't shave."

Finally taking a good look at him, I noticed the sleep-indentation running the length of his face from stubbled jawline, past his right eye, into his hairline.

"On the way over," he continued, "I saw that I had a voicemail message. Didn't want to take the time to check it until after I got a handle on what was happening here."

"Sorry," I said. I bit my lip. At the rate things were going, this man would never learn to trust me.

"Okay." His mouth set in a line, he turned to face me again, pulling out his spiral-topped notebook. "Now, tell me everything."

IT WASN'T UNTIL we made it to the police station almost an hour later that I remembered Lucy. "Oh my God," I said, with a clutch at Lulinski's jacket. "My sister."

"What?" His body language had shifted to one of swift urgency; he looked ready to bolt back to the car. "Is she home alone?"

"No," I said, holding a hand up to calm us both. We'd made it through the front door and stood now at the circular brick reception desk. "I need to call. Real quick."

Aunt Lena's tone made it clear she was none-too-pleased with me. "Lucy's been waiting all morning for you," she said. "I called your house, and when you didn't answer, I sent Moose over there."

My aunt hadn't yet jumped on the cell phone bandwagon, and she often forgot that I carried one. This didn't seem a good time to remind her she should have tried that number. "I'm at the police station," I said to hold off further rebuke. "Barton Vicks is dead."

"Jesus," she said in a whisper. "First his mother, now him. What happened? Was it a heart attack?"

"He was killed," I began, then caught Lulinski's wide-eyed warning. "I can't talk about it right now. But, please, tell Lucy I'll make it up to her. I promise."

"You can promise all you like, honey," she said, "but it won't do much good anymore. Lucy's been staring out the window since you were due to pick her up. She refuses to move."

"I couldn't come," I said.

"Well, I understand when plans get cancelled, but your sister's different. You know that." She sighed. "I probably shouldn't tell you this right now, but Lucy told me the other day that she thinks she's not important to you. She said she thought you wished she was back at school and out of your life. Now, after this, she's sure of it."

For the second time today, I leaned my butt against a nearby wall and stared at the floor, as my heart gave out. I swallowed the hurt this time, feeling empty. I didn't have the words to fix this. I didn't know how. When I finally spoke, my voice cracked. "Just tell her how sorry I am."

TWENTY-FIVE

Just as I finished giving my statement, my stomach let loose with a ferocious growl. Lulinski's gray brows shot up, gray gaze following. "Hungry?"

"After all I saw this morning, I can't believe I am."

"Come on," he said, "I have to drive you back to your car anyway. I'll buy you lunch. Let me just make a couple of calls."

I offered to walk out to the coffee room to give him privacy, but he waved me back into my chair. Since I had *de facto* permission, I eavesdropped on his two phone conversations, one regarding an update on Laurence Grady, which appeared to give him little information, but the man on the other end of the line had such a booming voice that Lulinski held the phone far away from his ear, and I could even hear his promise of more information soon. The second call was a more personal one; Lulinski spoke briefly to someone named Jenny, and promised to get back to her soon.

We stopped at a storefront Chinese restaurant, set up cafeteria-style where aproned men smiled as they lumped rice and stir-fry onto disposable plates. Lulinski paid for our two trays and we chose a table near the back, away from the rest of the hungry patrons.

"Now that we've got the official report taken care of," he said, "tell me the rest of it." Shoveling beef and broccoli into his mouth, he watched me with wary eyes.

"There isn't anything else." I pushed at my shrimp fried

rice with the plastic fork. "I still can't believe Barton's dead. I can't believe I found him. My God," I said, yet again, "if I'd only seen the blood right away, he might have survived."

Lulinski shook his head. "No," he said with authority. "You were there what, about five minutes? Even ten, fifteen minutes and it wouldn't have made a difference. Those were fatal shots he took."

"You're sure?"

He nodded, head down, apparently concentrating on his food. I was glad not to see his eyes. If he was lying to me, I didn't want to know.

We both ate in silence for a few moments until I asked, "Who do you think did it?"

"Good question," he said. "I'm having them run prints again. Fortunately we have yours on file for elimination," he said, heavy with sarcasm. "Look Alex, how about you try not to be involved in any more murders, okay?" When I shot him a conciliatory smile, he sighed. "But, that forty-two hundred dollars you told me about wasn't found in the room."

"Somebody stole it?"

"Either that, or he gambled it away last night." Lulinski responded to my skeptical look. "Yeah, I don't think he did, either. I think whoever killed him got away with his stash, too."

"You have any ideas?"

His food almost gone, speed-eater Lulinski seemed to weigh his decision to tell me. "Couple of thoughts. First and foremost, Barton Vicks was a gambling man, and we both know he was into his bookie pretty deep."

"You think this was a hit?" I said, just a bit too loudly.

Lulinski's eyes swept over the room before returning to me. "Could be."

"Wow," I said. "But if he's dead, then they never get a chance to recover that twenty-five thousand he owed, right? Killing him doesn't make sense."

He moved his head in a so-so motion. "Depends. If they've been waiting a long time, with nothing coming from Barton, then he's toast."

"Wouldn't the forty-two hundred be good-faith money?"

Lulinski barked out a laugh, but I didn't have a clue as to what was funny.

His eyes took on a hard glint. "Not everyone is 'nice,' Alex. There are bad people in this world. People who will gun down a woman and her three toddlers for ten bucks because drugs make them do it. They're not fair, they don't give a whit about promises, or good-faith gestures. They're cold. They want their cash. That's it. And if somebody is dead weight, and they figure they won't get any more out of him, maybe then he's worth more to them as a deadly example to their other lowlife clients."

I didn't have any response.

Lulinski sighed. "There's another possibility."

"What's that?"

"If Laurence Grady killed Evelyn Vicks, then chances are good he took Barton out too."

"Why would he have killed Mrs. Vicks? What's in it for him?"

"Barton was about to inherit half of the estate. With him out of the way, Grady's girl Diana will get everything."

"One problem with that," I said. "I don't think Diana knew she was related—or even knew anything about the will. So it stands to reason that Grady didn't either."

He pursed his lips, thinking. "You told me he was accompanying Diana to Dr. Hooker's, right?"

I nodded.

"So, Diana may or may not know that her landlady is her grandmother."

I interjected. "I'm betting she didn't know."

"Okay. But, Evelyn Vicks knew that Diana was her granddaughter, right? Over time, I'm sure they'd developed a close relationship. How could they not?"

The question seemed rhetorical, so I let him continue.

"Grady now has a window into Mrs. Vicks life, through Diana. Whether she meant to or not, Diana probably fed the loser enough information to let him know about the woman's finances, and her habits. Evelyn Vicks became an easy mark."

"But...to kill her?"

"My guess is he didn't plan on that. Criminals get nervous, too. Often with tragic results."

I shook my head. "Very iffy. Then why kill Barton?"

"Even if Grady doesn't know the true relationship there, Barton is in the way. And maybe he didn't set out to kill him, either. Maybe, like Evelyn Vicks, it was a robbery gone wrong."

"You really think that?"

Lulinski guzzled down the remaining coffee in his Styrofoam cup. "I've got three possibilities and I can't afford to dismiss any one of them until I have solid proof. Most likely scenario has Grady killing Evelyn Vicks. He's got the means, he had the opportunity, and all we need now is a motive. Second choice is a random act of violence. Thieves break into the victim's home and wind up killing her. And if that's the case, then Barton's murder coming on the heels of his mother's is just tragic coincidence."

He smiled, adding, "Of course, I don't believe in coincidences."

"So, what's number three? Owen Riordan?"

"You got it."

I'd about finished up my platter of Chinese food, amazed that I'd been able to eat so much in so little time. At the rate I was going, I might be able to race Lulinski next time we lunched together. With any luck, I thought, we wouldn't ever have to. Two murders in two weeks were too many. I'd be content never to have to deal with the good detective again—at least not in an official capacity.

"So you believe Maya and I might be onto something?" I asked.

"Could be," he said. "But I don't like the idea of the two of you skulking around in the bank by yourself at night."

"We'll be fine," I said, with a gusto I didn't feel. The specter of Bart's body moving from life to death before my eyes, still chilled me, down deep.

"You trust this Maya?" he asked, not for the first time.

"I do," I said with impatience.

"There's no way she can be setting you up?"

"Listen," I said, "I went to her with the information, not the other way around. And the reason I did was because I know she's okay." It sounded lame, but I knew I was right. "Okay?"

Lulinski made a face. "This kind of white collar crime is hard to carry out without help. I'm thinking there's a good chance he's working with at least one other person. Someone who can cover his ass."

My mind made the immediate connection. "Nina Takami," I said.

"Come again?"

"A woman who works for him," I said. "She was ready to haul off and deck me when I needed Mrs. Vicks' files."

"Give me her name again."

I did, spelling it from memory of the placard on her desk, then added, "If Owen's working with anyone, I guarantee it's her."

He nodded. "If you come up with the kind of information you're talking about, we'll have enough to investigate Riordan, and this woman, too. Mostly, I want to see if his blood samples and fingerprints match up to any of the ones we've found at any of the crime scenes." Holding up a finger, he looked like he wanted to say something else, but changed his mind. "I can't go in with you," he said. "Not without a warrant. But if you two find information that you believe points to someone's guilt, you have every right to bring it to my attention." He focused on a far corner of the restaurant for a moment. "It'll be best if you don't tell Maya that you plan to hand the information over to me. If she goes in there, with that knowledge…" he waggled his head in a so-so motion, "it could be construed that she acted as my agent. That'd screw everything up." Lasering his focus back to me, he added, "But as soon as you're out of there, I want to know. Make sure you're okay."

"What about Jenny?" I asked, remembering his phone call earlier. "Didn't I hear you promise to be home soon, or something like that?"

"Yeah," he said. "My daughter. She worried about me running out of the house so fast this morning."

"Your daughter?" That took me by surprise. "How old is she?"

I expected him to say eleven or twelve.

"Twenty-one. Graduating college in May, summa cum laude." The pride in his voice was nothing compared to the sparkle in his eyes. "She's home for spring break from Notre Dame."

"Wow," I said. "You don't look old enough to have a college grad daughter."

"Yeah, right," he said, but he grinned.

I was enjoying this glimpse into Lulinski's personal life. "Any other kids?"

"Nah." He shook his head, looked away. "Jenny's mom died real young," he said quietly. "She's had it rough all these years with just me for a parent."

Impulsively, I touched his hand. "Sounds like you did pretty well."

"Thanks. She's a good kid."

Leaning away again, I frowned at him. "You ought to lay off the smokes. For her sake."

He stood. "You women all like to nag, don't you?" Grinning, he cleaned up his dish and reached for mine, tossing them both in the nearby wastebasket. "But, we're not talking about smoking now, we're talking about you and this Maya pulling your little detective stunt. I don't like the idea of you taking chances. Too much can go wrong."

"Nothing's going to go wrong," I said, this time feeling a bit more confident. "Maya has the keys, the codes, and the authority to be there any time she wants. She told me she's gone in on weekends before, so this isn't going to raise any eyebrows."

"What time you meeting her?"

I glanced at my watch. Three o'clock already. "I'm supposed to be at her house about an hour from now. We better go."

On the ride back to my car, still parked in the Tuck Inn's lot, I thought about Lucy. I was torn. I wanted to call her, to apologize to her personally—but calling her now, when I still couldn't make time for her, seemed somehow worse than waiting. After all, I reasoned, Aunt Lena had probably come up with some diversion, and a call from me now would only serve to remind Lucy of my absence. Unsure of how to handle the situation, I chose to wait.

Lulinski made sure I got safely into my car, and waited till I pulled away, in the direction of Maya's, before taking

off again. He'd said something about following up with the
station regarding Grady before we left.

MAYA DROVE FASTER than I expected, zipping through the
scatter of slower-moving vehicles heading north on the
Dan Ryan expressway. We'd taken her car, a late-model
maroon Toyota, since it bought us free parking in the Banner Bank lot. In typical March fashion, the morning promise of spring had dissolved into yet another overcast, cold
evening. Gray sky, gray streets, and a certain heaviness in
the air sat like a chunk of bad food in my gut.

Wearing jeans, sweatshirts and black leather jackets, we
could have been two young women out for a night of fun
exploring Chicago. Instead, we were on a mission, and the
nervous tension put a damper on conversation.

She'd cracked her window open, slightly, and the breeze
that sneaked in had a promising feel to it. Maya's hair was
pulled tight into a ponytail, not moving, though the air current danced tendrils around my face.

"What if we're wrong?" she asked, her eyes on the road.

"We're not wrong."

She blinked acknowledgment, still staring straight
ahead.

I blew out a breath and watched the landscape zoom by.

My cell phone buzzed just as we passed fifty-first street
overpass. Fitting, since it was Lulinski on the phone. "Hi,"
I said, then added, "The eagle is in flight."

"Ha ha," he said, without mirth. "Listen, we need to
hold off on the plan for tonight."

"Why?" I asked. "What's wrong?"

Maya's face went slack and she glanced over at me with
panicked eyes.

I shook my head, in a "don't worry" movement.

"I can't get down there for another couple of hours. I'm

in the middle of taking a statement from one of the guests at the Tuck Inn motel. Guy just came in. Says he might've heard a scuffle, might've seen somebody leaving Bart's room. Didn't think much about it until he found out about the murder. Wants to come in and do the right thing." Lulinski snorted.

"You don't believe him?"

"I can't afford not to. Says he's thinking he might've heard gunshots. Thought they were tire blowouts, except there were two of them. There's enough here for me to want to follow up." He paused. "And, they picked up Grady. They're bringing him here."

"Where did they find him?"

"Back in town. Caught him leaving Diana's hospital room." Lulinski covered the mouthpiece and spoke to someone nearby. "Look, I have to go. Grady should be here in another hour or so. If I get finished with my motel witness and get the rest of this done, I can be down there by seven."

By seven I planned to be home, making amends with Lucy. "We'll be fine by ourselves."

Maya nodded, and her teeth were clenched. "Let's just get this done."

"Alex." Detective Lulinski's voice was serious. "I don't want you getting yourself into another situation."

"We won't. I promise," I said. "If anything goes wrong…anything at all, I'll call you, okay?"

I heard him blow out an exasperated breath, but before he could argue, I interrupted. "We're just about at the twenty-second street exit," I said. "By the time you're ready to go, we'll be finished. Okay?"

He mumbled something I didn't catch.

"What?"

"Keep the phone on. All the time," he said. "I'm going to call you to check periodically."

"Deal."

Maya and I made great time, pulling in just before four-thirty. As she handed her parking ID to the young black man in the booth, he looked up at us in surprise. "Ms. Richardson, what are you doing here, working on a Sunday?" he asked, with a bright smile.

"Hi, Jared," she said, smiling back. "I just need to pick something up."

He handed back her pass with his left hand, while operating the gate lift with his right. The red and white angle-striped bar began to rise.

I poked her arm.

"Oh, Jared?" she asked, still smiling.

He seemed happy that she wanted to talk with him further. "Yeah?"

"Anybody else come in? I mean, is anyone else from the loan department working here today?"

His face clouded momentarily. "No, can't say that anyone else has been here. Why?"

As we'd arranged, she forced a show of disappointment. Had Jared's answer been different, I would have piped up with a sudden remembered engagement elsewhere.

Maya sighed. "Darn. I have to talk to Mr. Riordan about something," she said. "He hasn't been in today at all?"

"No, ma'am," he said.

"Well, thanks anyway," she said. And with a wave, we drove in.

TWENTY-SIX

OUR FOOTSTEPS MADE echo-ey clicks in the tall atrium, their hollow tip-tap sounds bouncing upward from the marble floor and along the walls that reached heavenward toward the skylit roof. All four glass-walled elevators sat at the ground level, doors open, like wide, hungry mouths. Not one had any interior lights on, and I hesitated before stepping in.

"This one," Maya said, pointing to the one nearest me. Heading toward the security desk in the corner of the lobby, she reached around to unlatch a short door just behind it, allowing her access to the controls. She worked quickly, face down-turned, concentrating. I moved closer to her and stood, leaning on the chest-high cherry wood half-circle, watching as she inserted one of her keys into a metal control box.

"There we go," Maya said, her head popping up, eyes alert. The elevator chimed. "Our chariot awaits."

"No security staff?" I asked, looking around as we stepped in and pressed the button for the tenth floor.

She shrugged. "He must be making the rounds. We have a skeleton crew here over the weekends. You saw Jared—he's our first line of defense at the garage. During last year's budget cuts, we slashed the weekend security down to a bare minimum. It's dead here on Saturdays and Sundays. Since everything's under lock and key, anyway, and we have alarm codes everywhere, the bank directors said, 'What's the point?'"

The gold doors slid closed with a solid click, leaving us in vacuum-like silence. No music. Nothing.

She was right about it being dead here. I glanced down as the glass elevator rose slowly upward. The atrium lobby was darker than I'd ever seen it. The only light in the place came from low-beam security lamps and the evening-gray sky above.

Maya stared at the numbers above the closed door, her smooth dark face set in concentration. I wanted to talk, to lessen the tension somewhat, but I had nothing to say.

We both jumped at the "ping" that signaled our arrival at ten, and when the doors opened to the dark corridor, Maya stepped forward. "Come on," she said.

My eyes became adjusted to the darkness, appreciating the occasional pale bulb that graced the floorboards, illuminating the door to the loan department enough for us to see.

She unlocked it, with yet another key. "I don't want to turn on the lights in Owen's half of the office," she said. "There's no way I can explain us being in there. If we hear someone coming, we can just pretend we're on our way out."

The loan department itself was small, and once we passed the reception desk, Maya led me to the right side of the office where six-foot tall cubicle walls separated work areas. "I sit over there," she said, pointing to the left.

It looked like there were six desks between the two departments, three to a side. Maya's end of the office, the west corner, had a view of the atrium lobby along one wall of windows, a view of the street on the other. Owen's northeast corner view overlooked the cold streets below on both sides, and, bathed in blue light, we moved toward his desk.

The feeling that had come over me while staring down at Barton's suitcase full of dirty underwear rushed up, again. "You know," I said, "the faster we're out of here, the better."

Even in the dimly lit room, I could see the anxiety in her eyes. "Yeah. This is creeping me out. Like I'm doing something illegal," she said. "Any time I've come here before I've waltzed right in and never thought twice about it." She made a slow circuit of the room with her gaze, still whispering. "Right now I feel like someone's watching our every move."

I'd been in my own office late at night, many times. Contented, quiet times. Despite the fact that I'd been keenly aware of my aloneness, I'd never been afraid. Never felt a sinister force pressuring me to get out, the way I did now.

"Where are the files we need?" I asked.

"The files," she said, and I could tell that my question had focused her again. "This way."

I slid my jacket off as I walked. Anxiety made me sweat, and the heavy lining inside the leather added to the heat prickles dripping along my back. Maya noticed my movement and shook her jacket off too, sticking her tongue out and fanning her face.

She headed for a four-foot tall, three-drawer filing cabinet, its back to the windows. Pulling out yet another key, I questioned her about it. "You have keys to Owen's files?"

She shook her head, concentrating on the ring of choices. The keys' jangling and our breathing were the only sounds in the room. "All the files operate with the same key. Makes things easy for the support staff."

Dropping our jackets and purses on a nearby chair, we pulled open the middle drawer, labeled "L-Si". About two feet wide, its folders hung perpendicular to the edge of the drawer. Maya moved toward the end of the alphabetical file, and flipped through the last ten inches of records, using the tips of her fingertips, sometimes adjusting her position to make the most of the room's scant light.

"Hang on," I said, reaching for my purse. I pulled out my Mag-lite. Though small, its high beam would make all the difference in our expediency.

"Here we go," she said at last. "Siewicz, Ursula."

I thunked the drawer closed with my hip, and we opened the manila folder on top of the cabinet, both of us scrutinizing the signature on the enclosed application by flashlight.

"It doesn't look anything like the same handwriting to me."

"Me either," Maya said. She let loose a long sigh. "Okay good, now let's take a look at the repayment reports and we should be all set."

I tapped the original document. "Can we take this with us?"

She started shaking her head before the words came out. A look of angry frustration crossed her face. "Darn it anyway," she said, moving toward a location along the window that straddled the two sides of the loan department. "I knew we were going to want copies." Stepping close to a copier, she reached beneath an overhang at the back of it and flipped a switch that made it light up and break into a series of hums and clicks. A half-minute later the sounds quieted, but the digital screen warned that the machine wasn't ready for use, yet. "This thing takes forever to warm up," she said. "I should have turned this on when we first got here."

"Don't worry, we have more to do," I said. "Where are those payment schedules?"

"Those," she said, tapping a finger against her lips, "ought to be over along this wall." I followed her to a perimeter wall. A low table held at least a dozen flat files. Oversized cardboard covers, in light blue and navy, they

were binders that could be expanded as more and more
sheets were added. The ones before us held thick computer
printouts, some of them fatter than a phone book.

She flipped up the binders on two before finding what
she sought in the third one. She paged down several inches
and said, "Hmmph."

"What?"

"Give me that list of names and account numbers we
drew up."

I did.

She worked at comparing the information for a solid
minute while the hum of the copier finally lessened. Again,
we were in deep, dark quiet, with only Maya's page-flip-
ping breaking the silence, the narrow beam of light I held,
focused on the sheets before us. I pulled in a breath when
Maya glanced up. "It's here," she said.

"You're sure?"

Her dark eyes never leaving mine, she nodded solemnly.
"Part of me wanted it to be a big mistake. I didn't realize
how much I wanted to be wrong, till now." I wondered if
she could hear the trembling in her voice. "Owen has gotten away with…" her eyebrows came together, "millions."

"Let's get these over to the copier and get what we
need," I said. "Couple minutes, we're outta here, right?"

She handed me the fraudulent application for Ursula
Siewicz, then turned to unfasten the thin metal arms that
bound the computer printouts tight. Sliding the restraints
to one side, she lifted up one of the skinny metal arms.

"You hear that?" she asked. Even in the darkness I could
see the tension in her neck muscles as she strained forward.

I shook my head, listening, too. "I didn't hear anything."

We waited a long moment before breathing.

"It's okay," I said, "I'm just as nervous as you are."

She returned to her task, sliding those tiny metal restraints the other direction, in order to free the second arm, but this time, I noticed that her fingers shook.

Across the room, a phone jangled, splitting the silence with its shrill ring.

I yelped, as did she. I reached out a hand, grabbing Maya's arm to steady us both as the phone rang again. "Just the phone," I said.

Her head canted and she stared across the night-blue expanse. "I think that's my phone," she said, her voice hoarse. Her fearful eyes widened so much that I could see white all the way around her irises. She clutched my hand. "Who would be calling me? Is it Owen? Does he know I'm here?"

After five long rings, it finally stopped, but the noise echoed in my mind in the sudden silence. I let go of Maya and tried my best to keep my voice soothing and low. "Let's get this done."

She nodded, but looked unconvinced.

"Ten minutes," I said. "we're back in your car and on our way home."

"Ten minutes," she repeated so softly I could barely hear the breathy words.

"Come on." I opened the lid of the copier, placed the application face down on the glass, and hit the square green button. The machine whooshed to life, shooting a bright-light glow out from its edges as it scanned the page. "Let me get one more," I said, and hit the button again.

Maya held onto the inch-thick computer printout up to her chest like a school girl, and as soon as I finished, she lifted the lid and set the original in place. "Two," she said, changing the setting and starting her copies.

There were over fifty accounts listed on each page of the report, so within minutes, we had all we came for.

"Okay?" I asked, as Maya lifted the last original from the glass. "We done?"

She nodded, rearranging the pages back into their proper folds. "I'll put this back, you turn off the copier, okay? The switch is behind it."

One second later, the copier was utterly still, and the deafening silence returned, keeping us in whispers. "Almost ready?" I asked, as Maya slipped the silver brackets back over the top of the report then moved to lock the drawers we'd opened.

"Let's go," she said.

I'd just shoved all our copies in my purse and we'd donned our jackets when Maya made a little noise that stopped me.

"What?"

"We didn't put the original application back."

"Damn," I said, digging it out from my stash.

As Maya pulled out her keys again, I heard their now-familiar jangle.

And, I heard something else.

My hand shot out, of its own accord, silencing the musical clinking of the keys in Maya's hands. She stared at me. She'd heard it, too.

It was the elevator. And it was moving.

I shoved the original application back into my purse and grabbed Maya, pulling her toward her side of the office. I had the vague idea that if we were on that side, and pretending to leave, then no one would be the wiser about our true purpose here today.

"Turn the lights on," I said.

"I can't," she said, pointing to a corner near the door. "Too far."

I heard the sickeningly recognizable sound of the elevator doors opening. Someone had gotten off at this floor.

Flashlight off. I stuck it into my back pocket as we ran toward her desk, and once there, I slowed us both to a stroll, trying in vain to control my breathing. "We're okay," I whispered. "We're on our way out. Remember that."

Her head nodded, but her eyes were wild with panic.

We stood there, in front of her desk, me slightly in the lead with a protective hand extended behind me, like a parent would reach for a child before crossing the street. I felt every nerve in my body go taut, standing there, listening. Realizing that anyone in the hallway would be nearly invisible to us, but that if we stepped out beyond the cubicle separator, we would be backlit by the wall of night-sky windows, I yanked at Maya's arm. Forget trying to explain our being here. "Get down," I said.

We waited and listened for long minutes. Nothing. Not a breath, not a footstep, not a word.

"Maybe it's nothing." Maya's hopeful whisper seemed over-loud in the quiet.

I swallowed. Shook my head.

Pressing a finger to my lips, I pulled at her jacket sleeve, indicating she should follow me. I swung my purse so that the strap crossed my chest, to keep it from swinging free as we crawled. I turned to Maya, indicating she should do the same.

The oppressive heat made breathing through my mouth a necessity. Perspiration collected along my hairline, under my arms, and across my waist. As sweat droplets made their way down my forehead into my eyes I shook my head to clear my vision. We could continue creeping along the floor, and, if we were very careful, make our way back to the elevator.

As I put one hand flat on the carpet, followed by another, followed by my knees, I plotted out our path. If it was open, the elevator would be our best shot at escape. If not, the "ding" would alert anyone else on this level to our position and there wouldn't be enough time for the doors to open, us to get inside, and the doors to close again before he'd be upon us.

If the doors were open, we could creep in silently, hit the button for the first floor, and be on our way down just as he realized we were there. It could work.

Knee, hand, knee, hand. I glanced back at Maya. She was staying with me, her face a mask of intensity. Good girl.

We crawled to the far wall of filing cabinets; in our dark jackets and jeans we could be chameleons and disappear into the background. We just needed a minute's head start. A half-minute, even.

My right knee came down on the side of hard plastic push-pin. Biting the insides of my cheeks, I resisted the urge to cry out in pain. Concentrate, I told myself.

We had only about twenty more crawl-steps to go, but the elevator was around the doorway and I wouldn't be able to see if it was open or not without coming out into the pale corridor light.

Our only other option was the stairway. If we made it to the hall unnoticed, we could stand up and run to the stairs. With a good enough head start, we could make it down ten flights ahead of him. Sure we could.

With a lurch, my stomach remembered an article I'd read once about danger in stairways, and how they were particularly hazardous places. Most office building stairways didn't allow exit until one reached the first floor. We'd have to make it all the way down, or be trapped if the intruder beat us down by taking the elevator.

We would have to get to the elevator first, noise or no noise.

I'd been straining to hear any sound at all from anywhere on the floor. I heard nothing. Part of me wanted to believe that either the security guard had made a quick stop on ten and then left again, or that the elevator had mysteriously taken a trip down and back up by itself.

I could feel my heart. People always say that, but I never really believed it. Now, I knew it was true. My heart beat, and I felt the pulsations in my eardrums speed up as we neared the open loan department doors.

No one there.

Bracing myself, I moved forward just slightly, enough to peer around into the corridor. All I wanted was to see if the elevator was there. To see if it was open. To see if we could make our break.

A fast shadow movement from my left made me gasp, but before I could react, Owen Riordan jerked to a stop in front of my flat-on-the-floor hands.

"Don't move." I didn't. His voice was harsh and high, breathless. "Okay, now, slow," he said, "get up." Frozen to the spot, I stared up at him; he kicked at my shoulder with his foot. "I said, get your ass up."

Scrambling to my feet, I glanced at Maya, who cowered in terror.

When I turned back, I saw why. Owen held a gun close to my face, its long silver barrel lined up so perfectly at my eyes, that I could see the scalloped edges of the hollow bullets in its cylinder.

TWENTY-SEVEN

"YOU GODDAMN NOSY bitch," he said. The small baseboard lights from the surrounding corridor lit up Owen's face from below, emphasizing his scowl and hollowing out his eye sockets. I couldn't read him.

Shoving the gun into my shoulder, he pressed me back against the wall until I bumped into Maya, close behind. I grabbed her hand, squeezing it in a show of bravery I didn't really feel.

"What the hell is wrong with you, Maya? I thought you were a smart girl."

She didn't answer, but I could feel her body tremble against mine. If Owen had been the guy who'd attacked me and Diana—and right about now I decided he was—then I knew better than to underestimate him. Beneath that burgeoning layer of paunch, the man had power. But this time, I told myself—this time I was not going down so easily.

When he spoke again, his words were sharp. "Did you get everything you came for? Think you're some kind of detectives? Got old Owen all figured out?"

I'd gotten over the initial shock of being discovered, and my mind started to plot out escape routes. Something about the way he handled the weapon—the way he waved it between us, the way his body swaggered as he did so—seemed theatric. As if the gun imbued him with a power that he didn't know how to control.

"What do you mean?" I asked, working to achieve nonchalance, but the unevenness of my voice was a dead give-away. "We were just leaving."

"Cut the crap. I know goddamn well what you came for. And what you think you found." Moonlight glinted off the barrel of the gun that he waved between us, again. "Empty out your purses."

My pepper spray. It was in there. I reached into my cavernous bag, fingers making a quick search for the trusty weapon.

"No, wait," he said. "Drop your purses. On the floor."

"But—" I started to say.

"Drop them!" He screamed. We dropped our bags; they made clanging thunks as they hit the ground. "Now...back away from them."

With the tip of his tongue sticking out of the corner of his mouth, he kept an eye trained on both of us as he crouched to pick up both purses. The gun pointed upward, and if I'd have tried to smash his chin with a well-placed kick, I risked having him yank the trigger and the gun take off half my face.

Owen must have noticed me eyeing the gun, because he took a step backward, effectively out of my reach when he stood up again. Backing away two more steps, he upended both purses on the nearest desk, nabbing the original application I'd taken, and all the paperwork we'd so carefully researched and copied. One-handed, using the desk as a brace, he folded the information into quarters and shoved the thick wad into his back pocket.

I noticed, for the first time, that he wore skin-tight leather gloves. "Stupid," he said under his breath. Looking up at Maya, his voice took on a tone of blame. "Why can't you stupid women ever leave things alone? Goddamn nosy bitches. All of you." He kept watching us, even as he continued to dig through our belongings.

If I made a move, Maya would move with me. I forced myself to believe that she would, otherwise, I risked the paralysis of indecision.

"Did you know," Owen said, in an almost conversational tone, "that you were going to be dead today?" His pale eyes glanced up, waited for a response from us. When we gave him none, he set back to his purse-search. "Isn't that something? It's weird isn't it? Knowing when you'll die. And knowing there isn't a thing you can do about it."

Like hell, I thought, but hearing his words shook me.

"Ah," he said, "here's one." He held up Maya's cell phone. Even in the dark I saw his grin, the triumphant head-swagger. "Now where's the other one?"

My cell phone sat in my back jeans pocket, as always set to vibrate rather than ring. With a start, I remembered Lulinski had promised to keep in touch. I whispered a prayer that if he did call, I'd be able to stifle my reaction to the sudden buzz.

"I don't have mine," I said.

Owen stopped, mid-search. "I don't believe you."

"Fine," I said, forcing bravado into my voice. "Keep looking. Don't let me stop you."

"Then, where is it?" he asked, with just enough inquisitiveness that let me know he believed me.

"At home," I lied. "Charging the battery."

He seemed to weigh the answer, finally deciding to believe me, because he gave up on the pile on the desk. I tried hard not to show visible relief.

"Okay, over there," he said, gesturing with the gun.

"Where?" I asked.

He angled himself to my side, and pushed at the back of my shoulder. He must have pushed Maya, too, because she bumped into me, catching herself from falling by grabbing onto my arms.

His free hand did a quick sort of the desktop, grabbing Maya's keys in his fist. "Here," he said, thrusting them at her. "You clever girls can figure it out. Open up those files. The ones you thought you were so smart to uncover."

My feet were heavy; I took small steps back toward the window wall, as if moving slower could somehow keep me alive longer.

Maya fumbled with the keys, her fingers shaking worse than before. I watched her down-turned face as she tried to steady herself by gripping the key with both hands. When it finally clicked open, her dark eyes came up to meet mine, silently asking what we could do. Her teeth bit down on her lip, turning it almost white, and her chin trembled. I had no answer for her.

Owen pulled out another cell phone. Not Maya's. He held the bright screen at arm's length as he dialed. Whoever he called must have been waiting. "Hey," he said almost immediately. With a glance at his watch, he added. "You got what we need?" A smile shadowed his face for the briefest moment. "Good. It's all clear. Come on up."

An accomplice. Lulinski had been right.

"My office." he said, again into the phone. "Yeah. Both of them." He stared at us as he spoke, the blue ambient light giving his face a pale glow. He nodded. "Take your time," he said. "We'll be here."

When he ended the call, he lifted an eyebrow at me. In that small gesture I read all the smug superiority, echoing the fact that he stood on the right end of the gun and I did not—that life wasn't fair—that I'd lost. I moved, slightly, wanting to beat his ugly face with both fists, but the weapon pointed at my mid-section froze me in my tracks.

"Sit," he said, like he was talking to dogs. I turned fast, to glance at Maya, then behind us, stupidly looking for a chair. "On the floor," he said, his voice gaining intensity. "We've got work to do."

Maya and I sat next to one another, our backs to one set of unopened filing cabinets. Owen perched his butt on the corner of a nearby desk, one foot on the ground, the other suspended, swaying. His aim never wavered. "I could handle two of you by myself," he said with a shrug, "But there's too much at stake to take any shortcuts now."

I was less interested in what he had to say, than I was in figuring a way out. Whoever he'd spoken to on the phone, and I had no doubt that it was Nina Takami, was apparently en route. I knew she was small, but there'd be two of them and two of us, plus the gun, diminishing our chances even further. If we were going to move, we had to do it now.

Keeping my gaze on Owen, I snaked my right hand toward Maya, using my pinky finger to tap hers, hoping she'd understand. With a quick look toward the elevator corridor, Owen stretched out his back, and I chanced a look at Maya. I saw in her eyes a determination that matched mine.

I cleared my throat. "How much longer?"

"Shut up."

Maya shifted. "I have to go to the bathroom."

Owen rolled his eyes. "What, do you think I'm stupid? You gotta piss, be my guest. Piss all over yourself."

I ran a hand through my hair, trying to push the cold sweat out of my face, and he sat up, both feet hitting the ground, his eyes flashing with ready vigilance.

We couldn't try to stand without alerting him. His position was too far for me to reach with either my hands or my feet; so any wild thoughts about disarming him with some heretofore undiscovered superhero strength on my part was out of the question. My mind, fueled by the fear of that gun going off before I'd had a chance to really live, raced with crazed possibilities.

I still had my flashlight. If I could ease it out of my pocket and manage to toss it without him seeing my move-ment, it might create a momentary distraction. Enough for us to move.

A very long shot. But choices grew more slim every moment—I decided I would make this work. I had to.

I counted on the fact that Owen couldn't see into the darkest corners where the filing cabinets met the floor. I pushed my fingers into the split where my pocket opened, tugging at the flashlight by its rubber end—inching it up, into my palm with a slow, ferocious terror that released sweat at my hairline to trickle down my face.

It stuck.

I tugged harder, trying my best not to show any outward sign of movement. My fingers dug in deeper, but the wet-ness that gathered between them made the rubber-coated light slippery and hard to move. I wanted desperately to blow my bangs off my forehead, but didn't want to risk any undue attention.

As it was, Owen's unwavering gaze had begun to shift. He would watch us for long moments before chancing a quick look down the elevator corridor. We wouldn't have much time before Nina Takami joined us.

The next time he looked away, I leaned hard on my left palm, lifting my back end slightly off the floor—just enough to give the flashlight wiggle room. The fingers of my right hand got a solid grip and I had it in my palm.

At that very moment, my phone buzzed, shooting its vibration into the other pocket on my backside with a sud-denness that made me jump.

"What?" Owen started, stood, came a half-step closer now, the gun that much closer to my face.

The phone vibrated again. This time I didn't move. "Cramp," I said.

"Bullshit." Owen stared hard at my right side, his eyes flicking to mine as though he'd find an answer there. I remained as still as I could, hoping the vibration wasn't loud enough for him to pick up. When it buzzed a third time, I coughed.

"What's behind you?"

I shook my head. "Nothing."

He looked at me, as if trying to read my eyes. As if he'd find some answer there. "Show me your hand. Slow."

"Okay," I said, opening my fingers before pulling my hand forward. The flashlight dropped to the floor behind me with an almost inaudible thump. I held my empty hand out for his inspection.

Satisfied, he nodded, then looked toward the elevators and down at his watch. He must have had a hard time reading it because he leaned ever so slightly toward the cold night windows, adjusting the angle of the watch's face to catch the light.

I gripped the flashlight in a fast snatch, and threw it hard in an overhand arc, pulling my hand back behind me, fast—trying to look as though I hadn't moved. The tiny tool hit a far wall with a small, but noticeable bump.

He leaped up, shouting, "What was that?"

I scrambled to my feet, reaching for his arm, hoping to either grab the gun from him, or to force his hand back toward his own face. I *would* pull that trigger. It was kill or be killed, and I had no intention of going down.

"What the—" He twisted his body, but I'd latched on tight.

"Run," I said to Maya, but she'd grabbed him from behind, helping me.

Women don't have upper body strength. The adage

flashed through my mind and I fought the despair accompanying it. In my case, it was too true, and Maya's skinny arms couldn't be much stronger than mine.

Damn it. Every muscle strained to keep from losing, but his superior power was killing me. Hampered by my slippery hands, the tight fabric of my leather jacket, and the fact that we were slight women fighting a two-hundred pound man, I felt my hold on him lessen with every slow-motion second.

His arms had gone high over his head, both hands gripping the gun, and I fought to keep it pointed upward, away from us. We three danced like this, a vicious *ménage a trois*—his breath, coming in short pants across my face, souring my stomach with every hot blast. If I could jam his eyeballs, I might have a chance, but that meant dropping my straining arms from their protective perch—depending on Maya to keep that gun pointed away.

A woman's strength is in her legs.

I gritted my teeth—and shot a knee into his balls with strength borne of fury and disgust.

With a whoof, he doubled, his arms jamming down, an elbow grazing my head. Maya toppled to the floor behind him, and I heard a solid crack that could have been her head against the desk. I lunged for the gun, but he backed up fast, extending his arm, aiming at me again. His left hand cradled his private parts and the twisted expression on his face told me my life was a trigger-pull away from ending. His arm shook, the gun's barrel wavered.

We both heard the sound at the same time. The elevator.

I caught sight of Maya, behind Owen, still on the floor. She tried to stand, but Owen pushed her down, backing up as he did so, to keep us both in his sights at the same time. He'd gotten out of my reach, and his voice came out hoarse, cracked, as he screamed filthy names at me.

I took a small measure of satisfaction out of the fact that I'd hurt him. Small satisfaction, because he was ready to kill us both, now. Even in the dark, I could see the intent in his eyes.

Crouching, I helped Maya up. She rubbed at her left elbow.

The elevator doors opened with their cheery ping, as Owen continued to curse, shouting epithets in a pained rasp. Behind him, a shadow crossed the doorway, fast. She'd be here any second.

With another gun, no doubt. We'd blown our chance to get away.

Keeping a close eye on us, Owen half-turned to greet the newcomer, but his weapon stayed trained on us.

But the voice from the darkness behind him wasn't Nina's.

"What now, Owen?"

My stomach somersaulted downward to my feet as David stepped through a slice of faint blue window light before melting back into the far shadows again. For the briefest moment I held onto hope that he'd come to save us, like a knight in shining armor swooping for the rescue just in the nick of time.

"I knew you'd screw this up," he said, his disembodied voice coming from the corner's depths. "Give me the gun. Do I always have to come in and clean up after you?"

He emerged then, into our tiny section of light, dressed down in a dark turtleneck and dark pants, his face the only pale part of his body that I could see.

Owen handed the weapon over, then eased backward, head down, till he managed to brace himself against a nearby desk. Still cupping the family jewels, he ran his free hand over his sparse hair and blew out an anguished breath. "That one," he said, pointing to me. "Do her first."

"Owen, please," David said, as though addressing a mischievous child, "your temper's gotten us into enough trouble here. Let's handle this the smart way for a change, shall we?" I could see his face, half-blue, half-obscured when he turned to me. "Alex," he said, in the same soothing voice he'd used so many times since we'd met. "Are you all right?"

My heart leapt at his words—an instinctive response as my emotions reacted, holding fast to my last shred of hope. "We're okay," I said, wary. I could hear fear in my voice; I had no doubt he could, too. "What are you doing here?"

"Everything's gotten screwed up," he said. "I have to protect my assets." He moved closer, further into the light, as nonchalant as ever. It was his manner that chilled me most. "And to make sure nothing happens to you, of course." He smiled. "Yet."

All thoughts of a happy ending crashed through my brain with a soulful clang sounding like a death knell. Maya and I stood close to one another, arms touching. I couldn't tell which one of us shook more.

Owen's breathing had returned to almost normal. With his head up now, he glared our direction, then threw a glance at David. "Now what?"

"Let me think on this," he answered. "We have to plan well so it won't come back on us."

With the look of suddenly remembering a critical piece of information, Owen's body jerked. "The guard guy downstairs in the garage," he said. "That Jared guy. He knows I'm up here."

David made a sound of weary displeasure. "Taken care of," he said.

The implication of his words exploded in my brain.

Like a kid in trouble trying for an attaboy, Owen lifted

his chin in Maya's direction, "I got her cell phone, like you told me." Pointing to me, he added, "She didn't have one."

David rolled his eyes. "No wonder everything has blown up. You just can't do anything right, can you?"

"Hey, I checked. I emptied their purses, see? It wasn't there."

David moved toward the pile of purse debris on the nearby desk. From the light hitting him from the side, I could see him work his jaw. "Damn it, Owen. This is just another loose end you created. How do we explain their belongings dropped all over the place here?" He turned then, and I couldn't see his face, but I heard his hiss of frustration.

"I'll take care of it," Owen said, sullen. "But I had to make sure she didn't have a phone."

Turning back to face us, David made a tsking sound. "Of course she has one."

Shit.

"Maya," David said, still calm. "If you'd be so kind, would you please locate Alex's cell phone. I believe you'll find it in her back pocket."

When she didn't move, his voice deepened. "Maya. Now please."

She whispered that she was sorry as she pulled my phone out by its tiny antenna.

"Now toss it to Owen, would you?"

I took a small measure of pride in the fact that he winced when he caught it. David collected both phones from him and nodded. "You see, Alex," he said, "I really did pay attention to everything you told me. Everything. From your pride in your sister's musical prowess, to where you like to keep your phone."

I bit my lip. He'd conned me good.

"We can kill them right here," Owen said, making an

unsteady return to his feet. "Make it look like Maya was about to be exposed, and so she killed her. Then turned the gun on herself." His eyes were like mad things trapped in a frozen pond. "With records in her purse, it'll look like she knew she was caught."

David nodded slowly, walking toward him. "Actually, my thoughts were running along the same lines," he said.

He raised his arm so quickly, I didn't even see the gun in his hand until the flash exploded next to Owen's temple. He crumpled to the floor, the dark blood running out of the side of his head, forming a puddle on the carpet. I winced instinctively at the loud noise, my body turned away, my hands flew to my ears.

David looked down at him and smiled wistfully. He goddamn *smiled.* The sound of the shot rang in my head, echoing and strong. I could barely hear, but somehow I caught his words. "For the good of the firm, old chum."

I didn't wait. I grabbed Maya's sleeve and dragged her after me, back into the maze of the office. We ran through a lattice-work of those folding six-foot portable wall separators, my breath coming in ragged gasps.

"Alex," I heard David's smooth voice calling after me. "Don't run. We can talk this out. I promise."

I pulled Maya into one of the sections and forced her into a crouch. Her dark eyes jumped everywhere at once. Everywhere but at me. Her breaths came out in panicked whooshes. I thought she might hyperventilate.

"We're dead," she said. "He'll kill us both."

"How can we get out of here?" I asked, shaking her out of her stupor. A sudden crash to my far left made me jerk, but we both managed to keep from yelping aloud. Metal against wood, against plastic, thudding then, to the floor. Several of the nearby portable sections shook, and I knew

David must be systematically kicking them over. It would only be a matter of time before he found us.

I thought of Lucy. What would she do without me? I shook Maya again when another crash sounded. Closer this time.

"There's got to be a way out of here." I shook her hard. "Think."

"Alex," his smooth voice continued, "you know, I really believed you'd come to me if you uncovered any irregularities. We had a bond, you and I. I trusted you." He heaved a sigh, slammed the cubicle next to us to the ground.

We had to move. Now.

"I'm terribly disappointed in you."

Leaping like startled rabbits, we made it one cubicle over, just in time to hear his foot slam against the wall we'd just abandoned. He must have been getting tired because he kicked again, but this time, nothing fell.

"I had such hopes for us, Alex. I thought we could make beautiful music together." He chuckled. Moved nearer.

"It's not too late. I'm willing to…negotiate." I could hear him taking deep breaths. He was winded. "Owen killed Evelyn Vicks. You know that now. But, I didn't know about it until he told me. He was stupid. Out of control. Now, I have to come in and clean up his mess. But we can still escape. Together. All we need are a couple of fall guys."

I tried to estimate how close he was by his voice. We scurried. Like rats, I thought. Trapped rats.

"Owen already set things up for Maya to take the fall," his silky smooth tone continued. "She deserves it, too, believe me. Just call out where you are, and you and I can be on our way to the Cayman Islands to drink rum tonics on the beach for the rest of our lives."

Yeah, right, I thought.

I heard him grunt with effort, and then another crash. More partitions toppled.

"Listen to me, both of you," he said, his voice taking on a harsher tone. "You're smart girls. Think. Think hard. You can't get out of this alive. Not unless I let you."

We'd sidled up to a wide pillar, and I fought an exclamation of pain as I bumped against metal. David might have heard the sound of my hitting it, but I thought not. I looked at the mounted item, close-up. A fire extinguisher.

I lifted it from its hook, released the safety pin, and held the nozzle in my right hand, the tubing leading from the nozzle to the can I held in my left.

I kept close attention to his positioning, using the elevator corridor as the twelve on a clock to keep my bearings. We were at about the four, moving counter-clockwise around the maze of desks. He followed us, moving the same direction. I placed him at about the eight, maybe the nine. A few more steps around, he'd be behind us and we'd have our only chance to run.

He must have come to the same conclusion, at the same moment, because he stopped kicking the cubicle and I heard quick footsteps head toward the corridor.

We didn't wait. We didn't think.

We ran.

In the darkness, with all the strewn rubble from his kicking tantrum, he must have misgauged a step. I heard, rather than saw him trip, but not fall.

"Go," I shouted to Maya, then turned and aimed the nozzle at the open doorway we'd just left. David appeared and I sprayed him, directly in the face.

His hands flew up to his eyes in a futile effort to protect them from the onslaught of chemicals. I'd gotten him straight in the face. He bent over, coughing, retching. Some wafted my way and I tasted the chalky, yellow bitterness of the powdered spray, even as I turned to run.

Maya hadn't moved from behind me, so I threw the heavy fire extinguishing can aside and grabbed a handful of her leather jacket as I made for the wall buttons that would be our salvation.

My feet moved slow-motion, my left hand reached, like a Stretch Armstrong toy I remembered from my childhood, for the button that would open the waiting elevator doors.

It opened. Thank God.

We were inside before the doors fully spread, pressing the "close" button with four frantic hands. I heard Maya pray aloud, and I listened for movement from the corridor.

The doors weren't closing.

Because we hadn't picked a floor.

"Down," I shouted, pressing the button for the ground floor.

Whatever computer controlled the system gave us an indifferent click-reply, and ever so slowly, the doors slid shut. We stood, motionless, panting, not making any other sound—willing the golden panels to close. Now. To keep us alive.

Five inches.

Two inches.

Fingers thrust through the rubber linings, grabbing for Maya's coat. She jumped backward, fell to the floor, sobbing, eyes wild.

For a time-stopping second, I thought the doors, having encountered resistance, would make the faithful response and open again.

They didn't.

His fingers must not have hit the safety mechanism sufficiently, because the flexing digits yanked back just a fraction of a second before the elevator locked itself and made ready to begin its downward trek. I heaved a sick-to-my-stomach groan and, nearly blanking out from shock, dropped to lean against the inner wall. My mind flashed back to fourth grade when a boy I liked told me about a man who'd been decapitated by a set of elevator doors and how the body had danced around for long minutes before it finally died. Back then I'd believed that those door edges were sharp enough to chop through a man's neck. Right now, I wished to God those buggers had sliced David's hand right off.

Relief rushed through my body; there was no way he could beat us down by taking the stairs. I allowed myself to breathe again.

But our elevator stopped again, almost immediately. Maya pushed to her feet.

I stared out the glass walls for a split-second, trying to impel us to move by sheer force of will. The ground below remained immobile. The button we'd hit and lit up had gone dark now. I reached for the floor buttons, pressing "one" again and again, hoping to kick the computer into gear. Nothing.

I pressed "two, three, four."

We weren't going anywhere.

Maya stood transfixed, her eyes on the digital readout that indicated our floor. It was dark, too. As though the elevator system had been shut off completely.

"How?"

Maya blinked, shaking her head. "There's a control box on every floor."

"Shit," I said, then thought to ask, "Does it control all the elevators, or just this one?"

Maya blinked in concentration, looked up when the answer came to her. "All of them," she said. "If we're stuck, he can't use any of the others."

"Okay," I said, trying to make sense of our situation, trying to see how we could possibly survive.

Movement caught my eye, and I turned. Through the glass walls that faced the atrium a half-floor above us now, I could see David heading away from our position, back into the loan department. "What do we do?" I asked Maya.

She shook her head.

I tore open the brass control box inside, hoping to find some master command that would allow us to start moving again. There it was. A bulls-eye shaped keyhole, surrounded in red. White letters telling me that this was what we needed.

I grabbed Maya's arm. "You still have that key?"

Her face crumpled; she shook her head. She pointed back toward the loan department. "In my purse."

TWENTY-EIGHT

DAVID WAS BACK in less than a minute. He strode past the windows on his way to our glass prison, looking neither right nor left. A man on a mission. He held something long and shiny in his hand, like a pointer from a business meeting.

It dawned on me what he needed it for.

Every set of elevator doors had a small hole just above eye-level. In the event of an emergency, poking a long straight object inside would open the doors automatically. He'd have us then.

I looked up.

These fancy elevators had plastic-square dropped ceiling tiles. I jumped, pushing them aside with my hand, until I spotted the escape hatch, exactly where I thought it would be. "Boost me," I said to Maya.

With a stricken look on her face, she complied, wrapping her hands together and pushing my planted foot upward. We worked well together, Maya and I, and some auto-pilot part of my brain processed that nugget even as my fingers skimmed the square, knocking the small door off-center.

"One more time," I said.

This time my fingers strove for purchase over the edge of the open hatch, and I got it. Exerting muscles I didn't know I owned and pushing those harmful thoughts about my lack of upper body strength out of my head, I pulled myself through, using my right elbow as leverage. Once I

had my left elbow pulled up and set, I shimmied upward
with relative ease, working around vertical metal struts
on the elevator car's roof. Thank God we were both slim,
I thought.

The moment I made it to my knees, I reached back for
Maya's outstretched hand, pulling. No luck.

We both heard the sound of metal against metal as the
poker David used tried to find the doors' release level. I
laid flat on my stomach, giving me the best control I could
muster. "Come on," I said.

We locked hands, and she pressed a foot against the
sidewall railing. It was enough, and once she'd gotten her
torso through the opening, I grabbed her by her waist and
hauled her the rest of the way in.

I looked around. We hadn't dropped far at all. I could
see only the very top couple of inches of the tenth-floor
doors, where, from the sound of things, David Dewars was
having difficulty opening them.

I hate elevator shafts. I've always hated them. Looking
upward in an elevator shaft terrifies me. As a little kid I'd
visited a building on State Street with cage elevators that
were open everywhere—side-to-side, up and down. I'd
buried my head in my mother's stomach and didn't move
till my dad gathered me in his arms and carried me out. As
an adult, I recognized my irrational fear as a phobia. I lived
with it—believing that such an oddball phobia wouldn't
ever seriously impact my life.

Now, my life depended on me beating it.

I came through the small opening with nothing but sur-
vival on my mind. As I stood, in the worst of my night-
mares, I froze. I wouldn't look up. I couldn't.

But there was no way to go down.

Maya pointed at the wall near the doors. "A ladder."

Panic manifested itself in a cold flush that seared

through my body, making my heart hurt from its pounding, making my eyes see bright lights.

We heard a thud.

Those top two inches showed the tenth-floor doors wide open.

And David was inside the elevator.

"Go," Maya said, pushing me toward the ladder.

I followed her, working too many things in my brain at one time. I told myself not to look up. I repeated it like a mantra, hitting the words over and over as my feet clanged the stacked rungs. Maya stopped at the eleventh-floor doors, reaching.

She tried to force the panels open, but her center of gravity was off, and the doors wouldn't budge. Another memory flashed in my mind. Forcing open the windows in Mrs. Vicks' house during that storm, because she'd been locked out. This was how everything had started. If I hadn't helped her that night, I wouldn't be here now.

With a start, I realized that life moments were playing before my eyes.

I clenched them shut even as I put one hand above the other, climbing upward into the sum of all my fears. I couldn't let my childhood terrors be what stopped me now. I couldn't let David win that easily.

Looking down, I saw his head crown the opening. He'd be on top of the car any moment now.

We had enough light from the glass shaft surrounding us, but that meant that David would be able to see us just as easily as we could see him.

I looked up.

I thought my heart would explode from the sight of the dreadful abyss above me. I knew it only extended about two floors above us, but the panic attack had begun. My heart went into a long series of palpitations and my breath

came out in fast pants. I would not lose control. I couldn't.
I didn't have my father to carry me to safety. I had to do
it myself.

I did the only thing I could do at that point. I closed my
mind to all but the feel of cold steel rungs in my hand and
the muscles in my legs propelling me upward. I forced myself to envision blinders and from then on, I saw nothing
else but the path up the ladder.

"Look," I said, my voice barely audible. I pointed to another door, immediately above the end of the ladder, just
after "twelve," the top floor doors. "Where does that lead?"

She and I moved faster as David made a telltale whump
below. He'd hoisted himself onto the car's roof, and would
surely be on his feet in a moment.

Maya's face told me she didn't know. "Go," I said.

She did.

I watched her grab the set-in handle and thrust forward
with all her might, the hatch opening with rusty, shrill
shrieks. She toppled outward. I didn't know where, but I
couldn't wait to get there.

Seconds later, I followed, just as I heard David's feet
hit the first rungs.

He called to us, but I jumped out the small doorway, I
found myself hit by a cold wind outside on the building's
roof and a warm flush of relief for getting out of that shaft.
Maya and I spun, shutting the door behind us. There was
no lock on the outside.

I searched the flat area for something big to use as a
brace, but there was nothing.

The city surrounded us, taller on every side. I had a wild
hope that someone looking out their tall apartment window
would see us and call the police. But these weren't apartment buildings; these were offices. And I couldn't imagine
anyone working this late on a Sunday night.

I tried to think.

The door we held was set into a square rooftop structure, about six feet high, and the same dimensions on each of its sides. It was an extension of the shaft below. Stretching slightly, I could see four other similar structures in places that matched up with the three other elevators below, plus one extra. That meant that there must be other doors leading back down. If only we could keep him here long enough for an escape.

"Hold tight," I said. I ran around to where I'd detected a shadow that didn't 'fit.' Bingo. A piece of machinery—I was unsure what it was—stood against one of the nearby walls. It looked like a steel construction horse, but much heavier.

Wind whipped hair into my face, sent icy stings into my eyes. I dragged the metal horse, using every bit of untapped energy I didn't know I had. Every step felt like an hour, and as I drew nearer to Maya, pushing hard against the door, I felt as though I was being pulled further away. I grunted with the effort, finally coming around the rear, and pushing it into place.

We shoved it tight, wedging it as best we could, making it harder for him to break through. We needed time to find a way out.

"Shh," I said, holding my finger to my lips. I pressed my ear against the cold metal door, the iciness against the tender skin making me grimace. I listened.

I couldn't hear him coming. I heard nothing at all.

Maya listened, too. We stared at each other, faces inches apart, the steam from our breath curling upward toward the night sky. Nothing.

"Come on," I said, grabbing Maya, throwing one last hopeful look at the barricade we'd set up. "We gotta go."

I made my way to the closest shaft structure, feeling

my way around it in the dark, in search of the access door. Much is said about big city lights, but here, up on the twelfth-floor roof of a building dwarfed by neighboring superstructures, there was only the light from the sliver of moon above and leftover Chicago brightness from tall metal and glass walls. The sides of these upper shaft things were painted black, the door black, too, so I relied on my touch to find the opening.

We'd only been up here for minutes—three, maybe five at most—but my fingers already felt the paralysis of chill. "Go check that other one," I said, in a whisper. Maya raced around me to the third shaft and set to work. I didn't want to crawl through another shaft, but I knew now I could do it if we had to.

Moments later I heard her frustrated cry of effort. "I…can't…get…it."

Neither could I.

I tried squeezing my frozen fingertips into the narrow door indentation, running along the length of the perimeter by touch, trying to find some place where the door would give. Flat-handed I covered the door itself in a concentric-circle search, knowing there had to be some knob, or other device capable of providing access. "Damn," I said, pounding my angry fist against the metal panel. I glanced to my left; our barricade on the other shaft remained in place.

Something was wrong.

I moved back to the metal horse, leaned against the cold metal wall again. I heard nothing. No movement up the ladder, no sound of exertion from inside.

I knew.

"Maya," I shouted.

She was next to me in a second. "He's not coming up this way." I pointed toward the door that had given us roof access. My gaze swept the area. Four additional structures. Two wouldn't open for us. That left two more.

"Come on," I said.

Maya's teeth chattered; she hugged herself, knees bending up and down to keep warm. "Where is he?"

I shook my head.

"We'll go down the way we came," I said, starting to drag the horse barricade back, away from the door. I had a moment's terror thinking that he might just be waiting behind the metal door for us to open it. But I'd gotten to know the man. He waited for no one. He was on his way up here, from some other direction.

Together we pulled the heavy piece of machinery, moving it as fast as we could. So much easier with both of us handling it, we heaved it just far enough to give us clear access to the hatch. We wrenched at the squeaking metal door, and the hairs on the back of my neck zinged to attention.

I couldn't climb back into a shaft. I couldn't.

I had to.

"Go ahead," I said, keeping a shivering arm on the open door, lifting my head from our efforts, intending to keep a terse eye on the remaining empty areas of the roof. "I'll be right behind you."

"No you won't," David said.

I whirled.

He'd come up from behind me, and now pointed the gun at Maya, who'd just begun to lower her right foot behind her. "Get back up here."

David's eyes reflected the lights around us with an angry glitter. There were yellow streaks of firefighting chemicals on his clothes and in patches across his face. Grimacing, he blinked repeatedly, inching fingers under his glasses, to rub at his eyes, one at a time, never shifting his stare from us. I looked around the lonely expanse. How had he gotten here? As if in answer to my unasked question, he lifted his chin, tilted it sideways; I glanced that way. He'd come through the spare access door that led up from the stairway.

With the visceral impact of a body blow, the realization hit me that I had nothing left with which to fight.

"Did you really kill a man, Alex?" David shook his head, as though in appreciation. "You promised to tell me all about it. You promised me a ride on the Ferris wheel too." He sighed. "I'm very disappointed."

He was backlit by the thousands of pinpoint lights from nearby buildings, the crisp night wind lifting the short tufts of his hair. In another situation, I could have been enjoying the view, and the feel of freedom up here. Another flash-back, this one of his mustache grazing the side of my face as we gazed outward over the lake at Navy Pier. This time when my body shuddered, it shook with disgust.

Maya stood close to me, we stared together at the barrel of the weapon that seemed uncertain as to whom to kill first. My chin trembled from the cold and from fear; David words taking me back to the moment I'd pushed a man into the path of an oncoming train.

"You're not going to be able to kill me," he said with a curious lightness to his tone. "I'm indestructible."

I didn't have anything to say.

"But there's no other way out, is there?"

I shook my head, tried to keep my legs from giving out. The image of Owen's head taking the point-blank shot ric-ocheted through my mind and I saw my own head, a bullet in its center, jerking back with the impact of my last life experience. I tried to speak, cleared my throat, and tried again. "What now?"

He smiled. "Back downstairs." He wiped at his nose,

and coughed. "This way ladies," he said, stepping backward as though to allow us passage in front of him and indicating our direction with the gun. We didn't move.

"I am sorry about this, Alex," he said. The wind whipped his words from his lips, but I heard them.

In an instant I saw how it would go down. He'd kill me, then Maya, and somehow make it look like some tragic murder-suicide. George would know better. George would put it together.

But that gave me little comfort. I'd still be dead.

Desperation clawed through my paralysis of fear—and took over.

I couldn't stop myself. I leapt at David, swiping the glasses from his face with my left hand and scratching at his eyes with my right. The gun went off with a loud, powerful blast that made me clamp my teeth together in pained anticipation.

Though it took a split-second, time decelerated for me. My body went through a quick checklist of pain sensors even as I kicked and strove to deliver brutal blows—my single goal, to grab the gun.

I hadn't been hit.

But Maya had.

She fell backward—I was aware of her long nails grasping at David, trying to help me. Now they pulled away almost elegantly as gravity drew her body downward. I didn't know where she'd been hit. I couldn't take the time to find out. Fight or flight had kicked in, my instincts taken over by some wild animal within. The part of myself that remained human, begged me to stop fighting, to try to help her—as futile an effort as that may be.

Instead, I set into him with nothing more than blind, deaf, determination. I felt nothing, I heard nothing. The world had taken on a high-pitched wail that might have been coming from my soul. I attacked. Moving, writhing, biting, kicking—aware of nothing more than staying alive.

He twisted, turned, dragging me with him, then bumped into the open metal door, causing him to stumble, his grip on me to loosen.

The sound of the gun clanking to the rooftop floor near my foot was what finally broke into my screaming. David's voice, repeating my name as he struggled to subdue my flailing extremities, sounded like an echo from far away. He couldn't stop me because he didn't know what I was doing. I didn't know what I was doing. Sheer impulse urged me to drive hard against his bulk with the shaft yawning behind him.

Imbalance. His.

I sensed it as he tottered at the brink of the opening.

One more push.

I backed up a half step and then rammed my shoulder into his chest.

His arms flailed, his back jutted into the darkness behind him, but at the very last second his hands caught the sides of the door—suspending him there, his breath panting in labored grunts. I could almost see the rage gather in his chest as he dragged himself forward, bellowing, deep with effort. His knuckles whitened, he hauled himself up, about to stand.

I twisted, reaching down, and whisked the revolver from the ground, knowing this was the moment of decision. In the half-second it took to right myself, and steady the gun with both hands, I knew I was ready. With a deep hatred in my heart I'd never encountered before, I squeezed that trigger. Hard.

Light and sound burst forward in the night, as I felt the impact from a recoil I hadn't anticipated.

As though meant only for me to hear, over the din of

screams and exploding gunpowder, the bullet made a quiet chunk into the meat of David's flesh. I opened my eyes long enough to watch the soles of his feet tumble away.

TWENTY-NINE

"MAYA?" I DROPPED the weapon to lean over her body, lying prone—face-up where she'd fallen. I tapped my fingers along the side of her cheek, trying to determine, in the dark, where she'd taken the hit. Faint curls of breath wisped out of her mouth and nose at regular intervals. Thank God. She was still alive.

She'd fallen close to the shaft structure. In its shadow, with her wearing dark clothing, and my mind still processing David's attack, I had a difficult time finding the site of the bullet's entry. I didn't want to move her, but neither did I want to leave her alone, if there was anything I could do to keep her alive.

I needed to get help.

Pulling my jacket off, I used it as a blanket, to cover her till I got back. "It doesn't look bad at all," I lied, still not seeing where she'd taken the bullet. "You're going to be fine," I added, then headed back down the shaft.

Facing fears makes them go away.

I'd heard that enough times, seen enough reality shows, and read enough psychobabble to believe there might be some truth in that, but I hadn't ever seen the need to test the theory myself.

Now, as I made my way down the ladder, I found that my elevator shaft nightmare had less power to intimidate me. The fear of the unknown, the strange ominous feel I'd always had not knowing what loomed above, didn't paralyze me. I was at the top. I was here. And there was nothing but me and the sense that I'd made it.

I processed all this even as I made my careful way down the same ladder we'd climbed only short minutes ago. David's body had hit the top of the car below me, and he lay on his back, arms and legs spread like a fully-clothed version of the DaVinci depiction of man in a pentacle except for the tilt where his left thigh had impaled itself on an upright piece of metal. My stomach gave a queasy pitch at the sight; I breathed out my mouth and turned away.

His right hand lolled over the edge, into the open escape hatch. I moved it, none too gently, in my effort to rush.

"Alex."

I whipped my head around at the whispered word.

"Help me."

His lips curled back, baring teeth clenched in pain. Eyes tight, he took sharp, hesitant breaths.

I'd been about to lower myself through, with no thought other than getting help for Maya, but the realization that my words might be the last he'd ever hear stopped me for the briefest moment.

"Hang in there," I said, then realized with gut-punch impact that I'd said those very words to Barton while we waited for the parameds to arrive. "Help will be here soon."

AFTER CALLING 911, calling George, then getting back up to the roof via the stairway this time, I waited with Maya, encouraged by her occasional returns to consciousness. The bullet had torn through her left shoulder, and though she'd bled enough for me to find the wound in the darkness, I knew she was strong. I hoped and prayed that she make it.

The police and paramedics arrived simultaneously, allowing me to move off to a far corner of the rooftop while they scrambled to work on Maya. Moments after their appearance on the scene, they'd scoped out the area and called for a helicopter.

My teeth chattered, but I stayed up-top, hugging my knees as I sat far enough to be out of their way. One of the techs had given me a blanket, and I tugged it close, grateful for its warmth.

I winced at the throbbing shoop-shoop sound of the helicopter's whirling blades as it touched down. Turning my head from the cold gusts of wind particles it shot into my face, I whispered positive thoughts for Maya, as they loaded her stretcher and took off for Northwestern Hospital.

George found me there, huddled, too tired, too overcome, to move.

"I thought you promised me you wouldn't get into a situation again," he said, lightly, but the ambient light reflecting in his eyes told another story. He crouched to my position. "You okay?"

I nodded.

"Let's get you downstairs."

THEY'D TRANSPORTED DAVID Dewars via ambulance to Stroger Hospital, and I took a small measure of comfort in knowing he and Maya wouldn't be in the same emergency room. I worried for her.

George thought I ought to be checked out, too, but I hadn't suffered more than a few bad scrapes and a couple of hot bruises. "I'm fine," I said. "But is there any way we can know how Maya's doing?"

We'd settled ourselves in the bank's lobby, the three other glass elevators that had been sitting open-mouthed and dark on the main floor when we'd arrived, were now moving up and down between our level, ten, and twelve, filled with aftermath people.

George pulled a uniformed officer over, spoke to him briefly and then sat down by me. I'd taken a place on the tile floor, eschewing the building's security man's insistence that I sit in his wheeled vinyl chair. I wanted to ask where he'd been when we needed him, but I declined his offer politely instead.

Now, I leaned my head against the wall, staring upward at the dark skylit ceiling above.

"Start from the beginning," George said, pulling out a notepad.

I did.

By the time I'd gotten to the part about Owen's arrival, the young officer George had spoken to earlier returned, handing me a large Styrofoam cup of coffee. "Just cream?" the fellow said, with a look that asked if that was right.

"Perfect," I said, reaching up. The steam poured upward as I opened the lid, and the first sip, hot and familiar down my throat, brought a sting to my eyes. "Thank you," I said, in an uneven voice.

As he left, I started to resume the story, then suddenly remembering, I asked, "Jared. What about Jared?"

George shook his head, not understanding.

"When Dewars came, he said that the guy in the garage security had been 'taken care of.' What did he mean?"

The look in his eyes told me I didn't want to know.

He shook his head. "Point-blank to the temple."

My body began to shake then, as if reacting to a systemic toxin—struggling to work the poison out before it claimed my life, too.

"Talk to me," George said.

I did.

He received a call moments later; Maya was in stable condition. Despite the blood loss, she was expected to pull through.

David Dewars remained critical. I'd planted the bullet in his side. While I'd missed other major organs, the shot had pierced his bowel. The fall down the shaft had broken his back. Even if he survived, the chances of lifetime paralysis were enormous.

I felt no triumph, no relief.

I felt nothing at all.

AFTER I'D ANSWERED every question I could, George drove me home. We were quiet for the short ride from Banner Bank to Lake Shore Drive. As he merged into the southbound traffic, George turned to me. "You did good."

I shook my head. "This isn't the job I signed on for, you know. News research isn't supposed to be a life-threatening occupation."

He nodded, his face set—expressionless—alternating blue and dark as we drove past street lights along the shoreline. I stared out the window for the rest of the ride.

George came in with me to my aunt and uncle's house. Uncle Moose answered the door, but the look on my face must have been enough because Lucy and Aunt Lena, both pajama-clad and bleary-eyed, rushed me to sit on the sofa, full of questions.

Already tired of telling the tale, I gave them all the facts but very little flavor of the terror I'd felt on that icy rooftop. I told them all that we now knew that Mrs. Vicks had been killed by Owen Riordan, and that Riordan had been in collusion with David Dewars in a huge bank embezzlement scheme.

"One thing doesn't make sense," I said, turning to George. Uncle Moose had pulled out a few cans of pop and shoved a cold Pepsi into the detective's hand. He'd handed me one, too, but I waved it off with murmured thanks. "Why would Dewars steal from his own bank?

If he's the owner—the majority shareholder—he's only stealing from himself, isn't he?"

"I'll look into that," George said. He propped his notebook on his knee and scribbled.

"What about Barton?" I asked, starting to feel the grip of the story take hold, bolstering my energy, again.

"That witness I told you about *did* see someone at the approximate time Barton was shot," he said. "From the description of the man and his car, it sounds like Riordan killed Barton, too. We'll know for sure once I have the witness look at a photo spread. Plus, not only was that stash of money missing, but you told me you'd made a duplicate set of those bank record copies for Barton, right?"

I nodded.

"There was nothing in the room that had anything to do with Banner Bank. Not a single thing." George scratched his head. "We've taken a look at phone records. Barton called Riordan from his hotel room Saturday afternoon. What was said between them, we can only guess. Apparently Riordan paid a visit. Which explains how they knew you had the files." He made a face of discomfort. "Riordan must have tailed you today, both to Maya's and then to the bank. It's the only explanation for how he arrived there so quickly after you did."

I shuddered.

"I'm sorry," George said.

"Why?"

"I shouldn't have let you go there alone."

I thought about that. "Well, if he *was* tailing us, then it was just a matter of time before he made his move, right?"

George nodded. "Probably."

"There's no telling how it might have gone down in another situation," I said, sounding Pollyanna-ish with my explanation. "Maya and I survived. That's all that matters."

Lucy wrapped herself around my right arm and buried her head in my shoulder.

"So, it was Owen who attacked me and Diana?" I asked.

George nodded. "I got the guys running like crazy, trying to get all the pieces put together, but that's what it looks like. The blood type fits."

"He must have been looking for Mrs. Vicks' proof." I shook my head. "And it was in a safe deposit box somewhere else, the whole time."

My family sat, staring, listening to us try to piece it all together. My aunt tugged her robe close around her ample frame. "What about Grady?" she asked.

"He's in custody. I've got him charged with accosting Alex in the parking lot, but right now, there's not much more than that, and jumping parole. Apparently, he had nothing to do with any of this." George glanced at his watch. "It's after midnight. You folks ought to get some rest. And we'll know more tomorrow. I promise to be in touch."

I DECLINED AUNT Lena's offer to stay the night. One good thing had come out of all this—I sensed that Lucy finally realized it had been need, rather than desire on my part, that kept us from having our day together. I promised we would, soon.

Tomorrow was out, because I had Bass's deadline to meet, but after all this finished, I was determined to make her my priority.

George walked us the half-block to my house, Lucy holding tight to me. He waited till I had unlocked the door, then gave my shoulder an avuncular pat. "Good work, Alex. I'm proud of you."

With all that had gone on, I wanted to call Bass right now and tell him that I quit, that I didn't want to put my life on the line ever again. Common sense won the argument waging in my brain, however, and I shook my head, reconsidering.

I loved my job, and I knew that this story, with all its dangers, was an aberration. From here on out, I'd be living the safe life of a news researcher, behind my desk, and one day, when I was eighty years old, and looking back, I might recollect these past few days as fun and exciting. Right now, though, I needed to concentrate on kicking Dan Starck's station's butt with my coverage of this feature.

Inside, I got Lucy settled, then found myself wide awake with adrenaline-induced energy. I couldn't sleep. Visions of everything that had gone on the past two days rushed through my brain in snippets that made me blink in reaction.

At one in the morning, I knew exactly what would make me sleep better.

Bass answered the phone, groggy, after the third ring.

I interrupted his grousing expletives with a quick summary of the night's activities. "And here's what I need by noon tomorrow," I said.

By THE TIME I made it down to our station's studio the next morning, Bass had gotten everything I'd asked for: agreements for exclusive interviews with the board of directors at Banner Bank, the witness from the Tuck Inn motel, O'Shea Associates, the lawyers who'd drawn up Mrs. Vicks' real will, and some bigwigs at the FDIC.

I'd spent the morning holed up in my office recording every detail. William was back from San Francisco and would need me to be as precise as possible, in order to accurately write up the story for filming later in the week.

By eleven-thirty I finished and left the complete packet on his desk with a note to call me if he had questions. I made sure to include my phone number, to prevent any confusion again.

I still needed to visit the studio itself to coordinate locations with the crew—to ensure that the shots of the bank, of the motel, and of Mrs. Vicks' home, among others, would be set up just right. Since I was scheduled to appear on camera—I'd written up Gabriela's in-depth interview of me—I needed to coordinate that filming, too.

After today, I was taking vacation, and the sooner I got this stuff done, the better.

Bass caught up with me talking with one of our technicians, just outside the soundstage. Taking long strides with short legs, he closed the distance between us faster than I would've imagined.

"William's looking for you," he said.

"What for?"

"Don't know. He got your notes. Seemed disappointed." Looking around, Bass shot the tech a pointed, dismissive look. Taking the hint, the guy left.

"Disappointed?" I said, with not a small amount of anger. "How the hell can he be disappointed? I just about wrote the story for him. All he has to do is connect the dots." I wiggled my head, totally pissed. "And they're practically numbered, for crissakes."

"Settle down, all right?" Bass forehead creased and he held up a restraining hand. "I have no idea what's up with him, I just wanted to let you know, okay? Don't shoot the messenger."

"Whatever," I said, rubbing my eyebrows.

"He's coming down here to talk with you," he said. "Wanted to catch you before you took off." Bass looked from side to side then, as if to reassure himself that no one was listening in on our conversation. In a low voice he said, "I wanted to catch you, too."

I folded my arms, ready for a fight. "What?" I said.

Bass looked up at me. His hazel eyes held a look I'd never seen in them before.

"What?" I said again, in a nicer voice. Now I was curious.

"You did good, Alex. Don't get used to me saying that, but you did." He worked his jaw muscles and I sensed whatever was coming next was big. "I talked to Hank about promoting you to on-camera reporter. He's all for it."

Speechless, I blinked at him.

"More money," he said. "More exposure."

"I think I've had just about all the exposure I can take."

Bass shook his head. "Hank's spoken with a few of our consultants already. We're thinking you might be our ticket to knocking *UpClose Issues* out of the number one spot."

"You gotta be kidding," I said. Then as it hit me, I added, "What about Gabriela?"

"You'd share feature stories. We'll start you out doing a few small segments."

"But," I felt like I was sputtering, "what does she have to say about all this?"

"We haven't told her, yet." He winked at me as he left. "When you get back next week, we'll talk."

Fifteen minutes later, all I had left to do was my interview with Gabriela. She hadn't yet shown up, so I headed to the break room to wait.

William was there.

"Hey," I said, moving to the countertop to pour myself a cup of coffee.

"Alex," he said, half-standing. "How are you? I heard about everything that went on. Are you okay?"

"I'm great," I said. And I realized that was true. I'd been through trial by fire and my dad's constant mantra to "not let little things bother me" suddenly seemed like the best advice I'd ever received.

"I'm glad to hear that," he said, gesturing me into the seat across from him. "I guess I missed all the excitement."

"I'm sure you had plenty of your own," I said, with a light dose of sarcasm. "Just a different sort."

He winced at that, changed the subject. "How come you left that write-up on my desk?"

"Why, was there something wrong with it?"

"No, not at all," he said, looking confused. "It's just that we usually go over them together. Talk them through. I thought you'd want to do that again."

"It's all there," I said. "And if anything's unclear, let me know."

He closed his eyes for a long moment, as though weighing a momentous decision. "I'm sorry about that mix-up on the phone," he finally said.

"What mix-up?" I asked.

"You know, when I called you the wrong name."

"Oh, yeah," I said, waving my hand indifferently. "Don't worry about it."

"I didn't…" he began, then started again. "I wasn't entirely truthful with you."

I canted my head—smiled. "Really?"

He had the decency to blush. "Oh yeah, well." He scratched at his eyebrow. He blew out a breath and I wondered what sort of confession he was about to divulge. Looking up at me, he squinted, as though anticipating my reaction to his next words. "She…that other person… was…an old friend," he said quickly.

"An old girlfriend, you mean," I corrected.

"Yeah." He waited a beat before continuing. "She was one of the people running the conference. I had no idea she'd be out there, I swear. But she was. And we got to talking. It gave us a chance to reconnect."

I waited.

Behind me, the coffeemaker hissed.

William spoke again. "It was stupid of me to lie to you. I…" He shrugged and grimaced at the same time. "It surprised me when I realized I'd dialed wrong, and I wasn't sure about how things were going to…" He stopped himself. "I just made up the first thing that came to mind." One side of his mouth twisted downward. "I'm sorry if I hurt you."

"Don't worry about it," I said, feigning lightheartedness.

Another couple of silent seconds passed.

I spoke up. "So," I said, using his words to prompt the rest of the story. "You reconnected, huh?"

"Yeah."

Rather than endure another long interval of silence, I decided I needed to know how things stood. "She lives in San Francisco?"

He nodded.

I kept my voice just this side of chipper. "And so…are you two picking up where you left off?" I knew my upbeat approach was making this easy for him, but, just like whistling in the dark, faking composure made it easier for me, too.

"I…" he said, hesitating. "Yeah."

"Well, then," I stood, plastering on a tight smile. "I wish you guys the best. I hope I get the chance to meet her sometime."

He nodded, his look inscrutable.

Gabriela poked her blond head into the break room right then, and wiggled her perfectly manicured fingers my direction. "Alex," she called in a singsong voice. "We're ready for you."

THIRTY

LUCY AND I drove to Navy Pier Tuesday morning. As we strolled along the perimeter promenade, I experienced a peculiar gladness in my heart that she'd chosen the pier for our first outing. Being here with her, in the daylight, helped to dilute my recent memories of my date with David Dewars.

Still, after lunch at McDonald's, when she and I climbed aboard a Ferris Wheel car, I was struck by the promise I'd made to David less than a week ago to ride it with him. This morning I'd gotten an update on his condition. Paralyzed permanently from the waist down. He'd require years of physical therapy. Most of those years would likely be spent in prison.

"Whoa," Lucy said, as our car cleared the base area. We sat opposite one another, on molded plastic seats inside big enough to hold at least six people. These cars reminded me of Alpine ski-lifts, with doors on either side, and enough ceiling height to allow me to stand upright.

The young guy who'd helped us get in, slammed our car door shut and locked it. "Have a nice ride," he said as we drifted upward.

The wheel itself never stopped moving; passengers loaded and unloaded at snail speed. Lucy sat back, wide-eyed, her hands pressed against the seat at her sides, as if to steady us.

I slid back in my own seat and watched her across from me. We rose up, very slowly, to breathtaking views of

Chicago's skyline with the sun bright overhead, but still not enough to warm this cold day. I blew out a cloud of breath, and smiled.

Maya and George, not surprisingly, had both agreed to be part of my feature story. Maya was already back home, and though bandaged and a bit bruised, she was eager to get the truth out and start her search for a new job.

And my good friend, George, had discovered a key piece of information I'd never thought to look at.

Even though David was indeed the largest shareholder of Banner Bank, he wasn't the *majority* shareholder, like I'd been led to believe. He held only twenty percent of the stock. So, even though the embezzlement hurt the bank's bottom line, he was still clearing more than enough to make the effort worth his while. The bank wrote off bunches, got the tax benefits of doing so, and David was, in essence, stealing profits from the other shareholders who owned the remaining eighty percent of the stock.

Nice work, if you can get it.

"You having fun?" I asked.

Lucy nodded with vigor, then shot me a panicked look when the small movement caused the car to rock. "This is the most fun I've ever had."

I doubted that, but I didn't doubt her sincerity.

She was quiet for a long moment. "I told you about Bobby, right?"

"Yep." I made myself smile, even though I worried for her and her latest love. "I can't wait to meet him this weekend."

"Me too."

She was quiet again.

I looked out over the city below.

"Alex?" she said.

I pulled my attention away from the gray buildings, bright sky, and sparkling water below. "Yeah?"

Her eyes had welled up, and she stared at me over twin pools of blue. "I would miss you if you got killed."

The simplicity of her words caught me with a sting to the back of my throat. Moving slowly, so as not to upset the car's balance, I took her hands in mine. "I'm here for you, Lucy. I'll always be here for you."

She sniffed, then jolted up suddenly to wrap me in a bear hug that made the car rock. We both yelped at the sudden swinging, and Lucy sat back in her seat, laughing. "Wow, that was scary," she said.

"Yeah," I agreed.

She had no idea.

And thank God for that.

"How DID IT go?" I asked Dr. Hooker.

We'd stopped by his office later that afternoon. Lucy was trying to decide which of the many tea offerings she wanted to try. "Blackberry sage," she finally decided, holding up a round teabag in delight.

"Help yourself," Hooker said. He'd pulled over a third chair and as Lucy fixed herself tea I watched to make sure she didn't spill the scalding liquid on herself as he brought me up-to-date.

"Diana took the news amazingly well," he said. "I talked to her yesterday, before she was discharged. I thought that, just in case the revelation caused her a relapse, I'd rather she be in a hospital environment. She's home now, and she called her mother. Theresa's traveling from Iowa as we speak."

"Do you think that on some level, she suspected that Mrs. Vicks was her grandmother?"

Hooker shook his massive head. "No. She was completely surprised. In a case like this I might expect her to harbor some anger, some bitterness for not being told the truth sooner." He gave a big-bodied shrug. "But, rather than resent her mother and Mrs. Vicks, Diana is moved by the fact that her family cared enough about her to protect her."

I leaned forward, craning my neck to check on Lucy again. She'd finished steeping the tea and moved to join us, walking slowly, concentrating on the mug so as not to spill.

"What about Barton? How does she feel about him having been her father?"

"That one, and the circumstances that surrounded her birth, are a couple of the issues we still need to work through," he said. "But in time, I'm convinced Diana's going to shine. She's making great strides already."

"And Laurence Grady? What's going to happen with that situation?"

Hooker's smile split his face into a contagious grin. "I'm a psychiatrist, not a clairvoyant. Only time will tell on that one." He shrugged again, his eyes serious. "I can only promise you that Diana won't have to handle it alone."

FRIDAY AFTERNOON, as Lucy and I headed back to the house after a day of shopping and browsing up in the Long Grove historical village, my low-fuel indicator lit up.

"There's a Gas City," Lucy said, pointing down the street.

I nodded and Lucy grabbed my arm. "This is the place with the really good Slushies. Can I get one?"

I looked at her as I started to pull in. "It's cold outside. How can you want to drink a Slushie in this weather?"

"Look out," she said.

I turned just in time to see this red Firebird stop short.

We'd both been heading for the same gas pump, and I covered my mouth when I realized how close we'd come to hitting one another.

The Firebird driver, a big guy, sent me a furious look, but swerved over to a different pump. I shrugged, pulled up to pump eleven, and grabbed my credit card.

Just before I ran my card through the machine, I realized that I had to go inside to the convenience store anyway to buy Lucy's Slushie. I shook my head, mumbling about the cold and how it felt more like January than March, as I pulled open the door to the warmth of the mini-store for Lucy's drink and to pre-pay for gas.

Inside, an elderly gentleman wearing a plaid flannel jacket, leaned up against the protective glass window, talking to the cashier behind it. He had on a baseball cap, its brim pushed high over wiry white hair.

"Yeah," I heard him say to the girl behind the glass, "my son lives out of town, you know. He's got a real nice family and a real important job. And every year he sends me a Christmas card and tells me all about it." The guy nodded, staring out at the dark night, oblivious to the girl's pained looks of boredom.

Her dark brown eyes implored me to interrupt, but I had a mission. I headed over to the Slushie machine and poured a big cup of blue mush. The old guy continued to drone on about his son's life and how exciting it was. I heard him mention the Christmas card again. This was March and he was waxing poetic about a Christmas card?

I thought about Lucy. When she was back at the residence for special folks, next week, would she be telling everyone her memories from home like this fellow did? My heart went out to her, and to the old man, too.

The fellow whose car I'd nearly hit had come in, too.

He stood next to the old guy, shooting impatient glances between the two people waiting to pay.

I came up behind them all, Slushie and credit card in hand.

The old man ran a finger underneath his reddened nose, continuing with a sniff, "And my son writes everything that he's done for that entire year on the card, and, boy, does he write good, too. And I take my time reading it so I'll know what he's been up to." He shifted position, a wistful smile on his face. "I really look forward to getting that Christmas card."

Suddenly becoming aware that others waited in line, he moved aside. The dark-eyed girl asked Mr. Firebird, "May I help you?"

He paid for his gas with a twenty, and I'd expected him to head directly back out the door. Instead, he turned, and nearly bumped into me.

I got a good look at him, and knew immediately that I didn't want to mess with this guy. While he might have been handsome, he was badly bruised, which skewed the symmetry of his face. I willed myself not to react—anyone who looked like that was best avoided.

He must have been in a fight recently. From the looks of him, maybe more than one. He grimaced when he saw me there.

Solidly built, he moved well, effectively avoiding a collision with me. Beneath his open winter jacket, I could see he was well-muscled. I snuck a quick glance at the battered face again. I could only wonder what the other guy looked like.

Taking an involuntary step back, I said, "Oh, sorry. Today just isn't my day, is it?" His grimace faded, a little. All I wanted at this point was to pay for my stuff and get out of the man's way. If he proved to be a troublemaker I didn't have a prayer.

Kill 'em with kindness, I thought, and injected friend-liness into my voice. "Sorry about almost hitting you," I said. "I was talking to my sister."

"No problem," he said in a softer voice than I'd ex-pected. "I'm getting rid of the car anyway. In case you're interested."

A red Firebird. Yeah. Not exactly my style. I stepped back a little, leaning to look out the windows, pretending to consider it. "Hmm," I said. "Nice car. I'll think about it."

"Well, in that case," he reached in his jacket pocket and took out a business card. "That's me."

I read the card, feeling a paradigm shift in my brain. "Oh," I said, almost to myself. I looked him over again, seeing a bit more of the handsome and a bit less of the bruising. After a moment's hesitation, I pulled out a card of my own, and handed it over.

He studied it and nodded. "I read your magazine all the time," he said. "It's great."

I shook my head and laughed, wondering if anyone told the truth anymore. "It's not a magazine, it's a television show. Like *60 Minutes*. But I'm sure you meant you read the captioned version, right?"

"You got it," he said. He smiled then.

And I found myself smiling back.

Holding our respective cards, we gave awkward nods, and he headed out to his Firebird to start pumping his gas.

The Christmas card guy had started back into his mono-logue, and I waited for a break in the story to step up to pay.

Back out in the cold afternoon, I handed the card and the drink to Lucy before filling the tank.

When I got back in she asked, "What's this? Who's Ron Shade?"

"Take a look," I said. "He's a P.I."

I heard the soft purr of the Firebird next to me, and Ron Shade, private investigator, drove off with a roar.

"What does it mean?" she asked.

I thought about it for a moment before pulling into traffic. "You know how I accidentally got mixed up with all those bad people?"

She nodded.

"Well he does that sort of thing on purpose. That's his job." I wondered what this Shade character would think if he knew the excitement I'd just been through this week. Probably pooh-pooh it—all in a day's work for him.

"Oh." Lucy was silent a moment, then brightened as she handed it back. "Hey, maybe next time you have a problem with bad people, you should call this guy to handle them instead. That way you can stay safe."

I gave the card a look, pocketed it, and smiled at her. "Sounds like a plan to me."

* * * * *

REQUEST YOUR FREE BOOKS!

2 FREE NOVELS
PLUS 2 FREE GIFTS!

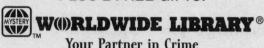

Your Partner in Crime

YES! Please send me 2 FREE novels from the Worldwide Library® series and my 2 FREE gifts (gifts are worth about $10). After receiving them, if I don't wish to receive any more books, I can return the shipping statement marked "cancel." If I don't cancel, I will receive 4 brand-new novels every month and be billed just $5.49 per book in the U.S. or $6.24 per book in Canada. That's a savings of at least 31% off the cover price. It's quite a bargain! Shipping and handling is just 50¢ per book in the U.S. and 75¢ per book in Canada.* I understand that accepting the 2 free books and gifts places me under no obligation to buy anything. I can always return a shipment and cancel at any time. Even if I never buy another book, the two free books and gifts are mine to keep forever.

414/424 WDN F4WY

Name	(PLEASE PRINT)	
Address		Apt. #
City	State/Prov.	Zip/Postal Code

Signature (if under 18, a parent or guardian must sign)

Mail to the Harlequin® Reader Service:
IN U.S.A.: P.O. Box 1867, Buffalo, NY 14240-1867
IN CANADA: P.O. Box 609, Fort Erie, Ontario L2A 5X3

Want to try two free books from another line?
Call 1-800-873-8635 or visit www.ReaderService.com.

* Terms and prices subject to change without notice. Prices do not include applicable taxes. Sales tax applicable in N.Y. Canadian residents will be charged applicable taxes. Offer not valid in Quebec. This offer is limited to one order per household. Not valid for current subscribers to the Worldwide Library series. All orders subject to credit approval. Credit or debit balances in a customer's account(s) may be offset by any other outstanding balance owed by or to the customer. Please allow 4 to 6 weeks for delivery. Offer available while quantities last.

Your Privacy—The Harlequin® Reader Service is committed to protecting your privacy. Our Privacy Policy is available online at www.ReaderService.com or upon request from the Harlequin Reader Service.

We make a portion of our mailing list available to reputable third parties that offer products we believe may interest you. If you prefer that we not exchange your name with third parties, or if you wish to clarify or modify your communication preferences, please visit us at www.ReaderService.com/consumerchoice or write to us at Harlequin Reader Service Preference Service, P.O. Box 9062, Buffalo, NY 14269. Include your complete name and address.

WWLI3R

ReaderService.com

Manage your account online!

- Review your order history
- Manage your payments
- Update your address

---

*We've designed
the Harlequin® Reader Service
website just for you.*

Enjoy all the features!

- Reader excerpts from any series
- Respond to mailings and special monthly offers
- Discover new series available to you
- Browse the Bonus Bucks catalog
- Share your feedback

Visit us at:
ReaderService.com

RS13